PRAISE FOR *HIDDEN*

"*Hidden* launches the Texas Murder Files with a bang, proving that Laura Griffin is the master of the romantic thriller. Intense, suspenseful, sexy, with an intriguing mystery and characters to root for. Griffin is at the top of her game."

—*New York Times* bestselling author Allison Brennan

"*Hidden* reminded me why Laura Griffin is an auto-buy author for me. The first book in her new Texas Murder Files series, *Hidden* is a stunning page-turner with the perfect balance of romance and suspense and a relentless pace that will keep you glued to its pages long into the night. You won't be able to put this book down!"

—Melinda Leigh, #1 *Wall Street Journal* bestselling author of
Cross Her Heart

"*Hidden* has Laura Griffin's trademark strengths: a fast-paced twisting plot and characters you want to know in real life."

—Kendra Elliot, *Wall Street Journal* bestselling author of
The Last Sister

PRAISE FOR LAURA GRIFFIN AND HER NOVELS

"Gritty, imaginative, sexy! You must read Laura Griffin."
—*New York Times* bestselling author Cindy Gerard

"Griffin never fails to put me on the edge of my seat."
—*USA Today*

"A gripping, white-knuckle read. You won't be able to put it down." —*New York Times* bestselling author Brenda Novak

Titles by Laura Griffin

FAR GONE

The Tracers Series

UNTRACEABLE	EXPOSED
UNSPEAKABLE	BEYOND LIMITS
UNSTOPPABLE	SHADOW FALL
UNFORGIVABLE	DEEP DARK
SNAPPED	AT CLOSE RANGE
TWISTED	TOUCH OF RED
SCORCHED	STONE COLD HEART

The Wolfe Security Series

DESPERATE GIRLS

HER DEADLY SECRETS

The Alpha Crew Series

AT THE EDGE	TOTAL CONTROL
EDGE OF SURRENDER	ALPHA CREW:
COVER OF NIGHT	THE MISSION BEGINS

The Glass Sisters Series

THREAD OF FEAR

WHISPER OF WARNING

The Borderline Series

ONE LAST BREATH

ONE WRONG STEP

The Moreno & Hart Mysteries, with Allison Brennan

CRASH AND BURN	FROSTED
HIT AND RUN	LOST AND FOUND

The Texas Murder Files

HIDDEN

FLIGHT

LAURA GRIFFIN

FLIGHT

BERKLEY
New York

BERKLEY
An imprint of Penguin Random House LLC
penguinrandomhouse.com

ISBN: 9780593197349

First Edition: March 2021

Printed in the United States of America
1   3   5   7   9   10   8   6   4   2

Book design by George Towne

For Doug

CHAPTER

ONE

THE LIGHT WAS perfect, but she didn't have long.

Miranda Rhoads dipped the paddle and glided smoothly through the water as she composed the shot. Cattails in the foreground, the tall lighthouse a distant spire. In between, the bay was a vast mirror that reflected the pinkening sky.

She lowered the blade of her paddle again, this time pushing off the spongy bottom to maneuver around a clump of reeds. This was it. She balanced the paddle on her thighs and adjusted the strap around her neck. Anticipation thrummed through her as she lifted the camera. Conditions were exactly what she'd hoped for when she saw the weather report last night and remembered one of her father's sayings: *Red sky at morning, sailors take warning.*

Miranda took a deep breath and waited. Seconds and minutes slipped by, and she let her mind drift like the kayak. The humid air settled around her. She listened to the hum of insects in the marshes behind her, a trilling chorus that swelled and subsided with the breeze. She took another deep breath and for a perfect, endless moment she felt truly okay. Her thoughts were clear and crisp. The sunlight-saturated air seemed to vibrate around her. The day was still new, limitless, and she gave in to the notion that she was going to be all right.

Movement in the corner of her eye.

She remained utterly still as a great blue heron stepped from the reeds, tall and elegant on his spindly legs. Another step. Miranda held her breath and brushed her fingertip over the shutter button. If he sensed her watching, he didn't show it.

She waited for the shot. It was instinct now. Like a hunter. Another deep breath and a long respiratory pause as she stayed motionless.

Click.

He stepped closer and dipped his head down. Then he lifted his head and turned toward her, regarding her with a regal look. Posing?

His silhouette was black and perfect against the fiery sky. Miranda's heart hammered.

Click. Click.

This was why she'd come here. This was why she put up with lukewarm showers and rusty water and a bleating alarm clock at four thirty a.m. This was why she schlepped her kayak to the dock all alone, slapping at mosquitoes before her first sip of coffee. Photography was all about light, and mornings offered the best chance of getting something useful. Not a guarantee but a chance, and it paid to play the odds. She couldn't sell what she didn't have.

Click.

Another careful step. *Click, click.*

The heron turned and took wing. She lowered the camera and watched him soar over the marsh, then swoop down into another clump of reeds.

Miranda sighed. Not bad for a day that had barely begun.

She shifted the camera under her arm and picked up the paddle, scanning the wetlands for new possibilities. She had thirty minutes left. More, if the distant line of storm clouds lingered off the coast.

Her paddle snagged on something. She spotted a slim yellow cord stretched taut across the reeds. She paddled closer and spied something green tucked among the cattails. A canoe.

An explosion of feathers nearby made her heart lurch as a trio of white ibis flapped away. Behind her, something thrashed in the water. A fish? A cottonmouth?

Her attention snapped back to the boat. Her heart was thudding now as she drifted closer. The air felt charged, and all her senses went on high alert. Habits kicked in. She noted the direction of the wind. She noted the height of the sun. She noted the air, damp and pungent, pressing around her. Her stomach clenched tightly as she took a slow, shallow stroke, careful not to bump the canoe with her kayak as she peered over the side.

They looked peaceful, with their long limbs intertwined. His arm around her was protective. Tender.

Obscene.

Miranda's vision blurred. Her brain recoiled from the sight in front of her, but she couldn't turn away, couldn't stop from registering every detail.

The man's head was nestled on the woman's shoulder just beneath her chin, and their pale skin looked rosy in the morning glow. An inch of water filled the bottom of the canoe. The woman's dark braid drifted there like a snake.

She stared unblinking at the morning sky.

* * *

ETECTIVE JOEL BREDA pulled into the marina parking lot and slid his truck into a space beside a dusty police cruiser. He scanned the boats bobbing in their slips before turning his attention to the caliche lot. He recognized most of the vehicles, including the hulking old Suburban that belonged to the Lost Beach police chief.

Joel surveyed the two-story building as he got out. The marina occupied the first level, and a seafood restaurant with sweeping views of Laguna Madre occupied the top. Neither was open yet, but the weathered wooden bait shop near the docks would have been busy since sunrise. The shop owner stood beside his hut now, smoking a cigarette and watching a cluster of boats about a hundred yards offshore.

"Thought you were in Corpus."

Joel turned to see Nicole Lawson trudging toward him. She wore a blue Lost Beach PD golf shirt and black rubber waders that were covered in muck.

"Not anymore," Joel said. "Who's here?"

"McDeere got here first. Then the chief. Still no sign of the ME." Nicole turned toward the water, and Joel followed her gaze to the boats. An LBPD speedboat and several small skiffs blocked his view of the crime scene.

"What do we know?" Joel asked.

"So far, not much. Two victims, both shot in the gut. Randy called it in."

Joel cast a glance at the bait shop owner as he flicked his cigarette to the ground. Randy chain-smoked when he was nervous. He'd probably gone through half a pack by now.

Nicole turned to face him. Her long auburn hair was tied in a messy bun instead of her usual braid, which made Joel think she'd been called out of bed.

"Male and female?" he asked.

"Yep. And they're young, too. Maybe early twenties."

Something in her tone caught his attention. He eased closer and lowered his voice. "What is it?"

She shook her head. "Nothing, just . . . freaky crime scene."

She'd been out there already, and Joel felt a stab of regret that he'd been off island when he got the call. He lived less than a mile away from here and should have been the first one on scene.

He studied Nicole's tense expression. "Does it look like a murder? A murder-suicide? A suicide pact?"

"Don't know." She wiped her brow with the back of her forearm. "Could be any of those. I didn't see a weapon aboard, though. Course, I didn't touch anything."

"Good." Joel stepped around her and reached into the bed of his truck to unlock the chrome toolbox.

"Don't bother with waders," she told him. "With the storm coming, they're bringing everything in."

He glanced at the sky. Given the angry gray clouds rolling in, it wasn't a bad call. He shoved his waders aside and grabbed his binoculars.

"Sure you want in on this?" she asked. "Technically, you're on vacation till Thursday."

"I'm sure." The department had only three full-time detectives—himself, Emmet, and Owen. Nicole was good, but she was still in training.

"I'm just saying," she went on. "You could probably let Emmet take the lead on this one."

Joel slammed the toolbox shut, not bothering to argue about it. "Fill me in as we walk."

She fell into step beside him, and her waders made little squeaking sounds. "So. How was the wedding?"

"Fine."

She cut a look at him. "Really?"

"Yeah. Anyone call the sheriff's office?" he asked. The last thing he wanted to talk about was the wedding he'd just attended.

"The chief called them. They're sending down one of their CSIs."

"Who?"

"Bollinger, I think."

Joel winced.

"You don't like him?"

"No."

"Well, he should be here soon." She checked her watch. "We called them forty-five minutes ago."

"He'll be late, count on it." Yet another reason the chief had probably decided to tow the canoe in. Joel passed a row of fishing rigs and catamarans, all neatly covered and secured in their slips. He reached the end of the dock and lifted the binoculars.

The distant crime scene snapped into focus. Chief Brady stood at the helm of the police boat as Emmet and Owen attached a line to the bow of the canoe. Joel studied the long green boat. It didn't look like a rental from one of the island's rec shops.

The police boat got moving, and the bow of the canoe tipped up. Joel muttered a curse as he imagined the canoe's contents shifting to the stern.

"We don't have much choice with the rain coming," Nicole said, clearly picking up on his concern.

"Tell me they got pictures."

"Emmet had the camera."

"Who found them?"

"Some woman in a kayak. She paddled to the marina to report it."

Joel lowered the binoculars. "Why didn't she call it in herself?"

"I don't know."

"Where is she now?"

"Um . . ." She turned around and scanned the parking lot. "McDeere was getting her statement. I'm sure she didn't leave yet. There she is. Just past the boat trailers."

"Black Jeep, red kayak?"

"That's her. Here, let me use your binocs while you talk to her."

Joel handed them over and returned to the parking lot, watching the woman as he approached. She stood on the running board of the Jeep, struggling with a bungee cord as she secured her kayak to the roll bar.

"Need a hand?" Joel asked.

"I'm good." The woman didn't look up. She had honey-brown hair pulled back in a ponytail. She wore stretchy black pants that clung to her curves and a loose white top over a black sports bra. Her cheeks were flushed from exertion, but the pissed-off look on her face warned Joel not to intervene as she wrestled with the final hook. After getting it attached, she stepped down.

"I'm Joel Breda, Lost Beach PD."

She gazed up at him and dusted her hands on her pants. "Miranda Rhoads." Her gaze dropped to the detective's shield clipped to his belt. When she looked up again, her caramel-colored eyes were wary.

"I already gave a detailed statement to Officer Mc-Deere," she said. "And I talked to someone named Lawson."

"I understand, ma'am. I just have some follow-ups."

She blew out a breath and tucked a loose curl behind her ear. "All right."

"Care to sit down?" He nodded at a picnic table not far from the bait shop.

"No, thanks. One second." She eased past him and opened the door of her Jeep, then reached across the seat and popped open the glove compartment. She pulled out a small red zipper pouch. "I just need to clean this," she said, propping her foot on the running board.

She wore silver flip-flops, and Joel saw a gash on the side of her little toe. The cut was bleeding. He hadn't noticed, probably because he'd been distracted by the rest of her.

"What'd you do there?" he asked.

She tore open a sterile wipe and dabbed at the cut. "I got out of my kayak to look at the canoe and stepped on a board covered in barnacles."

"You had a tetanus shot recently?"

She laughed. "Uh, yeah."

Joel looked at her. "Why is that funny?"

Her smile disappeared. "It's not."

She reached into the Jeep again to get rid of the wet wipe and tossed the pouch on the seat. Taking a deep breath, she squared her shoulders.

"Sorry. Okay. What were your questions?"

Joel looked her over, puzzled by her brisk attitude. Typically, innocent witnesses were pretty deferential with cops. Then again, she'd had a rough morning and people handled stress in different ways.

"Tell me how you found the boat," he said. "What were you doing out there?"

She rested her hands on her hips and gazed at the bay. Her arms were tanned and toned, as though she spent a lot of time in her kayak.

"I got to the marina about five fifteen," she said.

"That's early."

"I was photographing the sunrise."

"Okay. And you were coming from where?"

"The north end of the island. I'm renting a beach house about a mile from here."

"All right."

"I put in my kayak. Paddled about a hundred yards out, toward the marshes near the nature center. As the sky brightened, I took a series of photographs. Nautical twilight is the best time to get silhouettes. That's between first light and sunrise." She looked at him, probably sensing that he didn't know shit about photography. But fishing he knew, and he understood the different phases of daylight on this bay.

"Anyway, as I was paddling, I scared up some birds." A lock of hair blew against her face, and she peeled it away. Joel noticed her hand was trembling. "That's when I spotted a yellow line."

"A fishing line?"

"No, like a rope. A thin one. It was attached to a canoe hidden in some cattails." She paused, and a somber look came over her face. "That's when I saw them."

"The couple."

"Yeah."

"And you could tell they were dead?"

"Yes." She broke eye contact and looked at the bay again. The wind had picked up, and the water was getting choppy. "There was no mistaking it. I mean, you'll see when they bring them in."

"You know what time this was?" he asked.

"About six forty."

Joel watched her face as she looked out over the water. The boats were coming in, and he could hear the motors getting closer. But he was more interested in Miranda Rhoads's carefully calm expression.

"Do you recall any noises?" he asked.

She looked at him. "Noises?"

"When you were out on the water taking pictures. Did you hear any gunshots? Or yelling, screaming, anything like that?"

"No."

"Think back. Sometimes seagulls screeching can sound similar to—"

"I didn't hear anything like that." She was adamant. "I didn't hear anyone or see anyone until I got back to the marina and asked the guy at the bait shop for help." She turned to look at Randy, who was smoking another cigarette and talking with McDeere. "That guy there, with the beard."

"So you didn't have a cell phone out there with you?" Joel asked.

"Not on the kayak, no. I keep it locked in the console of my Jeep."

"All right. And when you arrived here, did you see any other cars in the lot?"

She shook her head. "I was the first one."

"Any other boats? Fishermen?"

"No."

"What about pedestrians? Dog walkers?" He nodded at the marshland between the marina and the nature center. "Some people use the trails in the morning."

"There was no one out when I first got here. At least, not that I saw. Only person I noticed was a cyclist on the highway. He was riding along the shoulder."

That caught Joel's interest. "Where, exactly?"

She blew out a sigh. "He was on a bike about fifty yards north of the turnoff for the marina. He was heading north. I described him to McDeere. He had on a light-colored T-shirt and a baseball cap. I remember noticing because he should have been wearing a helmet, especially riding in the dark like that."

Joel cast a glance at McDeere, who was watching him now with a look Joel couldn't read. He had no doubt the officer would have taken all this down. A former Marine,

McDeere was thorough and paid attention to details. It was one of the things Joel liked about working with him.

"As I said, I gave all this to the officer already."

Joel looked at the witness. Her cheeks were still pink, and she seemed antsy. Like she was itching to leave. She glanced over Joel's shoulder, and her brow furrowed.

Joel turned to see the ME's van swinging into the lot, followed by a white SUV. Both vehicles pulled into spaces near the bait shop. The door to the SUV opened, and Bollinger hopped out.

Joel checked his watch. Almost an hour since the chief had called the county for a crime scene investigator. Joel gritted his teeth.

"Detective? Is that all right?"

He shifted his attention back to the witness. Those caramel-colored eyes looked worried now.

"Ma'am?"

"I need to head out. I'm late for something." She nodded toward the bait shop. "If you have any more follow-ups, your officer there has all my contact information. And he gave me his card."

Joel didn't want to let her go, but he didn't have a reason to keep her here, either. The boats were pulling in, and Joel wanted to get a look at everything before the ME's people started.

"Let me see that card," he said.

She hesitated a moment before pulling a card from her bra and handing it over. Joel took out a pen and wrote on the back.

"That's my mobile," he said. "Call me if you remember anything else."

"All right."

"Thank you for your time today."

"No problem."

She stepped around him to open the Jeep, and Joel moved out of the way.

Bollinger was still with his vehicle, zipping into his white Tyvek suit. Meanwhile, the boats had docked, and Emmet was securing the canoe to a cleat.

Thunder rumbled, and Joel glanced at the sky just in time to catch the first fat raindrops. He looked at the canoe that held two dead young people, along with any forensic evidence he hoped to recover. All of it was going to get drenched.

Joel started for the dock.

"Detective?"

He turned around. Miranda wore a rain jacket now with a hood that covered her head. Wherever she was going, she was about to get soaked.

"Make sure they bag her hands," she told him.

"What's that?"

"The female victim," she said. "She's holding a feather. You don't want it getting lost in transport, so tell your CSI to make sure to bag her hands."

CHAPTER

TWO

M IRANDA PULLED OFF the highway onto the gravel road. Swerving around potholes, she approached the weathered wooden beach house she'd come to call home.

The place was gray, like today's sky. It looked small and dilapidated compared to houses in the nearby subdivision, where homeowners picked from a selection of pre-approved colors in a cheery Caribbean palette. Miranda had gathered these details at the neighborhood's sales office during her first week on the island. She'd also learned that if she'd been in the market for a house—which she wasn't—the pastel-colored bungalows were well out of her price range.

She pulled under the rental house and parked her Jeep. Perched on twelve-foot stilts, the house was lower than everything else on the island's north end. New regulations called for sixteen-foot stilts to protect against storm surges, but Miranda's place had been built in the seventies. The house didn't look like much, but she loved the location well off the highway. From the south, it was concealed from view by a sloping clump of oak trees that had been sculpted by countless storms off the Gulf.

Miranda gathered her cell phone and camera from the console and tucked both under her jacket before getting out. The rain was steady now, with no end in sight, and she was going to have to drag the Jeep's top from the storage closet before venturing out again. She made a dash up the wooden stairs to the door and was greeted by Benji's nose against the glass. With Benji on guard, she wasn't in the habit of locking up when she went out briefly. That was about to change.

"Hey, boy," she said as she stepped inside.

Benji wiggled and whimpered as she took off her jacket, dripping water all over the floor. She bent down to rub his ears, and his skinny body shook with excitement as he licked her hands. A greyhound mix who looked underfed, Benji wasn't winning any beauty contests, but for Miranda it had been love at first sight.

She set her camera on the kitchen counter and plugged her phone into the charger. Pausing by the window, she looked out over the beach. The surf was up, and gray water churned beneath the charcoal sky. Maybe the storm would blow through, maybe not. But either way, she needed to hurry.

She went to the sink and stood for a moment to get her bearings. She splashed water on her face, then grabbed a dish towel and blotted her cheeks.

Two vics. GSW. Point-blank range.

She pictured Officer McDeere beside his patrol car talking on his radio. Then she pictured the detective. Joel Breda. She thought of his wide shoulders and narrow hips, and the stern look in his blue eyes as he'd towered over her.

You could tell they were dead?

Miranda shuddered and squeezed her eyes shut, wishing she could get the images out of her head. But of course, she couldn't. The lifeless bodies were seared into her memory. She was a visual person, which had propelled her career, but sometimes it felt like a curse.

She tossed the dish towel away and opened the refrigerator. Usually after a sunrise photo shoot she brewed a pot of strong coffee and sat down to pore through her results. But she was wired to the point of being dizzy, and the last thing she needed was caffeine. She had a sudden craving for a cigarette, which made no sense because she hadn't smoked since college.

She reached for a bottle of water and took a long swig. Then she grabbed a beach towel off the stacked washer-dryer in the corner of the kitchen. The towel was gritty from her last trip to the beach with Benji, but she wrapped it around her shoulders and went to her workspace.

The corner of the living room was her office, and her laptop was perched on a rickety wooden card table that she'd found in the bedroom closet along with a stack of jigsaw puzzles. She brought the computer to life and plugged in her camera, then sat down. She checked the clock: 8:28. She didn't have much time, but this couldn't wait until after work.

Benji nudged her knee with his nose.

"I know, boy. But it's raining." She scratched his head. "We'll go later."

He grunted and licked her hand, and she knew he sensed her agitation. He always keyed in on her moods.

Miranda clicked into the photo software and watched her shots roll in. Thumbnail images flashed at warp speed—a sunset at the nature center, last weekend's regatta, a series of sand dunes.

"Come on, come on, come on," she muttered.

It had been far too long since she'd uploaded her memory card, and now today of all days, she'd reached capacity.

Miranda scooted her chair in and watched the screen as

her stomach filled with dread. Shuddering again, she pulled the towel tighter around her shoulders. Why was she so rattled? She'd seen bodies before. But that was different. Different place, different context.

Different everything.

Finally, today's fiery sky appeared, and Miranda held her breath. Sky, sky, sky. More sky. And then a blur of green.

She clicked an image to enlarge it. The great blue heron. The shot was good. Exceptional, even. She scrolled past it until she reached the clump of cattails.

Start big and get small.

Her photography instructor's voice echoed through her head again. That was exactly what she'd done. Even in her panic, she'd fallen back on her training.

She had several shots of the cattails, with the green canoe camouflaged among the reeds. She scrolled through the images, getting closer and closer until she came to the overview shot.

Miranda's chest tightened. The scene took her breath away, even now, separated from the horror of it by time and space.

She combed through her photographs, studying the legs, the faces, the hands.

Miranda bit her lip. She pulled the towel tighter. She scrolled and scrolled until there it was—the shot she'd been looking for.

Early this morning, she'd been totally hands-off, but now she could really *look*. She touched the screen and spread her thumb and forefinger apart to zoom in.

Miranda's pulse picked up. She leaned closer. She *hadn't* been seeing things or imagining. It was just as she'd thought.

"I'll be damned."

* * *

NICOLE STARED AT the picture taped to the murder board, transfixed by the young woman's face. Her eyes were half-open, her lips slightly parted. A tiny black fly hovered at the corner of her mouth.

Nicole tried to envision how those final moments had played out. Had she seen the gun and felt a jolt of terror? Or had she and her companion chosen this as some sort of twisted suicide pact?

Shifting her attention to the photo of both victims, Nicole considered their clothing. They both wore shorts, no shoes, and their legs were intertwined. The man's arm was draped over the woman's bare abdomen below the hem of her short-cropped blue T-shirt.

Nicole studied the picture, but she couldn't figure it out. The position of his arm seemed almost . . . sweet. Had he gone out there planning to kill her and dump her body? Maybe he'd felt remorse and killed himself, too? Or had a third party come upon them in an intimate moment and taken them by surprise?

Joel walked into the conference room and stopped short.

"Damn," he said, looking at the murder board. "You're fast."

"I didn't want to wait for you guys." Nicole perched on the edge of the conference table. "How'd it go out there?"

Joel peeled off his LBPD baseball cap and dropped it on the table. His shaggy brown hair was damp with sweat, and clearly he'd been in the sun for hours. After dumping an ungodly amount of rain, the morning storm had moved inland, leaving the island steamy and soggy.

"We went back to the scene," he said.

"You did?"

He stepped over to the coffeepot and picked up the carafe.

"That's been there all day," she said.

"Don't care. I missed lunch." He poured the dregs into a cardboard cup, then picked up the sugar dispenser and gave a few generous shakes.

"There are doughnuts in the break room. Tell me about the scene first, though."

"No new leads."

He downed the coffee and put the cup on the table, then stepped over to look at the board. He'd gone home at some point to change into his usual clothes: a navy police golf shirt, desert brown tactical pants, and brown ATAC boots—all terrain, all conditions—because island law enforcement frequently involved traipsing around in the mud.

"You got the pictures printed already," he said, stepping over to a close-up of the female victim's face. Still no IDs, so for now the victims were Jane and John Doe.

Nicole watched him examine the photos. His blue eyes were somber. The charming smile he used to disarm suspects and witnesses alike was gone now as he studied the victims whose death it was his job to solve. Joel was the lead detective. He was also her mentor, both officially and unofficially, and she'd worked with him on all sorts of cases, but nothing that came close to this.

He glanced at her. "What?"

"Nothing. You guys finish canvassing the nature center?"

"The nature center, the marina, the park." He finished his coffee and pitched his cup into the trash. "No one saw the canoe or heard any gunshots."

"Damn." Nicole blew out a sigh and turned to the board. "What about the ME?"

"Autopsies are scheduled for tomorrow morning."

"They can't do them today?"

He shot her a look. "We're last in line."

Nicole shouldn't have been surprised. Lost Beach was too small to have its own medical examiner and crime lab. They had to piggyback on the county.

"I'd really like to get his take on manner of death," she said. "It's a bizarre crime scene."

"Yep."

She studied the photograph again. *Bizarre* was an understatement. The woman's braid floated in the water, looking eerily like a water moccasin.

"Anything new with the IDs?" Joel asked.

"No, and there's not a lot to go on," she said. "No phones, no wallets, no keys, no driver's licenses. Just the backpack we recovered from the stern of the boat, along with a flashlight. How many twentysomethings do you know who go anywhere without a phone?"

"It could have been stolen with everything else."

She nodded. "So that would make this a robbery on the high seas. In a canoe, no less, which has to be a first for us."

Joel sank into a chair and leaned back, combing his hand through his thick dark hair. He looked whipped, and he had to be starving, too. Six-two and muscular, he had a big appetite and tended to get edgy when he skipped meals.

"With all the drug running around here, piracy's more common than you'd think," he said. "People don't exactly file a police report when their cargo gets grabbed."

Nicole crossed her arms. "Okay, but that logic doesn't add up either. If this *was* a robbery—as in they took the wallets, keys, phones, and whatever—how come they left the weed?"

"What weed?"

She picked up the manila folder on the end of the table and shuffled through the rest of the crime scene pics. She found the one of the unzipped backpack with a half-filled plastic baggie of marijuana. She stepped over and taped the picture to the whiteboard alongside the other crime scene shots.

"What else you have there?" Joel picked up the folder and thumbed through it. He stopped at an overhead shot of the canoe in which the victims were captured in the frame from head to toe.

"These really aren't bad," Joel said. "Bollinger's improving."

"He didn't take those."

"Who did?"

"The photographer lady."

He looked up. "Miranda Rhoads?"

"Yeah. She sent them over around nine."

His eyebrows tipped up. "You're telling me she took pictures of the crime scene before the police showed?"

Nicole shrugged. "She said she was worried about the storm destroying evidence, so she went ahead and photographed everything. We're lucky she thought to do it." Nicole took the overview picture from him and taped it beside the others.

Joel frowned at the board and rubbed his chin.

"What's wrong?" she asked. "I thought you'd be glad to have these. They're a hell of a lot better than Bollinger's shots. His are blurry and shadowed, and the canoe was already getting rained on by the time he got his ass in gear." Nicole taped several more photos to the whiteboard. "She thought to take *notes*, too, and emailed them with the pictures. Time of discovery: six forty-two." She uncapped a marker and jotted notes on the whiteboard. "Outdoor temp: seventy-eight degrees. Wind: moderate out of the southeast."

She turned around and Joel was staring at a stack of pictures. She leaned closer and saw that he was hung up on a shot of the woman. Her hand rested against her bare thigh. A small gray feather was stuck between her fingers.

Joel flipped through the pictures. "What kind of flash-light was it?"

"One of those camping ones that converts to a lantern. If they went out there in the dark, they could have used it as a running light."

He flipped to a close-up shot of the unzipped backpack. "Was this dollar sitting in the boat like this?" He held up the photo. A dollar bill sat on the backpack beside a long black feather.

"Oh, she mentioned that," Nicole said. "She didn't have a ruler with her, so she used that for scale."

Joel shook his head.

"What? You should be glad she got these before the sky opened up and all the evidence got ruined."

"I think it's odd."

"Odd . . . as in suspicious?"

"As in unusual," he said. "So far, Miranda Rhoads is our only witness. No one else has corroborated her story. And she discovered the crime scene and conveniently started documenting it?"

"So are you saying she's a suspect?" Nicole had been so glad to have the photos, she hadn't considered the possibility. Joel was a step ahead of her, as usual.

He closed the folder and handed it to her. "Everyone's a suspect until they aren't."

CHAPTER

THREE

JOEL TURNED ONTO the gravel road and saw the glowing yellow windows even before he spotted Miranda's black Jeep Wrangler parked beneath the house. The kayak was gone now, and she had put the Jeep's top on.

He parked behind her and got out of his pickup. The sun had set, and the last traces of daylight were fading over the sand dunes. Beneath the wooden staircase he spied the red kayak facedown in the grass beside a double-bladed paddle. Joel stepped over a pair of sandy purple running shoes and hiked up the stairs, pausing on the landing to admire the view. The old house didn't look like much and never had, but its location was impressive. To the south was the island's tourist center, consisting of colorful beach houses, inns, and Lost Beach's two high-rise hotels. To the north was a state park that stretched for twenty-four miles, or two-thirds of the island, and the distant flicker of a campfire was the only light.

Muffled barks erupted as Joel reached the top stair. The

back of the house was like a fishbowl, and he saw a skinny brown dog with his nose pressed against the glass door. Miranda crossed the living room, and Joel stepped under the porch light so she'd recognize him.

Gone were the snug-fitting yoga pants from this morning, and now she wore a black miniskirt and a silky gray blouse. She pulled her dog away from the door and opened it.

"Detective. Hi." She squeezed through the opening, blocking the dog.

"Hey there." He glanced down at her tall black heels. "I catch you heading out?"

"Coming home, actually." She tipped her head to the side. "What's up?"

"I had a couple more questions, if you have a minute."

"Sure." She scooted backward through the door. "Benji, *no*. Calm down."

Joel stepped inside and reached down so the dog could sniff his hand. Miranda kept a firm grip on his collar as he whimpered and strained against the hold.

"Sorry. He gets excited for visitors. Benji, *sit*."

He sat.

Joel crouched down and rubbed his head. "Is he a greyhound?"

She released the collar. "A mix, actually."

Joel was eye level with Miranda's knees now, and he tried not to stare at her legs. He wondered where she'd gone today all dressed up. Everything on the island was casual.

He stroked Benji's neck. A chunk of his right ear was missing.

"What happened to him?" he asked.

"I don't know for sure. He's a rescue."

Joel stood. Even with Miranda in heels, he still towered over her. She didn't seem intimidated, though, and for a moment, they just stood there looking at each other. Her hair was pulled up in loose bun. In the lamplight he saw that her caramel-brown eyes had gold flecks.

"Would you like something to drink?" She turned around and walked toward the kitchen, and Benji trotted behind her. "I've got beer, wine."

"I'm still on duty."

"Iced tea?" She looked over her shoulder.

"Sounds good."

He paused beside the window in the living room. "Nice view up here."

"That's what sold me."

"You bought it?"

"I'm renting." She pulled open the fridge. "The owner isn't interested in selling."

Joel smiled. "He's stubborn."

"You know him?" She set a pitcher of tea on the counter and took a pair of glasses down from a cabinet.

"I know his son," Joel said. "His family used to spend summers here. He and my brother were lifeguards together."

She took a lemon from a bowl and sliced two wedges.

Joel stepped into the kitchen and leaned back against the Formica breakfast bar. The place was just as he remembered it, including the dingy linoleum floor. Looking into the living room, he recognized the striped blue sofa and the black steamer trunk that served as a coffee table. He'd bet there was still a Monopoly game inside with half the hotels missing and a game of Clue with no revolver.

Miranda handed him the drink.

"Thanks." He took a sip. It was cold and sweet, and he chugged half of it.

She leaned her hip against the counter and watched him.

"Thanks for sending your pictures over." He set the glass down. "They're really good. Better than good. They're excellent."

"Thank you."

"How come you didn't tell me you were a CSI?"

She lifted her shoulder. "I'm not anymore. I left my job five months ago."

"But you're still licensed?"

"Yes."

"And you teach?"

She arched an eyebrow. "You've been checking up on me."

He smiled. "I was curious. Is that where you were today?"

She didn't answer, and he got the sense she wanted to tell him it was none of his damn business. She turned and put the pitcher back into the fridge. She was stalling for time. She leaned back against the counter and looked at him.

"Today I had a deposition in San Antonio," she said. "A case from last year that's on its way to trial."

He nodded. "And how many courses do you teach?"

"Just one. Beginning Forensic Photography at St. John's College."

"Good school. But that's what, a three-hour drive? You do that twice a week?"

"Only on Tuesdays."

"Pretty long haul to teach a class."

"I don't mind." She gave a tight smile. "Nature photography doesn't pay all the bills, unfortunately."

Joel watched her. She seemed guarded, and he could tell she didn't like the direction the conversation had taken.

"Your photographs are going to be critical to our investigation," he said. "We called a CSI from the county down here, but by the time he showed up and got started it was too late for some of the trace evidence. Your crime scene pictures really saved our bacon."

"Well. I was glad to help. Evidence is ephemeral."

He nodded. "Especially here. Weather changes on a

dime. Half the time we're dealing with outdoor crime scenes and we're up against the elements."

She folded her arms over her breasts and tipped her head to the side. "Why do I get the feeling you didn't come here to talk about the weather?"

"You're right. I came to see if you'd be interested in helping us."

"Us?"

"The department. Lost Beach PD."

When she didn't respond he kept going.

"We haven't had a CSI on staff in six months, and now we've got this murder case in our lap. The high season starts in two weeks, and that means our crime rate doubles. More car thefts, break-ins, assaults. We're buried already, and it's not even Memorial Day."

She just looked at him. "So . . . let me get this straight. You came here to *hire* me?"

"We could use your expertise."

M IRANDA STARED AT him, trying to get her head around the idea.

"You want me to work for you," she stated.

"No, actually." He rubbed the stubble along his chin. He had a strong jaw—strong features in general—and she was trying not to get distracted by his looks.

"You'd report to Chief Brady," he said. "He authorized me to offer you the job."

"Thank you. I appreciate the offer, but I'm not interested."

He smiled, and a warm flutter settled in the pit of her stomach. "You haven't even heard what it is yet."

"I'm not looking for a job, Detective."

"It's Joel. And I thought nature photography didn't pay the bills." His tone was easygoing, which made it hard for her to be annoyed that he was tossing her own words back at her.

"Nevertheless, I'm not in the market."

"No?"

"No." She forced her arms to her sides because she didn't want to fidget. She wanted to be decisive. "But thank you for thinking of me."

The side of his mouth curved with amusement, and the warm flutter was back again. Joel Breda was sexy and charming, and she'd already noticed he didn't wear a wedding ring. But she wasn't about to let him come in here and upend her life. She'd left her job without a backward glance, and she hadn't regretted it.

His phone buzzed, and he pulled it from his pocket. His expression quickly turned serious.

"Sorry," he said without looking up. "I have to go."

"I understand."

He glanced up at her, and the intense look in those blue eyes caught her off guard. Wow. Smiling, he was attractive. But his serious look ramped it up to a whole new level.

He tucked his phone away and headed for the door. Benji followed him.

Miranda walked around them and opened the door. "Thanks again for the offer. I'm sure you'll find someone to fill the bill."

He lifted an eyebrow skeptically instead of agreeing with her. "Be sure to lock up," he said.

"Of course."

"Good night, Miranda. I'll be in touch."

THE POLICE STATION was practically deserted. Their receptionist had long since gone home for the night, and the only officer in the bullpen was the rookie, Adam

McDeere. He sat at his computer, probably dealing with the blizzard of paperwork that had resulted from the day's events.

Joel traded nods with him as he cut through the cubicles. McDeere didn't stop typing. Given his agonizing hunt-and-peck method, he was going to be here all night.

Nicole stepped out of the interview room and caught Joel's eye. She closed the door behind her and walked over to meet him.

"Who is she again?" Joel asked.

"Her name's Jennifer Meznick, forty-six."

Joel ducked into the break room, and Nicole followed. He hadn't eaten anything since a chocolate glazed dough-nut six hours ago, and he was running on fumes. He went straight for the vending machine and fed in some quarters. "Meznick. I don't recognize that name." He jabbed a button for Dr Pepper, and a bottle thunked down.

"They're weekenders. *Were* weekenders," Nicole said. "They've owned a house on Bay View Drive for sixteen years. Now they're going through a divorce, and she's moved down temporarily to fix the place up to sell."

Joel twisted off the top and took a swig. It was fizzy and cold but didn't compare to Miranda's home-brewed iced tea.

"How come we didn't talk to her this morning when we canvassed?" he asked.

"She was off island. Visiting her mother in Kingsville, apparently. Said she didn't hear about everything until to-night when a neighbor called her. She said she came straight over." Nicole crossed her arms. "And that's about to be a problem, by the way. The word is out about the murders, and it's only a matter of time before we get big-city media down here. Brady's in his office fielding calls, and his phone's been ringing off the hook for the last half hour."

"We haven't confirmed manner of death," Joel re-minded her.

She rolled her eyes. "You know what I mean. Two dead bodies, possibly tourists, and summer season's about to kick off."

Joel glanced through the door at the chief's office. Brady hated dealing with reporters, and this was the second time he'd had to do it in less than a week. On Friday a group of protesters had showed up to picket the resort being built at the southern tip of the island. Police had arrested half a dozen people for criminal mischief, and photos of vandalized construction equipment had landed on the front page of the *Corpus Christi Gazette*. The media fallout from today was going to be worse by a magnitude of a thousand. Joel was glad he didn't have the chief's job.

He looked at Nicole, who was watching him expectantly.

"What's your impression of this witness?" he asked. "She on the level?"

"Seems to be."

"You want to sit in on the interview?"

"Sure."

Joel recapped his drink and stashed it in the fridge.

"So, did you talk to Miranda Rhoads about the job?" Nicole asked.

"She's not interested."

"Really? I'm surprised."

"I'll work on her."

Joel wasn't ready to give up on Miranda yet. He'd caught a tiny spark of interest when he'd first made the offer. He could build on that. She'd seemed intrigued by the case, and she didn't strike him as the type to want to sit this one out.

Miranda had an obvious talent for CSI work, and he was determined to convince her to join the team.

Nicole checked her watch.

"Let's get this interview done," he said. "Then you can get out of here."

"Roger that."

He led the way to the interview room. Opening the door, he was immediately hit by the smell of paint thinner. Jennifer Meznick wore a white T-shirt and torn jeans that were spattered with seafoam green. Her short dark hair was pulled back in a stubby ponytail.

"Ms. Meznick? Joel Breda, Lost Beach PD."

"Hi. Are you in charge of the case?"

"Yes, ma'am."

He and Nicole sat down in plastic chairs across from the witness, and Nicole pulled out a spiral notepad. Meznick eyed it nervously.

"Thanks for coming in," Joel said, trying to put her at ease.

She took a deep breath and blew it out. "Well, I don't know if this is helpful, but I thought I should talk to y'all."

"Can you reiterate what you went through with Detective Lawson?"

Another deep breath. "Well, I was gone all day, like I said. My mom lives in Kingsville, so I had to run up there and take her to a doctor's appointment."

Joel nodded. "Let's start with this morning."

"Well." She paused and seemed to gather her thoughts. "I got up early to fish. I'd checked the tide chart last night, and I wanted to get a line in the water while the fish were moving. I slept through my first alarm and—"

"What time was that?" Joel asked.

"That was five a.m. It went off again at five ten and I got up to put a line in." She folded her hands together and rested them on the table, and Joel noticed her fingers were smeared with more seafoam green. "I wanted coffee, so I put my fishing rod in the holder down by the dock—I've got one of those PVC things attached to the post on the boathouse? Anyway, I put the rod there and ran up to make some coffee. A few minutes later my dog—she's a Lab—she starts barking like crazy, and I knew I had a bite."

"Okay. You know what time this was?"

"I think about five thirty-five? So, I went down there, and sure enough I had a nice-size redfish. I reeled it in and was getting the hook out and putting it in the cooler; that's when a boat zipped by. It was going fast, like a bat outta hell."

"Which direction?" he asked.

"From the marina," she said. "North to south, right past my house."

Joel glanced at Nicole, who was writing something in her book.

"What kind of boat was this?" he asked.

"A skiff. I could tell by the motor."

"I would think you'd get a lot of skiffs back and forth with your house facing the bay like that," he commented. "Especially when the fish are moving."

"Sure, but this one was going so fast that I noticed it."

"Can you describe the boat?"

"Not really." She glanced from Joel to Nicole. "I mean, it was still pretty dark out, so it was really just a shadow streaking across the water. It was going fast, and I remember the front of the boat was tipped up."

Joel watched her, trying to gauge her credibility.

"Tell him about the running lights," Nicole said.

"Oh, well, yeah. It wasn't using any running lights. I noticed that, too," she said. "We get plenty of skiffs and fishing boats back and forth, but you'd be crazy to zip around on the bay without lights that time of morning. The sun wasn't even up yet."

"What time was this, when you saw the boat?" he asked.

"Five forty-five. I looked at my watch. It was just barely getting light outside."

Joel glanced at Nicole, and she lifted an eyebrow at him. The timing was about an hour ahead of Miranda's discovery of the bodies, so it could fit.

"One other thing that I forgot to ask." Nicole flipped to a new page in her notebook. "While you were fishing, did you hear any unusual noises?"

She frowned. "Like what?"

"Like gunshots," Nicole clarified. "Or maybe something that sounded like fireworks or a car backfiring?"

"No. Nothing like that."

"And any unusual sounds in the middle of the night?"

"No. Of course, I'm pretty far away from the place where they found them, so . . . I don't know if I *would* have heard anything." She looked from Nicole to Joel. "Sorry."

"It's okay." Nicole jotted a few notes.

"Is that it?" The witness checked her watch. "I hate to be rude, but I really need to get back now. I forgot to put my cat in the bedroom, and my cabinets aren't fully dry yet."

"We have all your contact info?" Joel asked.

"Yes."

"Then we'll be in touch if we need anything." He pushed his chair back and offered her a handshake. "Thanks again for coming in."

Nicole led the woman out. When they were gone, he sat down to flip through the interview notes. After three years of working together, he'd learned to decipher Nicole's scrawled shorthand.

She came back and leaned against the doorframe.

"What's your take on her story?" he asked.

"The timing works, but . . ."

He looked up from the notepad. "But what?"

"I don't know. A boat with no running lights? Given the traffic on the bay, it seems like a pretty thin lead."

Joel stood up and handed her the notepad.

"What's *your* take?" she asked. "You've been doing this a lot longer than I have."

He rested his hands on his hips. He was bone tired, and the day wasn't even over yet. He still had to go through a mountain of paperwork and circle back with the chief for a debriefing. And tomorrow he had to get up at the crack of dawn to drive to the mainland and attend back-to-back autopsies.

"I think we've got two young victims, no IDs, no suspects, and no discernible motive," he said. "Thin or not, this is the best lead we've got."

CHAPTER

FOUR

The smell of fresh-ground coffee greeted Miranda as she stepped into the Island Beanery. Even getting up early she hadn't managed to beat the crowd, and a line had already formed. She stood behind a pair of women in colorful yoga outfits as she studied the menu board.

"I heard it was kids," one of the women said in a low voice.

"You mean—"

"Teenagers. Can you imagine?"

"God, no. Their poor parents."

Miranda wasn't the only one eavesdropping on the conversation. A man had stepped into line behind her and was listening to every word as he pretended to be absorbed with his phone. He wore slacks and a crisp white button-down. He appeared slightly younger than she was—maybe late twenties—and his made-for-TV looks made Miranda think he was a reporter.

The yoga mamas paid for their lattes and stepped aside

to wait. Miranda ordered an extra-large house blend and collected it at the register. The maybe-reporter looked Miranda over as she took her drink to the condiment bar and added cream. She didn't recognize him from the local news stations, so he could have been from Austin or even Dallas. Two dead young people at a popular tourist destination was a big story.

Miranda scanned the parking lot as she returned to her Jeep. Sure enough, she spotted a white news van parked at the edge of the lot. Word was out. The logo on the side of the van was for a Houston station.

Miranda tucked her coffee into the cup holder and felt a pang of sympathy for Joel as she pulled out of the lot. This case promised to be a nightmare already, and now he had to deal with a media firestorm, too. She didn't envy him.

Miranda used side streets to avoid the tourist center as she made her way through town. No rain in the forecast today, and she'd left the Jeep's top at home so she could get some fresh air. She passed a couple of eateries and bike rental places before cutting over to the highway heading north. A few miles later, businesses gave way to neighborhoods. She passed an RV park and then a pasture where several horses grazed in a patch of shade beneath a water tower.

She sipped her coffee, savoring the rich flavor and the hit of caffeine. She hadn't slept well. Big surprise. She'd been haunted by dreams of dark water and long black snakes slithering around her. After tossing and turning most of the night, she'd hauled herself out of bed and stood under a tepid shower, trying to collect her thoughts. It was there under the anemic trickle with shampoo seeping into her eyes that she'd decided to bag the stack of grading she'd planned to do this morning and visit the nature center instead.

The sign came into view, and Miranda's pulse picked up as she made the turn. It was entirely possible she was wasting her time here. She wasn't even sure what she planned to say. But she had no choice, really. Certain elements of yesterday's crime scene were stuck in her head, and she knew herself well enough to know that they would stay stuck in her head until she tracked down some answers.

The Lost Beach Birding Center and Nature Conservatory, known locally as "the nature center," consisted of 160 acres of prairie and wetlands. The property's hub was a low wooden building painted moss green to blend in with the marshes. Surrounded by an intricate network of gravel paths and wooden boardwalks, the center offered eighteen miles of scenic trails, as well as a butterfly pavilion and sea turtle rescue center. The place's architectural focal point was a five-story wooden staircase leading to an observation deck where birders could peer through binoculars to spot a host of different species swooping over the marshes.

The center was busy for a Tuesday morning. Besides a half dozen cars, two yellow school buses were parked in the lot.

Miranda took a last sip of coffee before scooping up her file and heading in. She stood just inside the door for a moment, letting her eyes adjust to the cool dimness. Although she'd visited the nature center countless times to take photographs or walk Benji, she'd never been inside the building before now. It was bigger than she'd expected.

Miranda approached the reception desk, where a young man with a blond ponytail sat before a computer. He wore a blue shirt with a sea turtle patch on the front.

"I'm looking for Daisy Miller," Miranda told him. "Is she in today?"

"She's here, but—" He glanced behind him at a glass

window with a view of what appeared to be a science lab. "Think she's outside right now. You could try the tanks."

"Thank you."

Miranda cut through the lobby, passing the Discovery Center, where a group of preschoolers gathered around a low aquarium. A young woman, also wearing a turtle shirt, lifted a starfish from the water and held it up for the kids to see.

Miranda pushed through the door into the sweltering humidity. Not yet nine o'clock, and it was already in the eighties. The air smelled of brine and rotting vegetation. She passed through a low gate with a sign beside it: **BEWARE OF ALLIGATORS. NO UNLEASHED PETS.**

Miranda's sandals clacked over the wood as she made her way down the long boardwalk spanning the marsh. The path curved as she neared a wooden pavilion with a dark green roof. Beneath the roof was another group of children clustered around a large blue tank. Miranda scanned the adults in the group, and her gaze landed on a woman with curly gray hair and a wide-brimmed straw hat.

"That's Sparkle," she was telling the kids. "She was rescued on the Fourth of July."

A redheaded boy leaned over the tank. "Why does she swim funny?"

"Feet on the ground, please. She swims like that because she's missing a flipper. See? She can only go in circles."

The kids squeezed closer for a better look at the turtle. Some lifted cell phones and snapped pictures while others tossed in turtle food.

A young teacher clapped her hands. "Okay, it's our turn at the Discovery Center. Let's line up. Buddy system."

Miranda stepped out of the way as the kids scampered into formation. Then they tromped past her in pairs, leaving her alone with the woman in the hat. She looked to be a spry sixty years old and was dressed in khaki capri pants and a pink shirt with the turtle logo.

Miranda approached her. "Good morning. Are you Daisy Miller?"

She smiled. "That's me."

"Also known as the Butterfly Lady?"

She laughed. "I'll answer to that, too." Her gaze landed on the thick brown file in Miranda's hand. "Are you a reporter?"

"I'm a photographer. I read your book about birds on the island."

The woman's smile widened, and she took off her hat. "Oh dear. Now you're going to quiz me." She wiped her brow with the back of her arm and reached for a water bottle sitting on a stool near the tank.

"I'm doing some research and I wondered if I might have a few minutes of your time this morning? It shouldn't take very long."

Daisy replaced her hat and sighed. "Let's do it inside. It's hot as Hades today."

"Absolutely."

Daisy passed through a gate and joined Miranda on the boardwalk. They headed back toward the building together, quickly catching up with the stragglers from the school group.

"We get reporters from time to time." She gave Miranda a sideways look. "Especially just before summer starts. Everyone wants a feature story about vacation destinations. Do you work for a magazine?"

"I do freelance, mostly. Right now I've got a project with the Texas Birding Association. I'm doing their calendar."

"Oh, well, that's wonderful. I know the director there."

"Samuel. Yes, he's the one who hired me." Miranda hoped dropping the name would buy her a bit of credibility.

"Good for you. I love their calendar. Are you doing next year's edition?"

"That's right," Miranda said. "It goes to press at the end of August."

It sounded like a long lead time, but Miranda was already starting to get nervous. She had to submit sixty photographs, giving them a range to choose from, and they required a specific list of birds, all of which—supposedly—could be found along the lower Texas coast for at least part of the year.

They reached the building and followed the schoolchildren into the lobby.

"Let's go in my office," Daisy said, motioning for Miranda to follow her through a glass door marked **EMPLOYEES ONLY**. They ended up in the windowed laboratory behind the reception area.

Despite the windows, the laboratory didn't seem to be merely a showroom. A man in a white lab coat stood at a long slate table peering into a microscope. He had a shaved head and rimless glasses, and he didn't look up as Daisy and Miranda passed by. At the far end of the room, Daisy stopped beside a pair of computer workstations.

"My office, such as it is." She pulled out a chair and flopped into it with a sigh. "Gosh, it's hot." She set her water bottle by one of the keyboards. "Have a seat. Please. Would you like some water?"

"Thanks, I'm fine. I just had breakfast." Miranda sat, hoping she wasn't sitting at the bald guy's computer. She glanced over her shoulder at him, but he seemed absorbed in his work.

"Really, I don't want to take much of your time," Miranda said. "But I have this feather that I need help identifying, and since you're an ornithologist, I thought maybe you could help."

"Aha. I knew it." She tugged open a drawer and fished out a pair of reading glasses. "That's what most people want when they come to visit me. Let's have a look."

Miranda opened the accordion file and pulled out several photographs she'd printed at home.

Daisy frowned. "You don't have the actual feather?"

"I don't, unfortunately."

She put on the glasses. "Well, it's always better to have the real thing. Let's see what we can do."

Miranda handed her the close-up picture first. It showed the long dark feather that had been snagged in the zipper of the backpack on the floor of the canoe.

Daisy pursed her lips. "Hmm." She leaned over the photograph. This close, Miranda saw that Daisy's skin was dense with freckles and deeply lined, probably from decades of working outside.

"And this one is for scale. I didn't have a ruler handy." Miranda passed her the photograph that included the dollar bill placed parallel to the feather. "The length is fourteen point two inches, or thirty-six centimeters."

"Long," Daisy commented.

"Yes."

"It's symmetrical. Looks like a tail feather, given the shape." Her brow furrowed. "This color is interesting."

Miranda's pulse picked up.

"It's not *black* really, but more of an indigo."

"Yes."

Daisy looked at her, her pale gray eyes curious. "And it's shimmery, too. Or is that just the light?"

"No, that's what it looked like to me, as well." Miranda pulled out another photograph. She'd been saving this one for last. She'd taken it from a slightly different angle, and the feather had caught the sunlight. "Here."

Daisy took the photograph. She stared at it a long moment before muttering something.

Miranda leaned closer. "What's that?"

"Strange. I'm seeing a greenish tinge now." She met Miranda's gaze, her expression baffled now. "You said you found this feather around here?"

"That's correct."

"Well, I love a good mystery. Let's figure this out." She scooted her chair up to the computer and tapped the mouse to wake up the system. The desktop background image was an aerial view of Lost Beach taken from the north looking south toward the lighthouse. The sky was a dusky purple, and the causeway formed a glittery white arc connecting the island to the mainland.

"I use the Global Feather Index." Daisy clicked on a quill icon, and a sky blue screen appeared. "It's popular with birders and also law enforcement."

"Law enforcement?" Miranda asked.

"Customs people. They're trying to crack down on trafficking, you know."

Daisy clicked into a screen and ticked down a list. "Let's see . . . color. Length. Shape. This is definitely one of the tail feathers, or rectrices. A middle one, I suspect, because of the almost perfect symmetry. And it has a relatively short quill. See? This feather acts as a rudder, helping the bird steer in flight."

She answered several more questions on the screen and clicked SEARCH.

"Hmm. 'No results found.'"

Daisy went back to the form and navigated to the "Region" section. She unclicked "North America" and hit the SEARCH button again.

A result came back, and Daisy made a low whistle.

"Look at that. It's what I suspected. *Anodorhynchus leari.*"

Miranda's heart skittered. "What?"

She swiveled her chair to face Miranda. "The indigo macaw, or Lear's macaw."

"A parrot." Miranda had suspected the same when she'd seen the feather's greenish tinge.

"Not just any parrot. These are endangered."

Miranda leaned closer to the screen. "Really?"

Daisy clicked again. A photograph of a pair of dark blue birds appeared on the screen. The birds were long and elegant, with indigo plumage. Patches of bright yellow colored their cheeks.

"They're native to Brazil, and their populations have decreased dramatically in recent years," Daisy said. "There are just over a thousand left in the wild. Jason is really the expert." She nodded at the man in the lab coat. "He wrote his thesis on endangered species. You say the picture of the specimen was taken around here?"

"Yes."

"But not in *nature*. This was taken . . . Where is this, exactly?" Daisy held up the photograph showing a narrow glimpse of the canoe bottom.

"The feather was found in a boat."

"That I can see. I mean, what was it doing there? Whose boat is this?"

"I'm not at liberty to say." Miranda smiled to soften the message. "Sorry."

Daisy looked at her, lifting an eyebrow. "Is this a police photograph?"

"Why do you ask?"

"Because I've seen police pictures before, and that's what this looks like to me." Daisy set the photograph down and removed her glasses. Miranda tried to read her expression. She didn't look offended that Miranda had dodged her question. Instead, she looked worried.

"This is about yesterday, isn't it? Those two bodies they found out in the bay?"

Miranda's stomach knotted. Maybe she had made a mistake coming here. "I'm sorry, I can't—"

"I know, I know." Daisy held up a hand. "You can't tell me details. But tell me this, though. Are you working with the police here? Is this part of an investigation?"

A chill snaked down Miranda's spine. "Why do you ask?"

"Because you're not the first investigator to come to me with a feather."

"No?"

"A police detective brought me a feather last summer. He said he found it at the scene of a murder."

CHAPTER

FIVE

THE LATE-AFTERNOON SUN cast long shadows across the parking lot as Joel pulled into the marina. Nearing the water, he spotted an LBPD skiff in the bay alongside a boat that belonged to Lost Beach Fire and Rescue. Joel passed a pair of white vans and a couple of overdressed reporters who appeared to be setting up shots for the five-o'clock news.

He parked his pickup near a police unit and slid out. Randy stood in the shadow beside his bait shop, smoking a cigarette and eyeing the vans with suspicion. He waved Joel over.

"Hey." Joel stepped into the shade. "How's business to-day?"

"Shitty." He blew out a stream of smoke and nodded at the reporters. "The buzzards are scarin' off my customers. Any chance you can run 'em off?"

"They're on a public road."

"Hmph. That's what they said, too."

Joel looked at the reporters, then turned back to Randy.

"They'll pack up eventually. You see anything suspicious today? Anyone strange hanging around?"

"Nope." He dropped his cigarette to the gravel and stepped on it. "I'll call you if I do, though."

"Thanks, Randy. Be good."

Joel headed over to the blue tarp that had been erected near the dock and stepped over a swag of yellow tape that cordoned it off from the rest of the parking lot. He surveyed the plastic tubs that had been brought in to transport any evidence recovered by the diver. The tubs were empty except for a few crumpled beer cans and a barnacle-covered two-by-four—probably the same one Miranda had slashed her foot on yesterday.

Joel muttered a curse and turned to look at the water. Nicole was bringing in the skiff now, and he crossed the dock to meet her. She tossed him a line, and he crouched down to tie it to a cleat.

"How's it going out there?" he asked.

"It's freaking *hot*."

Her nose was pink from the sun. She wore sand-colored tactical pants and a navy golf shirt, same as he did, but she had on black rubber boots and had spent some time traipsing around in the mud this afternoon.

"Any luck?" he asked.

"Yep."

Joel gave her a hand as she stepped off the boat, and the excitement in her voice made him hopeful that his crap day was about to get better.

"You guys find a wallet or a purse?" he asked.

"No." She wiped her hands on her pants and walked with him toward the tent. "Emmet's brother found a slug, though."

"Oh yeah?"

"Yeah. *And* he said it's in good condition." She stepped

under the tent, peeling off her LBPD hat. She went straight for a cooler and popped open the lid.

Joel watched as she fished a bottle of water from the ice. They'd been searching for a slug at the crime scene ever since their examination of the canoe revealed a bullet hole, which explained why the canoe had been taking on water when the victims were discovered.

"Calvin's been down there for hours with a metal detector," she reported. "He said the silt is so soft, it's almost like ballistic gel."

Emmet's younger brother Calvin was a new hire with the Lost Beach Fire and Rescue team, and prior to that he'd been a Navy SEAL. The man was not only an expert diver; he knew a lot about ballistics, too.

"So, the slug's not mutilated," Joel said.

"Nope." She took a sip of water. "He said it has good markings, which means we can run it through the system."

Even so, a match was a long shot. The federal firearms database contained records of the unique markings made by a gun when a bullet was fired. The database included bullets recovered from crime scenes and victims' bodies, as well as test bullets fired from weapons seized by law enforcement. Problem was, running evidence could take months, and there was only a slim chance that the weapon used yesterday was in the database already.

"Why don't you look excited?" Nicole asked.

"I am."

"Uh-huh." She set her water bottle down on the table. "I take it since you're asking about a wallet, we didn't get IDs at autopsy."

"Nope."

"*Shit*. He printed them and everything?"

"Yep. Neither has fingerprints in the system."

"So, what *did* we get?"

"He ruled out suicide. No gunshot residue on their hands. So, we're officially investigating a double murder."

She sighed. "That's what we thought." Her expression clouded, and she looked out toward the bay.

"What?" Joel asked.

"Nothing. It's just they looked so, I don't know, *posed* in the canoe. I was thinking it could be some sort of creepy suicide ritual."

"Maybe the killer posed them."

She shuddered. "That's even creepier."

"So, like I said, no hits on the fingerprints. And no distinguishing scars or birthmarks. Both have tattoos, but nothing distinctive."

"What about time of death?" She dropped onto a plastic stool and pulled off one of her mud-caked boots.

"Within one to three hours of when they were discovered."

She took off the other boot. "Okay, so Miranda Rhoads found them about six forty, which means they were shot between three forty and five forty, or thereabouts."

"Given the bullet hole in the boat, I think we can narrow it down even more. If they'd been out there two hours, the canoe could have been at the bottom of the bay."

"We're lucky Miranda found them when she did or there'd be nothing left to find. What else?"

"No track marks or signs of drug use," he said. "But the tox screens will take a while."

"I bet they come back positive. This thing feels drug related to me. They were probably out there making a handoff."

Joel folded his arms over his chest. "What's the evidence of that?"

She glanced out at the bay. Calvin was climbing into the boat now and taking off his scuba tank. They were done for the day.

"What else would they be doing out there in the dark?" she asked. "Most sane people are asleep at that hour."

"Miranda Rhoads wasn't."

She shot him a look. "You know what I mean. They didn't have any fishing gear. It looks like they went out there in the dead of night, so what the hell were they doing? No one would sleep out there—you'd get eaten alive by mosquitoes." She heaved a sigh. "Any leads on their car or where they might have been staying?"

"McDeere's been looking for an abandoned vehicle, but so far nothing. And he checked in with the motels and campgrounds."

"So, we still have no clue where they were staying or what they were doing here."

Joel raked his hand through his hair, frustrated. The recovered slug was a good development, but what they really needed was IDs on their victims so they could start retracing their movements leading up to the murders.

Nicole stripped off her socks and dropped them into the boots, then retrieved a pair of flip-flops from under the table. She turned to watch as Emmet and his brother docked the boat. Calvin tied up, then hefted his scuba tank over his shoulder and walked barefoot up the dock. He wore only black swim trunks and a dive mask that dangled around his neck. The mask had left marks on his face, and it looked like he'd been underwater awhile.

Joel glanced at Nicole as the brothers walked over. Nicole and Emmet were like oil and water, but she'd had a thing for his brother Calvin for years.

"Hey, man." Emmet stepped under the tarp. "You hear about the slug?"

"Yeah. Good work."

Emmet went straight for the cooler while Calvin set his

scuba tank on the ground and started rummaging through a duffel.

"Mint condition," Calvin said as he joined them under the tarp. He scrubbed his hair, sending water droplets everywhere; then he reached out his hand for his brother's drink. Calvin guzzled water and plunked the bottle on the table.

"Here, check it out." Emmet tugged a small white envelope from his pocket and showed Joel the slug. It looked a hell of a lot better than the one pulled from John Doe's body at the autopsy.

Nicole stepped closer. "Amazing. So much destruction from something so small."

Calvin swigged more water. "I can put in a call, if you want," he told Joel. "A buddy of mine works in the county crime lab. He'll put a rush on it for us."

"Thanks," Joel said, although he doubted anything would come of it in time to be much use to them. If they arrested a suspect and recovered a gun, a match would be useful at trial. "We recovered another slug at autopsy, but it's mangled."

Calvin nodded. "This one's your best bet."

"What's your guess on turnaround?" Nicole asked him. "We don't have a lot of leads right now."

"Depends how backlogged they are."

Joel's phone buzzed and he pulled it from his pocket. His pulse picked up at the sight of the San Antonio area code.

"Breda," he said, stepping away from the group.

"Hi, it's Miranda. Miranda Rhoads."

Just the sound of her voice took some of the sting out of his mood.

"Sorry to bother you at work," she added.

"You're not. What's up?"

"I wanted to see if we could meet up later. There's something I'd like to show you."

He stepped away from the tent, picturing her at her house last night in her skirt and high heels. "Are you back from your class now?"

"I'm on my way. I have to pick up Benji at the dog sitter, but I can be at the station by six."

"I'm tied up until seven, at least."

"I'll come at seven, then."

There was a tension in her voice that hadn't been there the last time they'd talked.

"Hello?"

"I'll be there," he said.

"Good."

"Miranda . . . are you okay?"

She waited a beat. "No."

THE POLICE STATION was a madhouse.

The low-slung brick building sat near the waterfront, giving police boats easy access to the bay. It should have been a picturesque spot, but right now the place was besieged by visitors. The parking lot was overflowing, and Miranda counted four news vans and a half dozen police units from various agencies parked haphazardly on the grass. A red Suburban from Lost Beach Fire and Rescue occupied a front-row space near the flagpole.

Miranda surveyed the scene as she rolled through the lot, driving slowly so she wouldn't hit any distracted reporters. A press conference seemed to have just let out. Men in dress shirts and ties and women in miniskirts huddled with cameramen to review footage. Meanwhile, a wind gusted in from the bay, wreaking havoc on their overstyled hair and prompting them to use their vans as windbreaks.

Parking was impossible, so Miranda drove around to the back, hoping to find something near the boathouse.

A reporter darted in front of her, and Miranda slammed on the brakes. He glanced up from his cell phone and scowled.

"Idiot," she muttered.

The passenger door opened, and Miranda gasped, startled.

"Hey." Joel slid into the seat. "Bad place to meet. Sorry."

"It's a zoo here."

"I know." He raked his hand through his hair and looked out over the chaos. He was dressed the same as yesterday, in a navy shirt and brown tactical pants, with badge and holster at his hip. "Chief decided to hold a press conference, deal with it all at once." He turned to look at her. "You eaten?"

"What?"

"Are you hungry?"

She realized she was famished. "Yeah, actually. What are you thinking?"

"Drive north."

She maneuvered out of the lot, careful not to sideswipe any police cars.

"You can cut through this side street, then in four blocks pick up the highway."

Miranda followed his instructions and turned north onto the state highway that ran the length of the island. She glanced at Joel beside her. He had a strong profile. His mirrored sunglasses concealed his expression, but the tight set of his mouth hinted at the pressure he was under. He seemed tired and amped up at the same time.

"Long day?" she asked.

"You could say that," he said, rubbing his jaw. He was well past the five-o'clock-shadow phase, and she remembered how he'd looked last night at her door, all tall, dark, and sexy, like she'd conjured him up in a dream.

He glanced at her. "You been to Manny's?"

"No. Where is it?"

"Turn left after the marina."

The sign for the nature center appeared, snapping her attention back to the reason she'd called him. This was work, not a social visit, and she couldn't get distracted.

They passed the pasture with the water tower, but the horses were nowhere to be seen now. Joel looked toward the bay as they neared the marina, and she knew he was thinking about the investigation.

"Hang a left just up here," he said.

She turned onto a narrow road and bumped over potholes until she reached a row of warehouses along the waterfront. Rusted boat trailers filled half the parking lot. A chain-link fence topped with razor wire surrounded another lot with a sign pinned to the gate: **YOUNG'S BOAT STORAGE**.

The warehouse on the end had a blue awning above the door, and Miranda noticed the neon sign. Beyond the building, a row of picnic tables overlooked the water.

"I always thought this was a boat repair shop," she said, pulling into a space.

"That's next door," Joel told her. "Looks like a dive, but they've got the best fish on the island."

It was a high compliment given the number of seafood places in town, and her curiosity was piqued as they got out of the Jeep.

Joel waited for her to retrieve her purse from the back. They walked to the restaurant together, and he opened the door for her.

Inside, she paused beside the door to let her eyes adjust to the dimness. A large box fan hummed from the corner, circulating the humid air. The room had a concrete floor with a drain in the middle. Ice-filled cases displayed a selection of glistening fish. An array of big blue crabs had been arranged artfully in a case at the end. At the back of the narrow restaurant, a raised garage door provided a view of the docks.

"It's a fish market, too?" she asked Joel.

"Yep. They get it fresh every day. Or you can bring in your own catch and they'll cook it up however you want."

A man in a black apron came out from behind the counter. Joel peeled off his sunglasses and shook the man's hand.

"This is my friend Miranda," Joel said to him. "Miranda, this is Manny Ortega."

He flashed a smile at her. "Nice to meet you."

"You, too."

"You got a table free?" Joel asked.

"There's one outside. It's all yours."

"Thanks."

Joel ushered her through the restaurant, and the smell of fried shrimp wafted over as they passed the kitchen. Stepping onto the patio, Miranda saw that every picnic table was occupied except one on the far end. Joel led her to it and took the side with his back to the water.

Miranda sat down, swinging her legs over the bench, glad she'd changed into a T-shirt and jeans when she'd come home from work.

"Nice view," she said.

He glanced over his shoulder at the pair of shrimp boats moored at the weathered dock. "Are you being sarcastic?"

"Not at all. Look at the birds."

A flock of pelicans roosted along the roof of the neighboring building. They had a view of the boats, where men in waders were going through nets and tossing scraps into the water.

Joel turned back to face her. His blue eyes looked tired, and his thoughts seemed to be far away. It was a look she'd seen before on the faces of detectives she'd worked with.

"How'd the autopsies go?" she asked.

"Not good. Still no IDs."

"Damn. Really?"

"Really."

Oftentimes an autopsy provided information that could jump-start a stalled investigation. Such leads made sitting through the grisly procedure worth the agony—because it truly *was* an agonizing thing to watch. But Joel's grim expression told her that hadn't been the case here, which meant the pressure on him and his team was mounting.

"What did they find?" she asked.

"Cause of death, which is homicide, like we expected. Approximate age. Stuff we already knew, really."

"And what's the age estimate?" she asked. The Lost Beach rumor mill had the victims as "teens," but Miranda thought they'd looked slightly older.

"Early twenties," he said. "That's based on teeth. And something from the X-rays."

"The epiphyseal plates, probably. They stop growing in the early twenties."

Joel's frown deepened, and he watched her. She couldn't tell what he was thinking.

A young server stepped up to their table. She was tall and slender and had a mane of curly blond hair.

"Evening." She looked at Miranda. "Something to drink?"

"Um . . ." She picked up the menu tucked behind the condiment bottles and glanced at Joel. Was he on duty or off?

"I'll have a Dos Equis with lime," she said.

The server jotted it down and glanced up. "Joel?"

"Just water, thanks."

"Are y'all ready to order?"

"What's your rec today?" he asked.

"The snapper, hands down. It's just off the boat."

He arched his eyebrows at Miranda.

"Sounds great to me," she said.

"Make it two snapper dinners."

"You got it. I'll have those drinks out."

When she was gone, Miranda looked at him. "Everybody knows you."

"Yeah, well. I grew up around here."

Miranda wanted to know more. She wanted to ask about his family and his job and what it was like growing up in a beach town. But she hadn't come here for small talk.

"So, what's up?" he asked. "You sounded upset on the phone."

"Not upset, just . . . concerned."

"Concerned?"

"One more question about the autopsy," she said. "Did they remember to bag their hands?"

He nodded.

"So, they preserved the feather?"

"The ME collected it with other trace evidence. Nail clippings and all that. It went off to the lab. Why?"

"In terms of evidence, the feather is unusual."

He frowned slightly. "I figured it was from a seagull or some other scavenger bird."

"Maybe. But it wasn't the only feather at the crime scene," she said. "There was the other one caught in the zipper of the backpack."

His gaze narrowed. "The long black one."

"Not black."

"No?"

She took her phone out and opened a digital copy of the photograph that she'd sent to herself. "The color is indigo." She opened another photograph. "In this shot, you can see it has a tinge of green. See?"

She offered him the phone, and his fingers brushed hers as he took it. He stared down at the image.

"I thought this was from a buzzard that found the bodies before you did," he said. "Scavengers come quick out here."

"This feather isn't from a carrion bird. We've tentatively identified it as coming from a macaw."

His gaze snapped up. "Who's 'we'?"

"I stopped by the nature center this morning to talk to their ornithologist, Daisy Miller. She wrote a book about birds of the Texas coast. Anyway, she thinks this feather is from the indigo macaw, or Lear's macaw. It's a rare parrot native to the Amazon."

"A parrot." He sounded skeptical.

"There are only about twelve hundred left in the wild. They're on the endangered species list. Here." She took the phone back and brought up a picture of the macaw. "Here's one in its natural habitat. Which is a tropical rain forest, by the way, not a coastal wetland."

Joel stared at the picture, his expression unreadable.

"I don't know how this artifact came to be at that crime scene," she said. "But it's strange, don't you think?"

He scoffed. "There's so much strange about this case I don't know where to start."

Miranda put her phone away as the server stopped by to drop off their drinks.

"Have you had problems around here with exotic-animal trafficking?" Miranda asked when the server was gone.

"We get trafficking, yeah—drugs, people, counterfeit goods from Mexico. But animals? Not that I've heard about."

Miranda squeezed lime into her beer. "Here's the other thing that's weird. Daisy told me last year a detective came to her with another exotic feather he found at a murder scene."

Joel's eyebrows shot up. "Where?"

"Corpus Christi."

"Who's the detective?"

"Henry Lind."

"I know him."

Joel looked away, shaking his head, and his frustration was palpable.

"I've got two victims, no IDs, no suspects, and no apparent motive," he said. "And now I've got clues at the crime scene that don't make sense. Thirty-six hours into this case, and I'm nowhere." He gave her a sharp look. "Don't repeat that, by the way. That's between us."

"I understand."

He was treating her like an insider in the investigation, and it gave her a little buzz. She liked that he trusted her.

"Thanks for telling me," he said.

"Of course."

"I'll give Lind a call. See where things stand on his case."

"I think it's still open," she said. "I'm not sure, but I did some searching online and couldn't find anything about an arrest. The victim's name was Mark Randall."

"I remember the case. A shooting, right?"

"That's right."

"They never arrested anyone," he said. "I would have heard about it."

The waitress returned with two huge platters of pan-fried fish, French fries, and coleslaw. She set down a bottle of tartar sauce and a basket filled with hush puppies, then beamed a smile at Joel. "Enjoy!"

Miranda blinked down at the food. "How on earth can anyone eat all this?"

"You'll see." Joel dipped a hush puppy in ketchup and popped it into his mouth.

The conversation faded as they settled into their dinners. It was a nice evening to be outside. The breeze floated over them, and she shifted her attention to the birds as they flapped around the docks, vying for scraps from the boats.

Miranda tried to recall the last time she'd been out to

dinner alone with a man. Not that this was a date. But she couldn't deny how attractive he was. Every time she looked at him, she felt a warm *pull*.

She glanced up and caught him watching her.

"What?" she asked.

"You're good at this."

"At what?"

"Investigating. You've got an eye for detail. Any chance you come from a family of cops?"

She smiled. "No. My dad was an engineer and my mom was a teacher. They're retired now."

"Are they in San Antonio?"

"Nope. I grew up in Corpus, but they don't live there anymore. They retired down to South Padre Island."

"Not too far from here."

"Yeah, they love it there."

She dipped a fry in ketchup. Despite the ridiculous portions, she'd somehow polished off half her plate.

"So, why'd you quit CSI work?" he asked.

The word *quit* bugged her, but she shrugged it off. "I don't know. I wanted a change."

He pinned her now with those intense blue eyes. The look put a knot in her stomach. He knew she was lying. The man was a detective. He was skilled at reading people.

"Call it burnout," she said.

"That covers a lot of ground. What happened, specifically?"

"Specifically . . . I needed a break."

It wasn't a lie, really—just an incomplete answer. It didn't encompass the panic attacks and the night sweats and the constant low-grade anxiety that had permeated her life those last few months. She'd escaped all that when she'd left her CSI job and moved down here.

At least, she'd thought she had. Yesterday had rattled her.

Joel was still watching her, probably waiting for her to say more. For some reason she felt compelled to open up, which wasn't like her at all, especially with someone she barely knew.

"My specialty is forensic photography," she told him.

"You have a degree, right?"

"In criminal justice."

Apparently, he'd read her online bio on the college website.

"I've been doing nature photography for years, just on the side, selling pieces here and there," she said. "I heard about a calendar project for the birding association, and it sounded interesting, so I submitted a portfolio. They offered me the project, and the timing worked out, and so I moved down."

He nodded. "And you got down here when? April?"

"March. Just in time for the spring migration. My deadline is in August, so I signed a six-month lease."

The server was back to clear the plates and drop off a check, and Miranda was relieved by the interruption. She didn't want to talk to him about why she'd come here and when she planned to leave.

They split the bill and walked back to the parking lot. As they reached the Jeep, a flock of roseate spoonbills flew over in a V formation.

Miranda tipped her head back. "Look." She glanced at Joel, and he was smiling at her. "What?"

He shook his head. "Tourists."

Okay, so maybe she was a tourist. But he didn't realize how lucky he was to live on an island, surrounded by birds and beaches and beautiful scenery. Everywhere she looked there was something to photograph.

They drove back to the police station as the sky turned dusky pink and the sun disappeared behind the sand dunes. Miranda figured he was going back to work tonight. Day two of a homicide investigation, he would be working round the clock.

She glanced at him beside her.

"You ever think about going back?" he asked.

"What, you mean CSI work?"

"Yeah."

All the time.

"Not really," she said. "I like what I'm doing."

He nodded slowly, but she didn't know whether he believed her.

She turned into the police station parking lot, relieved for his sake that the reporters had cleared out. She pulled into an empty space beside the flagpole.

He turned to look at her. "My offer stands."

Nerves fluttered in her stomach. She didn't want to have this conversation again, but she'd brought it on herself by getting involved in his case.

"With the high season coming, we could really use your help," he added. "Our pay is consistent with big-city departments. You can look it up on our website."

"I'm only here through the summer."

"We could use you through the summer, then."

She sighed. "You're persistent, you know that?"

"So I've been told."

"Why are you so determined to convince me? I'm sure you could find someone else who's qualified."

"I've seen your work. I want you."

His words hovered between them as he looked at her. A warm tingle filled her stomach. She wanted to reply, but she couldn't think of a thing to say.

"The job's yours if you want it." He opened his door. "Think about it, all right?"

Before she could respond, he was gone.

CHAPTER

SIX

NICOLE TUGGED HER ponytail loose and drove with the windows down, letting her hair whip around her face. The wind felt liberating after hours stuck in the airless conference room, poring through reports and bickering with her team about next steps. It was good to get into her pickup and just drive through the darkness, letting the endless yellow stripes on the highway numb her brain. As she neared home, thoughts about the case were replaced by dreams of a long hot shower and the leftover pizza waiting in her refrigerator.

She passed the marina, and her food fantasies gave way to worries about the investigation again. Nicole's shoulders tightened. She hated bickering. Tempers were short today, and throughout the department frustration was running high. Everyone from Chief Brady on down was tense and snappish, and the army of reporters camped out in front of the station this evening hadn't helped.

Emmet and Owen wanted to keep the investigation tight.

They opposed reaching out to other agencies, especially off island. They'd even been reluctant to involve the fire department's search-and-rescue crew, although that decision was a no-brainer. Aside from that, not one person on her team—even Joel, who was usually pretty reasonable—had wanted to involve outside departments. But now that they were nearly two days in with no IDs, keeping the investigation close was becoming untenable. It was time to enlist help.

We should set up a task force, maybe get the sheriff's office to lend us a couple people, Nicole had suggested.

But Emmet had balked. *What, so they can come down here and take over? We can handle this ourselves.*

Since day one of the police academy, Nicole had become used to being surrounded by pushy alpha guys. She hardly even registered them anymore, except for times like today, when she went head-to-head with one of them.

She'd lost the argument, of course. As the department's sole female detective—not to mention a detective still in training—she had been outnumbered and outvoted by everyone. It was a waiting game now. If something didn't break soon, there would be no getting around the fact that the Lost Beach Police Department was in over its head with this one.

Nicole thought of the crime scene photos taped to the murder board. She couldn't get them out of her mind—and it probably didn't help that she'd spent half the meeting staring at them. The pictures were horrible. Gruesome. But as gruesome as they were, they didn't fully capture the chilling feeling of being there in person, looking down into that boat. The entwined victims had looked so *posed*, as if they'd arranged themselves for some macabre portrait. And now that the case had been classified as a homicide, Nicole knew the pose wasn't part of some bizarre suicide ritual. No, the killer had done that *to* them.

A shiver of fear went through her. The scene was . . . taunting, somehow. There was no other word for it. But who was the killer taunting? The investigators? Or was it a message for the general public? Either way, there was something sick about it. Something sadistic. Something utterly at odds with the friendly little beach town where Nicole had grown up.

Since the moment she'd seen the bodies, Nicole had had a deeply unsettled feeling in the pit of her stomach. It had her on edge. She hadn't slept well, and she was constantly looking over her shoulder.

Suck it up. You're a cop.

She'd be mortified if anyone on the job figured out how much this case had spooked her. She needed to stop obsessing. It wasn't the first disturbing crime scene she'd been to, and it certainly wouldn't be the last.

Nicole passed the sign for the Windjammer Inn. McDeere had been by there again tonight, and still no sign of an abandoned vehicle or guests who'd overstayed their reservation. Ditto the island's two high-rise hotels. Officers had been to every motel, campground, and RV park twice now, with no luck. Nicole's last task of the day had been to print out a map of Lost Beach rental properties. There were sixty-six houses and condos for rent on the bay side alone, and tomorrow they were going to have to start going street to street, knocking on doors.

A trio of flickering campfires came into view as Nicole neared Laguna Vista Park. On impulse, she turned in. An officer had been by here already, but what the hell.

She pulled up to the gatehouse, where an attendant sat with his feet propped up on the desk. He opened the window as Nicole rolled to a stop. The guy had long hair and eyebrow piercings, and she didn't recognize him.

"Evenin'." She held up her police ID. "How's it going tonight?"

He dropped his feet to the floor and clicked out of whatever he'd been watching on the computer, probably porn. "Quiet so far."

She put her ID away. "You guys full?"

"About half, I'd say."

"Any abandoned vehicles or tents?"

"Don't think so."

"Anyone who didn't check out on time?"

"No. Don't think so."

He sounded wary now. He either hadn't heard about the double murder that had rocked the island—which was unlikely—or hadn't put it together that the victims might have spent the night here before they died.

"So, no problems, then?" she asked.

"Nothing, really. Just a noise complaint on 12, but that's been it tonight."

"Good enough. I'll just take a lap around."

He nodded and reached for the button to lift the gate. Nicole drove through.

The island had three campgrounds—White Dunes, Lighthouse Point, and Laguna Vista, which was the only park facing the bay. Fifty percent occupancy meant twenty-two campsites occupied, and they were situated on two rows, with bayfront sites going on a first come, first served basis. She started with the row closest to the shore because wherever the victims had been staying, they'd managed to put a canoe in the water in the dark of night.

She passed several tents lit up by lanterns or computer screens. Even camping, people never really disconnected. She passed a pair of empty campsites and then an RV where a man sat outside in a plastic chair. He had a tackle box at his feet and was fiddling with a fishing pole by the light of a flashlight. A few more tents and RVs and Nicole spotted the sign for 12.

Site 12's occupants had pitched a large blue tent beside a black pickup with the tailgate down. Two men and a woman lounged in chairs around a campfire. All of them turned to look as Nicole rolled to a stop and parked her truck. She grabbed her Maglite and got out.

"Evenin'." She held up her police ID. "Lost Beach Police."

The two men exchanged looks.

"Hi," one of them said. He wore khaki shorts and no shirt and had a tallboy beer in his hand.

Nicole turned to the other man, whose feet were propped on a cooler. "That your Igloo?" she asked, beaming her flashlight at it.

"Yeah." He sounded defensive.

"What's inside?"

"Beer, mostly."

She turned to the woman, who looked eighteen, max. She wore a white bikini top and cutoff shorts, and her long blond hair was pulled back in a loose braid. "We had a noise complaint about this location. Was that you guys?"

"That was earlier," she said. "We turned it down."

"What's the problem, Officer?" Shirtless asked.

"No problem. Mind if I see some ID?"

The guys traded glances again. The one with the cooler stood up and dug a wallet from his pocket. His friend with the tallboy did the same. Nicole's attention was on the blonde.

"Um, mine's inside," she said. "I can get it if you want."

"How old are you?"

"Twenty-one."

"Go get it."

She got up and ducked inside the tent. Nicole checked out the IDs of the two guys. Twenty-five and twenty-six, both from Austin.

"That your kayak by the water there?" she asked Shirtless.

"It's hers."

Nicole handed back the IDs and stepped over to check out the yellow kayak. It was empty and had a paddle beside it.

The girl walked over and handed Nicole a driver's license. Amber Lynn Greeson. Austin address. The birth date checked out. Nicole studied the state seal, but everything looked legit.

"When did you get here?" Nicole asked her.

"Yesterday."

"You notice any canoes out since you've been here?"

"No."

Nicole lowered her voice. "How much have you had to drink tonight?"

"I don't know. Maybe two beers."

She watched the woman's eyes. "Are you here because you want to be?"

"Yeah. Why?"

"Just checking."

Nicole handed the ID back, then turned and skimmed her gaze over the water. The distant causeway formed an arc over the bay. From here, the refineries on the coast looked like a strand of twinkle lights, not a row of chemical-belching smokestacks. Nicole shifted her attention north, where the campground abutted private land. A pair of shadows near the water caught her eye.

No lights. The two shapes could be a pair of SUVs, or maybe an SUV and a camper. The shapes were about fifty yards away, past the boundary for Laguna Vista.

Nicole turned to the blonde. "Be careful out here, Amber."

"I will."

She gave the guys her stern cop look and returned to her truck, thinking about the weather the past few days and how soft the ground was likely to be. She continued down the road that started to loop back toward the gatehouse. She braked and studied the topography.

Screw it, she decided, going off road. It was sandy here, but not soft enough for her to get stuck. At least, she hoped not.

Her headlights illuminated some leaning posts and a sagging barbed-wire fence. In one section, the wire was missing completely. Nicole's pulse picked up as she felt her tires settle into previously made ruts in the dirt. Slowly, she passed through the fence posts. She hooked a left toward the water, and her headlights illuminated a silver camper and a black SUV.

"Son of a bitch," she murmured.

Nicole parked and grabbed her flashlight, ignoring the *ding-ding-ding* telling her she'd left the keys inside. The ground was soft and grassy but not wet. Her headlights created a long black shadow as Nicole trekked toward the camper.

It was a small Airstream. New, from the looks of it. The vehicle was a black Toyota with Oregon plates. It had a ball-and-socket hitch on the back, and the camper had been detached.

Nicole's heart thrummed as she shined her light over the SUV. A strand of Mardi Gras beads dangled from the rear-view mirror. Stuffed into the cup holder were a pink hair scrunchie and a bottle of Diet Coke. An orange-and-white fast-food bag littered the passenger floorboard.

She turned to the camper. Her heart was going double time now as she approached the door and knocked. She aimed her flashlight at the lock, checking for any sign of damage. Nothing. She knocked again.

Oregon plates. A woman's scrunchie. Nicole walked around the camper and shined her flashlight at the window, but a white curtain made it impossible to see inside. She circled around the back, and her shoes sank into the sand. It was wetter here.

Thunk.

Nicole froze and listened. Nothing. She switched the flashlight to her left hand and rested her right hand on the butt of her pistol. Still nothing. She thought she'd heard movement *inside* the camper.

Something rustled behind her. Footsteps. Nicole's pulse jumped as she whirled around, aiming the flashlight. But there was no one there.

She switched the light off and waited, listening for more rustling sounds. Maybe it was the wind.

Thud.

Nicole jumped, startled. This time she knew she hadn't imagined it. She unholstered her weapon. Creeping closer to the camper, she turned on the Maglite and aimed it at the back tire. A rat with beady red eyes glared at her and then darted into the field.

Nicole huffed out a breath, relieved. She was jumping at rats now. She continued around the back of the Airstream, looking for another window. The one at the back was blocked by curtains, too.

"Hey."

She whirled around with her flashlight. Emmet winced at the glare.

"Jesus, Nik."

"What are you doing here?" she demanded.

"Don't shoot me."

She flushed with embarrassment and holstered her weapon, trying to bring her heart rate back to normal.

"I'm checking out this camper," she told him. "What are you skulking around for?"

Emmet picked his way through the grass. He'd changed out of his work clothes and now wore a T-shirt and jeans with flip-flops.

"I did a loop through the campground and saw your pickup." He stopped beside her and looked at the Airstream. "Nice camper."

"It's abandoned."

He reached for her flashlight, and she handed it over.

"SUV has a roof rack," she said. "You could strap a canoe up there."

He aimed the light at the Toyota. "Plates?"

"Oregon. I was about to run them."

He stepped over to the vehicle to look, then handed back the flashlight. "I'll do it."

He walked off, and his broad-shouldered body was silhouetted by the headlights. She spotted his pickup, now parked on the same road she'd used. Why hadn't she heard him approach?

She'd been distracted by her discovery.

Nicole turned back toward the camper. This was it. She could feel it. Her heart was racing now, and not just because Emmet had scared the crap out of her. This location had bay access and was less than a mile north of where the bodies had been found.

But why set up here, away from the campground? Maybe someone was squatting here, using the bathrooms and avoiding the fees.

Nicole circled the car again, then searched the weeds around the Airstream, looking for trash or footprints or any other clues. Her flashlight beam fell on a pair of black Teva sandals on the ground near the camper door.

She crouched down. Men's shoes, probably size ten or eleven.

She stood up and examined the door again, itching to try the latch.

"Hey, Nicole," Emmet called from his truck.

She heard the excitement in his voice.

"What is it?"

"I think we've got something."

J OEL TREKKED UP the stairs to his house and cradled his phone on his shoulder as he unlocked the door.

"Did you talk to him?" he asked.

"Just got off the phone," Nick Brady told him. At Joel's request, the chief had checked in with a DEA contact, hoping to get a lead. "No run-ins with anyone who meets the description of our victims."

"Shit."

"I know."

Joel stepped into his dark house.

"I'm not surprised, though," Brady said. "If these two were running drugs on the bay, it was strictly amateur hour. No one makes a handoff in a canoe."

Joel knew he was right, but he'd hoped for a lead anyway.

"Thanks for checking," he said.

"No problem. You home now?"

"Yeah."

"Rest up. We've got a big day tomorrow," Brady said. "Try to get in early before the media invasion."

"I will."

"And if they corner you for a quote—"

"No comment. I know."

Joel ended the call and set his phone on the kitchen counter beside his keys. As he scanned his messy living room, his gaze landed on the tuxedo on a hanger draped over the back of his sofa. The tux was overdue, and now he owed a fee. Perfect. And the woman who ran the island's only formal-wear shop lived for weddings and would pump him for details the second he set foot in the store.

Joel grabbed a beer from the fridge and twisted off the top, then went out onto the deck. His house was small but solid. It had withstood a Cat 4 hurricane and three tropical storms, including one since he'd lived here. He'd been working on fixing the place up, and his current project was replacing splintered decking.

No wind tonight, just a light breeze. He walked out over the boathouse and leaned against the railing, looking down the canal toward the bay.

Elaina was married.

To Joel's best friend.

They were on their honeymoon right now in Hawaii, probably watching the sunset over the Pacific Ocean.

Joel sipped his beer and waited to feel something. Resentment. Jealousy. Regret. But he didn't. Just like at the wedding, he felt nothing but mild annoyance that people kept sneaking glances at him to get his reaction.

Maybe there was something wrong with him. After a three-year relationship, he should probably feel at least something watching two people he knew better than anyone stand at the front of a church and exchange vows. But he didn't feel a thing, and hadn't since he'd heard about the wedding. It was almost like the news had put his feelings for both of them on ice.

He sipped his beer. It was cold and bitter and felt good on his parched throat.

His sister said he was in denial. She had a degree in psychology, so maybe she was right. He'd trusted her judgment, too, which was why he'd planned to take a few vacation days after the wedding and head down to Cozumel to do some diving. But the callout on Monday morning had derailed that plan and, truth be told, he didn't mind. He wasn't big on vacations, and this one could wait until he didn't have a double homicide in his lap.

A boat motored by. Joel watched the running light get smaller and smaller until it became a pinprick. It was headed for the bay, probably to do some midnight fishing. Joel pictured Jennifer Meznick on her dock Monday morning, reeling in a redfish before witnessing someone who'd just murdered two people make a quick escape.

Or maybe not. Maybe the boat she'd seen had nothing to do with anything.

Joel checked his watch. Forty-two hours.

He counted because it mattered. The mythical "first forty-eight" in homicide investigations was real, and he knew that if he and his team didn't get a break soon, the trail would grow cold.

Evidence is ephemeral.

Miranda was right. And not just physical evidence—people's memories faded, too.

He thought of her at that picnic table tonight, with her loose curls blowing in the breeze. He pictured her plump mouth, which he'd been thinking about since yesterday. He pictured her brown eyes and the little worry line between her brows as she'd watched him talk about the case. She was right to worry. He was on a clock, and she knew as well as he did that time was ticking away.

So, was she onto something with the feather thing?

Joel didn't know. A Brazilian parrot was a strange twist. But everything about this case had been strange from the jump. He would follow up on the lead because he didn't have a choice. Right now he had no IDs and no motive, and the few clues he had didn't add up.

Yet.

And then there was the challenge of Miranda. Last night she'd been closed off. Defensive. Today, not so much. She'd seemed more relaxed tonight, smiling and talking and even laughing at some points. But still he could tell she was holding back, never truly letting her guard down.

And she continued to refuse the offer to join his team. Not that he blamed her. If she was dealing with burnout, the last place she should be working was his overwhelmed police department during peak tourist season. They'd be swamped with property crimes, drug crimes, sexual assaults. They'd recently seen an uptick in sex trafficking, too. Growth was a mixed blessing, and the same forces that brought jobs to the island also brought an increase in illegal activity.

Sometimes Joel felt like he was standing on the shore watching a wave form, one that had the potential to crash over him and wipe out the idyllic town where he'd grown up. Lost Beach wasn't the same now as when he'd been a kid, and he wanted to protect it. Unlike most people here, Joel had been born and raised on this island, and he felt a responsibility to help preserve it for future generations. He'd never actually said that to anyone, but the idea was in the back of his mind, always, motivating him to get up and do his job day after day.

So he understood burnout. But he was still hopeful that he could change Miranda's mind. They needed her skills, if only for the summer. Three months was better than no months. He planned to pour it on thick with her if he had to in order to change her mind.

Joel pinched the bridge of his nose, where he felt a headache forming. What he needed was a shower and about twelve hours of uninterrupted sleep. He'd take the shower, but trying to sleep would be pointless. He was better off working. He could fire up his laptop and comb through reports to see if he'd missed something—maybe some small detail from an interview that he could turn into a lead.

Joel emptied his beer over the railing. He went inside,

and the buzzing of his phone made his pulse pick up. Miranda? But she wouldn't call him this late. It was probably the chief again. He grabbed the phone and saw that it was neither.

"Breda."

"You still up?" Emmet asked him.

"Yeah." He caught the excitement in Emmet's voice. "What have you got?"

CHAPTER

SEVEN

MIRANDA PUSHED HARD until her muscles burned and her lungs felt like she was sucking in glass shards. She set her gaze on the horizon and ran flat out, ignoring the pain as the tip of the rooftop came into view. The wooden bridge grew bigger and bigger until finally she saw the yellow flutter of the beach towel she'd wrapped around the railing.

Just when she was feeling like a badass, Benji sprinted ahead, beating her to the finish line.

She staggered to a halt and tipped her head back to look at the pink sky. Benji galloped around her, showing off his boundless energy before darting to the shore to chase down a seagull. It flapped away, and Benji raced back, dancing and zipping in circles around her.

"You're killing me, Ben."

She trudged to the bridge that spanned the dunes and snatched up the towel. She'd left a water bottle there, too, and she took a long guzzle before sharing with Benji. After pouring some into his eager mouth, she unzipped the pouch clipped around her waist and made him sit for a treat.

"Good boy!" she said, and he ran off to chase sand-pipers.

Miranda blotted her face with the towel and hooked it around her neck. The beach towel was their signal for swim time, and Benji was already splashing around in the waves. The three-mile run had barely put a dent in his energy.

She turned her gaze to White Dunes Park and noted the shrimp boat just offshore, bobbing gently on the glimmering water. A lone man stood at the stern, pulling in a net as seagulls fluttered around him. Miranda shielded her eyes from the glare and watched him work, wishing for her camera. Maybe he'd be back tomorrow or later in the week.

She guzzled the rest of her water and sank onto the cool white sand. By lunchtime it would be scorching, but for now she leaned back on her palms and let the wind whip against her flushed skin. Benji barked and took off after a pair of gulls. He loved it here.

She loved it here.

Living near the water was a balm to her soul, and she felt grateful every day that the calendar project had come through. She'd needed a change. Not just a change, a life-line, and the photography project had given it to her. It wouldn't last forever, but for now the modest income and change of scenery were exactly what she wanted. It allowed her to procrastinate, to put off the decisions that had been weighing on her for months.

Should she go back to her old job? Her old life? Should she go back to school and maybe get a master's degree, along with a fresh load of debt? Should she apply for a full-time teaching position? For the past five months, she'd felt rudderless. All her life, Miranda had been goal oriented, and this feeling was new to her. She didn't know what to do about it.

I want you.

Joel's words came back to her, along with the determined look in those blue eyes. What must it feel like to have such brash confidence? She admired it, but it annoyed her, too, because she knew what he was doing. He was wearing her down, little by little, drawing her in. And she was letting him.

He'd lured her into his investigation, making his problem hers. She'd been up half the night thinking about it. And the night before that. She didn't even work for the man, and yet here she was, hooked on his case, analyzing the crime from every vantage point, trying to make sense of the bizarre clues.

And it wasn't just the case; it was the people. The camaraderie. The buzz of shared purpose that permeated a fresh crime scene.

Nature photography was a solitary pursuit, which was precisely what she'd wanted when she'd come to Lost Beach. But lately she'd been craving people, activity, human interaction. All her life she'd been an introvert, but now she found herself chatting up strangers in the grocery store and looking forward to Tuesdays on campus, when she would be surrounded by students.

She was lonely. She could admit it. But being lonely didn't mean she wanted to plunge right back into CSI work. Her last case had turned her inside out. Even now, all these months later, she still had the pictures of a lifeless child seared into her mind. The crime scene was every parent's worst nightmare, and she remembered every soul-crushing detail.

Miranda shuddered at the memory. And then the conflict was back, putting a knot in her stomach.

She missed police work, plain and simple. She missed the people. She missed the surge of adrenaline that came from looping a camera around her neck and approaching a scene, her pulse thrumming with anticipation. She missed the sense of foreboding. The challenge. The euphoria of finding that one overlooked clue that could break a case wide open. It was a high like nothing else. Not even sex came close.

Plus, Miranda was good at it. She had an instinct that set her apart from other CSIs, even ones with years more experience. She knew this about herself, and it gave Joel's words all the more impact.

I've seen your work. I want you.

Miranda felt a warm pull deep inside her as she pictured his blue eyes. How was it that a man she'd only just met could invade her thoughts so completely? Joel and his case had permeated every waking hour since she'd made her discovery. Was she obsessed with the man? Or was it the work she longed for because she needed to fill a void?

Maybe both.

But she couldn't have it both ways. If she worked with him, a personal relationship was out. And if she started seeing him, she could forget about accepting the job offer. Miranda had naïvely tried to mix professional and personal once before and it had backfired on her completely. After an intense four-month relationship—which had probably been more intense, she realized now, specifically *because* they'd kept it under wraps—her boyfriend had abruptly broken up with her. And then she'd had to cross paths with him every day while secretly nursing her wounds. She'd made a vow to herself not to go there ever again.

Miranda sighed. She knew what she needed to do. What she wanted to do. But the thought of actually doing it made her heart race. Forensic work was high stakes, the very highest. Not like nature photography. In police work, if you missed your shot, you didn't get another one. The possibility of failure was always there, swirling beneath the surface like a current ready to pull you under. She'd been pulled under before.

The job was risky, which attracted her and scared her, both at once.

Miranda unzipped her pouch and took out her phone. Before she could change her mind, she scrolled through the call history and found Joel's number. Her thumb hovered over it.

Maybe calling his cell was too personal. She should keep things professional and call him at work.

She found the website for Lost Beach Police and tapped the number. As it rang, Miranda remembered the time. It was barely seven. He probably wasn't in yet.

"Lost Beach PD," a woman's voice said.

"I'm calling for Detective Breda."

"Which one?"

Miranda didn't respond. Did he have a brother on staff? Maybe a sister or a cousin?

"Joel, please."

"He's out," the woman told her. "Would you like to leave a message?"

"No. Thank you."

Miranda hung up, uncomfortable now. Things with Joel had felt friendly last night—almost intimate. But in reality, she knew almost nothing about him.

She found his cell number and called it.

"Breda."

"Hi. It's Miranda."

"I know."

Her heart skittered. Damn it, she'd thought she knew what she wanted to say to him. She stood up now, brimming with nervous energy.

"Hello?"

She cleared her throat. "I'm calling about your offer. I'd like to accept."

No response. She waited a beat. And another. And another.

"Joel?"

"Let me call you back."

He clicked off, and she stared down at the phone.

Benji bounded up to her. He halted at her side and shook water all over her feet. She looped the towel around his neck and scrubbed him dry. Then she walked over to a piece of driftwood and sank onto it. Benji plunked down on the sand beside her, panting.

Miranda stroked his head as she gazed out at the waves. Her pulse was thrumming again now. Was she making a mistake? She wasn't sure how she'd expected Joel to react, but that hadn't been it.

Benji scrambled to his feet and darted toward the surf again just as her phone chimed.

She took a deep breath. "Hi."

"Sorry about that," he said. "Where are you?"

"At the beach."

"You have your camera with you?"

"No. But I can get it."

"Hang on."

She heard muffled voices in the background as he talked to someone.

"Get it," he said.

"You mean—"

"You're officially hired," he told her. "And we've got a crime scene."

* * *

NICOLE POPPED OPEN the trunk of the patrol car and rummaged through the heap of equipment. Traffic cones, waders, extra ammo. She found the box containing disposable Tyvek suits. She handed the box to Miranda.

"Thanks for coming," Nicole said.

"No problem."

Nicole offered Miranda a pair of gloves, too, but she shook her head.

"I brought my own."

Nicole eyed the tackle box at her feet. "And you have your own kit?"

"Yep."

Miranda zipped into the suit. Then she pulled her hair back into a ponytail and secured it with an elastic band from around her wrist.

"Where's Joel?" Miranda asked, looking toward the campground.

"On his way. He's getting the warrant."

"You sure?"

"The judge just signed off. The vehicle's registered to the female victim, tentatively identified as Elizabeth Lark, age twenty-two."

Miranda nodded. "In that case, I'll go ahead and get started with the outside." She looped her camera around her neck. "Don't walk on anything till I'm finished, okay?"

"Sure."

"And don't touch anything."

"I know."

Miranda trekked across the grass and set down her tackle box by a police barricade. She ducked under the yellow tape that Nicole and Emmet had set up last night. After the driver's license photo had come back, she and Emmet had cordoned off the scene and stationed an officer nearby while Joel got the ball rolling on the warrant.

Nicole slammed shut the trunk and looked around, wishing Joel would hurry. It was humid as hell. She'd been here an hour already, and the can of mosquito repellant she'd doused herself with was having little effect.

She leaned back against the trunk and watched Miranda Rhoads circle the Airstream with her camera. Smart. Pretty. Pushy attitude. The woman was one hundred percent Joel's type, and Nicole wondered how much flirting he'd done to get her to take this job. Not that she cared, really. They were headed into the high season shorthanded, and Nicole was glad he'd managed to find someone before Memorial Day.

The CSI knelt beside the door of the camper and looked over her shoulder at Nicole.

"What size shoe do you wear?" she asked.

"Six."

"Anyone else been walking around here?"

"Just me and Emmet. He's a thirteen."

She turned and photographed something before continuing around the Airstream. Nicole slapped at mosquitoes, thinking wistfully of the sixteen-ounce coffee she'd decided not to buy this morning because she didn't want to have to pee while stuck at a crime scene.

A low rumble had Nicole turning around. Joel's gray pickup bumped across the field. Emmet was in the passenger seat. Joel slowed as he drove through the fence posts and then parked beside her patrol car. He got out and looked at Miranda.

"You get the warrant?" Nicole asked him.

"Yep."

Emmet walked over, swilling a Red Bull. "Where's Hartman?"

"I sent him home. He was out here all night."

Joel nodded at Miranda. "How long's she been here?"

"About fifteen minutes."

They watched as Miranda crouched beside the camper door with her tackle box open beside her. Using a fat black brush, she dusted the doorframe for fingerprints.

Joel swung his long legs over the crime scene tape. Emmet followed. Nicole grabbed the boxes of gloves and shoe covers and joined them by the Airstream.

Miranda knelt beside the door, flushed cheeked. She adjusted her camera lens and took pictures of the doorframe. Next, she took out a piece of clear tape and carefully stretched it over a trio of black fingerprints.

"Morning," Joel said.

"Morning." She didn't look up as she slowly lifted the tape. "You get your warrant?"

"Yeah."

"I'm almost done here."

She placed the tape over a white index card and slid it into an evidence envelope. Then she stood up.

"You plan to jimmy it?" Miranda asked as everyone pulled on gloves and shoe covers.

Emmet held up a battery-powered lockpick. "We'll use this."

"Wow. Fancy."

Miranda moved out of the way as Emmet inserted the pick into the lock. It made a low hum, and metallic dust sprinkled down. A soft *click*, and Emmet moved aside.

Miranda stepped toward the door, but Joel held up his hand. "We need to clear it."

"Okay, but *don't* move anything," she instructed.

"I won't."

"Don't even touch anything."

"I won't."

Joel took out his pocket flashlight and entered the

camper, followed by Emmet. The Airstream was small, so Nicole kept Miranda company outside while she packed up her evidence kit.

"All good," Emmet called.

Miranda went in first and placed her kit by the door. She lifted her camera and immediately started clicking away.

Nicole stepped into the Airstream. The space was stuffy and dim, with only natural light streaming through the open door. Thick white curtains covered the windows.

The guys moved to the back, and Nicole scanned the living space, cataloging impressions. Her first one was that Elizabeth Lark was a meticulous housekeeper.

The camper's countertops were spotless, the sink empty. A pair of lemon yellow plates sat in a drying rack beside a toaster oven. A half dozen different-colored coffee mugs hung from evenly spaced hooks beneath the kitchen cabinet. Nicole noticed the mint green Mixmaster and did a double take. She tried to imagine whipping up a batch of cupcakes in a kitchen this small. While on a road trip, no less.

Miranda was crouched beside the fridge now, photographing the contents. Nicole stepped around her to the small booth by the window. The seats were white vinyl and they looked like they could fold into a bed.

On the wall beside the booth was a strand of twinkle lights. Polaroid photos were clipped to the strand with small pink clothespins. Nicole leaned close to look. Each photo featured Elizabeth by herself or with her as-yet-unidentified boyfriend. One photo showed the couple on a beach at sunset with their hands pressed together in the ubiquitous heart shape. Another picture showed Elizabeth doing yoga, then another in tree pose on a rock bridge. Another photo showed her in full splits at the top of a cliff.

"Damn." Emmet leaned over her shoulder. "Can you do that?"

Nicole rolled her eyes. "Get a life."

"What? I'm curious."

She ducked under his arm. "Any evidence in the bedroom?"

"Yeah. Evidence they're schizo."

"What?"

"This room's perfect." He turned around to look at it. "The bedroom's a dump."

Nicole squeezed around his oversize body and stepped to the back of the trailer.

Joel stood there, looking around, his gloved hands tucked obediently in his pockets. The bedroom was indeed a complete crap hole. Shoes and clothes were strewn everywhere. The sheets were in a tangle atop the mattress. A pizza box sat open on a pillow, a gelatinous glob of cheese stuck to the bottom.

A magazine lay open on the floor, and Nicole stooped to see what it was. *Entertainment Weekly*. The date on the header was three weeks ago.

Joel crouched beside the mattress to look at something with his flashlight. Nicole could tell by his expression that it was something important.

"What is it?" she asked.

With a gloved hand, he picked up a yellow scrap of paper. "Check it out."

She stepped over to look. It was one of those wristbands they gave out at bars and waterparks.

"This could really help us," Joel said.

"How? They hand those out everywhere."

"This one's from Buck's Beach Club. See the palm tree logo?" He held up the wristband, and she noticed the design. "They use them to differentiate over-twenty-one and under-twenty-one customers. Different color for every night, so—"

"So we can figure out what night they were there, which might tell us when they showed up on the island," she said.

"Exactly. And possibly who they hung out with, too," he said. "They have security cams at the door there."

"Wow. Good lead."

Emmet stepped into the room and made a face. "Smells like piss in here."

He was right, and Nicole searched for the source.

Thunk.

She whirled around. The sound had come from the closet. She drew her weapon.

Ka-thunk.

Nicole's heart lurched. She reached for the door, but Emmet stepped in front of her.

"Emmet, wait. Don't—"

A yowl erupted as he opened the door and a gray animal leaped out.

CHAPTER

EIGHT

MIRANDA TROMPED ACROSS the grass to the pickup truck. Emmet stood beside it with his shirt off, cleaning the gashes on his chest.

"Here." She held out a tube of antibiotic ointment from her first-aid kit.

"I'm good."

"Really, you should use it. Cat scratch fever's no joke."

He reluctantly took the ointment, and Miranda rounded the back of the pickup as Joel ended a call with someone and slipped his phone into his pocket.

"You about done?" he asked, looking her over. She'd stripped off her Tyvek suit and now wore a tank top and yoga pants.

"For now." The breeze felt good against her skin after the stifling coveralls. She looked at the patrol car, where Nicole was using a pocketknife to puncture holes in the top of a cardboard box. "Is that for the cat?"

"Yeah. She's taking it to a shelter."

Miranda shot him a look.

"Relax. They don't euthanize."

Nicole walked back to the camper, probably to retrieve the traumatized kitty, which had likely been stuck in the closet for days. After clawing Emmet, it had raced into the bathroom to hide behind the toilet.

"What do you mean 'for now'?" Joel asked her. "What's left to do?"

"I'd like to come back after dark with some luminol. I didn't see any traces of blood or signs of a struggle, but I want to be sure. Someone could have cleaned up in there."

"Couldn't we cover the windows and do it now?"

"It's easier just to wait."

Joel's brow furrowed as he turned to look at the camper. He rubbed the stubble on his chin, which was thicker than last night. The scruffy look suited him, and Miranda was annoyed with herself for noticing. She'd accepted his job offer, and they were co-workers now. She needed to stop thinking about his looks.

"What's your take?" he asked.

"My take?"

"I want your opinion." He turned those vivid blue eyes on her. "You've seen a lot of crime scenes. What stands out to you?"

She felt flattered that he'd asked—which was probably his intent.

"Well, for starters, the obvious," she said. "No wallets, no IDs, no phones. Which makes me think they had those things out on the boat, maybe in the backpack, and that the killer took them."

"Why?"

She shrugged. "To stall identification? Or if he knew them personally, maybe to hide phone calls or text messages? Could be a combination of reasons."

Joel nodded, and she felt a twinge of irritation. This was Homicide 101, and he didn't need her to tell him this stuff.

"Also, no sign of hard drugs," she said. "No paraphernalia that would make me think they were moving product for someone. No cigarettes, no alcohol, no prescriptions of any kind. Just some over-the-counter allergy meds. And no evidence of visitors that I could see, although we'll need to run the prints I lifted. As far as I could tell, it was just the two of them using the place."

"We'll get the prints to the ME today. It shouldn't take us long to confirm her ID. Then we can notify her next of kin and hopefully figure out who the boyfriend is."

"That's big progress."

"Yeah."

"So, why are you frustrated?"

He glanced at her, then looked back at the camper and shook his head. "Something about their place seems off."

Nicole emerged from the Airstream with the cat bundled in a T-shirt, probably to keep it from scratching her arms to ribbons. The cat hissed and squirmed as she lowered it into the cardboard box.

Miranda turned to Joel. "Off, as in something illegal going on or—"

"Just, I don't know, off."

"You should track down their social media accounts," she said. "And I'd do it soon."

"Why do you say that?"

"I'm betting they're pretty active. Or she is, at least. The place has a certain *staged* look about it."

"Not the bedroom."

"Besides that." She surveyed the silver camper, gleaming in the morning sun. Everything from the twinkle lights to the mismatched-yet-color-coordinated coffee mugs had looked Instagrammable. "It's very photo ready, you know?

Even the Airstream itself looks like an ad for glamping. And then the bedroom is a pigsty, which makes me think that's where they really lived."

"Interesting point."

She shrugged. "It's just a hunch, but I wouldn't be surprised if they post a lot. You could learn about their friends, their lifestyle, wherever they've been lately."

Nicole walked over, dusting tufts of fur off her shirt. "I'm headed out," she told Joel.

"Quick question before you go," Miranda said. "Have you touched any of the windows since you've been out here?"

"You mean the camper? No."

Miranda glanced at Emmet, who was on his phone now. "What about Emmet?"

"Not that I saw, and he would know better," Nicole said. "Why?"

"I lifted a karate-chop print from the outside surface of multiple windows."

Joel's eyes flared with interest. "Which ones?"

"All of them."

"A 'karate chop'?" Nicole asked.

"The side of the hand," Miranda said. "The FBI's got a database. It's not nearly as extensive as their database of fingerprints, but it's worth a shot. I mean, it could be nothing."

Joel looked at Miranda, and she could tell he understood what she was thinking.

"Or," he said, "it could mean someone came by here and cased the place."

THE ISLAND BEANERY was busy with the lunch rush when Joel walked in. They made the best paninis in town and attracted a crowd seven days a week.

He caught the eye of the barista and took a seat beside the big bay window overlooking the sand dunes. The weather was clear today. Parents with beach toys and sunscreen-slathered kids crossed the bridge spanning the dunes. May was a big month for families with toddlers whose lives weren't yet ruled by the school calendar.

Joel tapped a quick message to his team letting them know that Brady wanted all hands on deck for a press conference at four. Another media gig that no one wanted to do. Nicole replied to his text with a gagging emoji.

"Hey."

He glanced up. Leyla slid a plate with a croissant in front of him and plunked a water bottle beside it.

"You look like shit," she said.

"Thanks."

His sister took the seat across from him and dusted crumbs off her apron. Her long brown hair was pulled back in a ponytail, and she tucked a loose strand back in place.

"Busy morning?" he asked.

"We've been slammed since six."

Leyla ran two coffee shops in town, the Beanery and the smaller but even more popular Java Place at the Windjammer Inn. The hotel provided a steady stream of customers year-round.

Joel picked up the croissant. "Thanks for this. I'm starving. Is it cheese?"

"And jalapeño."

He chomped into it, and the flakes practically melted on his tongue. His sister made the best pastries he'd ever put in his mouth. She'd won awards and been written up in magazines.

Like Joel and his two younger brothers, Leyla had moved to the mainland after graduating from Lost Beach

High School. She'd gotten a degree in psychology from UT but then decided therapy was too depressing and applied to culinary school in New York. She'd lived in the city for five years before moving back following a bad breakup.

"How was the wedding?" she asked. Leyla was one of the few people with the guts to ask him about Elaina.

"Fine."

She rolled her eyes. "That's it? Fine?"

"What?"

"I want details."

He twisted the top off the water. "There was a church, a cake, flowers. Your basic wedding."

"What kind of cake?"

"No idea."

"Open bar?"

"Yeah."

She smiled. "Did you get drunk?"

"A little."

"Good." She picked up the water bottle and took a sip. "Maybe you're not *totally* in denial, then."

"Listen," he said, ready to change the subject. "I came by to ask something. The press doesn't have this yet, but we've IDed our two victims."

"Hey, that's good."

He picked up his phone and pulled up the pair of driver's license photos from the Oregon DMV. He slid the phone across the table. "Do you recall seeing these two around recently?"

She picked up the phone and studied the photos. "Her, yes. Him, no."

"She came in here?"

"Yeah. I think it was Sunday."

That would have been the day before her murder, which

made it critical to the timeline. Joel and his team were still piecing together the victims' movements leading up to their deaths.

"Was she with anyone?" he asked.

"Nope. Came in by herself. She ordered a soy latte."

"Damn. You remember her order?"

She shrugged. "It was late afternoon, just before close. We were out of soy milk, so she got a berry frappé instead." Leyla nodded at the table behind him. "She sat in that chair right there until closing and looked through her phone."

Leyla was a good resource because she interacted with people all day long and she had a steel-trap memory. She was particularly good at picking up on people's quirks.

"Was she alone the whole time?" Joel asked.

"Yep. We were pretty empty by that point."

"You remember how she paid?"

She blew out a sigh and paused to think. "Probably credit. That's what most people use here."

He'd been hoping she might have used a phone app, which could have given them a new lead.

"Sorry," Leyla said. "That's all I remember. You have any idea how long they were in town?"

"We're working on that. They were down from Oregon, possibly on a road trip. We're trying to piece together their movements over the last few weeks."

"Well, I definitely don't remember the guy in here, but I can ask the staff in both of the shops."

"Thanks. After the press conference, I'll shoot you these pictures."

She crossed her arms and watched him. "So, I hear you hired a new CSI."

"News travels fast."

"And I hear she's pretty."

"Where'd you get that?"

She smiled. "Owen."

Joel felt a prick of annoyance. As far as he knew, his brother hadn't actually met Miranda, but he'd probably noticed her at the crime scene. Every man there had noticed her.

Leyla lifted an eyebrow.

"What?" he asked.

"Is that why you hired her?"

"We've been looking for a crime scene tech for months."

"But not actively recruiting."

"We've got a double homicide," he said. "We're underwater, and we're about to be neck-deep in tourists."

He sounded defensive now, and Leyla raised her brow again. She communicated a lot with that eyebrow. In this instance Joel knew that she—like every other business owner in town—was hoping Joel and his team would solve the case quickly and make an arrest before Lost Beach got more bad publicity ahead of the high season.

Joel wanted nothing more, and it wasn't only about tourism. He'd felt a weight on his shoulders from the moment he'd seen the victims' bodies intertwined in that canoe. They had been posed. Whoever had done that was sick, and the thought of that person roaming his hometown with impunity made Joel's blood boil. As lead detective, he was responsible for bringing that person to justice. The investigation was off to a slow start, but things were ramping up now, and Joel planned to be laser focused until he had the killer in custody. He couldn't let anything, including Miranda, distract him from that goal.

"So, is Owen on this case, too?" Leyla asked.

"Everyone's on it. We're thinking of forming a task force and bringing in some resources from the sheriff's department."

She looked surprised, probably because she knew about

the turf wars around here. Lost Beach was like any other small town.

"Whose idea was that?" she asked.

"Nicole's."

"You should do it. Tell Brady to get over his ego and get some help."

Easier said than done.

Joel finished off his croissant as some new customers walked in, all men wearing dress shirts and ties.

"Geez, more media bros. I have to go." She slid back her chair.

"Thanks for lunch."

"Sure." Leyla squeezed his arm. "And don't work too hard," she said, even though she knew he would. "I'm serious, Joel."

"Same to you."

M IRANDA HEFTED HER tripod onto her shoulder and trekked through the cordgrass. The last bit of daylight faded over the wetlands as birds and other creatures settled in for the night.

The marina glowed like a lantern, and the parking lot was busy with fishermen securing their boats before taking home their catch or heading to the upstairs bar for a beer. Even on a weeknight, the place was busy.

Miranda's duck boots squished in the mud as she neared the parking lot. A man stood there watching her, and his tall, wide-shouldered build was unmistakable. A warm tingle went through her as he walked out to meet her.

Joel looked good again. His hair was windblown, and he had the scruffy-beard thing going. He was attractive. Very. There was no denying it, or denying the zing of excitement she felt every time she saw him.

He stopped in front of her. "Hey."

"Hey," she said, suppressing a smile. "What brings you out here?"

"Interviewing regulars."

"Any luck?"

"Not much. Here." He reached for her tripod, and she handed it over.

He swung it onto his shoulder as they set off toward the lot. He was in his work clothes still, with his gun and badge clipped at his hip.

She matched her stride to his as they crossed the field. She felt ridiculously happy to bump into him here—a pleasant surprise at the end of a tedious day.

"I talked to a couple fishermen," he said. "They were out on the bay early Monday morning around the time of the murders, but no one saw anything."

"Bummer."

"No one heard anything, either." He glanced toward the bay. "That's three people—including you—who were out there that morning but didn't hear any gunshots."

Scanning the parking lot, she spied a white LBPD pickup next to her Jeep.

"Wind does funny things to sounds out on the water," she said.

"True."

They walked in silence, and she glanced at him. He looked tense, and his thoughts seemed far away.

"What about you?" he asked. "You get any good photos?"

"Some wade birds. Mostly ibis."

They reached her Jeep, and she unlooped the camera from her neck.

"You want this in back?" he asked.

"Yeah. Thanks."

He stowed the tripod on the floor, securing the end

under the passenger seat so it wouldn't bounce out. He turned to her and rested his hands on his hips, and she marveled again at his broad shoulders. He somehow managed to look athletic just standing there.

"What were you hoping for?" he asked.

"What?"

"Your photo shoot."

She stashed her camera bag in back with the tripod. "A reddish egret. Preferably a breeding adult male."

"Why?"

"They have the best plumage." She dusted her hands on her pants and turned to face him. "Seen any around?"

"No idea. How do you tell an egret from an ibis?"

"An egret's bill is long and pointed. An ibis has a curved bill for hunting prey in the shallows. The ibis is closely related to spoonbills, actually, but those have a spatulate bill."

He lifted an eyebrow.

"Sorry." She grinned. "Bird nerd here."

He smiled slightly. But his expression turned serious as he looked out at the bay. "You should be careful hiking out there alone."

"I am."

"Especially at night."

"I am. Anyway, I saw Nicole out there earlier. She was alone."

"Nicole is armed. You're not."

"Says who?"

Interest sparked in his eyes as he looked her over, and his gaze lingered on her hips. Her form-fitting yoga pants didn't leave room for a pistol.

"I carry pepper spray." She patted the zipper pouch clipped around her waist. "Never leave home without it."

He scoffed.

"What? This stuff could fell a bear."

"Not much good unless you're quick on the draw."

His tone was joking, but his eyes were deadly serious. His protectiveness put a warm glow inside her. How did he manage to do that? Usually men telling her what to do pissed her off.

Their gazes locked, and she felt another buzz of physical awareness. She wondered what he was doing tonight. She pictured him going home to an empty apartment and had the sudden urge to invite him to her place. How would he respond if she asked him?

Of course, she shouldn't ask him. They were working together now, and she should keep things professional.

She unclipped her pouch and dropped it into her back seat with her camera. "So." She cleared her throat. "Where are you off to now?"

"Work." He cast another glance at the bay. "I need to write up these interviews and go through some reports." He heaved a sigh and looked at her. "You?"

"Home," she said lightly, covering her disappointment. "Benji's been cooped up awhile now, so he needs a walk."

He opened the door for her and stepped aside.

"Thanks." She looked up at his somber blue eyes. He seemed to have the weight of the world on his shoulders tonight, and she felt a pang of empathy. He was under intense pressure right now. Yet he still found the time to carry her tripod and show concern about her safety.

She went up on tiptoes and kissed him. His mouth was firm and warm, and she eased back to see his startled expression.

"What was that for?" he asked.

She stepped back, and he caught her hand.

"Do it again."

Her heart skittered. She went up on tiptoes again. This

time he slid his hands around her waist, pulling her snugly against him as she pressed her mouth to his.

He tipped his head to the side and coaxed her lips apart, and she slid her tongue against his. He tasted sharp and musky, and every nerve in her body caught fire as his big hands glided over her hips and squeezed. She combed her fingers into his hair, pulling his head down, drinking in his kiss and letting it go on and on until she felt dizzy. His mouth was demanding, like he wanted more of her, and she pressed against him, feeling the hard ridge of him against her stomach. He made a low sound deep in his chest, and lust shot through her.

Finally, she eased back and blinked up at him. *Holy hell.*

Heat flared in his eyes, and something else. Frustration. His fingers curved into her hips, holding her in place.

Then he loosened his grip.

"Wow." Her lips tingled as she stepped back.

"I'm still on duty," he said, and his gruff voice sent another shot of lust through her.

"I know. I didn't mean to . . ." She slid into the driver's seat, needing to put some space between them.

"What?"

"Start something."

She should really shut up now. And leave before she did something else that was stupid. Like ask him what time he was getting off work.

She reached for the door, and he closed it for her with a soft *click*.

His eyes simmered as she started the Jeep. She fastened her seat belt and hoped he didn't notice that her hands were trembling.

"Be careful," he told her.

"I will."

NINE

EMMET STOPPED BY Nicole's cubicle and dropped into a chair.

"You get rid of the devil cat?"

She didn't look up from her computer. "No."

"No?"

"They were full."

"So, where is it?"

Sighing, she swiveled her chair to look at him. Emmet had cleaned himself up for the press conference earlier and somehow still managed to look cool and collected more than five hours later. He picked up the stress ball on her desk and tossed it into the air.

"You ate already, didn't you?" she asked.

"Grabbed a burger. Why?"

She growled. "I skipped dinner to work on this."

"You didn't answer my question." He tossed the ball and caught it one-handed.

"What question?"

"The cat."

She turned back to her screen. "The shelter was full, so I took it to my neighbor. She fosters strays."

"And what are you working on now?"

"Social media. Joel thinks this could be important."

"Why?"

She rolled her chair back and sighed. "We heard from the sheriff's deputy in Oregon who handled the death notification. The mom said her daughter set off on a road trip three months ago, and they haven't been in touch much. Last time she talked to her daughter was five weeks ago when she called from the Grand Canyon."

"What does she know about the boyfriend?"

"Not a lot besides his name, Will Stovak."

"Did the mom know what they were doing for money?" Emmet asked.

"Not really. Said her daughter had moved to Portland two years ago. She was waiting tables there and doing some modeling, apparently. That's where she met the boyfriend."

Emmet set down the stress ball. "Modeling. You think that's code for porn?"

"No idea. It definitely crossed my mind. Anyway, the mom wasn't exactly a fountain of information. She said she and Elizabeth haven't been close since she remarried."

"So, she doesn't even know her social media accounts?"

"Nope."

"Damn."

Nicole rubbed a kink in her shoulder. "Joel has a phone interview with the boyfriend's family tomorrow to try to get more. But in the meantime, I'm coming up with jack." She sighed. "I found a Facebook page for Will Stovak, but he hasn't posted in over a year. I've got zilch for her."

Emmet leaned in closer to look at the screen. It showed a profile page for Will Stovak. The banner photo was a beach. In the profile picture, Will wore a full wet suit and had a surfboard under his arm.

"You check Instagram?" Emmet asked.

"I've checked everything."

"Under what name?"

"That's the problem. 'Elizabeth Lark' turns up no matches, but she probably used a handle. Her mom calls her Liz, and I've tried a ton of potential nicknames—Liz, Beth, Lizzie, Lizzo—nothing. And then I tried nicknames with Lark—because she likes to travel, right? I searched Liz on a Lark, Girl on a Lark, Lizzie's Lark—but nothing matches." She swiveled her chair to face him and sighed.

"You look tired."

"I got three hours of sleep last night."

"So take a break."

"No." She turned back to the screen and clicked into Instagram. "I really need to come up with something. Joel put me in charge of this angle, and I think it's important."

"Well, I'm out." He pushed his chair back and stood up. "Don't work too late."

"Yeah."

He leaned over her and studied the Instagram page of someone named Beth Lark. The photos showed a fifty-ish woman who apparently loved knitting and Instant Pot recipes.

"Where's she from in Oregon?" Emmet asked.

"Coos Bay. Some little town on the coast."

"Try Betty."

"Betty?"

"You know, *Betty*. Like a hot surfer chick?"

"Hmm." She turned to her screen and started entering search terms. Three minutes later she pulled up a page showing a smiling young woman with sunglasses and braids.

Nicole's heart lurched as she scrolled through row after row of pictures.

"No freaking way. It's her."

Miranda parked her Jeep and gathered up her groceries, skimming her gaze over the dunes before she got out. The privacy of her location had been a draw from the beginning, but since Monday she'd been feeling uneasy about it. Maybe she should stop doing her shopping at night, but she preferred the stores when they weren't crowded with tourists.

She heard Benji's muffled barks as she slipped off her flip-flops and walked up the stairs laden with bags. As she reached the deck, she looked over the dunes to the beach. It was deserted—which wasn't unusual for a weeknight. Turning her gaze north toward the park, she saw a lone bonfire flickering in the distance.

Benji scratched at the door, and she transferred her bags to one hand as she fumbled with her keys.

"Hey, boy! You miss me? I got you your treats."

Miranda's phone chirped from her purse as she dumped the groceries on the counter. The cricket ringtone told her it was her sister.

She grabbed the phone. "Hey, what's up?"

"*Finally*, I caught you," Bailey said.

"I got your message. Sorry I didn't call you back yet. It's been a crazy day."

"I saw Lost Beach on the news this morning. There was a double homicide down there?"

Bailey worked for a paper in Austin and constantly followed the news. Miranda should have known she'd catch the story.

"It happened Monday morning," Miranda said, unloading a six-pack of yogurt into the refrigerator.

"That's horrible. I thought the crime rate was low there."

"Yeah, well, you know how that goes."

As a newspaper reporter, Bailey knew better than most people that violence had no boundaries.

"Actually, something really weird happened, too." Miranda cleared her throat. "I happened to be the one who found the victims."

Silence.

Benji whimpered, and Miranda fished the new box of treats from the grocery bag.

"*You* found them," Bailey stated.

"Yeah."

"You're serious."

"Yes. I was in my kayak doing a sunrise photo shoot, and I came upon their canoe."

"Holy crap, Miranda. What did you do?"

"Called the police. What do you think?"

Miranda motioned for Benji to sit and gave him a treat to tide him over until she could take him out.

"Miranda, *how* does this stuff happen to you?"

"What's that mean? It's not like I've ever found a body before."

"No, I mean, you move all the way down to Paradise Island to get away from the murder and mayhem that surrounds you at work, and you end up in the middle of murder and mayhem."

"I'm not in the middle of anything."

But that wasn't true. Miranda hadn't intended to be in the middle of anything, but as of this morning she was officially involved in the case.

"Although I did offer to do some freelance work for them," she said.

"Come again?"

"The police here. My background came up when I was dealing with investigators, and their CSI recently quit, so the lead detective asked if I could help out."

"Oh my God. Miranda."

"They're shorthanded. I didn't want to leave them in the lurch."

Benji had polished off his treat and was standing at attention now, waiting for his walk. Miranda stashed the coffee creamer in the fridge and grabbed the leash off the counter.

"So, what, you mean like helping them with this one case?" Bailey asked.

"However many they need. They're expecting an uptick in crime during the summer, so I said I'd do it for a couple months."

"A couple months."

"It's not like I'm busy all day. I may as well earn some extra money."

"Hmm. So, is he single?"

"Who?"

"The lead detective that you didn't want to leave in the lurch."

Miranda hesitated. She should have known her sister would see right through that.

"He's single, but that's not why I'm doing this."

Which was mostly true. Joel was certainly part of the reason. He'd been very persuasive. But she hadn't accepted the job to start a romance with him. If anything, the job made her want to avoid one.

Except for tonight, when she'd hauled off and kissed him for no good reason whatsoever.

"I hope you know what you're doing," Bailey said. "I've got to be honest, I'm worried now."

Of course she was. Bailey was one of the few people who understood what Miranda's last major case had done to her. All child death cases were difficult, but this one had been particularly heart wrenching. And when the case had fallen apart due to a flaw in the forensic evidence, Miranda had been devastated. She'd gone into a funk after the trial. For months, Bailey had prodded Miranda to see a therapist or, at the very least, take a vacation, and she'd been immensely relieved when Miranda announced her plan to take a hiatus and move to the coast for six months.

"Please don't worry," Miranda said. "It's good that I'm busy. You know how I am."

Bailey sighed.

"If it gets to be too much, I can always quit."

"Right."

"I did it before, didn't I?"

Bailey didn't respond. Meanwhile, Benji gazed up at her, thumping his tail.

"So, how's Jacob?" Miranda asked, changing the subject. "When are you guys going to come down and visit?"

"Soon, I hope. Maybe Fourth of July."

"That's 'soon'?"

"It's the soonest we can get a weekend off together."

Bailey's fiancé was a cop, and he worked unpredictable hours, just as she did. Miranda figured there was a fifty-fifty chance they'd actually make it down for the holiday. But at least she could hope. She already had a mental list of all the places she wanted to show them.

"Listen, I just pulled up to Coco Loco's," Bailey said. "Hannah and Matt got a babysitter, and we're meeting for drinks."

Miranda felt a twinge of envy as she pictured her sisters at their favorite margarita spot together. One downside of moving to the coast was that she hadn't seen them in months.

"Say hi for me," Miranda said. "And have fun."

"Keep me posted on how it's going, okay? And please be safe."

"I will."

"I mean it, Miranda."

"I *will*."

She stuffed her phone into her pocket and clipped the leash to Benji's collar.

Wind gusted over the dunes as she walked downstairs, glancing around. Why did she feel paranoid tonight? Joel's warning came back to her, along with the stern look in his eyes.

And then she thought of that kiss and the warm slide of his hands over her hips. Her body tingled just from the memory. The man could *kiss*. She'd suspected it all along, but her daydreams hadn't come close to reality. Why did he have to be an amazing kisser?

Benji tugged on the leash, and she glanced around again.

"No beach tonight, Ben. Just poke around here, okay?"

She unclipped the leash and let him sniff around the property. Of course, he wanted to go bounding over the bridge to the shore, but since she was standing right there, he obediently stayed close.

Another gust of wind blew up, making sand sting her eyes. Maybe there was a front blowing in.

Her gaze fell on the bottom step, where she'd left her flip-flops. Beside them was a muddy shoe print. She walked over to look.

It was a partial—just the toe of a boot—and it wasn't hers. She'd left her muddy duck boots in the Jeep. And anyway, the tread was different. A trail of partial footprints went up the steps.

"Benji, come on."

She walked up the stairs, taking care not to mar the

prints, which led straight to her door. The threshold was a strip of wood painted white, and the print was clearest there. Someone had stepped on the threshold, probably leaning forward to peer through the glass.

Had her landlord stopped by?

Maybe Joel?

It could have been someone looking at beach houses. She'd seen plenty of couples driving around the island checking out For Sale signs and picking up flyers, especially in the Caribbean Sands neighborhood next door. Sometimes they even got out and walked around the houses. But Miranda's place was isolated.

Worry needled her, and she tried to shake it off. Anyone could have stopped by here. It was probably her landlord.

Benji whimpered and scratched at the glass. With a last glance over her shoulder, Miranda took him inside and locked the door.

CHAPTER

TEN

JOEL STOPPED BY the break room to grab a soda. The team meeting was already underway, but he needed the caffeine after another restless night. He'd stayed late finishing reports and then battled the urge to swing by Miranda's to see if she was up. He'd resisted going, not because he didn't want to but because he didn't want her to think he was desperate to finish what they'd started in the parking lot, even though he was. Her kiss had hit him like a sucker punch, and he was having a hard time reconciling her usually reserved demeanor with that one bold move.

Joel stepped into the conference room, where the team was seated around the table listening to Nicole. The only person missing was Owen.

"One point two million," Nicole was saying. "And that's on Instagram alone."

Joel took the chair next to Emmet and twisted the top of his drink. "Who are we talking about?" he asked quietly.

"Elizabeth Lark," Nicole answered from the other end

of the table. She had a laptop computer open in front of her and a coffee mug at her elbow. "She posted a crap-ton of photos on Instagram. She's got accounts on several other platforms, too."

"What kind of photos?" Joel asked.

"Hiking, climbing, kayaking, yoga. She does it all. Or *did* it all, I should say. And she looked good while doing it, too. In almost every picture, she's in the latest and greatest activewear."

"So, is she an influencer?" Emmet asked.

"There are a few brands she tags a lot, along with some outdoor sports groups," Nicole said. "I'm still going through all these posts."

"How come the mom didn't tell us any of this?" Brady asked.

The chief sat at the head of the table with his arms crossed. In any discussion, he was usually the skeptic, quick to point out holes in people's logic.

"I don't know." Nicole looked at Joel. "You said she wasn't close to her family, right?"

"That's what the sheriff's deputy told me."

"So, maybe she didn't talk about it. I mean, her mom knew she was doing modeling. Maybe this is an extension of that."

"What about timing?" Emmet asked. "Any of these pictures tell us what she was up to the week before her murder?"

Nicole tapped her computer, and a collection of photographs appeared on the screen on the wall. The pictures were arranged in a grid, and Joel instantly recognized the smiling young woman. The shots were similar to the Polaroids he'd seen in the camper. She was practicing yoga, climbing a rock wall, doing cartwheels on the beach. In several pictures, she and her boyfriend were taking a selfie while kissing.

"She posted from Big Bend last Saturday," Nicole said. "By Wednesday, she was in Marfa checking out art galleries."

Joel skimmed the shots as Nicole slowly scrolled.

"Stop. There's the lighthouse." He leaned forward in his chair. "What day was that?"

"Where?" Nicole frowned down at her computer.

"The close-up," he said. "They're wearing mirrored sunglasses. You can see the lighthouse reflected in the lenses."

"Damn. Good eye." Nicole clicked the photo, enlarging it on the screen. It was a close-up shot of Liz and Will, so close you could count the freckles on Liz's nose. She wore a pink baseball cap, and her hair was in one long braid that draped over her shoulder.

"That's definitely the island," Nicole said. "From the date stamp it looks like . . . they were here as early as last Friday, three days before they died."

"We know from the wristband we found in their camper that they were on island Saturday and they went to Buck's Beach Club," Joel said. "But this puts them here at least a day earlier."

"Still not a big time window," Emmet said.

"Big enough," Brady countered. "I want to know where they were from the second they crossed the causeway."

"I interviewed some people at the beach club," Joel said. "The bartender remembers her but not him. Said he doesn't recall her hanging out with anyone in particular, just ordering a beer."

"What about the security cam at the door?" Nicole asked.

"I took a look. They've got footage of them arriving and leaving, but it's just the two of them."

"So, we still don't know who they were hanging out with here," Emmet said.

"I'll shop the photos around, starting at the campground,"

Nicole said. "Maybe we can learn more about what they were up to."

"Sounds good." Brady turned to Emmet. "What's the news on the ballistics?"

"Still waiting. Calvin said we might hear something later today."

Brady looked at Joel. "What else are you working on?"

"The autopsy report just landed in my inbox," Joel said. "And I've got a call later today with Will's sister. Apparently, he was in closer contact with her than with his parents."

"How about Corpus Christi?" the chief asked. "Didn't you have a lead there?"

Joel hadn't revealed much yet, because he didn't have much to reveal. So far, all he had was a detective's name and Miranda's hunch about an exotic feather.

"I've got a message in to the detective," Joel said. "I should know more today."

"What detective?" Nicole wanted to know. She didn't like being kept out of the loop, but Joel hadn't wanted to talk up this lead until he knew more about it.

"Henry Lind," Joel told her. "There may be a similarity with one of his cases. I'm checking into it."

Brady pushed back his chair, signaling an end to the meeting. "Let me know what you find. All of you. And I want everyone back here at three, so we can get squared away before the press briefing at four."

As they adjourned, Joel caught sight of Owen ducking into the break room. At a glance, he could guess why his brother had missed the meeting.

Joel stepped into the doorway. "Hey."

Owen peeled off his shades and winced at the light. "Hey." He took out his wallet and fed a bill into the machine.

"Rough night?"

He smiled and shook his head. "More ways than one."

Joel didn't want to hear about it. He and Owen were only two years apart, but sometimes it felt like a decade.

"What are you working on?" Joel asked him.

A drink thunked down. Owen twisted the top off and took a long sip. Joel waited in the doorway, tamping down his impatience.

"Dude. You have any aspirin?"

"No."

Nicole walked in and stopped short at the sight of Owen. "You missed the meeting."

"I know."

"I guess that means you were busy breaking the case for us?"

"Absolutely. You have any aspirin?"

"No."

"Advil? Midol?"

Nicole rolled her eyes and walked out.

Owen turned to Joel and sighed. "Catie Vasco."

"What about her?" Joel didn't know the woman, except that she was a game warden.

"I'm meeting up with her soon." He checked his watch. "She ticketed five people on the bay Monday morning, and I'm interviewing them to see if they saw or heard anything."

It wasn't a bad idea, but he didn't tell Owen that. He wasn't about to praise his brother when he'd spent the night partying and come into work hungover. Owen had the potential to be a good detective, but he needed to focus.

"I tracked down three yesterday," Owen said. "So far, no one knows anything useful, but I've got two to go."

"What's the holdup?" Joel asked.

He swigged his drink. "Two of them speak Spanish, so I need Catie to come with me." He looked at Joel. "How's it going with Miranda?"

"How's what going?"

"How's she working out?"

"Fine."

"Does she know what she's doing?"

"Yeah." Joel asked the question that had been nagging him since yesterday. "You met her yet?"

"Just briefly. She was in here dropping off paperwork." Owen paused and looked at him. They had the same blue eyes, but Owen's were bloodshot. "I know what you're thinking, bro. Relax."

"I'm not thinking anything."

"Yeah you are." He lobbed his bottle into the recycle bin across the room. "Elaina made you paranoid."

"I'm not paranoid.

"Whatever." He checked his watch. "I gotta go. I'm meeting Catie in ten."

"Let me know how it pans out."

"Will do."

MIRANDA UNLOCKED THE storage closet and gave the knob a hard pull, but the door didn't budge. The damn thing was warped from the humid air. She braced her foot against the wall, pulled again, and stumbled back as the door popped open.

The closet light was burned out, but she didn't need it. Batting away the spiderwebs that had formed in the short time since she'd last been in here, she stepped into the cramped space. She moved the dusty Weber grill and reached for the folded Jeep top propped against the wall.

A low rumble had her turning around. Joel's gray pickup made its way up the road, and Miranda's nerves did a little dance. She wiped the dust off her hands.

"Hi," she said as Joel got out. He was dressed in his usual work clothes and held a small manila envelope.

He took off his shades and walked over. For a moment he simply gazed down at her. He'd shaved this morning, and she remembered how his beard had felt against her skin last night.

He looked at the closet. "Clean-out day?"

"I'm getting the Jeep top out. It's supposed to rain later, and I don't want to get caught on the highway."

He looked down at her, and butterflies filled her stomach. She could tell he was thinking about last night.

"Brought you something." He held up the envelope.

"Let me guess. My ID badge?"

He handed her the envelope, and she slid out the badge. Seeing her name and photo beneath the official Lost Beach Police shield brought a rush of emotion—apprehension, mostly, with a touch of pride mixed in.

"You're official," he said.

"I am."

She met his gaze again, and a little warning bell went off in her head. They were officially co-workers now, and she needed to stop thinking about his tongue in her mouth.

He turned to look at the Jeep. "Where you headed?"

"I've got an errand in Corpus Christi."

"No kidding? Same. What's in Corpus?"

"A camera shop. I've got to get my macro lens fixed. What about you?"

"I'm interviewing that detective."

He was following up on the lead she'd given him. Good.

"Want to ride together?" he asked. "It'd save you the hassle of putting the top on."

She gazed up at him, trying not to bite her lip as she debated the seemingly casual question. Should she or shouldn't she? She was tempted to go with him. She didn't care about putting the Jeep top on, but she *did* want to know more about the Corpus Christi murder case in which a feather had been recovered at the crime scene.

"It's your lead," he said. "Aren't you curious?"

Okay, so he knew exactly which buttons to push.

"You don't mind swinging by the camera store?" she asked. "It's just a drop-off, so it shouldn't take long."

"Not at all."

"And I have to be back by one."

"Same here."

Miranda locked the closet and retrieved her camera bag and purse from the Jeep. Errands were good. This would give her a chance to be around him while conducting official police business, which would help get things back on a professional footing after her temporary insanity last night.

"Hang on," he said, opening the passenger door. He reached inside and grabbed a Dr Pepper can and some newspapers off the floor, making room for her stuff.

She climbed inside and looked around his truck, taking in every telling detail. It was neat, but not immaculate. The faint smell of leather told her the truck was fairly new. He had his cell plugged into the charger and a tackle box stashed in back, alongside a brown accordion file.

Joel hitched himself behind the wheel. So, errands with Joel. Not what she'd expected to be doing this morning. She snuck a look at him as he pulled onto the highway. Just seeing his strong hand on the steering wheel put a warm tingle inside her.

She distracted herself with her phone.

"The camera shop is on Pecan and Second Street," she informed him.

"My appointment's at eleven, so we'll do that first."

"Eleven? That's cutting it close."

"It's on the south side of town."

They picked up the highway, and Miranda looked out the window. A line of gray clouds was moving in from the Gulf.

"So, what's a macro lens?"

"For macrophotography," she said. "Extreme close-ups. Like hair and fiber evidence, marks on shell casings, things like that."

His eyebrows tipped up.

"Not something I've been doing much of lately, so I've been putting off getting it fixed, but I like to be prepared. You never know what you're going to need, and I hate getting caught with the wrong equipment."

She was babbling.

She looked out the window again and thought about that kiss. What had she been thinking? Really, she hadn't. It had been pure impulse, a response to that world-weary look in his eyes.

The second kiss had been something else entirely.

"I went back to the camper last night with Emmet," she said. "No sign of blood spatter or unexpected bodily fluids."

"I heard."

She'd expected he would have heard by now, but she was trying to fill the silence. Maybe this outing was a bad idea.

They reached the causeway, which was lined with signs showing how all lanes of traffic would become one-way in the event of a hurricane evacuation. Miranda gazed out at Laguna Madre, one of only six hypersaline bays in the world. It was a rare and beautiful ecosystem, teeming with wildlife. No boats out at the moment, which wasn't surprising given the forecast. The wind had picked up since earlier, and little whitecaps formed in the bay.

She glanced at Joel. Time to summon her courage and get it out there.

"So, I want to apologize," she said.

He cut a look at her. "For what?"

"Last night. That was poor judgment on my part."

"I thought it was great judgment."

"Well." She glanced out the window. "Now that we're working together, it's probably best if we don't . . . you know."

"What?"

She looked at him, and he was smiling slightly, like he was enjoying her awkwardness.

"Work and personal relationships don't mix. Trust me. Things can get messy, and it's totally not worth it."

He didn't respond. A few seconds ticked by and she tried to read his expression.

"So . . . can we agree?" she asked.

"We can agree to disagree."

She tried to come up with a response to that. What didn't he agree with? That things could get messy, which they could? Or that the risk wasn't worth it?

And did any of it matter, really, if she was just here for the summer? What was so bad about a summer fling? By the time anything got messy, she'd be leaving.

Her heart thrummed as she thought about it. A fling with Joel. The idea had been lurking in her mind since the day she'd met him, and she'd tried to ignore it, but it wouldn't go away.

"Miranda?"

She looked at him.

"Relax. I won't kiss you unless you ask me to. How's that?"

"That's . . . fine," she said.

He looked at the road again, and she had no idea what he was thinking.

"So, you were right about social media," he said.

"What'd you find out?" she asked, relieved by the change of subject.

"Nicole dug up several accounts. Elizabeth Lark has a huge Instagram following."

"How huge?"

"One point two million."

It wasn't crazy big, but big nonetheless.

"You should look her up," he said. "Betty's Lark. She's posted a lot, and we're piecing together her timeline now leading up to the murders." He cut a glance at her. "How'd you know?"

She shrugged. "I follow a lot of online photography. You get a feel for it. Different platforms have a different vibe."

"Well, maybe when you check her out, you'll come up with more insights. I know jack about social media, to tell the truth. Same for the rest of the team, except for Nicole."

"You should get educated. It's a useful investigative tool."

"I know. I keep meaning to take an online class, but something always comes up."

"You guys do training, don't you? Suggest it to Brady."

They reached the mainland. Miranda was startled when Joel changed lanes and signaled to exit.

"Already?" she asked. "I thought you said Corpus."

"We're meeting at his house in Bayside. Did I mention he's retired?"

"No."

"He retired at Christmas after thirty-one years on the job."

They turned at the first intersection and passed an oil refinery partially concealed by a high fence covered in vines. After several stoplights, Joel hung a right into a neighborhood called Rippling Shores. Miranda caught a glimpse of the bay, where no doubt the waves weren't exactly *rippling* during tropical storms. The neighborhood was only a few dozen homes, all smallish seventies-era houses on stilts.

"The case is still open?" Miranda asked.

"Yep."

Joel pulled up to a stop sign and checked an address on his phone. He glanced at her.

"I wanted to talk to the original detective," he said, reading her mind. She would have expected him to want to interview someone currently with the department.

"Why?"

He hung a right onto a street called Ghost Crab. Trucks and cars filled the driveways, even some boat trailers. The neighborhood looked to be year-round residents versus weekend people.

Joel swung into a driveway and turned to look at her.

"You know how you walked through that camper and got a hunch about the victim? It's like that. Those impressions don't translate when you hand off a case file."

"I get it."

She looked at the one-story house painted sky blue and felt a flutter of apprehension as the reality set in. Joel had come all the way here to interview a veteran detective at *her* suggestion. All because of a feather. She hoped to hell this wasn't a waste of time.

She glanced around. At the end of the cul-de-sac was a marshy area. Beyond it, several wade fishermen stood in the water.

She looked at Joel. "You should talk to him alone."

"Why?"

"You said you know him, right? He'll probably open up more if it's one-on-one."

He seemed to think about it. "What will you do?"

"Go exploring with my camera."

"You sure? I bet you'd ask good questions."

"I'm sure you have plenty of your own."

HENRY LIND HAD spent thirty-one years as a police officer before retiring to his house on the bay. Not a bad life, if you still had time to enjoy it.

"Damn prostate cancer," he said now, leading Joel down a creaky wooden staircase. "And as soon as I got through that mess, my heart started giving me trouble."

Maureen Lind had poured Joel and her husband tall glasses of lemonade before shooing them off to "the workshop," which seemed to be her name for the pass-through garage where Henry kept his boat. Joel stepped into the space, which could have held two cars if not for the boat trailer smack in the middle. Both garage doors were open, creating a breezy tunnel where Henry could work.

"Before Christmas, I finally said screw it." Henry set his glass on a workbench stacked with toolboxes, hoses, and power tools—few of which related to boat engines, as far as Joel could tell. "I didn't want to spend my last years cleaning up other people's shit."

Henry straightened his green John Deere cap and nodded at his boat. "I've been working on the engine all week. She crapped out on me in Farland's Channel, had to get a tow from a buddy. Mechanic was out here last month, but he only made it worse."

Joel approached the boat—an eighteen-foot Grady White with a Yamaha engine. It was a nice boat, but it had to be at least twenty years old. The engine cover was off, and an array of tools littered the floor.

"What's your horsepower?" Joel asked.

"Three hundred." He looked at Joel. "You fish?"

"When I can."

"Don't guess that's a lot with all y'all got going on down there."

Joel figured he was referring to Lost Beach's economic boom, which was fueling development, traffic, and crime on the island.

"So, you're here about Randall." Henry leaned back against his workbench, evidently finished with small talk. "That's one of those cases you don't forget."

"There's a chance there could be a connection to my case."

"The feather."

"That. And the murder weapon."

"Oh yeah?" His bushy gray eyebrows arched, and Joel could tell it was a detail he didn't know. "A .38?"

"That's right. We just heard that this morning. We recovered a slug, but we're still waiting to see if it matches anything in the federal database."

Henry pursed his lips. "Interesting."

"I understand Mark Randall was shot twice with a .38 pistol."

"That's right."

"No witnesses?"

"No one saw or heard a thing. He was out there fishing by his boathouse, and they got him in the chest from two to three feet away, according to the ME. His wife came home from the grocery store and found him sprawled on the dock with a buncha buzzards pecking out his eyeballs."

"You guys zero in on a suspect?" Joel asked, wording it carefully so it didn't sound like criticism.

Henry snorted. "I was up to my ass in suspects. That was the problem. Mark Randall had two ex-wives and four grown kids who hated him, plus a business partner he screwed out of hundreds of thousands of dollars. Not to mention his third marriage being on the rocks. They had a kid together, too. He was in kindergarten, or he probably would have been on the suspect list with everybody else."

Joel sipped his lemonade, hoping Henry would keep talking. He seemed to be on a roll.

"Bottom line, this guy had spent fifty-two years stockpiling money and enemies. He was a prick, and we had no shortage of people who wanted him dead."

Joel had read about Randall in newspaper articles. He'd made a fortune putting in housing developments along the lower Texas coast, making friends and enemies along the way. He'd run for a seat in the state senate at one point but lost the primary after a local newspaper got hold of a police report showing that cops had been called out to Randall's house for a domestic dispute.

"You look at the current wife?" Joel asked.

"Yep." He tossed the cap on his workbench and picked up a folded red bandana. He used it to mop up the sweat on his brow. The breeze had died down and it was hot, even in the shade. "She got all the money, along with their big-ass house in Laguna Estates. We took a good look at her, but she had an airtight alibi."

"What was it?"

"She was at the grocery store when it happened. Some other errands, too. We got her on videotape in and out of different stores in town."

Joel waited, hoping he'd keep going so Joel wouldn't have to ask questions that would come across as insulting.

"Course we also checked out her bank records and poked around to see if maybe she hired it out." Henry walked over to a wall switch and turned on the ceiling fan, which hung from the rafters. "Nothing there. We checked over and over and couldn't make anything of it."

"Who else was high on your list?"

Henry blew out a sigh. "Kid number four, Reed Randall. He's a mess."

"Oh yeah? How old is he?"

"Nineteen at the time, so twenty now. He's got a rap sheet, and he hated his dad."

"Any idea why?"

"Never did pin it down, but it started around the time of the divorce, when Randall was screwing around on wife number two. Anyway, kid got into drugs, apparently, racked up a few DUIs. We brought him in a few times for questioning, but nothing ever came of it."

Joel sipped his lemonade. "What would be his motive? If wife three got all the money, what would he have to gain by killing his dad?"

"Who knows. Revenge? Like I say, the pieces didn't come together, but we took a hard look at him."

"How about the physical evidence?" Joel asked, circling back to what had brought him here.

"You want to know about the feather."

"Yeah. Any idea what that was about?"

"Damned if I know. I took it to a bird expert down at the nature center y'all got there."

"Daisy Miller."

He nodded. "She ran it through her computer program and said it was some kind of rare toucan from the rain forest in Peru or someplace."

"We recovered a feather from an endangered parrot at our crime scene. An indigo macaw."

"Indigo, huh?" Henry shook his head. "Our feather was green with some red on the tip. I've got a picture of it in the file up in my office, if you want to see."

"You have the file in your office?" Joel didn't hide his surprise.

"I've got the whole damn case box up there. Copies,

anyway. I copied all the reports before I left. I still work on it when I can."

Joel watched him, wondering how his department felt about a retiring detective taking home cold-case files. Joel didn't know the brass over there, but he knew that they were tight on money and manpower, like everywhere else. So maybe they didn't mind if one of their veterans spent time on a case that was collecting dust.

"That feather was strange." Henry finished off his lemonade and plunked down the glass. "But it wasn't the only thing strange about the case. The murder happened right on that boat dock, in full view of the neighbors, on a clear summer evening. But no witnesses. No one heard a gunshot." He shook his head. "It was bold, I'll tell you that."

Joel subtly checked his watch. He needed to wrap up.

"Back to the feather," Joel said. "Any chance it somehow got there by accident?"

"No."

Joel waited for him to elaborate.

"That feather was put there."

"How do you know?"

"Because I know. It was tucked in his pocket like some kind of calling card, maybe. It was deliberate."

Joel pictured the victims in the canoe, locked together in an embrace. They'd been posed that way deliberately by someone. Joel couldn't say how he knew that, but he did.

Henry looked out toward the water and his empty boat slip, and his expression turned pensive.

"You ever get a case that stuck with you afterward, eating away at your guts like battery acid?"

Joel nodded. He knew this case had the potential to be like that.

"I can't get rid of it. This thing happened almost a year ago. And I been retired—what is it?—five months now."

He looked at Joel. "Still, I wake up every morning thinking about that prick on his boat dock with his eyeballs pecked out."

JOEL DIDN'T TALK much as they drove into Corpus Christi. Miranda was burning with curiosity, but she resisted the urge to pump him for info and instead navigated him to the camera shop. She made quick work of her errand and also purchased a new memory card, and then they got back on the road.

When they started seeing signs for Lost Beach, Miranda couldn't contain her curiosity any longer.

"So, what did you think of Lind?" she asked.

Joel waited a beat before answering. "He misses the job."

"Oh yeah? Retirement doesn't agree with him?"

"Healthwise, it probably does. But I could tell he misses it."

Miranda felt a twinge of sympathy. She knew how it felt to be floundering. Adrift. At a loss for motivation after years of driving hard.

"He had some interesting thoughts about the case, too, so I'm glad we came."

Now they were getting somewhere.

"Any new leads?" she asked.

"Possibly."

Joel walked her through their conversation, ending with Henry Lind's certainty that the feather had purposely been left at the crime scene by the killer.

"He have any idea why?" she asked.

"No. And neither do I. But it has to mean something." Joel looked at her. "Those feathers aren't just floating around."

Miranda looked out the window, frustrated. They'd come all the way to the mainland to pursue her lead, but Joel was no closer to solving the case than he'd been before.

"Hey, you mind if I stop for gas?" he asked.

"Sure, go ahead."

"You're not late?"

She didn't want to tell him that her time limit hadn't been about work, really, but her reluctance to spend the entire day with him. She was determined to put their relationship back on professional footing, and spending too much time alone together wouldn't help.

"It's fine," she said.

He pulled into a gas station, and she went inside the store to buy a drink. She returned with a water for herself and a Dr Pepper for him.

He hitched himself behind the wheel. "How'd you know?" he asked.

"I noticed your empty one."

They got back on the feeder road, and Miranda spied a sign up ahead.

"Look. That's the neighborhood," she said.

"What?"

"Laguna Estates. Where Randall was murdered. You have time to take a look?"

"We'll make time."

He changed lanes abruptly, earning a honk from another car, and turned into the subdivision. At the entrance was a giant water fountain set against a backdrop of king palms. The palm tree theme continued as they proceeded down Laguna Boulevard, which was divided by a landscaped median.

In contrast to the homes in Rippling Shores, these two-and three-story houses stood shoulder to shoulder, maxing out their spacious lots. Even the small homes had to be five thousand square feet. All the houses had manicured landscaping, and many of the arc-shaped driveways showcased luxury cars.

"Wow," Miranda said.

"He lived on a point, apparently. Can you pull up a map?"

Miranda was already on her phone looking at the layout of the neighborhood. "We're coming up on an intersection. Looks like . . . Sunset Cove? Hang a left there and it curves around to a point overlooking the bay.

Joel followed her instructions, passing one mansion after another, all with bay views.

"These homes aren't on stilts," she said.

"The whole development is elevated to protect against storm surges," Joel said. "They used thousands of tons of sand. I read about it when it was happening."

"That's a lot of sand to bring in. There have got to be what, a couple hundred houses in here?"

"They didn't bring it," Joel said. "They dredged it up when they carved out this cove here. Another selling feature—the neighborhood sits on its own private harbor."

They curved around until the street ended in a wide cul-de-sac. The house at the very end looked like a Tuscan villa, with beige adobe walls and a tile roof. All the upstairs windows had ornate wrought-iron balconies.

"It's for sale," Joel said.

She skimmed the yard and noticed the understated wooden sign beside one of the flower beds. Even the sign looked expensive.

Joel rolled to a stop. "Let's look around."

"What if someone's home?"

"Then we're prospective buyers."

Miranda grabbed her camera and got out. She walked over to the **FOR SALE** sign, which had a covered container that held a stack of flyers. She fished one out. *Luxury waterfront estate, 9,500 square feet. New hardwood floors. Italian marble. Updated finishes throughout . . .*

"How much?" Joel asked, coming down the cobblestone sidewalk toward the street. Had he just rung the doorbell?

"Doesn't say. I guess if you have to ask, you can't afford it, right?" She folded the flyer and tucked it into her pocket.

"No one's home," he informed her.

"You rang the bell?"

"Come on. I want to see the boathouse."

"But we're trespassing."

"Police business."

She followed him up the driveway of embossed concrete made to look like cobblestones. A separate path led to a vibrant green lawn that sloped down to the water. The concrete bulkhead started with Randall's property and continued in a graceful arc around the man-made cove. All the homes facing the water had sloping green lawns and impressive boathouses, some big enough for two or three boats.

Randall's had four slips, all vacant at the moment.

"I don't think anyone's living here," Joel said. "The house was dark, and one of the porch lights by the door was burned out."

They reached the boathouse. Each slip had an electronic boat hoist. The only boat, though, was a flaccid rubber dinghy stashed in the rafters alongside a rusty crab trap.

"So, looks like the third Mrs. Randall is either selling the house, or she already sold it, and someone has it on the market again," Miranda said.

"Looks like."

Miranda turned to look at the neighboring lot. That house was definitely occupied. A game of croquet was set up at the top of the green lawn. Water toys, including an inflatable banana that could probably seat three or four kids, sat on the wooden dock beside a gleaming white Boston

Whaler. Above the boathouse was a spacious deck with a pair of Adirondack chairs that faced west.

"It's not that far away," Joel said.

"What's not?"

He was staring at the neighbor's property with a furrowed brow.

"The next-door neighbors. Hard to imagine no one heard a gunshot."

"Maybe they weren't home."

"They were. Lind showed me copies of the police reports. Two adults and four kids home that night, and no one heard a thing. It's weird." He looked at her. "No one heard any gunshots Monday morning, either."

"No one you've been able to find."

He nodded, conceding the point.

"But you're right—it is weird." She lifted her camera and took several pictures of the dock. She didn't have a reason, really, except that it had been a crime scene. "Have you considered maybe the assailant used a suppressor?"

"I hadn't. Until now."

"So, you think the crimes are connected?"

"Maybe." He turned to face the other side of Randall's lot, which looked out over a marsh. In the distance, a small skiff was anchored in the bay with a fisherman at the stern, casting a line.

"Pays to be the developer," Joel said.

"How do you mean?"

"He got the best lot in the neighborhood. The biggest house. An unobstructed view of the wetlands."

"It's a shame the place is sitting empty now."

Miranda turned back to look at the neighbor's deck again. There was something charming about the red Adirondack chairs. She pictured a couple sitting there together and watching the sun go down over the water. For a fleeting moment, she felt a pang of envy.

Miranda turned away and spotted a tall white crane at the edge of Randall's property. Slowly, so as not to spook it, she walked over and lifted her camera.

The crane paused to look at her as she neared it. She took another step. And another. It was a beautiful bird, nearly four feet tall.

Click.

It didn't move.

Click, click.

It dipped its head down, almost like a nod, then flapped its wings and took off, soaring over the water.

Miranda snapped another picture. She turned to look at Joel as he walked over.

"Beautiful, isn't it?"

He stepped closer. "I was just thinking that." He reached out and tucked a lock of hair behind her ear.

Miranda's heart skittered, and she stared up into those mesmerizing eyes. She held her breath, waiting for what he'd do.

Her gaze dropped to his mouth, and she remembered how it felt and tasted. Warmth flooded her. She looked into his eyes and could tell he knew exactly what she was thinking.

He stepped back. "Let's go," he said. "You need to get back, remember?"

ELEVEN

NICOLE STRODE INTO the bullpen with a Whataburger bag in her hand and a pissed-off look on her face. She dropped the bag and a manila folder on her desk and slumped into her chair. Then she got on her computer and started muttering at it.

"Missed you at the press conference," Joel said from his desk as he typed an email.

"I was at Lighthouse Point."

The smell of French fries drifted over as she unloaded the bag.

Joel went over and leaned against her cubicle. "You're sunburned."

"Really? You're kidding. I hadn't noticed that."

He stole a fry off her pile. "Any leads today?"

"No." She blew out a sigh. "I spent five freaking hours canvassing all three parks, interviewing everyone and their grandmother, and nobody spent any time with this couple. I only talked to one person who even saw them at all."

Nicole's auburn hair was up in a ponytail, revealing sunburn on her neck, too. The burn on her nose looked even worse up close. She was going to blister.

"Most of the people I talked to weren't even there last weekend," she said. "I found a retired couple who's been at Laguna Vista Park all month in their RV, but they don't remember them."

Joel noticed the photograph peeking out from the manila folder. "These the pictures you've been shopping around?" he asked, opening the file.

"Yeah."

He recognized the photos from Elizabeth's social media posts. She had several individual pictures, along with a selfie she and Will had taken together at the beach. From the angle of the light, Joel could tell it was a sunrise shot. She took a lot of sunrise shots, he'd noticed, and may have been taking one when she was killed.

But that was speculation at this point. He didn't know for sure what they'd been doing out in that canoe, and they still hadn't recovered the cell phones, which might give them a clue.

"Then I talked to one guy at Laguna Vista who *was* there last weekend and remembers two people in a green canoe. But he didn't have a conversation with them or even get a look at them up close."

"What day?" Joel asked.

"Friday." She picked up her drink and sipped from a straw. "And that part was interesting, actually. This guy says they took the canoe out around sunset, which matches up with that picture they posted where you can see the lighthouse reflected in their sunglasses."

Nicole leaned her arm on her desk and winced. Even her elbows were burned.

"How'd it go with Henry Lind?" she asked. "Any links to our case?"

Joel gave her the highlights of their conversation, including how—just like with their case—no one heard any gunshots, even though people were nearby.

"So, does Lind think he used a suppressor?" she asked.

"He thinks it's possible."

"You think our guy used one, too?"

"He could have."

Nicole shook her head. "Damn. Sounds like organized crime. Who were their suspects?"

"They never arrested anyone, but they took a long look at the third wife, who inherited about six and a half million dollars, as well as one of the grown sons, who has a rap sheet. His name is Reed Randall."

Nicole picked up a fry and popped it into her mouth. "Interesting. So that's two possible links to our case."

"Three. The location, which is just over the bridge. The feather. And the type of gun used."

"Possibly with a suppressor," she added.

"Maybe, maybe not." He nodded at her computer. "What else did you find with their social media?"

"That's one area I *did* make headway. Look at this." She scooted her chair in and brought up an Instagram page for Elizabeth. "You saw some of this before, right? Kissy pictures, cartwheels on the beach, their cat, their cat, their cat"—she rolled her eyes—"more sunset and sunrise pictures. Okay, now look."

She clicked on a photo of Elizabeth rock climbing. She wore a helmet, but Joel recognized her by the long brown braid down her back.

"Okay, she posted this and wrote, 'Last days in Big Bend' and then hashtag 'bigwall yolo getoutside.' And here are the comments on her post."

Joel leaned over her shoulder to look. People had posted

emojis mostly, along with a few short responses such as "nice!" and "go girl."

"What am I looking at?" he asked.

"Nothing yet. Hang on." She clicked on one of the commenters. "Check out the profile picture."

The photo showed a young woman looking over her shoulder and smiling. On her shoulder was a tattoo that looked like a sideways eight.

"Look familiar?"

"Yeah." Joel stared at the tattoo. "Will Stovak had a tattoo like that."

"Yep."

Nicole flipped open another file folder—this one filled with case notes and autopsy photos. She pulled out a photograph of Will's lifeless gray forearm on the stainless-steel table. The tattoo on his forearm was a snake in the shape of a figure eight.

"What's it mean?"

"No idea," she said. "I mean, in math it's the symbol for infinity, but this design is a snake. And look." Nicole turned to her computer again and clicked into another profile picture. "I've come across three other commenters with the same tattoo, a woman and two men. You think maybe they're in some sort of club?"

"Could be."

Joel's phone buzzed and he pulled it from his pocket. Miranda. He had dropped her off five hours ago and hadn't expected to hear from her again today.

"Hey," he said, turning away from Nicole.

"Hi. I just wanted to tell you this." She sounded breathless. "I'm out here at the nature center with Benji. I'm walking him on the trail, and on my way in here I saw that cyclist."

"Cyclist?"

"The guy on the bike from Monday morning."

"The one without a helmet," Joel said.

"Yes. And this time I recognized him. He must have had his hair up in a bun or something the other day, but today it was in a ponytail, and I recognized him right away. He works at the nature center. I spoke to him briefly when I was there Tuesday."

Joel had thought the cyclist lead was a dead end. He spied a notepad on an empty desk and grabbed it.

"You happen to get his name on Tuesday?" Joel asked.

"No. But he has long blond hair that he wears in a ponytail. And he rides a black bike, no helmet. I was going to ask someone inside about him, but the building's closed for the day."

"Where's he work exactly?"

"The reception desk. He looks about nineteen or twenty."

Joel turned to Nicole, who was watching him and eavesdropping. "You know the name of the guy who works the front desk at the nature center?" Joel asked her.

"No idea."

He got back on the phone. "Thanks for the tip. I can ask Tom."

"Who's Tom?"

"The groundskeeper over there. He's worked there for years and knows everyone."

"The guy with the riding mower?"

"Yeah."

"Okay, well . . . I wanted you to know," Miranda said. "Maybe he saw or heard something that could be useful."

"I'll follow up. Thanks."

"Sure."

She clicked off as Joel jotted some notes.

"How's Miranda?"

Joel looked up and pretended not to catch the meaning in her tone.

"Fine. She just saw the cyclist from Monday when she was pulling into the nature center, said he works the desk there."

"Could be worth an interview."

"Yep." He tore the paper from the notebook.

"So, what about this symbol? Don't you think we should figure out what it is?"

"Just because one of our victims has a tattoo of it?"

Nicole pulled another photograph from the file. It was a profile shot of Elizabeth Lark's head and shoulders, also taken at autopsy. On the ghostly pale skin just behind her left ear was a small tattoo of a snake in the shape of a figure eight.

Joel's blood chilled. He hadn't noticed the tattoo at autopsy.

"Not just him—her, too. That's the point." Nicole looked at him, clearly worried. "This symbol is everywhere. We need to figure out what it means."

MIRANDA STEPPED THROUGH the door of the restaurant and nearly smacked into Joel.

"Whoa. Hey there," he said.

"Hi." She looked up at his blue eyes, startled to be face-to-face with him after thinking about him all afternoon.

"Takeout tonight?" he asked.

"What?"

"Dinner?" He nodded at the plastic bag in her hand.

"Oh. Yeah."

A young couple walked up, and Joel touched Miranda's elbow to steer her out of the way. The pair stepped into the restaurant, and then it was just her and Joel on the sidewalk in front of the Calypso Café.

"You mind hanging on a sec? I need to ask you something," Joel said.

"Sure."

"One minute."

He stepped into the restaurant, letting out a waft of Caribbean chicken and reggae music. Through the window Miranda watched the cashier hand over a bag of food and ring him up. He still wore his work clothes, including the holster and badge, and she wondered if he was on his way home from work or headed back in.

He stepped outside, tucking his wallet into his back pocket.

"Are you eating alone tonight?" he asked.

"Yes."

"Want to come over?"

She smiled. "That's what you needed to ask me?"

"One of the things."

She stalled for time as she debated what to do. "Where do you live?"

"Just over there." He nodded at the neighborhood behind the shopping center. "Three-minute drive."

He seemed perfectly at ease as he waited for her answer. She was tempted to say yes, and he seemed to know it. Nerves fluttered inside her as she considered the pros and cons.

Pro, dinner with Joel. At his house, too, which meant she'd get to see where he lived, and she was definitely curious. Con, seeing where he lived was personal, and she'd intended to put things back on a professional level.

If they went to his house, they could end up in bed. But she had the willpower to resist that. Or at least, she thought she did.

He watched her, smiling slightly, as though he knew exactly what she was thinking.

"I'll follow you," she told him.

"Sounds good."

CHAPTER

TWELVE

A S SHE TAILED his pickup truck, Miranda realized she looked like crap. Cutoff shorts, faded T-shirt, hair twisted into a bun. She'd meant to shower after her walk with Benji, but hunger had won out and now here she was, having dinner with Joel for the second time in three days. It wasn't a *date*, because it had just sort of happened, same as last time. But she would have liked to have showered at least.

He turned onto a street lined with houses on stilts, probably two- and three-bedroom bungalows from the looks of them. Some of the homes had cars in front. The ones with empty driveways and storm shutters down looked like weekend places. It was clearly an older neighborhood, but the houses were painted cheerful colors and looked well kept.

Joel turned onto a street facing a canal and pulled into the driveway of a plain white house flanked by palm trees.

Miranda parked behind him and got out.

"Nice," she said.

He took her bag of food. "Thanks."

"How long have you lived here?"

"Almost a year."

They walked under the house to a wooden staircase. Out of habit, she kicked off her shoes at the base of the steps.

"Watch for splinters," he said.

A motion-sensitive light came on as she followed him upstairs. At the top he shifted the bags into one hand and slid a key into the lock. His door was wood, not glass like hers, which was better for security.

He flipped on a light as he ushered her inside, and she immediately noticed the quiet. She was used to being accosted by a frenzied dog the instant she set foot through the door.

"It's kind of a mess," he said. "I wasn't expecting company."

She followed him to the kitchen, checking out the living room as she went. Bleached oak floors. No rugs. Not much in the way of furniture, either—only a brown leather sofa, an armchair, and a simple glass coffee table arranged in front of a wall-mounted TV. No framed photos, or color-coordinated throw pillows, or any other sign of a woman's touch. If he'd lived with anyone, it didn't appear recent.

Her gaze went back to the coffee table, where she spied a file folder with a series of photographs fanned out beside it. Next to the table was a pair of worn-looking running shoes.

"This isn't a mess," she said as he deposited the bags on the breakfast table. Then he dropped his keys and phone on the bar.

"Mind if I change?" he asked.

"No."

"Help yourself to a drink. I've got some stuff in the fridge."

He disappeared down a hall, leaving her alone in his kitchen.

Joel's kitchen. Nerves flitted in her stomach as she looked around.

The kitchen was even more spartan than the living room. No clutter on the countertops—not even a coffeepot, which was unfathomable to her. Several photos were taped to the fridge, and she walked over for a closer look. One showed Joel and four other men, all in firefighter gear, standing in front of the lighthouse. Another picture showed the causeway with a trio of hot-air balloons in the distance. Studying the angle of the light, Miranda could tell the hot-air-balloon shot was taken in the early morning.

She heard water running on the other side of the house and hoped he wasn't taking a shower. Then she'd feel even grungier.

She opened several cabinets and found an extensive collection of barware before discovering the dishes. She took down two plates.

Joel returned to the kitchen, and he'd most definitely changed. He wore faded jeans and a gray T-shirt that stretched taut over his pecs. His feet were bare. He stepped closer, and she felt a warm pull in the pit of her stomach.

"So, are you moonlighting for the fire department?" she asked, nodding at the fridge.

"That was Fourth of July. I'm on the crew that puts on the fireworks display. We go all out."

"So I've heard."

"Guess this will be your first Fourth on the island, huh?"

"Yep." She nodded at the photos again. "The hot-air-balloon picture is a beautiful shot."

"Can't take credit. My sister, Leyla, took it from the top of the lighthouse. You ever been up there?"

"It's been under renovation since I got here."

He opened the fridge, and she admired his back as he leaned down to peer inside. "How about a drink? I've got beer, water." He moved some stuff around. "Hard lemonade."

She smiled. "You drink hard lemonade?"

He shot her a look. "They're Leyla's."

"I'll have one."

He took out a beer and a lemonade and twisted the tops off.

"Thanks," she said as he passed her the drink.

He clinked his bottle with hers and leaned against the counter. "You hungry?"

"Starving."

Together they unpacked the bags, and he opened the boxes. "I can't believe you went all the way to Calypso's and only got salad."

"I love their salad. The mango lime dressing is my favorite."

He shook his head as they loaded their plates. "Next time try the jerk chicken. It's legendary."

"Noted."

"Want to eat outside? There's probably enough breeze to keep the mosquitoes away."

"Sounds good." And it had the added advantage of being away from the bedroom.

She followed him onto the spacious deck that extended above the boathouse. He had a glass table and four chairs. As she sat down, he took a lighter from his pocket and lit a citronella candle in the center of the table.

"So," she said as he scooted his chair in. "You have a wedding to go to?"

He froze.

"I saw the tuxedo bag inside."

"Oh." He took a sip of beer. "That's from last weekend. I was a groomsman."

"Was it a family wedding or . . . ?" She trailed off, noticing the tension in his shoulders.

"My best friend. And my ex."

Her mouth fell open. "Seriously?"

He shrugged.

"That sucks."

"Not really." He dug into his food, and that probably should have been her cue to shut up, but she was too curious.

"Was it, like, a long-ago breakup or—"

"It's been . . . a little over a year."

So, not long before he moved in here. Interesting.

"And you dated her for how long?"

"About three years."

"Wow."

Miranda thought about how she'd feel if her best friend, Jamie, married Ryan, the only boyfriend Miranda had been serious about since college. It would never happen. Jamie was too loyal. Miranda couldn't imagine it, and she sure as hell couldn't imagine *going* to their wedding.

Joel sipped his beer and put it down. "What?"

"Nothing. You're just very . . . mature about it."

"Mature?"

"Yeah."

He smiled and shook his head.

"What? That's a compliment. If it were me, I'd probably want to claw their eyes out. Especially hers."

He laughed. "Why hers?"

"Because. If someone's your *best friend*, then your exes are off-limits to each other."

"Yeah, well. They didn't exactly ask my permission."

"Did you have to give a toast at this thing?"

"No." He sighed, and some of the amusement faded from his expression. "His brother did it. He was the best man."

"Sorry." Miranda opened the plastic container of dressing and drizzled it over her salad. "It's totally none of my business, but . . . I don't know. I'm sorry you had to go through that."

She forked up a bite. He was watching her now with a look she couldn't read.

"What?" she asked around a mouthful of salad.

He shook his head.

They got quiet then, and she wondered what he was thinking. Probably that she was nosey.

She looked out at the canal, which was wide enough for two boats to pass with plenty of room. The decks along the opposite side were empty, but a few houses over, a man stood on the dock with a fishing pole.

"So, how's the case going?" she asked, hoping for a neutral topic.

He took another bite of chicken—which she had to admit smelled amazing.

"Slow," he said.

"That must be frustrating."

"Very. But at least we got the autopsy report back."

"Already?"

"It's just the preliminary. There wasn't anything in there we didn't already know."

"What about the tox reports?"

"Those will be a while longer."

She watched him. The candle cast a warm glow over their table, and she felt herself relaxing with him. He took a sip of beer, and she noticed his long fingers around the bottle.

"I saw the pictures in your living room," she said.

He smiled and set the beer down. "You really don't miss much, do you?"

"Sorry. Force of habit." Miranda had lost the ability to step into a room and *not* notice every detail. "I could take a look if you want."

"At the autopsy pics?"

She shrugged. "I might spot something useful."

"Hey, have at it. I'll take any help we can get, at this point. You really don't mind?"

"Not at all."

"The first few days are critical, and we're running behind."

"I know."

For a while they ate quietly, enjoying the breeze and the food. The man down the canal got a bite on his line. The fish got away, and he rebaited his hook and recast.

It still seemed weird to Miranda that she was living on an island, where people boated and fished and went for walks on the beach every morning, like they were on vacation. Maybe it didn't feel like vacation if you lived here permanently, but for her the novelty still hadn't worn off. She suspected working with the police department might be a reality check. Nothing like being called out of bed late at night to take the sparkle off a vacation. She didn't know if she was ready for it, but she'd committed to them for the summer, and she had no intention of flaking out. She'd abandoned a lot of things about her former life, but not her work ethic.

Miranda looked at Joel, and he was watching her again. The candle flickered, shifting the shadows on his face. He had strong features, and again she felt that warm pull of attraction. By the way he looked at her, she could tell he felt it, too.

Maybe she'd made a mistake coming here. She probably should have come up with some excuse. But he had a way of talking to her, of looking at her, that melted her resolve.

She thought of that moment earlier today when they'd been standing by the water and he'd brushed the hair from her face. That one small touch had set off a firestorm inside her. How did he do that?

How was it possible she'd known him less than a week and already he'd turned her world upside down? It wasn't just that he'd offered her a job and persuaded her to take it. He seemed to be offering something else, too, and she felt tempted. He'd never overtly said it, but he showed it in those long looks and brief touches, and that soul-searing kiss that had seemed to go on forever.

Her cheeks warmed as she watched him in the candle-light, wondering what he was thinking.

The distant buzz of a phone broke the spell, and he looked over his shoulder.

"That's you," she said. "Mine's in my pocket."

They got up and cleared their dishes, and she followed him into the house. He set his plate by the sink before going to check his phone. She started rinsing the dishes, but he came over and bumped her out of the way with his hip.

She dried her hands on a dish towel and offered it to him. He tossed the towel on the counter and took her hand instead.

Her heart skittered as she looked up at him. *I won't kiss you unless you ask me to.*

He tugged her closer, and her pulse sped up. She wanted to say something but couldn't think of the right words.

His phone buzzed again. Cursing, he dropped her hand and stepped over to grab it.

"Breda."

Miranda watched his face, and she could tell it wasn't good news.

"Where?" His jaw tightened. "When?" Pause. "No, I'll be there." Another pause. "Ten minutes."

Miranda put the plates in the dishwasher as he hung up.

"I need to go in," he said.

She turned around. "Anything big?"

"Probably not, but I won't know till I get there."

She grabbed her purse off the counter and hitched it onto her shoulder.

"I'll walk you down," he said.

"No need."

"Just hang on, okay?"

He went to the bedroom and she waited by the door. He came back wearing his badge and holster and the boots he'd had on earlier. He stepped over to the coffee table and scooped the photographs into the folder.

"Thanks," she said as he handed her the file. "I'll let you know if I see anything."

She followed him out, slipping on her shoes at the base of the stairs. He opened the door to her Jeep with his usual manners, and she slid inside, precluding an awkward good-bye moment.

"Sorry to cut our evening short." He sounded frustrated, and she knew exactly how he felt, having been summoned into work at night more times than she could count.

"No worries, I get it." She smiled. "Duty calls."

EMMET ANSWERED THE phone, but Nicole could barely hear him over the background noise.

"Did you talk to your brother?" she asked.

"What's that?"

"Calvin," she said louder. "Did you talk to him? He was going to follow up on that slug for us."

"Yeah, he—" Whatever Emmet said was drowned out. "—at the latest."

Nicole pulled into the parking lot in front of her apartment building.

"Where the hell are you?" she asked. "I can hardly hear you."

"We're at Finn's."

She didn't ask who "we" was because she already knew. It would be Emmet, Owen, and probably Calvin and some of his firefighter friends, all hanging out at their favorite bar on the strip.

"Did you hear what I said?" Emmet asked.

"No."

"Calvin's contact should have something possibly by tomorrow, Monday at the latest."

"Monday? Seriously?"

"He's doing the best he can," Emmet said. "They're really jammed up. Hey, are you still at the station? I thought you were off tonight."

"I just got home."

"You want to come meet us?"

"Not tonight. I'm beat."

Nicole crossed the parking lot, scanning the rows of cars for any suspicious shadows. She'd always been cautious, but the double homicide had ramped up her vigilance.

"You sure?" he asked.

"Yeah."

"Okay. Later, then."

Nicole stopped to get the mail from her box and then mounted the steps to her second-floor unit. The building was old and kind of dumpy, but it was four blocks off the beach, so she couldn't complain.

Her neighbor's kid had left his electric scooter on the breezeway again, and Nicole knocked on the door. She heard a television on inside as she waited. Finally, the door opened, and four-year-old Olivia stood there in a lavender nightgown with a unicorn on the front.

"Hey, Livvy. You should ask who it is before you answer the door, hon. Is your brother home?"

She scrunched up her nose. "What happened to your face?"

"I forgot my sunblock."

Olivia stepped aside as Drake got up from the carpet, where he was playing a video game.

Nicole held up his scooter. "You're gonna lose your scooter, Drake."

"Oh. Thanks." He took it from her and parked it by the door.

"Is your mom at work?"

"Yeah."

"Don't let your sister answer the door by herself, okay? Lock up now.

"I know."

Nicole waited until she heard the lock click to walk two more doors to her unit. She stepped inside and flipped the bolt.

For a moment she simply stood there in the quiet darkness before switching on the light. It felt good to be home, and she was glad she hadn't let herself get roped into going to Finn's tonight. Even if she didn't look like a tomato, the last thing she felt like doing was listening to a bunch of guy talk.

She crossed her living room and dumped her mail on the kitchen counter. A cat jumped down from the refrigerator, and Nicole's heart lurched.

"*Shit!* What are you doing up there?"

The cat mewed and pranced across the stove to the breakfast bar. She stood beside the mail and made another pitiful sound.

"All right. Geez."

Nicole grabbed the bag of cat food from the pantry. It was the same brand she'd seen in the camper. Lucy sprinted over as Nicole poured a serving into the bowl on the floor.

Lucy. Nicole only knew the name because Elizabeth had posted captions with her endless cat pics. Based on the posts, she'd only had the cat for seven months, and she was still practically a kitten.

Nicole watched her chow down, purring noisily while she ate. That was what had done it. Nicole wasn't a cat person, and if not for the purring, she might have taken her back to the shelter when her neighbor said she couldn't adopt any more strays. So now, after years of resisting, Nicole was officially a cat owner, and she had the outrageous vet bill to prove it.

She opened the fridge and immediately regretted her decision not to stop on her way home. She was out of almost everything. She grabbed the second-to-last beer and pressed the icy bottle against the back of her neck as she checked out her freezer.

"Hot Pocket or Lean Cuisine, Lucy. You decide."

Lucy didn't glance up from her bowl.

"Yeah, me, either."

She walked to the bathroom, still pressing the ice-cold bottle against the back of her neck. It was the best thing she'd felt all day. In her bathroom she set the beer beside the sink and stripped off her clothes. Standing before the mirror, she blew out a sigh. Her entire face was bright pink. Ditto her arms. The back of her neck was the worst of all, bordering on magenta.

How had she let this happen? She'd conducted all her interviews in the shade, but somehow she'd still managed to get burned to a crisp walking around the parks. She twisted the top off her beer and took a sip as she surveyed the backs of her arms. She was going to blister, no doubt about it.

Her phone chimed, and she dug it from the pocket of her crumpled pants. It was Emmet.

"What's up?" she asked. The music in the background seemed to have gotten louder.

"We just snagged a pool table," he said over the noise. "Come meet us. We need a fourth."

"I'm making dinner."

"They have food here."

She glanced in the mirror again. It felt weird to be talking to Emmet naked. She opened the cabinet beneath the sink and rummaged through the bottles and medicines. No aloe, damn it. She knew she should have stopped at the store.

"Come on, Nik. We need you."

"Sorry."

"Calvin's coming."

She felt a dart of annoyance. He seemed to think she had a thing for his brother. Joel did, too. Men could be so dense.

"So, there's your fourth," she said. "What are you calling me for?"

"Because. We need your skills."

"Not tonight. I'm beat."

"Your loss."

She got off the phone and sat on the edge of the tub, setting the water to lukewarm. No aloe, but she had a bag of Epsom salts, which was her grandmother's cure-all for everything from bug bites to bruises. She dumped about half the pack in the bathwater, then grabbed her beer and stepped into the tub.

Even the tepid bathwater stung. She stirred the salt with her foot and carefully lowered herself. Slowly, cautiously, she leaned back against the cool slope of the tub and let out a sigh. She closed her eyes. Even her damn eyelids burned.

She pictured Emmet and Owen standing around the pool table at Finn's. She pictured Calvin with them, and maybe Kyle or Reese from the fire department. What did they need with her? Even if she hadn't looked hideous, she wouldn't have felt like going out, especially not with Emmet. Not that she and Emmet were romantic or anything, but there had always been something simmering beneath the surface. Neither of them had ever acknowledged it, and probably never would, but she definitely didn't enjoy watching him slip into bar mode and pick up other women.

Nicole dipped her toes under the faucet, letting the rushing water soothe her tired feet. She couldn't remember the last time she'd been so whipped, both physically and mentally. This case was getting to her. Only four days in, and she felt overwhelmed. Maybe she wasn't cut out for detective work. Emmet and Owen could put in a full day investigating and then kick loose at a bar. Nicole was different. She couldn't turn her thoughts off. Ever since Monday morning, she'd done nothing but think and even dream about this murder case.

The crime scene photos haunted her. They seemed to be stuck in her head, like a slideshow on a continuous loop. She couldn't even imagine what it was like to be Miranda. After years as a CSI in a major city, she must have countless gruesome images lodged in her brain. How did she manage to sleep at night?

Nicole's phone chimed again. She glared at it on the counter. Muttering a curse, she leaned over and grabbed it. It clattered to the floor, and she scooped it up.

"What now?"

Silence.

"Hello?"

"I'm calling for Nicole Lawson."

She checked the screen, and her heart skittered. The caller ID said US GOV.

"This is Lawson."

"I'm Special Agent Meacham with the FBI. I have the results of a query you submitted."

"Oh. Thank you." She checked the time. "I didn't know you guys worked this late."

"This request was marked 'urgent.'"

"It is. Thanks." Nicole reached over and tugged a towel off the rack. "Tell me what you found."

THIRTEEN

Emmet crossed the bullpen toward him, and Joel knew his plan to slip out this morning without getting sidetracked was blown.

"Hey, I heard the team meeting got bumped," Emmet said. "Where is everybody?"

Joel finished off the last of his lukewarm coffee and tossed his cup into the trash. "Owen's working the gas station robbery and Nicole's on the mainland following up on something."

Emmet leaned his arm on the top of Joel's cubicle. "So, listen, I interviewed that biker kid," he said.

"You're talking about the cyclist?"

"Yeah, the one Miranda saw Monday morning when she was driving to the marina," Emmet said. "Alexander Kendrick, twenty-three years old. Works at the nature center front desk."

"Yeah, I talked to Tom Miller, the groundskeeper. He told me he goes by Xander."

"Whatever. After you got us his name, the chief had me go

interview him. McDeere and I tracked him down at his apartment last night. He said he didn't see or hear anything suspicious when he was riding home Monday, which would have been shortly after the murders."

"Is he credible?"

"Yeah."

Joel sighed. Another dead end. "What was he doing on his bike so early? Doesn't sound like he's a serious athlete, riding around without a helmet like that."

"He told us he was coming back from his girlfriend's. He crashed there after hitting the bars and wanted to clean up before his shift. Said he was pretty hungover when he left her place."

"Any chance he could have—"

"Nah, we checked with the girlfriend. She backed up his alibi."

The cyclist lead had always felt like a long shot, but it was frustrating to have another lead eliminated.

"Hey, I thought you were off today," Emmet said.

"I am. Just finished my report from last night. A lady in Saltwater Glen reported her husband missing. We were about to put out a Silver Alert on him when someone found him asleep in his car in the parking lot of his favorite restaurant."

"Alzheimer's?"

"Dementia."

"Well, at least they found him." Emmet looked over Joel's shoulder. "What's Miranda here for?"

Joel turned around, and his pulse gave a kick as he saw her. She stood in the reception area talking to Denise at the front desk.

"I don't know," Joel said.

Miranda glanced over and caught his eye through the glass partition that divided the bullpen from the reception room. Joel walked over and leaned his head out the door.

"Hey, what's up?"

"I'm looking for Nicole," she said.

"She's off island."

"So I hear." She held up a file folder. "You have a minute? It's about the case."

"Sure."

Joel held the door for her and ignored Denise's interested look as he ushered Miranda back. She wore dark snug-fitting jeans and a loose white shirt. Her hair was back in one of her messy twists that told him she'd left the top off her Jeep today.

"You said she was looking into the social media angle," Miranda said. "I wanted to show her something interesting I found."

"Come on back."

Joel led her to the nearest conference room, where many of Miranda's crime scene photos had been taped to the whiteboard. Joel had drawn a timeline, and different members of the team had added dates and other details as the victims' movements became clearer.

"Whoa." Miranda set her file down and approached the board. "It's weird to see it laid out like this."

"Helps us to visualize things. And make connections."

She stepped up to the photograph of the victims intertwined in the canoe. Joel had spent hours analyzing that one picture, either in this room or in his head. He couldn't shake the feeling that the pose meant something—he just hadn't figured out what.

"So, what'd you find?" he asked.

Miranda turned around. Instead of taking a seat, she propped her hip on the edge of the table. She smelled good again today. Yesterday the scent of her perfume or her shampoo or whatever it was had lingered in his truck after he'd dropped her off, distracting the hell out of him.

"Well, you gave me those photographs last night," she said, "and one of the first things I noticed was their matching tattoos. That design appears on the social media pages of some of Elizabeth's online followers."

"Nicole noticed the same thing. You think that's relevant?"

"I don't know. That's why I'm here." She flipped open the folder and pulled out a stack of papers clipped together. "I was up late combing through her posts and her commenters' posts. Check out what I found."

She unclipped the pages and fanned out three across the table. Joel didn't recognize any of the pictures. Two were cat pictures with the snake symbol on the lower right-hand corner. One picture showed a beach scene with a surfboard stuck in the sand. Again the symbol, this time in the lower right corner.

Joel pulled the beach picture toward him. "Weird."

"I know, right? I spent hours going through this stuff and found a total of fifty-three images with this symbol somewhere, either in a post or in someone's profile picture. Several of these photos were taken here on the island." She tugged a paper from the stack and slid it in front of him. Joel recognized the landscape instantly.

"This is in White Dunes Park."

"Exactly." She tapped the corner where the serpent symbol had been superimposed on the picture. "This was photoshopped. And this picture was posted a week ago today, which is three days before the murders."

Joel looked down at the fan of pictures. Then he thumbed through the stack. "Fifty-three images with this snake thing?"

"Those are just the ones I found last night. She has more than a million followers, so who knows how many of them have posts with this symbol."

"What does it mean?"

"I don't know," Miranda said. "I know someone who would, though."

"Who?"

"Mike Conner, one of my colleagues. He teaches cultural anthropology at the college, and he's an expert in symbology. In fact, he wrote a book on the subject: *Symbols through the Ages: Hieroglyphics to Emojis*."

Joel rubbed his jaw as he gazed down at the photographs.

"I brought you his contact info, in case you or Nicole want to give him a call. He's done some consulting work with the FBI's gang unit in San Antonio." She pulled a slip of paper from her purse. "He teaches classes today at eleven and one, so you should be able to catch him at his office. That is, if you're interested."

Joel took the slip of paper and read the name. "I'm definitely interested, but I'd rather talk to him in person."

She looked startled. "You want to drive to San Antonio? Wouldn't it be easier just to call him?"

"Easier, yeah. But I always get more out of a face-to-face interview. Henry Lind is a case in point. If I hadn't gone to his house, I never would have gotten a firsthand look at that case file."

"Don't you have work to do here?" she asked.

"Technically, I'm off today because I've got to be on call this weekend. But you know how that goes. I was planning to work from home." He folded his arms. "What do you have going on? You up for a road trip?"

She looked surprised again. "You want me to come with you?"

"Sure. You can introduce me."

She checked her watch and seemed to consider it. As the silence stretched out, he realized how much he wanted her to say yes. Since the day he'd met her, he couldn't stop drumming up reasons to spend time with her.

"If you can't get away, no problem," he said, trying to

sound casual. "I can track him down myself and show him your research."

"No, I'll go." She slid from the table. "I was up half the night on this. I'd like to get some answers."

ST. JOHN'S COLLEGE was a twenty-five-acre oasis in the middle of bustling San Antonio, just ten minutes from the Alamo and five minutes from the apartment where Miranda had lived before she'd put her stuff in storage and moved to the coast. The architecture on campus consisted of white stucco buildings with red-tile roofs, with the glaring exception of the newest dorm, a glass high-rise that towered over the south lawn. Huge oak trees dotted the campus, offering shade to students who wanted to eat, nap, or otherwise slack off between classes.

Miranda pulled into a lot and whipped into a front-row space beside the visitors' center, a mission-style building with a bell tower at one end. She'd insisted on driving because she had a faculty parking sticker, even though that meant they had to stop by her house and put the top on the Jeep.

"Nice campus," Joel said. "Looks bigger than I thought."

"Four thousand students."

"When do they get out for summer?"

"Ten days." Miranda smiled as she gathered her file and tote bag from the back seat. "Can you tell I'm counting?"

She locked the Jeep and stepped onto the sidewalk. Joel stretched his arms over his head and shook out his stiff legs, and she admired his athletic build for the millionth time. He was in street clothes today—a black T-shirt and jeans, along with a scarred leather bomber jacket, which he wore to conceal his gun.

"Conner's office is a bit of a hike," she told him. "You're going to be hot in that jacket."

The corner of his mouth curved up. "I'll survive."

They took the sidewalk that led past the dining hall, which was crowded with students eating lunch around outdoor tables. They crossed a grassy quadrangle where people seemed evenly divided between reading and sunbathing.

"Oh, to be a student again," she said wistfully.

Joel made a face.

"No?"

"College wasn't my thing," he said. "The whole time I was there, I wanted to get out and work."

Interesting. And she could totally picture that.

"Where'd you go to school?" she asked.

"University of Houston. Then straight to the police academy."

"So, you got your start with HPD?" She had been wondering about his background since the very first day.

"Spent six years as a uniform, then two as a detective before I moved back."

"What made you want to move back?"

He glanced at her. "My dad died."

Guilt needled her. "I'm sorry."

"Thanks." He looked up at the trees. "I liked Houston, but I wanted to reconnect with my family, help out my mom. I'd been thinking of moving back anyway, and the timing seemed right."

Miranda could relate. The photography project had come up at just the right time, the exact moment when she desperately needed a change. It had felt like fate. Or necessity. Maybe a combination of both.

"How long have you worked here?" Joel asked.

"Three semesters. One of my former professors told me about the opening, and I decided to apply."

"You like teaching?" He glanced over at her, and his

eyes were a startling shade of blue-green because of the leafy tree cover.

"Love it," she said. "I didn't think I would but . . . I don't know. I like working with students. Showing them how to do things for the first time. Forces me to keep up with innovations in my field, too, so that's a plus."

"It's good that you want to."

"What? Keep up?"

"Yeah. So many people get into a rut. I see it all the time in law enforcement."

"You ever thought about training cops? I bet you'd be great at it."

He slid her a sideways look. "Why?"

"You're a natural leader."

He didn't bother to deny that. It was one of the first things she'd noticed about him. When he showed up at a crime scene—or anywhere, really—he assessed the situation and took charge. And people looked to him for direction, as though they expected it.

"I've trained a number of our recruits," he said.

"Oh yeah?"

"And I'm Nicole's TO right now. She's working her way up to detective."

"I thought she was one."

"That's by design. We treat her that way so she grows into the role."

They reached another quadrangle. A scooter zoomed up behind them, and Joel caught Miranda's arm and tugged her out of the path.

Miranda noticed women's reactions as she crossed the campus with Joel. He definitely turned heads, and it wasn't just because of the leather jacket in eighty-degree weather.

It felt strange to be around him in a completely new setting, one where she'd spent so many days as her former self.

CSI Miranda. Forensic Photography Miranda. Living on the island, she'd grown used to being the quirky nature photographer who was always traipsing around the marshes or stalking birds in her kayak. Which version of herself was the real one? She didn't know anymore. She felt caught between worlds.

She looked at Joel. He had a certain intensity that permeated everything he did. He seemed to believe solving this case was his personal responsibility, and he had no intention of delegating the task. When it came to his job, he was driven. Focused. Impatient with anything that got in his way. His need for answers festered inside him and wouldn't leave him alone. Miranda knew because she had the same need festering inside her, too.

That relentless drive was a trait shared by the best investigators Miranda had ever known—people she considered mentors. It was a trait she hadn't expected to find in a small-town police force.

Maybe she was being a snob. She'd let her stereotypes influence her opinion of an entire police department, Joel included. She'd underestimated him.

He cut a glance at her. "What's wrong?"

"Nothing." She nodded at a three-story building behind a tile fountain. "That's it."

"The library?"

"There are offices in the back."

They stepped through double glass doors into a two-story foyer with a huge wall of glass. Behind the glass were rows and rows of tall bookshelves. Joel peeled off his sunglasses and glanced around as Miranda approached the information desk, where a student with earbuds sat in front of a laptop computer.

"I'm looking for Professor Conner's office?"

The student plucked a bud out. "Through that hallway,

all the way past the rare-book room. It's the third door on the left."

"This floor?"

"Yeah."

They followed the instructions down a long glass corridor that looked out on a grassy courtyard filled with students either reading or using their books as pillows. The corridor opened into a spacious room with a vaulted ceiling. Bookshelves lined the walls. A spiral staircase in the corner led to a second-floor balcony also lined with books.

Miranda stopped and tipped her head back, admiring the grand architecture. On the ceiling was a religious fresco depicting St. John.

"There's a gatekeeper," Joel said.

Through the doorway, Miranda spotted a gray-haired woman at a desk in a waiting room. Behind her was a long hallway, where professors had offices, presumably. Miranda was glad she'd called ahead from the road.

She approached the receptionist with a smile. "Hi, I'm here to see Professor Conner."

"Do you have an appointment?"

"Yes, for twelve thirty. I'm Miranda Rhoads."

The woman looked from Miranda to Joel and then turned to her computer. "Looks like he has you down, but he's not back from class just yet." She nodded at the chairs on the other side of the room. "You're free to have a seat until he's available."

"Thank you."

Miranda turned around. Joel had wandered back into the rare-book room and was checking out a glass display case. Miranda joined him. The volume was an illuminated Bible opened to the book of John. The yellowed pages were filled with Latin writing. Intricate drawings decorated the margins. Miranda turned to check out another display, this one showing an antique hymnal.

Boots thudded on metal, and she turned to see Joel going up the spiral staircase. She followed him.

The balcony level was warmer and mustier. Tall shelves made accessible by sliding ladders held hundreds and hundreds of leather-bound tomes. One of the four walls was devoted to a glass case containing a collection of stuffed birds. The taxidermy reminded her of childhood field trips to the science museum.

Joel approached a placard. "What's with all the birds of prey?"

"I don't know. Maybe because the mascot here is an eagle?"

She stepped closer and surveyed the selection. "Some of these are endangered, too. The Andean condor, for example."

"The bird theme continues. We can't escape it."

She surveyed a golden eagle clutching a stuffed rabbit in its fierce three-inch talons.

"Ms. Rhoads?"

They glanced over the balcony to see a bald man looking up at them. He wore black-framed glasses and had a stack of books under his arm, and Miranda barely recognized him from this vantage point.

"Dr. Conner, hi," she said.

"Call me Mike. And sorry to keep you waiting."

Miranda picked her way down the spiral staircase, followed by Joel. The professor was thinner than she remembered, and he'd shaved off his beard since the last time she'd seen him, at the faculty picnic in September. She didn't know his age, but she guessed late thirties.

He switched his stack of books to the other arm and offered Miranda a handshake. "Good to see you again."

"You, too. This is Detective Joel Breda, with the Lost Beach Police Department."

The two men shook hands and seemed to be sizing each other up. Joel was bigger and taller, but the professor didn't seem intimidated at all. If anything, he looked keenly interested in his badge-wearing visitor.

"Thanks for making time for us," Miranda said.

"Absolutely. Come tell me about your case."

They followed him back to a small office. The professor dropped his books on his desk and moved a stack of binders from a side chair onto the floor.

"Let me grab another chair from next door," he said and walked out.

Joel nodded at the chair. "Sit down."

Miranda took a seat and glanced around the room. What it lacked in size it made up for with a scenic view of a giant oak tree. The sidewalk outside was filled with students shuttling between classes. As a part-time teacher, Miranda hadn't achieved windowed-office status. Instead, she had a PO box and a classroom in the art building that she shared with four other teachers.

A shelf beneath the window was filled with books, and Miranda tilted her head and read some of the titles. The subjects ranged from medieval symbolism to digital encryption.

The professor reappeared with a chair for Joel.

"I read about your case online. Sounds horrible." He looked at Miranda. "I have to say, I'm at a loss as to how I might help. I've consulted with the FBI on occasion, but the news article I read didn't make it sound like a gang-related crime."

"We're still determining that," Joel said.

"We've been going through the victims' social media posts," Miranda said, tugging a file out of her tote bag. "We've come across a number of references that we aren't sure about. In particular, a symbol that comes up over and over again."

She opened the file and pulled out the three best photographs she had. Two of the pictures were nature scenes with the infinity symbol on the lower right-hand corner. The third picture was a close-up of Will Stovak's forearm.

Mike leaned forward, immediately zeroing in on the tattoo picture. "This is an autopsy photo." He looked up.

"Both of our murder victims had the same tattoo," Joel told him. "And a number of their followers on social media have it, too."

"The ouroboros, or infinity serpent," Mike said.

Miranda felt a flood of relief. This trip wasn't a waste of time. "It has a name?"

"Yes." He pivoted to his computer and tapped the mouse. "The image is based on the infinity symbol, obviously, which has roots in ancient Egypt." He tapped a few keys, and a photo appeared on the screen. It was a row of hieroglyphics carved into a stone. He tapped the screen with a pencil. "See?"

Miranda scooted closer.

"Now, the serpent imagery here adds another layer of meaning. The snake is eating its tail, you see. Instead of 'everlasting life,' it takes on a more sinister meaning. The destruction of the afterlife. Or self-destruction, however you want to view it, depending on your biases."

"Biases?" Joel asked.

"Well, in modern times, yes." Mike shrugged. "The image is associated with a number of current-day causes. The climate crisis. Deforestation. The destruction of nature at the hands of technology, just to name a few. The symbol has been appropriated by a particular group, if I'm not mistaken." He leaned closer to his computer and typed some words into a search engine. "Yes, that's it. Alpha Omega Now."

Miranda and Joel both leaned closer.

"This is their symbol?" Miranda asked.

"There may be other groups that use it, too, but this is

the one that comes to mind. They had a demonstration recently, didn't they?" He looked at Joel. "I thought I read something—"

"Last Friday. They demonstrated at the construction site at the south end of the island." He glanced at Miranda. "Three days before the murders."

"You guys made some arrests, didn't you?" she asked.

"Minor property damage," he said. "Nothing violent." He leaned back in his chair and rubbed his chin.

"Is that their website?" Miranda asked.

"No, this is a site that simply lists various organizations, like an online glossary. I'd be surprised if Alpha Omega has a website per se." He turned back to his computer and scrolled through some search results. "I'm not seeing one. Groups like this often try to stay under the radar, so to speak."

"Groups like what?" Miranda asked.

"Groups that are potentially monitored by law enforcement," Mike said. "It's the same with gangs. As you can probably guess by the name, Alpha Omega Now is on the extreme end of the spectrum. They're all about the end of the world. They've been known to use illegal or even violent tactics to get their message across."

"Such as?" Miranda looked at Joel.

"They took credit for an explosion at a logging company up in East Texas several years ago," Joel said. "That's one reason we responded so quickly when we heard they were on the island. But their protest turned out to be kind of a dud. Just about fifty people with handmade signs and some cans of spray paint. Looked to me like they were looking for media attention more than anything else, and they got it, too. There was a front-page news article in Corpus."

Miranda frowned down at the papers in front of her. So, now they had a lead on the symbol, but the posts still didn't make sense to her. And if their two victims were part of this group, why would they be targeted by it?

"What is it?" Joel asked her.

"I still don't get what all these posts mean."

"Maybe they're messages to followers of the group Alpha Omega Now." The professor pulled the pages closer.

Miranda took out a few more pictures and arranged them in front of him. Each photo showed the infinity serpent in the lower right-hand corner.

"But these shots aren't exactly a call to action," Miranda said. "We've got beaches, sunrises, sunsets, latte art." She pulled out a picture of a coffee cup with a heart drawn in foam.

Mike tugged out a picture. "And the ubiquitous kitten photo," he said with a smirk.

"Right. These shots aren't at all controversial."

"Maybe that's the point," Joel said.

Miranda looked at him. He was studying a trio of pictures, all posted by Elizabeth Lark over the past four months.

"How do you mean?" she asked.

"Could be the message isn't obvious unless you know what to look for," he said.

"Yes, they could be employing steganographic techniques," Mike said.

She leaned her elbow on the desk. "How do you mean?"

He lined up several pictures in front of him and gazed down at them for a moment. "Steganography." He looked from Miranda to Joel. "From the Greek *steganos* meaning 'covered' and *graphia* meaning 'writing.' It references a technique where a secret message is hidden in plain sight." He leaned back in his chair and laced his hands behind his head. "There's an old story about a Greek ruler who tattooed a secret message onto a slave's scalp, then waited for his hair to grow out before sending him through enemy territory. When the messenger got to his destination, he shaved his head to reveal the writing. In the digital era, steganography can refer to hiding a file within a file. Or, another example, sending a hidden message using microscopic variations in certain letters within a font system."

"I've heard about this for photography." Miranda looked at Joel. "You can use certain software to embed a smaller text message within an image file, which is much larger."

Joel arched his eyebrows.

"But from what I understand, the software runs into problems with social media platforms," she said. "Photo-sharing sites typically compress or otherwise alter images as they're processed, and so the embedded data is lost or damaged."

"Maybe we're making it too complicated," Joel said. "Maybe the symbol on the picture here is meant to flag it for followers. A handful of these photos were taken in Lost Beach during the two-week window before the protests. The picture itself tells people where to go—Lost Beach. They just have to figure out the date and time."

"How?" Miranda asked.

"I don't know."

"It's possible my FBI contact has more on this group," Mike said to Joel. "I can give you the agent's name and number."

"Thanks."

"No problem. I'll text it to Miranda."

Mike glanced at the clock on the wall, and Miranda knew he had a class. Joel seemed to pick up the cue.

"Thanks for your time," Joel said, standing up and offering a handshake. Miranda stood, too.

"No problem. I don't know if it was useful."

Miranda smiled at the professor. "It definitely was."

* * *

T HEY SWUNG BY Miranda's mailbox and made a stop at
the dining hall before heading back to the parking lot.
Joel checked his watch. They'd been gone almost four hours
and probably wouldn't be back on the island until five.

"I can drive if you're too tired," he said as they neared
the Jeep.

She gave him a puzzled smile. "Why would you think
I'm too tired?"

"Because you ordered a triple-shot latte."

And because she looked tired. But Joel didn't think
she'd appreciate hearing that.

"I'm fine."

As he got in the Jeep, she stowed her giant beverage and
checked her reflection in the mirror.

"Okay, so I look like crap. I know. I was up all night,"
she said.

"Working on this?"

"Yeah."

He wondered if there was more going on with her. She
seemed stressed-out. Edgy. He was, too, but as lead detective it went with the territory.

Miranda pulled out of the parking lot and merged into
downtown traffic. She'd gone above and beyond to help him
with this investigation, and he should probably feel guilty for
using so much of her time. But he didn't. He needed her. The
clock was ticking on the most challenging case of his career,
and Joel wanted all the help he could get. Miranda was sharp
and thorough, and she'd managed to spot critical clues that
other CSIs would have overlooked. She was an asset.

Not to mention—if he was honest with himself—he
really liked spending time with her. He liked her insights

and her opinions. He liked *her*, and it wasn't just about work.

"Thanks for introducing me to Conner," he said. "It was a good idea to consult him."

She cut a glance at him. "Are you glad we came in person? By the time we get back, this will have burned a whole day."

"It was worth it," he said. "We have a new lead. I'm not sure how it fits, but it feels significant."

"Alpha Omega Now, you mean."

"Yeah. It's a connection we didn't have before. It gives us an idea of why our two victims were on the island when they were killed. They weren't just tourists. Still . . ."

"What?"

"The whole thing raises more questions than answers."

"Well, the link to this group might explain the feathers at the crime scene," she said. "Maybe the feathers are some kind of message about the destruction of fragile ecosystems or the loss of endangered species."

"An ideological killer. Just what I *didn't* want to learn today." Joel raked his hand through his hair.

"Why?"

"That would mean our case isn't a one-off." He shook his head. "A person like that is trying to rid the world of some evil by killing people. For example, the Unabomber, Eric Rudolph, killers like that."

"So, they're on a mission."

"Exactly. In terms of motive, it doesn't really fit, though," he said. "When it comes to Randall, yeah, I can see it. But what about Elizabeth Lark and Will Stovak? They were so devoted to their cause that they got matching tattoos of the group's logo. And Elizabeth used her social media platform to help promote the group to all her followers."

"What do you know about Randall's business?" Miranda asked. "I'm wondering how he got permission to carve up all that land on the coast."

"I'd be willing to bet it was through a wetlands swap program. Companies can sometimes get a permit to develop land in certain areas if they donate land somewhere else."

Miranda rolled her eyes. "What a sham. Wetlands aren't just interchangeable. If you destroy breeding grounds and disrupt migratory patterns, the long-term impact can be devastating."

Joel pulled his phone from his pocket and entered some search terms. He wanted to know more about the Corpus Christi victim.

Miranda sipped her coffee and then offered him the cup. "Want some?"

"I'm good.

He didn't need a caffeine fix. He was already wired from the barrage of new clues flooding his brain.

"Are you reading about Randall?" she asked.

"And about Randall Enterprises, LLC. I need to find out whether his company had any run-ins with this protest group."

What he really needed to do was call up Corpus PD and see if their detectives had pursued this angle, either before or after Henry Lind's retirement. An Internet search was one thing, but really exploring this lead would require digging deep. Had Randall's company faced threats or protests or possibly litigation at any point?

Joel scrolled through search results until a headline snagged his attention.

"Bingo."

Miranda looked at him. "What?"

"'Flash Mob Protests New Development in Rockport,'" he recited.

"That's, like, fifty miles up the coast."

"Yep. And looks like it's one of Randall's projects."

"What's the date on the article?"

Joel scrolled to the top. "Almost two years ago."

"So, that means almost *one* year before Randall was murdered on his boat dock."

Joel read the full article, filing away names and dates. He needed to follow up on this, and it wasn't going to be easy to do it from the car. His first impulse was to call Nicole for help because she was up to speed on the Corpus Christi connection. But she was off island today running down a lead from the FBI. She'd been excited about it this morning, but the fact that Joel hadn't heard from her yet put a damper on his hopes.

"I don't understand the link between this environmental protest group and our two victims," Miranda said. "A millionaire real estate developer, yes. But how do a couple of weed-smoking road trippers get into the crosshairs of an ideologically motivated killer?"

Joel didn't know. But he had that niggling feeling in his gut, the feeling he got when he pulled a thread and a mystery started to unravel. This was one of those threads, and Joel felt certain that he needed to keep pulling.

"Joel?"

He looked at Miranda.

"No idea," he told her. "But I plan to find out."

CHAPTER

FOURTEEN

MIRANDA STOOD IN the knee-deep water and composed her shot. She had ten, maybe twelve, minutes till sunset, and she was determined to get this egret while the sun looked like liquid gold shimmering on the water.

She lifted her camera and waited.

Click.

She zoomed in closer and adjusted the focus.

Click. Click.

The reddish egret stepped away from the reeds, and Miranda followed his movements.

"Yes," she whispered. "That's it. Now, turn this way . . ."

Click.

Her heart skittered. She *had* it. She took another few shots just to make sure, but she knew deep down that she already had exactly what she wanted, what she'd been searching for, for weeks.

With a satisfied sigh, she lowered her camera.

Across the channel, a wade fisherman looked her way

and nodded before casting his line. He was up to his thighs already, and her stomach tensed with worry as he moved farther out. This waterway looked placid at the moment, but beneath the surface was a powerful undertow.

The egret flapped away, and Miranda lifted her hand to shield her eyes as she watched the bird veer toward the sun.

She turned around and sloshed back to shore, grateful that she'd followed her instincts and come out here this evening. Crossing the causeway earlier, she'd felt the irresistible lure of Lighthouse Point—something about the sky and the clouds and the quality of the light. She couldn't put her finger on it exactly, but she'd wanted to capture it, so after dropping Joel at the police station and swinging by the dog sitter's, she'd grabbed her camera and come straight here.

Thinking about her day with Joel gave her a heady buzz. She'd enjoyed driving in her Jeep with him. She'd enjoyed talking with him. She'd enjoyed being on a mission together, a mission no one understood or even knew about besides the two of them.

She'd never met a man like Joel Breda—so self-assured and secure about who he was. He was confident without being arrogant. He was smart and capable but willing to give credit to others when it was due—something that mattered to Miranda because she'd worked with so many men who were utterly unwilling to acknowledge other people's help.

Joel was different. And the more time she spent with him, the more he intrigued her.

She thought of the feel of his mouth on hers and his stubbled jaw and his warm hands sliding over her hips. Just the memory made her insides tighten. Why had she made the mistake of kissing him? That one moment of weakness had changed the balance between them in a major way. She'd revealed her attraction to him. She could no longer go back to *not* knowing what it was like to kiss him and feel all that intensity focused on her. And if that was how he kissed, she could only imagine what it would be like to spend an entire night with him.

But she shouldn't imagine it. They would be working together all summer. If they started up a fling, things were bound to get complicated.

Besides, she didn't even think that a fling was possible with him. He was too intense. Too serious. And whatever this . . . attraction thing they had going was, it felt a little too potent. She had a sneaking suspicion that if she gave in to temptation and slept with him, she'd be unleashing a force she couldn't control—or wouldn't want to—and there would be no going back.

Miranda slid her feet into her flip-flops and glanced around. Some shirtless guys near the RV park were tossing a Frisbee and drinking beer. They had their tailgate down and their music up, and they seemed oblivious to all the signs prohibiting glass and alcohol on the beach. Miranda trudged over the dunes toward the parking lot, surveying the lighthouse as she neared it. It sat atop a gentle green hill, towering above everything on the island.

She remembered seeing the lighthouse in the distance when she'd first driven over the causeway in March. Back then it had been a beacon of hope, quelling her anxiety after she'd quit her job. It seemed to offer solace, and every time she spotted it from somewhere on the island, she felt a renewed sense of reassurance that she'd made the right decision in coming here.

She cast a glance at her Jeep in the parking lot, then changed directions and hiked up the grassy hill. The south side of the lighthouse was covered in scaffolding, and five-gallon buckets lined the sidewalk. An orange barricade blocked the entrance, but the door stood ajar.

Miranda stopped at the top of the hill and tipped her head back to study the vertical brick building. Up close, the white paint was dingy and peeling. Sidestepping the barricade, she touched the wooden door and peeked around it. A tarp and paint cans covered the floor. The air smelled of turpentine. She stepped inside, bumping the door against a metal ladder. The air felt warm and still, and dust motes floated on shafts of light streaming through the windows.

The great metal staircase spiraled up like a nautilus. Miranda adjusted the settings on her camera and peered through the viewfinder. She took a few shots and then followed the curving stairs to the first window.

A lone sabal palm cast a skinny shadow over the lawn outside. She followed the staircase up and up and up, keeping her gaze on the top window to ward off the dizziness. After what seemed like thousands of stairs, she finally reached the top. Her throat felt dry and her heart hammered against her rib cage. She climbed one last steep trio of steps to the 360-degree lookout.

Laguna Madre stretched out before her, shimmery pink now in the fading sunlight. The windowpane was cracked and dirty, and Miranda used the tail of her T-shirt to wipe off the grime. Then she lifted her camera and snapped a few shots. A line of brown pelicans soared over the channel on their way to the marsh. Once nearly extinct due to pesticides, the pelican had made a comeback in recent years. To Miranda, they were a symbol of hope. She'd photographed them hundreds of times, but never from this lofty vantage point.

Thunk.

She glanced down. The floor below looked miles away.

Creak.

A chill snaked down her spine.

"Hello?" she called.

Silence.

Miranda peered over the railing. No sound. No movement. Only a faint curl of smoke drifting up from beneath the ladder. A flash of orange caught her eye.

Fire.

Miranda's heart lurched. She rushed down the stairs.

"Fire!"

No sooner had she screamed the word than another flame licked out from behind the paint cans. The fire was alive, leaping from one wall to the other. Miranda slipped on a step and landed hard on her butt. She grabbed the handrail and hauled herself to her feet.

"Fire! Help!"

Smoke stung her eyes as she neared the bottom step. She reached for the door. A flame leaped in front of her. Pain seared her arm, and she lunged away.

"Help!"

Panicked, she raced back up the stairs as she swiped at her stinging flesh. Coughing and choking, she took the steps two at a time until she reached the first window. She pounded on the glass.

But there was no one. The Frisbee people were gone. The fisherman was gone. The campground had some RVs and trucks but no *people.*

Miranda's heart jackhammered as she cast a frantic look down at the flames. They were getting closer. Smoke burned her throat and her eyes as she yanked off her T-shirt. The shirt tangled in her camera strap, and she jerked it free, then wrapped it around her fist. She punched at the glass, but it didn't break. A bolt of panic shot through her. Good Lord, was it hurricane glass? She punched again and again, finally busting through the window. Pain tore up her arm. She kept punching, knocking pieces loose until the lower half of the pane was open.

"Help!" she shrieked, sticking her head out.

Miranda looked down. She had to be twenty feet off the ground. She glanced around desperately. A man ran from the RV park, waving his arms and yelling.

Miranda pulled her head inside and looked down again. The base of the lighthouse was an inferno. Her heart seized. Swinging her leg through the opening, she clutched the frame around the window. People were running now from every direction, waving and shouting at her.

She sat on the windowsill and pulled her other leg through, and her flip-flop fluttered to the ground. Smoke poured through the window. She felt the heat of the flames against her back.

"Oh my God. Oh my God. *Oh my God!*"

Miranda coughed and choked. Tears stung her eyes as she tried to blink away the smoke.

Please, God, please, please.

She looked out at the marsh through a blur of tears, and a strange calm settled over her. She looked down at the grassy hill. She was going to have to jump.

FIFTEEN

NICOLE STRODE INTO the bullpen and looked around. Where was everyone? She passed the conference room and spotted Joel at a table with his laptop in front of him.

"Hey, I've been looking for you," she said. "Did Brady tell you what happened?"

"No." He didn't stop typing.

"I followed up on that lead."

"The ViCAP thing." He stopped and looked at her.

"Yeah." She sat on the end of the table. "I submitted the details of our case to the FBI violent crimes database, and they got a hit."

"You told me that part this morning. You're saying it panned out?"

"*Yes.* Listen to this." She pulled off her LBPD baseball cap and dropped it on the table. "There's a cold case in Houston. Three years old. I drove all the way up there and interviewed the lead detective about it, and I think it's our guy."

He lifted an eyebrow. "You *think*?"

"No, I know. I'm almost positive." She glanced through the door to the bullpen. "I brought back copies of the reports—"

"Just tell me what you found."

Joel sounded impatient, and she didn't blame him. Brady hadn't wanted to read the reports either. He'd wanted the bottom line.

"Okay, the upshot is that I found striking similarities between the Houston case and ours, and I think we could be dealing with the same perpetrator."

Joel leaned back in his chair and folded his arms over his chest, making his biceps bulge. He was skeptical. Or maybe he was just waiting to be convinced. Nicole could never tell with him.

"The victim up there is a forty-seven-year-old man," she said. "This guy's leaving for work one morning when he goes out to his driveway and gets shot in the chest, point-blank range."

"They know the caliber?" Joel asked.

"A .38," she said. "There are no eyewitnesses. No one heard anything either. No robbery. The assailant left behind this guy's wallet, his Rolex, and his Mercedes. Just shot him in the chest and left."

"So, same kind of weapon."

"But there's more," she said. "Investigators found a long red *feather* in the pocket of his suit jacket. No idea where it came from. His wife didn't know either. Nobody could figure out what to make of it."

Joel stared at her, and she tried to figure out what he was thinking. She'd expected him to be more excited.

"Any suspects?" he asked.

"Suspects, yes. Arrests, no. They zeroed in on a few people but could never make it stick. I got the details down for us to go through."

"What did this guy do for a living?" he asked.

"Chief financial officer for some company. EastTex Petroleum, I think it's called."

Interested flared in his eyes. "No shit. An oil company?"

"Yeah. Why?"

"We found a link today between our victims here and the environmental group that was protesting on the island last Friday."

"The flash mob thing."

"Yeah. The group's called Alpha Omega Now. We think Lark and Stovak were both members."

"Who's 'we'?" Nicole asked.

"Miranda and I. She's helping me follow up on this. We talked to one of her professor friends in San Antonio who works with the FBI gang unit, and he identified the tattoos on the two victims. It's a symbol of this group."

"Is this group on the FBI's radar?"

"I'm looking into it."

"Are they violent?"

"I'm looking into that, too. But listen to this." Joel leaned forward. "Alpha Omega *also* protested the company owned by that real estate developer in Corpus Christi—"

"Mark Randall."

"Yeah. They protested his company a year before his murder. We need to find out if this Houston case has a connection like that."

Emmet leaned his head into the room. "Yo, you guys hear the radio?"

Nicole turned to face him. "No. What?"

"There's a fire down at Lighthouse Point."

"When?" Joel asked.

"Right now. Calvin just called me. The fire department's not even there yet. They've got two trucks en route."

"Like, a brush fire or—"

"I don't know."

Owen stopped and leaned his head in. "Hey, the chief called. There's a fire at the lighthouse." He looked at Joel. "He said Miranda's there."

MIRANDA SAT ON the tailgate of the red pickup, trying hard not to puke. For the last twenty minutes she'd felt queasy. Nauseous. Like everything she'd eaten in the past twenty-four hours was about to come up.

She looked across the parking lot to the lighthouse. Fire-fighters had set up klieg lights to illuminate the scene as they combed the grounds, searching for evidence. Miranda watched them, feeling strangely disconnected from everything, as though she were watching a movie.

She hadn't jumped.

Two men had rushed over from the campground and yelled at her to wait while they dragged the scaffolding over. One of them had scaled the bars like a gymnast and helped her climb down, all before the first fire truck made the scene.

Miranda looked around the parking lot now. She wanted to thank the man—she'd been practically incoherent earlier—but she didn't know where he'd gone.

She bent over and rested her hands on her knees, acutely aware of Joel only a few feet away, watching her every move. He hadn't taken his eyes off her since he'd arrived, even when he was interviewing witnesses.

Miranda examined the long cut in her forearm from when she'd punched her fist through the glass. The bleeding had stopped, and Emmet's brother Calvin had given her a bandage for it. Both he and Joel had offered to take Miranda to the clinic to get it checked out, but she'd refused.

She peeled the gauze back to look at it. The blood was like glue and she pulled up a layer of skin. The pain hit, and she felt queasy all over again.

Miranda pushed off the tailgate and walked to the water's edge, turning away from the chaotic scene behind her. The last bit of sunlight had faded over the marsh, and the sand now felt cool under her feet. She focused on gripping the sand with her toes to take her mind off how badly she wanted to puke.

"You okay?" Joel's voice was low and gruff behind her, and she didn't turn around.

"A little dizzy."

"You sure you don't want to get your arm checked out?"

"It's fine. Just needs a butterfly bandage, and I've got some at home."

She turned to face him. His brow was furrowed, and his blue eyes were filled with worry.

"I'd like to go home now," she said.

"I still have to interview a couple more witnesses."

"I'm not asking for a ride. I've got my car here."

He looked at her for a long moment. "Hang on."

He walked off, and she turned back to face the water. She didn't want to be here. She wasn't sure how much longer she could hold it together. She'd gone through her story three separate times, with three separate people, including Joel, and each time she'd done it she'd felt her stomach churning.

"Screw it," she hissed.

She hiked across the beach to the fire department pickup truck and collected her shoes and camera from the tailgate.

Joel walked over. "McDeere's going to follow you home."

"Why?"

"Because I asked him to."

"That's totally unnecessary."

"I'll come by as soon as I wrap up here."

"You don't need to—"

"Miranda." His sharp tone cut her off.

"Fine," she said. She didn't want an argument. Not now,

and definitely not here, in front of half the police department. She just wanted to leave.

"It shouldn't be too long," he said.

She returned to her Jeep and stashed her stuff in the front seat. The parking lot was jammed, and she maneuvered around all the emergency vehicles.

The lighthouse was a stark tower in the glare of the lights, and she noted the blackened streak where smoke had billowed from the broken window. As she pulled onto the highway, she caught McDeere's patrol car in her rearview mirror.

Miranda focused on the road in an attempt to steady her nerves. She felt shell-shocked, and the shriek of the fire engines still echoed through her brain.

She tried to get her head around what had happened, but it still felt unreal. She'd been trapped in a burning building. She'd been seconds away from making a twenty-foot jump. If those men hadn't helped her, she could easily be in a hospital right now with a slew of broken bones. Or worse.

And what if that window had been hurricane glass?

Just the thought made her queasy again. She bit the side of her mouth and prayed she wouldn't have to pull over and get sick in front of McDeere.

The drive whisked by in a blur of yellow stripes. When Miranda made the turn into her driveway, the headlights followed. She pulled up to her little house and cut the engine, and the rookie cop slid from his car.

"Thank you," she said.

"I'll walk you up."

She forced a smile. "That's not necessary."

"It's no problem," he said, and his steady look told her that he had orders he intended to follow.

Miranda walked up the stairs. The muffled sound of Benji's barks brought tears to her eyes, and she felt a rush of relief to see his nose pressed against the glass.

McDeere waited patiently as she unlocked the door.

"Thank you," she told him again.

"Yes, ma'am. Be sure to lock up."

Inside, Miranda secured the latch and sank to her knees beside Benji. She gave him a fierce hug, relishing the familiar scent of his fur as he licked her face. He smelled like home.

She, on the other hand, smelled like a bonfire.

Miranda dropped her phone and camera on the table. Crossing the living room, she yanked off her T-shirt. It had slivers of glass in it, and she planned to throw it away. Her clothes reeked; her hair reeked; her skin reeked. She went into the bathroom and turned the shower on, then stripped everything off and stepped under the warm stream. She squirted a ridiculous amount of shampoo into her hands and lathered up her hair.

Pain tore up her arm, taking her breath away.

Cursing, she stepped out of the spray. Somehow she'd forgotten her cut. With a trembling hand, she unwound the gauze and braced for more pain as she rinsed out the soap. Then she quickly finished her hair and stepped out.

Miranda grabbed a towel and dried off. She retrieved the shoebox of first-aid supplies from under the sink and carefully dabbed disinfectant on her wound. The cut was about three inches long, and fairly deep. She was lucky she hadn't nicked a vein.

Whimpers in the next room told her Benji wanted out. She applied a row of butterfly bandages, popped an ibuprofen, and went into the bedroom to throw on some clothes and comb her hair. When she came out, Benji was scratching at the front door. As she opened it for him, she spotted her zipper pouch on the counter.

"*Crap*. Benji, wait!"

But he was already down the stairs.

She grabbed the pouch and checked to make sure she had her pepper spray. Then she grabbed her phone and followed Benji outside.

At the top of the staircase, she paused. The beach looked deserted beneath the rising moon. She glanced south and then north toward the campground but didn't see the flicker of even a single campfire.

A chill crept down her spine. She didn't want to be on the beach alone. Not tonight, not even with pepper spray. Benji could poke around in the yard.

"Benji?" She walked down the stairs, scanning the salt grass around the house. "Benji, here, boy." She glanced at the nearby dunes, which were covered with a thick carpet of vines.

She gave a sharp whistle and waited. No answer but the distant crash of waves and the hum of crickets.

She looked around, annoyed. Usually Benji's fluorescent yellow collar made him easy to spot. She switched on her phone flashlight and walked down the driveway to one of his favorite clumps of bushes.

"Benji? Here, boy!"

She turned and walked toward the sand dunes. If he'd run across the bridge, she would have heard him.

A sharp yelp had her whirling around.

"Ben?"

She aimed her light at the weeds surrounding the bridge. She jogged toward the sound she'd heard, but she didn't see him. Dread filled her stomach.

A flash of yellow caught her eye. And then her heart lurched.

"Benji!"

CHAPTER

SIXTEEN

JOEL STOOD AT the top of the stairs and cursed. Where the hell was she? Her Jeep wasn't here. Her dog wasn't here.

Joel's phone buzzed and he recognized McDeere's number.

"Sorry, I had a traffic stop," McDeere said. "What's up?"

"Where's Miranda?"

"At home. Why?"

"She's not here."

No response.

"McDeere? Didn't you say you walked her to the door?"

"Yeah. And I waited until I heard the lock before I—"

"Did she say she was going anywhere?"

"No."

"Well, I'm at her house and she's not here. Neither is her car or her dog."

Joel walked down the steps, feeling a sense of panic that he didn't know what to do with. She'd been rattled earlier—that was obvious. So, where would she have gone? It suddenly hit him that he didn't know much about Miranda's personal life. In fact, he knew crap about it. Would she go to visit a friend? A boyfriend? Was it possible she'd gone back to San Antonio? Joel felt completely clueless and he fucking hated that.

This was his fault. He'd realized she was in shock back at the fire scene. She'd told him she was fine, but he'd known that was bullshit, and he should have called her out on it right there and forced her to talk to him. Now she'd gone off somewhere, and he couldn't even get her to pick up the phone.

"Are you there?" McDeere asked.

"Yeah."

"You want me to drive over there or—"

Joel's phone beeped.

"She's calling me now. Forget it." Joel grabbed the call. "Hey, where are you?"

"Almost home."

Relief flooded him at the sound of her voice. And then he saw her Jeep's headlights, high and close together, coming up the drive.

"I'm here," he said.

He slid the phone into his pocket and walked over, trying to calm down. Since the moment he'd jumped into his truck and raced to Lighthouse Point, his heart had been going a mile a minute. And it had practically stopped when he caught sight of the black plume of smoke billowing from the lighthouse.

That fire was arson. They had nothing official yet, but Joel knew it with every fiber of his being.

Miranda pulled to a stop beside his truck, and he took a deep breath. *Calm the fuck down.*

She pushed open her door and got out.

"Hi," she said, but she wouldn't look at him.

"What's wrong? Where were you?"

"I took Benji to the emergency animal clinic." She walked around the front of the Jeep to the passenger side. As she opened the door, he saw Benji curled into a ball on the seat.

"What happened to him?"

She reached for the dog.

"Here, let me get him." Joel stepped over, and she moved aside so he could slide his hands under him. His body was completely limp, but his eyelids fluttered open as Joel picked him up. His snout was swollen up the size of a grapefruit.

"A snake bit him," Miranda said.

"Oh no."

"I think it was a cottonmouth. I found him in the ditch over there."

The dog felt like deadweight as Joel carried him to the stairs, with Miranda trailing close behind.

"The vet gave him some antivenom and said there's nothing to do now but wait it out. She gave him something for the pain and said it would make him sleepy."

On the deck, she sidestepped Joel and reached over to open the door.

"You left it unlocked?" he asked.

"I didn't think about it. I was in a hurry."

Joel bit back his criticism as he stepped into the house. "Where should I put him?"

"On his bed by the sofa. It's the softest one in the house."

Joel wasn't surprised her dog had multiple beds. Miranda doted on him, and it must have scared the hell out of her when he'd been bitten by a venomous snake—especially after everything that had already happened tonight.

Joel sank to one knee and placed Benji on the big plaid pillow by the sofa. The dog opened his eyes briefly and then settled his head on his paws.

Miranda knelt beside him and stroked his ears. He didn't

move. Joel looked at Miranda, and the pained expression in her eyes made his chest tighten.

"Is he going to be all right?" Joel asked.

"He should. That's what the vet said, anyway."

She stood and walked into the kitchen. Joel followed. She picked up one of the two silver bowls on the floor by the pantry.

Joel raked his hand through his hair. "You scared me," he said, leaning against the counter. "I thought maybe you were hurt."

I thought maybe someone hurt you. Maybe the same someone who started that fire.

"Sorry." She rinsed the bowl and filled it with water.

Joel watched her with a knot in his stomach. She seemed calm and controlled, but he wasn't buying it. He'd seen this before, at the marina the morning she'd discovered the bodies.

She washed her hands and dried them on a towel.

"We need to talk," he said.

"I know." She grabbed the bowl and took it into the living room. She placed it beside Benji's bed and sat on the edge of the couch, looking down at him.

Joel sat on the armchair beside her.

"Was it arson?" she asked.

"We don't know for sure yet. But it's looking that way." He paused, debating how much to tell her. She was a CSI, for fuck's sake. He could be straight with her. "The fire chief found pour trails."

Miranda nodded stiffly. She knew exactly what that meant.

"We'll test a sample of the drop cloth, but it looks like mineral spirits."

"The turpentine." She still wouldn't look at him. "I smelled it when I stepped inside the building. There was a can of it next to the paint."

"That's likely the source."

So, was it a random crime? Miranda was simply in the wrong place at the wrong time? Or was she specifically targeted? Had someone been following her with the intent to harm her, and they spotted their chance?

Or maybe Joel was being paranoid, and Miranda just happened to be inside what looked like an abandoned building when some pyromaniac decided to do their thing. Joel wanted to believe it was random. But his gut instinct told him there was more to it.

He watched her gazing down at Benji, completely still. She seemed so composed, but he knew this tough demeanor was an act. Was she doing it for him? He didn't know what to say to her. Maybe he should just be honest.

"Miranda."

She lifted her gaze to his, and the fear in those caramel-colored eyes pulled at him.

"I don't fully understand what's going on here," he said. "But I want you to trust me that I *will* figure it out."

She didn't look convinced.

"I'll tell you what I know as soon as I know it."

As he said the words, he wondered if he was making a mistake. She was potentially the target of a crime, and he shouldn't be making promises. But he needed to reassure her. He needed her to understand there was nothing he wouldn't do to figure out who had put her in danger and hold them accountable.

She cleared her throat. "Thank you. I appreciate being kept in the loop."

She looked at her dog again, and the tense set of her shoulders got to him. She started to say something, then changed her mind. Her chin began to quiver, and that was it.

"Hey. Come here." He moved to the sofa beside her and pulled her into his arms. She stayed stiff at first. Then she relaxed a fraction, and he felt her arm slide around his waist.

"It's okay." He pulled her closer, settling her head on his shoulder. Her hair smelled amazing again, and he tried not to think about it.

"I've never been so scared in my life." Her arms tightened around him. "And then when I couldn't find Benji . . ." Her shoulders hunched and he felt the tension radiating from her. "I saw him in that ditch and I thought he was dead." The last part ended with a hiccup, and he wrapped his arms tighter. A tremor went through her, and he knew she was fighting for control.

"It's okay." He stroked her hair. "He's fine now. You both are."

She pressed her face against his chest, and he felt the warmth of her tears seeping through his shirt. She curled against him, crying silently as he held her, and he wished he could take away the fear.

"Hey. Look at me."

She sniffled.

"Miranda."

She looked up, and her watery eyes tore at his heart. "Benji's all right. You took care of him. He'll be okay."

She rested her forehead against his shoulder again, and he gathered her closer. A soft sob escaped. And then another. She wrapped her arms tighter, and he felt her breast pressed against his side. He caught her thigh and pulled her close, tucking her head under his chin, and she nestled into him. It was a special kind of agony, feeling her soft curves pressed against him as she quietly cried. He looked at the ceiling, desperate for a distraction—anything to help him think about something other than taking her clothes off while she cried her heart out. She was coming down off a trauma. From the moment he saw her at the crime scene, she'd been practically catatonic. She'd managed to hold it together until the thing with Benji opened the floodgates.

She curled into him, and he tortured himself by bending his head down to inhale the sweet scent of her hair. Never in his life had he wanted a woman this badly. And he couldn't have her. Not tonight, at least. Not like this. She was scared and vulnerable, and probably still in shock from everything that had happened. She'd been rescued from a burning building, for Christ's sake. She was traumatized, and if he took advantage of her now, he'd never forgive himself. Especially when she'd explicitly told him she wanted to keep things platonic.

The decent thing to do would be to lift her luscious body out of his lap—where it had somehow migrated—and make an excuse to leave before he did something really selfish, like try to talk her into bed.

Her shoulders went still, and she eased back.

"Sorry." She looked at him, and her tear-streaked face made his chest hurt. "I got you all wet." She rubbed the damp spot on his shirt.

"It's fine." He reached up and feathered her hair away from her face. "You've had a rough night. I get it."

She gazed up at him, and her lips parted slightly. The pain in her eyes faded, and he saw the moment it was replaced by something else.

She could feel what she did to him. *That's right, honey. Holding you while you cry turns me on.* He gazed down at her, waiting for her to pull away or scramble off his lap, but she simply looked up at him with an expression he couldn't read. Then her gaze dropped to his mouth, and lust shot through him. *That* look he knew.

"Miranda."

She glanced up at him. Her gaze settled on his mouth once again, and he felt like he was going to catch fire right there.

"Tell me what you want," he said.

She looked up at him with those golden-brown eyes. Time seemed to stop, and he held his breath, waiting for her answer.

"I want you to kiss me."

THE INSTANT THE words were out, he dipped his head down.

His kiss was strong. Demanding. But in a different way from last time. He seemed hungry, almost desperate to taste her as he combed his fingers into her hair. His intensity sent a jolt of desire through her, obliterating all the other emotions she'd been juggling till now. The fear was gone, the confusion, the stark terror that had gripped her when she thought Benji would die.

Everything was gone, replaced by this thick, hot *yearning* flowing through her veins.

His hand slid to her breast. He stroked his thumb over her nipple, and she moaned against his mouth. She slid her hands around his neck and leaned back on the sofa, pulling him with her until the delicious weight of him settled between her legs, right where she wanted it, and the hard ridge of his erection sent fiery darts of desire through her. She shifted under him and groaned softly.

He pulled back. "You okay?"

She nodded.

He pulled away again, sitting back on his knees as he removed his holster, and just the sight of those strong hands on his belt buckle gave her a heady rush of anticipation. He placed the belt and holster on the coffee table, then added his wallet and keys to the pile.

Miranda sat up to check Benji.

"He's asleep," she whispered.

Joel was watching her now with a mix of worry and need. Maybe he thought she was getting cold feet. She took his hand and pulled him back where he'd been before. Hooking her leg around his calf, she pulled his head down for another kiss that went on and on until their bodies were moving in sync.

She couldn't believe she was doing this. She couldn't believe they were here, finally alone together where anything could happen. She'd thought about this, about him, but the weight of his body and his hands moving over her made her realize this was real, and it was much better than a daydream.

He murmured something as he pushed up on one hand and slid the other under her tank top. He moved the shirt up and freed her breast from the cup of her bra, and she felt a chill against her skin until he swooped down on it.

"Oh."

The hot pull of his mouth was an electric shock, and she felt it in every cell of her body.

"Oh my God."

She combed her fingers into his thick hair, loving the silkiness of it as she savored the feeling of his mouth on her nipple. He shifted his attention to the other side, and she moved under him. He felt so *good*, and she knew she should resist this. Or put the brakes on while she was still able to think. But the only thing she wanted to do was wrap her legs around him and feel the full power of his body.

He tugged on her shirt, and she sat up. Taking care not to touch her cut, he pulled the shirt over her head and tossed it to the ground. He unclasped her bra with a smooth motion, then slid it from her arms and tossed it aside, too. His eyes simmered as he gazed down at her.

She propped herself on her elbows, hoping he'd take the hint and return to her breasts again. He did, stroking his big hands over them, cupping them gently before using his mouth.

"God," she breathed, closing her eyes and tipping her head back.

She pulled his shirt loose and ran her hands under it, sliding them over his muscular back, tracing the deep valley of his spine. His stubbly beard rasped her skin as he slid down her body, kissing her sternum and then her rib cage and then her navel. He reached the button of her cutoff shorts and kept going, and every nerve in her body sparked as his hands slid up the backs of her thighs. He hovered over her, and she could feel the heat of his breath through the denim. Then she felt the warm press of his mouth against her thigh, and she nearly shot off the couch. She combed her fingers into his hair and arched her hips, but he didn't move.

She opened her eyes, and he was gazing at her with a hungry male look that sent another jolt of lust through her.

"Do you have a condom?" she whispered.

Heat flared in his eyes. "Yeah."

Relief flooded her and she gripped his hair. "Oh, thank God."

She closed her eyes and tipped her head back, and the next thing she felt was the warm press of his mouth against her navel. And then he was shifting over her again, and she felt the brush of his knuckles as he unbuttoned her shorts.

She slipped her hands under his shirt and tugged it up. He yanked it over his head and added it to the growing pile of their clothes. He hooked his fingers into her shorts and panties and she watched, holding her breath, as he slid everything down her legs.

Miranda's skin heated as he looked her over. She closed her eyes.

"You're staring."

He leaned over her, and she felt the rasp of his jeans over her most sensitive skin. "You're beautiful."

The compliment set off another ripple of desire, and then another as his mouth closed over her nipple at the same moment his hand slid between her legs. His mouth gave a hard pull as he touched her, teasing and stroking and making her crazy.

Every thought seemed to empty from her mind as she gave herself over to the heat of his mouth and the fiery touch of his hands. She felt the tension building and building until she knew she was going to snap.

"Joel. I need you."

"What do you need, honey?"

"Everything."

His hands slid over her thighs.

"Now. *Please*. I can't wait."

He pulled back and reached for his wallet on the table, and she squeezed her eyes tight, desperate to hold on while he stripped off his pants and put on the condom.

"Hurry," she said.

And then he was back, sliding her legs apart.

"Open your eyes."

She did. And the pure male desire she saw on his face nearly sent her over the edge. He hitched her thigh over his hip and pushed into her, and she closed her eyes at the bittersweet pain. She dug her fingernails into his hips as he kissed her neck beneath her ear.

"Okay?"

"Yes," she gasped.

He took her hands and placed them over her head, resting them on the sofa arm behind her. He held them in place with one hand and planted the other on the cushion beside her head. She wrapped her legs around him, and he set a rhythm, thrusting into her over and over. His body felt warm and solid, and she loved the weight of him on her as the tension inside her built and built until she knew she couldn't hold on. He felt so good, so amazingly perfect, and she never wanted it to end.

"Joel. Oh my God. Oh my *God.*"

He released her hands to touch her right where they were joined, and she came in a blinding-hot rush that went on and on and on as she gripped his shoulders and held on. She squeezed him tightly, and he gave another hard thrust and collapsed on top of her as she shuddered through the aftershocks.

Miranda's mind reeled. Her body felt lax and boneless. And flattened from Joel's weight. For an endless moment she couldn't think or move or even take a breath.

He propped himself on his forearm, taking some of the weight off her chest as she let her eyelids flutter open.

The stunned look on his face snapped her out of her daze. He brushed a lock of hair from her face.

"You okay?" he asked gruffly.

"Mmm-hmm." She couldn't even speak.

He leaned down and kissed her softly. Then he got up and disappeared into the hallway, and she suddenly felt a chill.

She lay on her back and gazed at the wooden rafters above her. What had she just done? Her pulse thrummed and her skin was damp with sweat. And she felt a strange swell of pride. When was the last time she'd done something so impulsive?

She rolled onto her side and looked at Benji curled on his bed, snoring softly through his swollen nose. He looked completely oblivious.

Joel returned, and the sight of his gorgeously naked body made her throat tighten. His muscles rippled as he reached down and tossed one of the sofa cushions to the floor to create more room on the sofa. Then he gazed down at her with a hungry look that made her cheeks warm.

The side of his mouth curved up. "Damn," he said, stretching out beside her.

"What?"

"I've never seen a full-body blush before."

She turned her face into his chest. "You were staring."

He hitched her leg over his thigh. "I was."

She nestled closer, not wanting to look at him. She didn't want him to see her emotions written all over her face.

His warm hand slid over her hip, sending a flurry of sparks through her.

From the day she'd met him—from that first snippy conversation—she'd known they had chemistry. And she'd predicted that sex with him would be amazing. But it was more than that.

His fingers stroked lazily over her arm—up and down, up and down. She nestled her head against him and tried not to think about the sudden knot in her chest.

She'd had a meltdown.

There was no other word. First, she'd cried all over him. And then she'd dragged him on top of her and come completely undone. She'd sensed that if she ever let her guard down with him, she'd be in trouble, and now she was.

Tomorrow she would have to get up and go to work and be around him and all his co-workers while pretending nothing had happened. She'd been in this situation before, and it sucked, especially when everything went sideways and got uncomfortable.

"I can hear you thinking, Miranda."

She sighed. "I'm not thinking."

"No?"

"I'm . . . analyzing."

"Well, stop."

"I can't. It's what I do."

He tipped her chin up to make her look at him. "You don't need to worry."

"Why not?"

"Everything's the same as it was before."

She snorted. "Um, no, it's *not*." She reached between them and grasped him, and his body went rigid.

"Jesus. What are you trying to do?"

He was still hard. How was that possible after all that? She released him, and he took her hand.

"I'm not saying don't do it. I'm saying give me a little warning next time." He smiled down at her, and Miranda's heart skittered.

She stroked his chest, admiring the defined muscles. She couldn't believe they were here, joking around while tangled together naked on her sofa. And tomorrow, and the next day, and the next week, they were going to have to work together and act like nothing was going on. And then things would get contentious, like they always did, and one of them would end it, and everything would be awkward and unbearable until one of them quit their job—which would obviously be her, since she was the newbie and Joel had been here for years.

Just the thought depressed her.

"Miranda, stop. I mean it."

She looked at him.

"You worry too much."

"We can't do this again."

Hurt flickered in his eyes, but then it was gone. He smiled slyly. "Why not?"

"Because. We're working together now. I don't want things to go south and get awkward."

"So . . . we can't do this again tonight? Or ever?"

"I'm serious."

"I am, too. I need to know what you want."

I want you.

She didn't say it.

He traced a finger over the top of her breast, making her shiver, and she caught the look of satisfaction in his eyes. Her cheeks heated as she thought of his mouth on her nipple. Everything he did turned her on, even the way he looked at her. And especially the way he touched her as though he somehow knew exactly what she wanted.

He traced her nipple, and she shivered again.

"How about this?" He propped up on his elbow. "How about we just have fun tonight and worry about the rest in the morning?"

It sounded heavenly. She nodded.

He kissed her. It was soft and sweet, and her heart squeezed as he eased back. He watched her with those intense blue eyes, and she felt a pang of yearning. Working together wasn't the only thing that worried her. With every day she spent with him, she could feel herself becoming more attached. She couldn't help it.

He took her hand and placed it on his shoulder. "Hold on to me."

She gave him a suspicious look. "Why?"

He slid his arm under her. "Because." She gasped and clutched his neck as he stood up. "The things I want to do to you are better in bed."

NICOLE DESPERATELY NEEDED a shower and some food. Her stomach had been grumbling for an hour, but the shower was going to have to come first. Nicole's clothes and her hair and even her skin smelled like smoke. She hadn't set foot inside the lighthouse, but after three hours of working the scene, the campfire smell permeated everything.

She swung into the parking lot of her building and

pulled into a space, cutting the engine with a sigh. Even her truck would probably smell like smoke tomorrow.

From the cup holder her phone chimed, and she instantly knew who it was.

"Shit." She checked the screen. Emmet.

"Hey, sorry I blanked," she told him. "I meant to call you."

"Where the hell are you? You said you were coming."

"I got sidetracked. You guys still at Finn's?"

"I'm just leaving. Why'd you get sidetracked?"

"McDeere was on patrol and spotted that white pickup we've been looking for," she said. "It was at the Windjammer Inn."

"You're talking about the Frisbee guys."

"Yeah, we went over there and interviewed them. Talked to all three of them separately."

"I thought the witnesses said they left the park ten minutes before the fire started."

"Yes, but we wanted to get these guys on record anyway."

"You get anything?"

"Not really." She sighed. "They said they weren't even aware of the fire. Said they were at Dairy Queen downtown and had no idea what the sirens were all about."

"You believe them?"

"McDeere interviewed the manager, and he confirmed that they were there eating, and the timing checks out. I mean, I don't really see these guys torching a building and then sitting down for burgers and Blizzards a mile away, do you?"

"You never know."

She felt a surge of irritation as she got out of her truck. "Well, I got their contact info, so feel free to haul them in and take another crack at them if you want."

"Chill out. I'm just saying, you never know. People are fucked up."

Nicole tamped down her irritation as she crossed the parking lot. Yes, she was being prickly. But she'd spent the last two hours working after Emmet and everybody else had knocked off for the night. Not that she had really been in the mood for Finn's, but still.

"How's Miranda doing?" Emmet asked, changing the subject. "I heard McDeere took her home."

"Yeah, he said she seemed pretty out of it. I think she's in shock."

"Well, can you blame her?"

"Nope."

Nicole glanced at the wall of mailboxes and decided to skip it. It would just be junk mail and bills. She turned to go upstairs and nearly tripped over Drake's scooter at the base of the steps.

"Dang it, Drake."

"What's that?"

"Nothing," she said.

Nicole checked her watch. It was too late to knock on their door. She should probably leave the damn thing down here to get stolen, so he'd learn his lesson.

On the other hand, his mom worked two jobs and had given it to him for Christmas.

"So, I'm going back down there tomorrow morning with Calvin," Emmet said.

"You mean the lighthouse?"

Nicole grabbed the scooter and headed toward the storage locker beside the maintenance closet.

"Yeah. We're going to see if we missed anything," he said. "You want to come?"

"What time?"

"Early. We're meeting at six thirty, before any gawkers show up."

So much for sleeping in.

"Yeah, I'll come."

She passed a row of dumpsters. The garbage reeked, and trash day wasn't until Tuesday.

"See you there, then," Emmet said. "You can bring the coffee."

"Ha. Bring your own coffee."

Nicole ended the call and fumbled with her key chain as she approached the storage locker. It consisted of a walk-in cage made of chain-link fencing where tenants stored beach chairs, bikes, and water toys. Nicole had stashed a boogie board in there a year ago but hadn't used it since.

She glanced over her shoulder at the shadowy walkway between the maintenance closets. She didn't like being down here alone, and especially not at night. She unlocked the gate and pulled it open with a creak. The wind gusted and she got another whiff from the dumpsters. It smelled like spoiled meat.

She went still.

A low buzzing noise filled her ears. She set the scooter down as an icy trickle of awareness slid down her spine.

Nicole put her hand on the butt of her pistol and stepped over a yellow pool noodle. Heart thrumming, she scanned the row of bikes and wagons and half-inflated rafts. Slowly, silently, she pulled her weapon from the holster.

The buzzing grew louder, the stench stronger. She wasn't breathing now as she stepped around a rusty red wagon and peered into the shadows.

"What the . . . ?"

Nicole blinked into the dimness. At first she didn't understand what she was looking at.

And then, all at once, she did.

SEVENTEEN

MIRANDA AWOKE TO the low murmur of conversation. She felt a zing of panic and sat up in bed.

Joel.

She closed her eyes as the memories flooded back. The fire, the snakebite, the clinic.

Joel pinning her beneath him on the sofa.

Miranda glanced at Benji on the floor beside her. Joel had brought him in here, bed and all, without even being asked, and settled him right beside her nightstand.

Miranda got out of bed and grabbed a T-shirt from the chair. She slipped it over her head, careful not to pull her bandage. Her arm was sore, and the ibuprofen she'd taken earlier had completely worn off.

She padded barefoot into the living room. Joel stood beside the coffee table zipping his pants and cradling the phone on his shoulder as he spoke. Miranda halted in the hallway. His beautifully sculpted torso looked silver in the moonlight, and desire rippled through her.

He turned and spotted her as he ended the call.

"I have to go."

"So I gathered." She walked over, tugging the hem of her T-shirt. "Who was on the phone?"

"Brady."

He buttoned his pants and grabbed his holster off the table, and she watched as he buckled his belt with brisk efficiency.

"Anything serious?" she asked.

He tucked his wallet into his pocket. "I don't know all the details," he said, evading her question.

Miranda walked him to the door. He stopped and gazed down at her.

"Sorry I have to leave," he said.

"I understand."

"Lock up behind me."

"Of course."

She watched him go as she flipped the lock. Then she glanced at the clock in the kitchen. It was 12:25. If not for the callout, would he have spent the night?

He hadn't kissed her good-bye. She felt a twinge of hurt even though she knew she was being ridiculous. He'd been distracted.

She returned to her room and knelt beside Benji. His poor nose looked swollen and miserable, but he was snoring peacefully, so maybe the painkiller still hadn't worn off. Miranda stroked his silky head between his ears. She thought of how Joel had lifted him from her car and carried him up the stairs as though he weighed nothing—not unlike the way he'd carried Miranda off to bed an hour ago.

Her throat felt parched, and she realized she was starving. She couldn't even remember what she'd been planning to do for dinner tonight. Her sunset photo shoot felt like days ago, rather than a few short hours.

She went into the kitchen and grabbed a loaf of bread and a jar of peanut butter from the pantry. As she took down a plate, her phone chimed on the counter.

She eyed it, dreading what she already knew.

She picked up the phone and cleared her throat. "Miranda Rhoads."

"Hi, it's Nicole Lawson."

Miranda put away the bread and peanut butter. "What's up?"

"We could use your help at a crime scene. You know the Driftwood Apartments north of the marina?"

"No."

"Two-story building. Blue with white trim?"

"Okay, yes, I know it."

"We'd like you to meet us here ASAP. Bring your kit."

"I'm on my way. What's going on?"

"I'll explain when you get here."

Miranda hurried into the bedroom to dress, taking the time to put on socks and sneakers instead of flip-flops. She retrieved her evidence kit from the hall closet, then grabbed her camera and a diet soda before heading out. She hated leaving Benji, but hopefully she would be home by the time he woke up.

Miranda twisted her hair into a quick bun and secured it with a scrunchie before getting on the highway. The night was muggy but clear, and the nearly full moon cast a silver glow over the marshes. Miranda popped open her soda and took a long swig, hoping the caffeine would snap her awake.

She still felt groggy from her dream. She'd been in a burning house, running from room to room searching for a way out, but each time she ran for an exit a flame leaped into her path. Finally, she found a window with one of those inflatable yellow slides used to evacuate airplanes. But just as she started to climb on, the slide vanished.

The dream seemed silly now, but it had been searingly vivid, so vivid she could taste the smoke in the back of her throat.

Miranda gripped the steering wheel as she thought of the lighthouse and the petrifying feeling of being trapped. Her stomach clenched, and the faint scent of smoke tickled her nostrils.

Joel had held her through her meltdown. He'd listened to her and soothed her and then distracted her with mind-blowing sex.

But it was more than sex. He'd been kind and sensitive and genuinely concerned about Benji. And she added all of that to the list of things she liked about him.

As if she needed more.

She spotted the apartment building, and nerves fluttered inside her as she put on her turn signal. She'd given in to temptation. The rapid-fire series of events had obliterated her willpower, and she'd slept with Joel. Had it been a mistake? She was about to find out.

She turned into the apartment parking lot, which was packed with police vehicles. Her stomach tightened with dread as she surveyed the scene. This was no car theft or apartment burglary. She passed a trio of black-and-white patrol units. She spotted a space beside Joel's gray pickup, but she drove past it and found another space on the edge of the lot closest to the street. Miranda grabbed her camera from the back seat and looped the strap around her neck. Then she picked up her tackle box and got out.

The apartment complex was built on stilts, with the apartments on the second level and the bottom level devoted to storage closets and empty space. The building had an open staircase on each end, and an area near the back staircase had been cordoned off with yellow tape.

Miranda glanced at the breezeway, where tenants in

bathrobes and warm-up suits loitered beside the railing, watching the scene play out below. Several more onlookers stood in the parking lot, but they were set apart from the police, as if they'd been herded away from the heart of the action.

Miranda crossed the lot to a group of cops who—thank goodness—were *not* tromping around inside the yellow tape and making her job harder. Scanning the faces, she saw many she recognized, including Chief Brady, who was talking to Joel.

Joel's gaze homed in on her as she approached. Did the chief know that when he'd called his lead detective to this scene he'd been in Miranda's bed?

She tried to make her expression neutral as she neared the officers—all men, she couldn't help but notice. This was exactly the circumstance she'd wanted to avoid.

"Miranda."

She turned around to see Nicole Lawson walking toward her. She was dressed in the same clothes as earlier—a navy LBPD polo and beige tactical pants, with her duty weapon holstered at her side. Miranda immediately noticed her gloves and shoe covers.

"Thanks for getting here so fast." Nicole stopped in front of her. Her nose was pink and peeling, and her auburn hair was pulled back in a long braid. "The scene's back there." She nodded toward a row of dumpsters. "The body's in the storage locker. See the wire mesh near the recycle bins?"

"Show me."

Miranda followed her toward the yellow tape, skimming the area for potential paths of entry and exit. She halted near a tall hedge of oleander.

"Hold up," Miranda said, setting down her kit.

She opened the tackle box, zipped into a white Tyvek suit, and then pulled paper booties over her shoes.

"You have a mask with you?" Nicole asked.

"Yeah."

"You're gonna need it. It's bad."

Miranda found a plastic bag with several paper face masks. She took out a vial of orange oil and applied some to the mask with an eyedropper.

"You want one?" she asked Nicole. "It helps with the smell."

"Absolutely. Thanks."

Miranda handed the mask to Nicole and prepared another. She arranged it on her face and then started photographing the area. Walking all the way around the flower bed, she took photos of the soft dirt around the hedge. Then she returned to Nicole.

"Okay, ready," she told her.

They ducked under the tape, and Miranda immediately caught the stench, even through the orange oil. Nicole led her across a concrete slab decorated with brightly colored sidewalk chalk. They passed a pink tricycle and went through a narrow corridor with closets on either side, both marked MAINTENANCE. At the end of the corridor Miranda turned left to find a storage closet made of wire mesh. The door had been propped open with a brick.

"Who found the body?" Miranda asked.

"I did."

She whirled around. "*You* did?"

"I live upstairs. I was stashing something in here when the smell hit me. I didn't touch anything, obviously, but at first glance, it looks like a gunshot wound or possibly a stabbing."

Miranda turned to face the metal gate, which had a heavy-duty lock.

"You have a key to this gate?"

"All the tenants do. I propped it open with a brick because it kept blowing shut. It locks automatically."

Miranda studied the gate, paying particular attention to the lock. It didn't appear damaged.

Shoot your way in, shoot your way out.

It was the mantra that Miranda taught to her forensic photography students. Miranda took dozens of pictures of the door, including the lock. Peering through the wire mesh, she scanned the contents of the closet: bicycles, beach chairs, half-inflated rafts.

"No sign of forced entry."

Joel's voice had her turning around. He wore latex gloves and paper shoe covers.

"There are some footwear impressions in the flower bed on the other side of the closet," Miranda said.

His eyebrows arched. "By the hedge there?"

"Yes."

"Don't touch anything," she said as he moved toward the bushes. "And don't step in the dirt."

He gave her a pointed look. "I know."

Miranda took a few more photographs of the door lock and then stepped inside the closet. No footprints on the concrete, no blood trails.

The breeze kicked up, and she held her breath against the stench. Even with the mask on, it was nearly overpowering.

Miranda stepped over a foam pool noodle and sidestepped a bicycle with dirt-caked tires. She snapped a few pictures.

The low noise sent a chill down her spine. Flies. Lots of them. Gritting her teeth, she lifted her camera to take a few more shots as she moved deeper into the closet. The space back here was dim and airless. Flies zipped toward her, and she batted them away.

She saw the shoes first. Men's basketball sneakers, laces untied. Miranda took a photograph, looking at the body through the viewfinder, as if the lens might somehow shield her from the grotesque scene.

Black flies swarmed the face, concentrating their attention on the nose and mouth. Miranda stepped closer and took a picture, and the flash illuminated him.

She gasped and lowered her camera. "Oh my God."

Joel stepped up behind her. "What is it?"

"Joel, it's *him*."

CHAPTER

EIGHTEEN

JOEL WATCHED MIRANDA with an eagle eye as she rummaged through the back of her Jeep. She'd spent the past few hours ignoring the flies and the god-awful smell as she photographed every inch of the crime scene. And then she'd taken out her evidence kit and lifted prints from the gate.

"Joel?"

He turned to Brady. "What's that?"

"I said, it's confirmed," the chief told him. "They checked the wallet. Alexander Kendrick, twenty-three."

Joel turned to watch as a pair of ME's assistants loaded a gurney into the back of their van.

"Also, it's a gunshot wound," Brady said. "Not a knife wound."

"Thanks."

The chief looked at Miranda. "This is the person she saw on his bike the morning of the murders?"

"That's right."

"She's sure?"

"Yes," Joel said. "And we confirmed it was him earlier this week. Emmet and McDeere interviewed both him and his girlfriend. Kendrick was at her place at the time of the murders—or so he said. He confirmed that he was riding his bike along the highway within an hour of when the bodies were discovered, but he said he didn't see anything suspicious."

"So, we don't have a reason to think this murder is connected to the others."

Joel looked at Brady. The chief didn't really believe the crimes were unrelated any more than Joel did. This was his way of asking Joel to speculate. But Joel wasn't ready to do that.

"No official link, no."

Emmet walked up. "So, is it him?"

"Alexander Kendrick," Brady said.

"He goes by Xander. Shit." Emmet looked at Joel. "What do you think it means?"

"I don't know yet."

Emmet offered Joel a bottle of water.

"Thanks." He took it and glanced across the parking lot at Miranda.

"Soon as we get official identification, I can go with you to notify next of kin," Emmet said. "I already met the girlfriend, and we'll definitely want to interview her again."

"Autopsy should be later today." Brady looked at Joel. "You up for it?"

"Yeah."

Brady pulled out his phone. "I'll pin them down on a time. We can't wait on this one."

The chief stepped away, and Joel walked over to check on Miranda as she slammed the tailgate of her Jeep. A paper mask dangled around her neck, and her cheeks were flushed.

He offered her the bottle of water, but she shook her head.

"What's wrong?" he asked.

"I had some quick-dry plaster in my Jeep, but now I can't find it."

"I've got some in my truck."

"You do? I need it."

He walked her across the lot to his pickup, looking her over. She'd been taking pictures for the last two hours in ninety-degree heat, and it was humid as hell.

But he knew that wasn't the only thing bothering her.

"You all right?" he asked.

"Yeah. Why wouldn't I be?"

"You look upset."

"I want to get this shoe print in the flower bed before it gets lost."

Joel dug his keys from his pocket and unlocked the chrome toolbox behind his cab. He rummaged through waders and fishing gear and found the jug of quick-set plaster. He handed it to her, and she started to walk away.

"Miranda, wait."

She turned around.

"Maybe you should take a break."

Annoyance flared in her eyes. "Why?"

"You were injured in a fire just a few hours ago. It's okay if you need to go home and get some rest."

She laughed. "Who's going to collect evidence at this scene if I go home and *rest*? Evidence gets trampled on and rained on and blows away." She gestured to the parking lot still crowded with emergency vehicles and curious onlookers. "It's probably happening right this second, as we speak."

"We can call the county to help."

"No. This is *my* job."

He stepped closer. The frightened, vulnerable woman

who'd cried on his shoulder earlier was long gone. For the
last two hours, she'd been terse and defensive.

"I'm just saying, you've been through a lot—"

"Stop." She held up a hand. "Please don't do this. This
is exactly what I *didn't* want you to do."

"What?"

"I don't want special treatment, okay? You can't treat me
different from everyone else."

"I'm not giving you special treatment."

"Oh yeah?" She tipped her head to the side. "Where's
Nicole, then? She's canvassing the neighbors and taking
people's statements. She's the one who *found* the body, and
you didn't send her home to take a nap."

Joel gritted his teeth. She was right, he hadn't. But he
also wasn't worried that Nicole was somehow wrapped up
in this case the way Miranda was. Joel didn't like the fire
tonight, and he sure as hell didn't like another body turning
up just a short time later. He didn't know what the fuck was
going on yet, but way too much of it had somehow involved
Miranda.

She glanced past him. "People are watching us. Don't
make a scene. Please?"

The pleading look in her eyes tugged at him, and he
knew she was worried about the same shit she'd been worried about when they were lying together sweaty and naked
on her sofa.

He took a deep breath, trying to tamp down his frustration.

"I'm just doing my job, Miranda. I'm trying to figure out
what the hell this is about."

"I've got a job to do, too." She held up the jug of plaster.
"Now, let me do it, okay?"

CHAPTER

NINETEEN

THE SKY WAS pale gray by the time Miranda pulled into her driveway. She eyed the bedroom window. She'd left the lights off, and her little cottage seemed to be asleep. She hoped Benji was, too. She didn't want him to wake up groggy and disoriented with her not there.

Miranda gathered her evidence kit and trudged up the stairs, pausing at the top to look out over the beach. No campfires or lanterns to the north. To the south, lights in the cottages and beachfront hotels were starting to wink on.

Miranda cast a worried look at the glass door as she fumbled with her keys. Fear coiled tightly in her stomach as she unlocked the door and stepped into a silent house. She flipped the lock and dumped her things on the table before hurrying into her bedroom.

Benji was asleep in his bed, just where she'd left him. He lifted his head from the pillow as she knelt at his side.

"Hey, boy." She kissed his head and stroked his back. "You still sleepy?"

The swelling on his nose had gone down, but his eyes still looked droopy as he rested his head on his paws. His temperature felt normal, and Miranda breathed a sigh of relief as she ran her hand over his fur.

She slumped against the nightstand. Home. *Finally.* She was exhausted. She'd been exhausted when she came home from the lighthouse, and that was before the trip to the clinic, and before Joel, and before the crime scene.

She leaned her head against her unmade bed and thought of Joel. The memories were a blur, really. A good blur—exciting and erotic and even sweet at some points—but definitely a blur. She hadn't yet had time to process what had happened. Her sleep-deprived brain wasn't fully functioning.

She thought back to the look on his face as he'd hovered over her in the dimness. Just remembering his heated, half-lidded gaze sent a ripple of desire through her.

She shouldn't have done it. She knew that. Her one impulsive decision had made her work life—and her personal life—infinitely more complicated. But she couldn't bring herself to be sorry. It was too good. Just the memory alone filled her with a bone-deep yearning.

Miranda sighed.

She needed a shower. And food. She was sweaty and gross after five long hours of working a crime scene. But her limbs felt leaden and she couldn't bring herself to move.

Benji snorted softly but didn't open his eyes. Miranda stroked his head.

"It's okay, boy. I'm home."

She pulled the comforter off the end of the bed and wrapped it around her shoulders. Then she curled up on the floor beside him. She needed a nap—just a short one—before she could do anything at all. She let her eyes drift shut.

A faint chime dragged her awake. She tried to place the sound. Sitting up, she pulled her phone from the back pocket of her jeans.

"Hello?"

"Is this Miranda?"

She blinked down at the screen, shaking off the fog. She didn't recognize the number. Her room was bright now and seagulls screeched outside the window. How long had she slept?

She cleared her throat. "This is Miranda."

"It's Mike Conner. Sorry to call you on a Saturday, but I didn't think this could wait."

She sat up straighter as the words sank in.

"It's no problem," she told the professor. "What's wrong?"

DENISE BROUGHT IN a box of doughnuts from the Beanery, but Joel couldn't even look at food. He was too wired. He tapped his pencil on the table and stared at the whiteboard as he waited for Brady to kick off the meeting.

"Let's start with Joel." The chief scooted in his chair. "Tell us about the autopsy."

Joel had spent the better part of the morning at the ME's office. Their case had jumped to the front of the line after Brady made a few well-placed phone calls.

"We got confirmation on the ID," Joel told the group seated around the conference table. "Alexander Kendrick, twenty-three. His prints were in the system."

"Why?" Owen asked.

"DUI from a few years ago. Other than that, he doesn't have a rap sheet." Joel flipped open the notepad in front of him, even though he knew the information by heart now. "Cause of death, single gunshot wound to the chest. ME recovered the bullet. He says it's in decent shape." Joel darted a look at the chief. "And we're still waiting on the ballistic results from the other cases."

Brady surveyed the faces around the table. The group included detectives and several uniforms who'd been enlisted to help with the legwork—which was extensive now that they had a third homicide to deal with.

"Where's Emmet?" the chief asked. "Isn't he taking the lead on the ballistics?"

"He's on his way here," Nicole said. "I just got a text from him."

Brady looked at Joel. "Okay, what else?"

"Time of death, based on the state of the body, eighteen to twenty-four hours before discovery, give or take. He said it's an estimate."

"So . . . between midnight and six a.m. Friday morning, give or take," Nicole said.

"That's right."

"We talked to people at the nature center," Owen said. "Kendrick was seen by a co-worker leaving on his bike about fifteen minutes after closing, so around six forty-five."

"Who'd you talk to?" Brady asked.

"One of the scientists who works in the lab there. Jason Freeman. He says he saw him leaving on his bike. Then Emmet and McDeere went to his apartment and interviewed him around nine, and that's the last we know of his whereabouts until the body was discovered late last night. Also"— he flipped open a notebook in front of him—"we had another interview with his girlfriend."

"Who's 'we'?" Brady asked.

"Me and Emmet."

"Okay. How was she?"

"Seemed genuinely distraught. Said she had plans with her friends Thursday night, and she texted Xander a couple times Friday. By the time she got off work and hadn't heard from him, she was starting to worry. She said she went by his place yesterday, but he didn't answer his door, so she started pinging his friends to see if anyone had heard from him. She showed us the texts, so that checks out."

"We still need to confirm her alibi," Brady said.

Owen nodded. "I know. We're on it."

Joel turned to look at the murder board, where he'd taped up half a dozen new pictures. The first was a driver's license photo of Alexander Kendrick. Beside it was a series of graphic crime scene photos that Miranda had taken early this morning. Joel studied the shots, thinking about Miranda stoically working the scene just hours after she'd been caught in a fire and had an emotional meltdown.

"What happened when he didn't show up for work Friday?" Nicole asked. "Did anyone think to check on him?"

"We asked that," Owen said. "They assumed he was out sick and assigned an intern to cover the desk."

Emmet strode into the room. "Sorry I'm late," he said, grabbing an empty seat by the chief. "I just heard back from my ATF guy. Our ballistics results are in."

Joel could tell from Emmet's face that he had something important. "What'd you find out?" he asked.

He took a deep breath. "The bullets that killed our two victims, and Mark Randall in Corpus Christi, and the oil company executive in Houston, were all fired from the same gun."

Silence settled over the room.

Joel leaned forward. "*All* four victims. At three separate crime scenes."

"That's right."

Joel looked at the chief. The stony expression on Brady's face told him he was thinking the exact same thing Joel was.

"You're sure?" Joel asked Emmet.

"Yes. He just emailed the report. You can read it for yourself."

Brady leaned back in his chair. "So, we're dealing with a serial killer."

No one spoke, and the chief's words hovered over them.

Joel got up and walked to the murder board. "So we've got four linked deaths, all involving the same gun," he said.

"Five, including Alexander Kendrick," Nicole added.

"That one's not confirmed yet," Brady said.

It was linked. Joel knew it. He figured Brady knew it, too.

"And in all of those four linked cases, a feather was recovered on or near the victim," Joel said.

"What about Kendrick?" Owen asked.

Joel shook his head. "No feather. But as Miranda pointed out, it was windy last night, and the body had been there awhile."

"What the hell do the feathers mean?" Emmet asked.

"I don't know," Joel said. "But it could go to motive. We know at least two of the feathers are from endangered birds, so it could be some kind of message the killer is sending."

"Another link is that protest group," Nicole said. "Alpha Omega Now. They held protests at the Houston oil company where the executive worked and at one of Mark Randall's developments. And we think our two victims—Liz and Will—were members of the group." She looked at Joel. "You went to the autopsy. Did you see—"

"No tattoos," Joel said. "But he might still be part of the group. We need to check with his friends and look at his social media accounts."

Chatter erupted around the table, as everyone reacted to the idea that they could be dealing with a serial killer.

Joel turned to the board. He studied the photograph of the couple in the canoe. The damn image had been stuck in his head for days.

"Okay, so assuming this group is somehow involved, I

don't get why Kendrick was targeted," Owen said. "And the couple from Oregon. I mean, if we assume this is some kind of ideologically driven killer who is into environmental causes—then an oil company executive and a real estate developer would fit the motive. But the couple in the canoe—they were members of the protest group. And Kendrick worked at a nature center. Why would *he* be targeted?"

Joel didn't understand it either. He stepped over to the satellite map of the island where someone—probably Nicole—had put tiny orange stickers at each of the death scenes. They now had three.

"Maybe we're making it too complicated," Joel said, staring at the map. "Maybe it's all about location."

"How do you mean?" Owen asked.

Joel turned around. "Maybe Kendrick was targeted because he was a witness to the double homicide Monday. Miranda reported seeing him near the marina right before the bodies were discovered. Just look at the map. Kendrick lives here." Joel tapped the Driftwood Apartments. "He was riding his bike home from his girlfriend's place not long after two people were murdered here." He put his finger on the orange dot representing the canoe crime scene. "It's possible he saw something—maybe a vehicle or a person—leaving the marina after the murder happened."

"But we interviewed him," Emmet said. "He said he didn't see anything suspicious."

"Maybe someone *thinks* he did," Joel said. "He was in the area. The timing works. Maybe he didn't actually see anything, but someone saw *him* and decided to get rid of him. So in this case, no feather. This was about eliminating a witness, not making some ideological statement."

Joel glanced around the table. Everyone looked skeptical.

"That's pretty damn cold-blooded," Nicole said. "You're

talking about ending someone's life because they *might* have witnessed a crime?"

"Every one of these is cold-blooded," Joel countered. "We've got a guy who gets a bullet in his chest as he's on his way to work. Another who gets whacked while he's fishing off his boat dock." He gestured to the murder board. "And another two victims barely old enough to buy beer who get gutshot while they're watching the sunrise from a goddamn canoe. Whoever's doing this has ice in their veins."

"Or maybe they're crazy," Emmet said.

Joel turned to the board. Crazy or not, it didn't matter. Anyone who would commit a murder—let alone four—to make a statement had no boundaries. They were dealing with someone cold and ruthless. Someone who wouldn't hesitate to shoot a man in the chest—or start a fire—to get rid of a potential witness.

Joel's stomach filled with dread as he studied the map and thought about Miranda. He couldn't shake the feeling that every strange thing happening here was somehow connected.

"Joel?"

He turned around. The chief was watching him, along with everyone else.

"If we're going to do this, we need you on board," Brady said. "You'll still be the lead, but we'd have more resources. I think it's clear we need them."

He was talking about the task force. It was way past time to put aside the turf wars and bring in some help.

Joel nodded. "I'm all in."

M IRANDA STEPPED INTO the police station, and the sympathetic look from the receptionist told her that news of last night's fire had made the rounds.

"Oh my goodness, how *are* you?" Denise got to her feet and hurried around the counter to give Miranda a hug. "I can't believe it about the fire. How are you feeling?"

"Fine." Miranda forced a smile. "No injuries, thanks to some helpful bystanders."

Denise darted a worried glance at Miranda's bandaged arm.

"Nothing serious, that is. Just a scratch." Miranda looked through the glass partition, but she didn't see Joel or any of the other detectives in the sea of cubicles.

"I stopped by to talk to Detective Breda," Miranda said. "Do you know if he's here?"

"Joel or Owen?"

"Joel."

"He's out right now. Would you like to leave him a message?"

The door behind her opened and Nicole walked in, accompanied by a uniformed officer Miranda hadn't met.

Nicole stopped and peeled off her sunglasses. "Miranda, hey. How's the arm?"

"Fine," she said, wishing she'd thought to wear a long-sleeved shirt. "I came by to see Joel, actually, but I understand he's not in."

"He's on the mainland with the chief. Anything I can help with?"

Miranda hesitated. She'd wanted to give this information to Joel, but Nicole was up to speed on the social media angle. And Miranda didn't want to sit on this lead.

"You have a minute to talk?" Miranda asked.

"Sure, come on back."

"There are doughnuts in the break room," Denise said, returning to her chair. "Somebody better eat them. I don't want to have to take them home."

"Thanks, Denise," Nicole said, holding open the door.

Miranda smiled at Denise and followed Nicole back through the bullpen, scanning the room for anyone she recognized, but everyone she knew appeared to be out.

Maybe they were home asleep after being up all night.

"Pretty quiet around here," Miranda said.

"Everyone's following up on leads," Nicole said. "The first forty-eight hours are crucial." She stopped beside a cubicle and tossed her baseball cap on the desk. "But why am I telling you that? You know." She smiled and gestured to the desk chair. "Have a seat."

"Thanks." As Miranda sat, Nicole dragged a chair over from the neighboring cube.

"What a night, huh?" She wiped her brow with the back of her hand. Nicole smelled like sunblock, and Miranda guessed she'd been out either knocking on doors or conducting interviews outside. "We haven't forgotten about the arson case. Don't worry. It's just that everyone's a bit sidetracked with this new homicide."

"You guys must be overwhelmed."

"A little." She made a face. "A lot, actually. But we're hoping to get some help. Chief Brady and Joel are at the sheriff's office right now. As of this afternoon, we're forming a task force and bringing in some additional resources."

"Sounds like a good idea."

"Yeah, I've only been suggesting it since Monday." She rolled her eyes. "But, hey, better late than never, right?" She nodded at the folder in Miranda's hand. "So, what brings you in?"

Miranda set the folder on the desk, which was cluttered with paperwork, coffee mugs, and a yellow stress ball. Nicole moved the mugs aside.

Miranda looked at her. "Joel told you all about that protest group, right?"

"Alpha Omega Now," Nicole said.

"We think both Elizabeth Lark and Will Stovak were members."

"Based on the tattoos."

"And their social media posts," Miranda added. "I've been trying to learn more about them, but it isn't easy. Evidently, their group is loosely structured. I think that's by design. They don't want to attract the attention of law enforcement, so they don't seem to have a designated leader, and their public-facing communication is pretty cryptic."

"Okay."

"But I have a colleague who works with the FBI gang unit in San Antonio and he turned up an interesting lead. He believes the person running things is a guy named Trevor Keen. He's from Denver." Miranda pulled out a printout of an article from the *Denver Post*.

"'Protest Halts Mining Project,'" Nicole said, reading the headline. "This was in Denver?"

"The protest happened three years ago in a town east of Denver where a private company had gotten permission to mine in a federally protected forest. This was one of Alpha Omega's first protests, and this guy Trevor was their spokesperson. He's quoted several times in the article. Since then, looks like he's been keeping a lower profile. But according to my friend, the FBI has him in their records as an affiliate of the group."

Nicole pivoted to her computer. She tapped the mouse to wake it up and clicked into a new screen.

"You have a middle name?" she asked.

"No," Miranda said. "But he's from Colorado, like I said. And three years ago, he was twenty-four, according to the news article."

Nicole entered some information and waited. A mug shot appeared on the screen, and Nicole scooted her chair in. "I got him. Trevor James Keen, twenty-seven. Looks like . . . he's got a sheet, but nothing too serious. An arrest for criminal trespass and vandalism. And a public intox." She scrolled through some more information, then went back up to the mug shot and enlarged it. The man had dark hair, blue eyes, and a tan that suggested he spent a lot of time outdoors. "Check out the ink."

She pivoted her computer screen for Miranda to see. On the man's shoulder was a tattoo of the infinity serpent.

"Same as our two victims," Nicole said. She tipped her head to the side and studied the mug shot. "Nice-looking guy. I'd definitely remember if I'd seen him at the protest last week. Was he there?"

"Not sure. But he was in Lost Beach almost two weeks ago, when he posted a picture from White Dunes Park. And then this morning he posted from Padre Island National Seashore."

Nicole's eyebrows tipped up. "That's only an hour from here. He posted from there this morning?"

"Yep."

Miranda watched Nicole and knew exactly what she was thinking. This guy easily could have been on the island when all three of the murders happened.

Not to mention the fire.

"Damn." Nicole turned to look at her screen. "What else did you get?"

Miranda pulled a handwritten list from her folder. "That's about it for Trevor Keen. I only found that one article that quoted him. But I got more info on Alpha Omega Now."

Nicole leaned in.

"I didn't print all of the news stories, but I made a list of dates and places. Here are the most recent ones." Miranda cleared her throat. "Two years ago, they protested a drilling project near Yellowstone. Then they protested a logging company in East Texas, followed by an oil-and-gas company in Houston. That's the one you discovered."

"EastTex Petroleum," Nicole said. "The CFO was later murdered in his driveway."

"How much later?"

"About eleven months after the protest."

"Okay. Next protest I found was at a development in Rockport that was built as part of the wetlands swap program."

"Mark Randall's project," Nicole said.

"Right. Then last fall they were in Houston again at the headquarters of a cruise line."

Miranda looked at her notes again. "Then . . . earlier this spring they were out in Sedona, Arizona, where they assembled a flash mob to protest a resort that was going in near a nature reserve. Last month, they were at Joshua Tree National Park in California, where they were protesting a highway project. Then this week they turned up here."

"Sounds like they really get around."

"Those were just the incidents that generated media coverage I was able to find. Who knows what else they've been doing." Miranda closed the folder.

"Mind if I make a copy of that?"

"You can have the whole file. I've got it saved on my computer."

Nicole picked up the stress ball and squeezed it as she stared at the mug shot on her computer screen. She looked deep in thought. Or maybe she was just dazed from lack of sleep.

Miranda checked her watch. She glanced at the reception area, but still no sign of Joel. She had been apprehensive about coming to talk to him, but now that he wasn't here, she was eager to see him. It made no sense.

"Miranda?"

She snapped her attention back to Nicole, who was eyeing her with concern.

"Are you all right?" Nicole asked.

"Yes. Why?"

She hesitated a beat before responding. "Joel's worried about you. We all are."

Miranda's stomach knotted. "Why?"

"Because. The fire. And your injury. And then you were up all night working another death scene." She shook her head. "This new homicide is . . . well, it's pretty unnerving. Especially coming so close after the other two."

Unnerving. That was one word for it.

"I appreciate your concern, but I'm fine." Miranda forced a smile. "Just a little sleep deprived, like you." She checked her watch again and stood up. "I need to go. Can you relay all this to Joel?"

"Sure. Thanks for the help."

"No problem." She started to walk away.

"And Miranda?"

She turned around, and Nicole looked worried again.

"Be careful."

JOEL WATCHED THE line of storm clouds rolling in off the Gulf. Just what they needed. A Saturday rainstorm would clear the beaches and fill up the bars early, and by sundown they'd be dealing with more than the usual number of drunken hotheads.

Joel focused on the road as he crossed the causeway. Driving typically helped him think, but today everything was a chaotic mess inside his head. He was trying to unravel three homicides, two cold cases, and a fire. Somehow all of it fit together—he felt sure—he just didn't understand how. The only thing he knew for certain was that somewhere along the way, Miranda had gotten tangled up in everything.

Guilt needled at him. He never should have hired her. From an investigative standpoint, it was a win, no question. Miranda had a keen eye for detail and good instincts. Without her, Joel wouldn't have half the leads he was currently pursuing. Her idea about the feather, which he'd initially thought was pretty out-there, now seemed to be central to the case. But whether through her work on the case or her proximity to the original crime scene, she'd caught the attention of someone dangerous. A person who apparently would go to any lengths to silence a potential witness.

It was only a theory at this point, but there was something to it. Joel didn't believe in coincidences, and he didn't buy into the notion—as much as he wanted to—that the murders and the fire were unrelated.

The lighthouse came into view. Joel's gut churned as he spotted the sooty black streak above the window. Miranda could have been killed last night if those bystanders hadn't jumped into action.

This situation was his fault. She'd repeatedly rejected his job offer, but he'd pressured her. And now she was deep into this thing, and Joel didn't know how to get her out. He was in a state of constant tension, and he knew he'd stay that way until he made an arrest.

His phone buzzed from the cup holder as he turned onto the highway. Nicole.

"Hey," Joel said.

"How'd it go at the sheriff's office?"

"They're lending us two deputies. They'll be here tomorrow for the team meeting."

"Two? That's it?"

"Plus, we've got the FBI looped in, which might help speed up some of the evidence."

Joel rolled to a stop at the intersection in front of the Sand Dollar Inn. A group of girls in bikini tops and shorts rushed across the street, followed by a pair of guys carrying coolers. With the rain coming, they were moving the party inside, apparently.

"Well, at least we have help now," Nicole said. "You think they're lending us good people?"

"We'll find out soon enough. What's going on there?"

"We finally got the phone dump on Lark and Stovak."

"It's about damn time."

"Yeah, I know. I'm going through it now."

"Anything useful?"

"Not yet. And Miranda came by with some interesting info."

Joel's stomach clenched. "What kind of info?"

"She's been doing some research on Alpha Omega Now. She's put together a timeline of their protests over the last few years. When you line it up with the murders we know about, it's pretty compelling."

The murders they *knew* about. Joel wasn't the only one who'd realized there could be additional victims they weren't aware of yet.

"She left a file for us," Nicole continued. "You should go through it. She turned up a name for some guy who may or may not be the leader of the group."

"Of Alpha Omega Now?"

"Yeah, she consulted a co-worker who's got an in with the FBI gang unit. This is a name they have on file in connection with the organization. We definitely need to look at him. His name's Trevor James Keen, and he's from Colorado. I just sent you his mug shot."

Joel checked his phone as a text landed.

"What's on his sheet?" he asked, studying the picture.

"Nothing major. Trespassing, vandalism, public intoxication. You can look at all this when you get in. Wouldn't hurt to loop the feds in, see what else they might have on him. But, listen, get this."

Joel's shoulders tensed.

"He was here in town within the last couple of weeks," she said. "And he was on South Padre Island this morning."

"Where'd we get that?"

"Miranda checked out his social media posts."

Joel gritted his teeth. Once again, she was way more involved than he wanted her to be. "We need to get a bead on this guy, ASAP. We need a vehicle description—"

"The chief already put Emmet on it," she said. "Brady called from the road, so I filled him in on this."

"Good."

"So, are you almost back?"

"Yeah. I'll be there in twenty."

"Okay, I'll probably go get dinner, and then I can go over this stuff with you. See you soon."

Joel ended the call and drove through downtown, scanning the sidewalks for anyone who looked like Trevor Keen. As if he might just be strolling down the street with a surfboard under his arm, waiting to be hauled in for questioning.

Was he their guy? Just because he'd been on the island and was affiliated with Alpha Omega Now didn't make him a murderer. But the timing raised a red flag. He was on the island before the first two murders and he was within an hour's drive around the time a third body showed up. It was worth checking into.

Joel passed the pastel-colored beach houses of Caribbean Sands and slowed as he neared Miranda's driveway. His spotted her Jeep parked in front of the house and battled the urge to swing by and see her. He wanted to. Miranda had been stuck in his mind all day, and he couldn't stop thinking about her warm body and her smooth skin and the way she'd fallen asleep with her head tucked against his chest. Joel definitely wanted to see her, but he needed to pursue this new lead more than he needed to get distracted.

Joel neared the turnoff for White Dunes Park and spied a lone woman at the top of one of the dunes. He tapped the brakes as he passed her.

Miranda. What the hell was she doing?

Joel watched in the rearview mirror as she lifted her camera and took a shot, then trudged down the dune toward the beach.

Joel swung into the next park entrance. He passed a black pickup with a surfboard strapped to the top and a white convertible loaded with teenagers who were about to get soaked. The gravel road turned to sand. Joel drove between the dunes and hung a right onto the beach.

Miranda was walking north now, away from her house. She stopped and faced the water, lifting her camera. Joel slowed as he neared her, and she turned around.

He rolled down the window as she walked over. She wore snug-fitting yoga pants and a loose T-shirt. He noticed the bandage on her arm.

"Hi," she said.

"What are you doing out here alone?"

She gave him a quizzical look. "Working. Why?"

"Get in."

"What?"

"Get in and I'll give you a ride home. It's about to pour."

Annoyance flickered across her face. "I'm not done yet. And anyway, I can walk."

As if on cue, the rain started coming down.

"Get in, Miranda."

She glanced at the sky and stuffed her camera under her T-shirt. She looked at him again, and Joel clenched his teeth to keep his cool.

Another quick look at the sky and she walked around the front of his truck. She climbed in and slammed the door.

"I *don't* need a ride. It's, like, a tenth of a mile." She turned to look at him. "And I don't need you bossing me around, either."

"Too bad."

He put his truck in gear.

"*Too bad?* What the hell does that mean?"

He shook his head.

"Forget it. Let me out. I'll walk."

He didn't stop.

"Let me *out*, Joel!"

He rolled to a stop, and she reached for the door handle.

"Wait. Just—hang on."

She turned to look at him, her eyes blazing.

"I'm sorry." He took a deep breath. "I didn't mean to boss you around."

"What is your problem?"

He put the truck in park. "Nothing. I just don't like seeing you walking around alone in the rain."

It started drumming on the windshield, making his case for him and preventing him from looking like a complete idiot.

"Sorry." He raked his hand through his hair. "I'm tired and I've had a shit day."

"Well, don't take it out on me." She unlooped the camera from around her neck and settled it on the floor. Then she turned to face him. "Why have you had a shit day?"

God, he wanted her. Just being alone with her in his truck was making him want to take her back to her house for a repeat of last night.

He looked through the windshield as the rain thrummed down. "We got the results back on the lighthouse fire. The accelerant used was turpentine." He looked at her. "No can recovered, so the perp likely used the can that was there and took it with him when he left."

Worry flickered in her eyes, and Joel felt guilty again for getting her involved in this. He felt guilty every time he looked at that bandage on her arm.

"I saw you out here alone and—I don't know." He shook

his head. "Until we get a handle on what's going on, until we make an arrest, I won't feel good about your safety."

Her eyes softened at that.

Joel picked up her hand. "Sorry I snapped at you."

She leaned in and kissed him. It was soft and brief, and she started to pull away, but he touched her cheek and held her in place. He wanted more. He kissed her longer, and she tasted as hot and sweet as she had last night.

He combed his fingers into her hair, and she slid closer, running her hands over his shoulders. She scooted over and hitched her hip onto the console, and that was all the encouragement he needed to pull her into his lap. She never broke the kiss and made a soft sound in her throat as she melted against him. He glided his hand over her warm thigh. She squirmed on his lap, and all the blood in his body went straight to his groin as she kissed the hell out of him.

She pulled back. "We're in your truck," she said breathlessly.

He kissed her again, pulling her closer, and she ran her fingers into his hair. Rain pelted the windshield as the kiss went on and on. Then she pulled away. She shifted her weight, and he thought she was sliding off, but instead she straddled him. Lust shot through him, and he gripped her hips. She settled her arms on his shoulders and rested her breasts against his chest. He slid his hand under her shirt.

"Joel." She squirmed closer as he filled his hand with a perfect breast.

"Yeah."

"I thought about you today."

She tipped her head back as he leaned forward and kissed her neck. Her skin was smooth and warm, and she smelled even more amazing than she had last night. He reached around her and unclasped her bra, and she shivered as he slid his hand around to touch her.

A loud *whelp* of a siren made her jump. She scrambled off his lap, and Joel looked in the rearview mirror to see a Beach Patrol unit stopped behind them.

"No parking on this beach," said a voice over a megaphone.

"Oh my gosh."

He glanced at Miranda, who'd turned a deep shade of pink as she sank down in the seat and refastened her bra.

The patrol unit rolled up alongside them, and Joel glared at the kid behind the wheel. The guy recognized Joel and gave a quick wave before driving on.

Miranda closed her eyes. "Crap."

"Relax. I know him."

"I know! That's why I'm embarrassed."

Joel put the truck in gear. He moved slowly down the beach and took the first right turn to the highway. The rain was really coming down now, and he switched the wipers to high.

"Joel."

"What?" He turned toward her house.

"We can't keep doing this."

He shot a look at her. "Why not?"

"Because."

Her house came into view. She didn't say a word as he turned onto her driveway and bumped over the ruts. He rolled to a stop behind her Jeep and shoved it in park again.

She started to say something, but Joel's phone interrupted her, and he dug it out. Emmet. He tucked the phone back in his pocket.

"Do you need to answer that?" she asked.

"Later." He looked at her. "I meant what I said last night. Everything's the same as it was before."

"No, it's *not*. I wasn't making out with you on a public beach before." She closed her eyes and squeezed the bridge of her nose.

"What's wrong?"

She shook her head.

"Miranda, look at me."

She looked out the window instead. "What's wrong is I'm completely stressed. But, hey, what else is new?"

She met his gaze, and the anguished look in her eyes pulled at him. He wanted her to talk to him, and he tried to pick his words carefully so she wouldn't shut him down this time.

"It seems like you're dealing with something," he said. "You referenced it at dinner the other night."

She'd called it burnout, but he knew there was more to it. She looked away again.

"Want to talk about it?" he asked.

She shook her head.

"I can't help you if I don't know what's wrong."

She looked at him. "It's not your job to help me."

"Okay. But I want to."

She stared through the rain-slicked windshield, and he could see the debate going on in her head. She was analyzing again. Weighing the pros and cons of letting him in. The humid air in the truck was thick with tension as she stayed silent.

Joel was in uncharted territory here. Usually he was the one who kept his feelings on lockdown. As a rule, he avoided emotional conversations, and now here he was asking Miranda to open up.

His phone buzzed again, and he cursed.

"Sounds like someone needs you." She reached for her camera. "Thanks for the ride."

MIRANDA DASHED UP the stairs with her camera tucked under her T-shirt. She ducked under the narrow overhang and dug the house key out of her pocket. The sight of Benji on the other side of the glass flooded her with relief.

She stepped inside, shaking off the water, and crouched to give him a hug. His nose looked better. She tried to hold his head still so she could examine it, but he wiggled away and made excited circles around her as she dropped her stuff on the armchair.

Her phone chirped from the kitchen where she'd left it charging, and she hurried to grab it.

"Hi," she said to Bailey.

"I got your message. Miranda! What the *hell*?"

She'd left her a brief message about the fire, downplaying everything. She'd also mentioned the new homicide case, which might end up on the news in Austin, where her sisters lived.

She hadn't mentioned Joel.

"Are you all right?" Bailey asked. "I can't believe you were in a fire. The pictures look awful."

"What pictures?"

"It's in the Corpus Christi paper. I googled it. Did you seriously climb down from a four-story window?"

"It sounds more dramatic than it is."

"Right. Uh-huh. It's totally normal that you had to be rescued from a burning building. What does your detective think?"

Miranda plopped into the armchair. "He's not *my* detective."

"Well, does he have any leads in the case? I read an AP article that said they're conducting an arson investigation."

Miranda sighed. Dodging Bailey's questions was pointless, so she gave her a rundown of everything she knew, including her suspicion that whoever set the fire knew she was in the building.

Bailey was uncharacteristically quiet.

"Are you there?" Miranda asked.

"I'm thinking."

"What?"

"I'm truly worried about you."

"Please don't worry."

"Well, I am. And I'm glad you're involved with a cop. Don't pretend you're not—I can tell by the way you talk about him."

She leaned her head back against the chair. "It's confusing."

"Why?"

"Because. I like him a lot."

"That's good."

"But we're working together now. I don't want to do this again."

"Well, too late. You did it." Amusement crept into her voice. "Was it good?"

"Very."

She squealed. "Yes! *Finally.*"

Alarmed by the noise, Benji nudged his head against her knee.

"Finally what?"

"Finally, you're getting over Ryan. It's been almost two years."

"I've been over him forever."

"But now you're *over him* over him. Good sex makes it official."

Miranda smiled. But then her stomach knotted because it wasn't nearly as simple as she was making it out to be.

I can't help you if I don't know what's wrong.

It's not your job to help me.

Joel hadn't liked that response. But at the moment, it was the only one she was prepared to give, and she couldn't feel guilty about that.

"Seriously, though, what's he like as a detective?" Bailey asked.

"How do you mean?"

"I mean, is he good at his job?"

"Yes."

"Well, do you have confidence they're going to figure out what the hell's going on?"

"Yes."

"You sound sure."

"I am."

Joel was very good at his job. And she didn't doubt for a moment that he was one hundred percent committed to solving this case. Still, worry gnawed at her. Her concern had more to do with the Lost Beach Police Department than Joel. Such a small department wasn't accustomed to dealing with three homicides and an arson in the space of one week.

"They've formed a task force," Miranda said, not sure whether she was trying to reassure Bailey or herself. "It includes the sheriff's office, the FBI. So, it's a coordinated effort, and they've got a lot of good leads. I wouldn't be surprised if they zero in on a suspect soon."

Her sister's silence told Miranda she was skeptical.

"You sound optimistic," Bailey said.

"I am."

CHAPTER

TWENTY-ONE

L OST BEACH HAD more than a dozen hotels that catered to families by offering complimentary breakfast, kitchenettes in the rooms, and giant pools with elaborate kiddie slides.

The Sand Dollar Inn wasn't one of them.

The place offered highway views, spotty Wi-Fi, and a pint-size pool that emitted a funky smell. But what it lacked in amenities, it made up for with cheap rates and a prime location next to Lost Beach's liveliest strip of bars. Families avoided the place, but it did a booming business with college groups and bachelor parties, and Nicole was only mildly surprised to see the flickering **NO VACANCY** sign as she pulled into the parking lot.

Nicole checked her watch. She'd been at it for two hours, and the Sand Dollar was her final stop tonight. If it didn't pan out, she'd likely get tapped to spend half of her Sunday checking out the campgrounds again and interviewing regulars.

After scanning the parking lot, she walked into the unimpressive lobby, where she was greeted by an electronic doorbell and the smell of onion rings.

The guy behind the desk didn't look up from his computer. Early twenties, skinny, goatee. Nicole didn't recognize him—which was good. After a string of drug busts on the property, the police department wasn't exactly a favorite of the Sand Dollar management team. Nicole approached the desk, and the guy glanced up from his game of solitaire. He had a napkin at his elbow and a pile of rings.

"Help you?" he asked, wiping a crumb from his goatee.

"I hope so." She smiled and held up her police ID. "I wanted to see if you recognized this guest." She held up a printout of Trevor Keen's Colorado driver's license photo. It was a better picture than his mug shot and had the added benefit of not putting people on guard when she flashed it around.

The guy pursed his lips and looked at the printout.

"Mind?" He reached for it.

Nicole handed it over, and her pulse picked up because she could tell he recognized him.

"He looks familiar."

"This would have been sometime in the last two weeks."

"Yeah, I've definitely seen him." He handed the picture back. "Don't know if it was here, though."

Score.

"Could you check your computer? The name's Trevor Keen, two *e*'s."

He closed out of his game. "Trevor Keen?"

"That's right."

Nicole held her breath as she waited. She'd already resigned herself to another day in the sun tomorrow, but maybe her luck was turning. It was about freaking time.

The only surprise was that the Sand Dollar Inn had anything to do with it.

"Nope."

She felt a stab of disappointment. "You sure?"

"K-E-E-N, you said?"

"That's right."

The door behind the desk opened, and a heavyset woman bustled out. Her eyes narrowed when she saw Nicole talking to her staffer.

"There a problem?" she asked.

Nicole smiled and held up her ID. "Nicole Lawson, Lost Beach PD. I'm looking for someone who might have stayed here recently." She slid the printout across the counter, but the woman didn't even glance at it.

"You got a warrant?"

"No."

"Our guest records are confidential." She shot a look at the clerk, probably wondering what he'd already revealed.

Nicole glanced at her name tag and smiled again. "Ms. Grady, our department is investigating three homicides right now. I'm sure you—like other local residents—are hoping we can bring a quick resolution to these cases, especially with Memorial Day just around the corner. Anything you can do to help us is much appreciated."

Her jaw tightened, and Nicole could see she was torn. She glanced down at the computer. Nicole glanced, too, and noticed the guest registration screen was gone now, replaced by a generic desktop.

"What's the name?" The woman stepped over, and the clerk rolled his chair out of the way as she reached for the keyboard.

"Trevor Keen. K-E-E-N. This would have been sometime in the last two weeks."

She tapped at the keyboard. "He's not in here."

Nicole wanted to ask if she was sure, but the woman's defiant glare made her bite her tongue.

"Thank you." She nodded at the clerk. "Y'all have a good evening."

She left the lobby and pulled the small spiral notebook from her back pocket. The clerk had recognized the picture, but the guest wasn't in the records. So maybe he'd registered under a different name. Or maybe the clerk had seen him somewhere else on the island. Nicole jotted down the clerk's first name and glanced around the parking lot.

The tiny pool was deserted. On the opposite side of the patio, the door to one of the rooms stood open and a housekeeping cart was parked outside. Nicole glanced at the lobby and then crossed the lot. It was after seven, which seemed late for housekeeping, but Nicole heard someone in the room as she approached. She leaned her head in the door.

A thin woman with short brown hair bent over the bed, stripping the sheets. Sunny Luciano. She'd gone to high school with Nicole's older brother.

"Hi, Sunny."

No response. Nicole stepped into the room, and Sunny jumped.

"God, you scared me." She plucked out an AirPod from her ear.

"Nicole Lawson. I'm with LBPD."

"I know who you are." Sunny looked wary.

"You got a minute? I'm investigating a case, and I'm making the rounds."

"I really don't, sorry. I have three more rooms left and our dryer conked out, so I'm already behind." She wadded the sheets into a ball and brushed past Nicole on the way to the cart, where she stuffed the bundle in a hamper.

Nicole racked her brain for details about Sunny. Nicole

knew she was divorced and was fairly sure she had a young kid at home.

Sunny strode back into the room and cast a wary look over her shoulder. "Marge will chew me out if she sees me talking to you."

Nicole stepped farther into the room. "This will only take a minute." She held up the picture.

Sunny cast a furtive glance outside. Then she swung the door almost closed and stepped over to look at the picture.

Up close, Nicole saw that Sunny's nose was pink and her skin looked wan. She seemed like she might have a cold or allergies.

"What about him?" Sunny asked.

"Have you seen him around in the last two weeks? His name's Trevor Keen."

She dug a tissue from the pocket of her sky blue uniform and blew her nose. "He drives a black Honda."

Nicole's heart skittered. That was the vehicle registered to Trevor Keen in Colorado.

"You've seen him?"

"Yeah. Him and his girlfriend." She turned and grabbed a stack of sheets off the dresser. "Look, I really have to finish this." She snapped the sheet up, and it floated down over the mattress pad.

Nicole grabbed a folded pillowcase off the dresser and reached for a pillow. "So, where did you see him?"

Sunny sighed. "You're going to get me in trouble."

"Just a few more questions." Nicole stuffed the pillow into the case. "Where'd you see him?"

"Here." She moved around the bed, expertly tucking the sheet under the mattress.

"And the girlfriend? You remember what she looked like?" Nicole tossed the pillow on the chair and reached for another one.

"Young. Blond. Hair to her butt." She rolled her eyes. "You can't miss her."

"And do you remember anything else about them? Did they have any visitors?"

She whipped out the top sheet, and it floated down. "Not that I saw."

"You remember anything else about either of them?"

"Yeah, they left their cigarette butts everywhere." She tucked the sheet. "But they left me a tip, so I didn't mention anything."

Nicole stuffed another pillowcase. "You remember which room they stayed in?"

"On the end. Room 125. Now they're in 102, I think."

Nicole froze. "Now?"

"Yeah." She reached for the last pillow and grabbed the case off the dresser. "They checked in again earlier."

"They're here today?"

"Yeah. At least, they were." She tossed the pillow on the bed and glanced at the door. "Look, not to be a bitch, but I really need to finish this. If Marge sees me talking to you—"

"Don't worry. I'm gone." She dropped the pillow on the bed. "Thanks, Sunny. I appreciate it."

She gave a weak smile. "Sure. And tell your brother I said hi. He was always a sweetie."

"I will."

Nicole scanned the patio for Marge before crossing the parking lot to her truck. She was in her personal vehicle because she wanted to keep a low profile. She slid behind the wheel and called Joel.

"Where are you?" she asked.

"At the station. Why?"

"He's here."

"Who's here? Where are you?"

"At the Sand Dollar. The desk guy *and* the housekeeper

recognized Trevor Keen's photo. The housekeeper said he and his girlfriend checked in earlier today."

"Black Honda?"

"Yep. The manager told me Keen's not registered, but maybe it's under the woman's name. Or maybe he's using an alias and trying to keep his presence here under wraps. Anyway, their car's not here right now, but they're staying at this motel."

Silence on the other end. Nicole scanned all the cars in the lot but didn't see a black Honda. She set her phone in her lap and started her truck.

"Joel?"

"You're sure they're not there?"

She pulled around the side of the building and checked the alley. No cars.

"Their vehicle isn't here. And the room they're supposedly in is dark. What do you want me to do?"

"Sit on the place. I'll put a BOLO on the car. Maybe they're out."

"Okay. Should I talk to the management?"

"No, I don't trust them. Just sit tight. And park somewhere inconspicuous."

"What do you want me to do if they show up?"

"Call me."

TWENTY-TWO

JOEL SLID INTO Nicole's pickup.

"They pulled in twelve minutes ago," Nicole informed him. "Room 102, the second one from the right."

He trained his binocs on the door. A black Honda with Colorado plates was parked in front of it. Nicole had found a good vantage point in the parking lot of a drive-through taco place across the street from the motel.

"Just the two of them?" Joel asked.

"Yep."

"They bring anything in with them?"

"No luggage. They must have taken it inside already."

He lowered the binocs and looked at Nicole. "Emmet's around back, watching the bathroom window in case either of them tries to slip out. We want to know everything they've been up to the past two weeks. Places, timing, everything. We'll interview them separately and see if their stories match."

Nicole looked alarmed. "You just want to go over there and knock on the door?"

"Yep."

"You wouldn't rather take them to the station?"

He looked at the motel. "I'll read the situation, but probably not. My guess is we'll get more information if we keep it low-key and talk to them here."

Joel looked at her, noting the tense set of her jaw.

"You want to trade places with Emmet?" he asked.

"No."

"You sure?"

"Yes. Let's go."

Joel pulled out his Glock, checked it, then slipped it back into his holster as Nicole did the same.

"You take the woman, I'll talk to Keen." Joel pushed open the door. "And keep an eye on their hands."

They walked half a block to the intersection and waited for the light to cross, even though traffic was thin for a Saturday night. Music from the nearest bar drifted over as they crossed the highway. The Sand Dollar was full, and someone's party had spilled onto the breezeway on the second floor.

Approaching room 102, Joel caught the flicker of a television through a gap in the curtains.

He and Nicole stood on either side of the door, each with a hand on their weapon. Joel made eye contact with Nicole and then rapped on the door.

Someone moved in front of the window. The door opened a fraction and a pair of pale blue eyes peered out over the security latch. The woman had long blond hair and wore a black bikini top and white cutoffs.

"Who are you?" she asked with a frown.

"Lost Beach Police, ma'am. We'd like a minute," Joel said.

"A minute for what?"

"Open the door, please."

She closed the door, and Joel kept his hand on his weapon. The TV volume went off, and Joel watched through the gap in the curtains as a shirtless man got off the bed and crossed the room.

The door opened fully, and Trevor Keen stood beside the blonde. Keen wore blue board shorts, no shirt. Both of them had bare feet.

"Lost Beach Police," Joel said. "Could you step outside, please?"

"Why?" Keen asked.

"Step outside."

Keen stepped out, followed by the woman, and Joel looked them over to make sure no one had a weapon tucked in the back of their shorts. They weren't wearing enough clothes to conceal much of anything.

Joel flashed his police ID. "Are you Trevor Keen?" he asked.

His gaze narrowed. "Yeah. Why?"

Joel looked at the woman. "And your name?"

She darted a look at her boyfriend. "Gillian Copeland."

"We're investigating an incident from several days ago," Joel said. "We'd like a word with both of you."

"Care to come with me, ma'am?" Nicole said to the woman.

She darted a look at Trevor, and he turned to Joel. "What's this about?"

"Just a few questions. We can ask them here or at the police station, your call."

Trevor's expression hardened. He shot a look at his girlfriend.

"Sure, whatever." He opened the door wider. "Come on in."

Joel stepped through the doorway, positioning himself between Trevor and anything he might decide to reach for.

"Ma'am, we'll talk outside," Nicole said. "Step over here, please."

She and her boyfriend exchanged looks, and then Trevor closed the door. He turned around and looked at Joel, folding his arms over his chest. Joel noticed the serpent tattoo on his left shoulder.

Joel did a quick scan of the room. A duffel bag was parked on the floor beside the closet and a silver laptop computer sat open on the bed. Cigarette butts filled a soap dish on the nightstand.

"What's this about?" Trevor asked.

"Have a seat," Joel said, nodding at the chair by the door. He wanted the man well away from the nightstand and the duffel, just in case he might have a weapon stashed nearby.

Trevor walked over to the chair and sat down. "Did Romero tell you to talk to me?"

"Who's Romero?"

Trevor's gaze narrowed.

"That your PO?"

His jaw tightened. "I don't have a PO."

Joel stepped over to the cheap wooden dresser, eyeing the duffel bag on the floor. His interest in it seemed to make Trevor uncomfortable.

"Who's Romero?" Joel repeated.

"No one. Forget it. Ask me your questions."

Joel watched him for a long moment, trying to read his expression. He leaned back against the dresser and rested his palms on it.

"So, Trevor, where you been the last few weeks?"

His look turned wary. "Why?"

"I'm curious."

"We're on a road trip."

"Where?"

He lifted a shoulder. "California. Arizona. Texas."

"How long you been down here?"

Another shrug. "I don't know. Couple of weeks."

"Were you part of a protest at Joshua Tree National Park last month?"

Surprise flickered across his face, but he covered it. "Yeah. So?"

"And Gillian?"

"Yeah."

Joel folded his arms over his chest. "What about a protest at the Saguaro Hills golf resort in Sedona, Arizona?"

Trevor didn't respond.

"Were you there, too? On April fifth?"

"Yeah."

"And Gillian?"

"Yeah. So what? It's a free country."

Joel nodded. "And when, exactly, did you first arrive on the island?"

He sighed and seemed annoyed. "I don't know, man. We've been driving a lot."

"Think about it."

He rested his elbows on his knees and looked at the floor. Joel watched him staring down at the dingy blue carpeting. "Ten days ago. Last Wednesday."

"Two days before the protest."

"Yeah."

"And where'd you stay when you were in town?"

"Here."

"And then where'd you go?"

He sighed. "Padre Island. We went there Sunday afternoon. And we stayed at a Motel 6 there, case you're wondering."

Joel tugged a piece of paper from his back pocket and unfolded it. "Do you recognize either of these two people?" He stepped over and handed Trevor the paper.

Trevor frowned down at the driver's license pictures of Elizabeth Lark and Will Stovak. He rubbed his chin and shook his head. "Nope. Don't recognize them."

"You sure?"

"Yeah. Who are they?" He handed back the paper, and Joel folded it and tucked it back into his pocket.

"Elizabeth Lark and Will Stovak. Both from Oregon." Joel watched the kid's expression. "They were found dead in their canoe on Monday."

"I heard about that. What's it got to do with me and Gillian?"

Joel watched him carefully. He seemed uneasy now. But not as nervous as Joel would have expected if he'd been involved in the murders.

"They're both members of your group."

"*My* group?"

"Alpha Omega Now," Joel said.

"We have a lot of members. I've never met them."

"How many?"

"You want, like, an exact number?"

"Ballpark."

"I don't know. About five fifty, maybe six hundred."

Joel nodded. "Including you and Gillian?"

"Yeah."

"And are you the group leader?"

"Me? No. No, I'm not."

"Who is?" Joel asked.

"We don't have one."

"Oh yeah? Then who's in charge?"

"No one. Everyone." He shrugged again. "We're pretty egalitarian."

Joel watched his expression, looking for signs that he was lying. He didn't like Joel being here, but that didn't make him guilty of murder.

A knock sounded at the door, and Trevor darted a look at it.

"That's probably our pizza," he said.

Joel stepped over and checked the peephole. A young guy in a red cap stood at the door holding a pizza box.

Joel looked at Trevor and caught him glancing at the duffel bag again.

"How long you guys in town this time?" Joel asked.

"A couple of days."

"Are you here for a protest?"

His jaw tightened.

"The golf resort going in down by the lighthouse maybe?" Joel asked. "They're scheduled to break ground on Tuesday morning."

Another knock, and Trevor looked at the door, then at Joel. "Like I said, it's a free country. I assume you're familiar with the First Amendment? There's nothing illegal about congregating with like-minded people."

Joel stepped over and opened the door, startling the pizza kid, who was scrolling through his phone.

Joel turned and gave Trevor a long, hard look. "Stay out of trouble, Trevor. Gillian, too."

TWENTY-THREE

"D AMN," NICOLE SAID. "How'd you know?"

Joel drove with the windows down, letting in the warm breeze off the Gulf. The rain had blown through and the strip was now in full swing.

"Just a hunch," he told Nicole over the phone. "What did you find?"

"Special Agent Brian Romero. He's in the Houston field office. Looks like . . . the counterterrorism division. That's weird."

"Not really," he said. "They've probably been on the radar for domestic terrorism since they planted that pipe bomb at that logging company." He scanned the sidewalks for any trouble. Saturday was typically their peak night for arrests, mostly on drinking-related charges.

"Do you want me to call him up?" she asked. "It's almost midnight."

"Text me his info and I'll do it in the morning," Joel

said. "We don't want to piss him off right before we ask for a favor."

"And what's the favor?"

"We need him to share whatever he's got on Trevor Keen."

"Assuming he has anything. Could be a coincidence that there's an FBI agent in Houston with this name."

"Working counterterrorism?"

She didn't respond, probably because she knew it was a stretch. Joel pictured Trevor in the motel room. He'd had his guard up. *Did Romero tell you to talk to me?* From the way he'd asked the question, Joel could tell Romero was a cop.

"I'll call him early," Joel said. "See what I can dig up."

"Ask about the girlfriend, too. Maybe she's in the mix."

"I will. And good work tracking down Keen."

"Sure. Thanks for the assist."

Joel ended the call as he neared the entrance to Caribbean Sands. He passed the pastel-colored houses in tidy rows. North of the neighborhood was the turnoff to Miranda's, and Joel slowed, muttering a curse when he saw that her house was dark. He made the turn anyway and switched off his headlights as he bumped over the gravel road. Rolling to a stop, he looked up at the little cabin.

She was asleep, which was probably good. The past two days had been crazy, and she'd been up all last night working a crime scene.

Joel glanced at the seat beside him. A ziplock bag sat beside his binoculars. Inside it was the folded piece of paper with the two murder victims' pictures. Joel wanted Miranda to lift Trevor Keen's fingerprints from the paper. But it could wait until tomorrow.

Joel studied Miranda's house, and emotions churned through him. Worry. Impatience. Frustration.

Lust.

He wanted to see her. All day—and all night, too—he'd been thinking about her, even at the crime scene. It was distracting as hell, but he couldn't help it.

We can't keep doing this. She'd said that minutes after climbing into his lap.

Joel knew she was torn. He was, too. He understood full well that sex was going to complicate their working relationship. But so what? He couldn't remember the last time he'd felt this way about anyone, even Elaina, and he and Elaina had been together for three years. It didn't make sense, but this thing with Miranda felt different. Joel didn't know why.

But he knew that he liked her. A *lot.* He liked spending time with her, even though he knew spending time with her was distracting him from his case. He didn't want to stop. If anything, he wanted more of her.

Joel glanced at the plastic bag again. As much as he wanted to, he couldn't wake her up right now, not for something she could just as easily do tomorrow morning.

Joel put his truck in reverse and turned around. In his rearview mirror, Miranda's house got smaller.

Hooking a left onto the highway, he headed south back toward town. As he neared the turnoff into his neighborhood, he spied a familiar black Honda parked in front of the island's only twenty-four-hour convenience store.

Joel whipped into the lot. He pulled into an empty space beside the Honda and looked past the neon Bud Light sign hanging in the store window. He got out of his truck and waited.

Two minutes later, Gillian Copeland emerged from the store. She had a six-pack in one hand and a carton of cigarettes under her arm. She wore the same bikini-top-and-shorts outfit, but now she had on silver flip-flops.

"Hey, Gillian."

She glanced up from her phone and halted.

"Got a minute?"

She cast a furtive look toward the highway in the direction of the Sand Dollar Inn, confirming Joel's guess that she was alone.

"What do you want?" She tucked her phone into her pocket and pulled out a set of keys.

"Just a quick question."

"I already talked to your partner."

"It's something she forgot to ask. About your organization."

"My organization?"

"Alpha Omega Now."

She popped the car's locks and opened the back door, then stashed her purchases in the back seat. She closed the door and looked at him.

"What about us?" she asked, and her tone was more curious than wary.

"How long have you been involved with them?"

"About a year now." She tipped her head to the side. "You know, I know what you're investigating, and you've got us all wrong."

"I do?"

"Yeah. We're not *violent*. We're basically just a bunch of socially conscious people committed to stewardship of the planet."

"It's an important cause."

Surprise flickered in her blue eyes. But then it turned to suspicion.

"I'd like to see a list of your members," Joel said.

"A list?" She brushed her long hair over her shoulder and rested her hand on her hip. "We don't have a list. It's not like we're a rotary club."

"Was that your laptop I saw in the hotel room?" he asked.

"Yeah." She frowned. "Why?"

"How do you communicate with other members?"

"Social media, mostly."

"I'd like a list of social media names, then. Twitter handles. Emails. Whatever you have."

She eased closer, and Joel caught the scent of marijuana. So, Trevor had sent his girlfriend out for beer and smokes while he sat in the motel room getting high. Very egalitarian of him.

"Why should I help you? All you do is hassle us. And now you're trying to pin something on Trevor that he didn't do. I told your partner, we left here on *Sunday*. Trevor told you that, too. Check our cell phone records if you don't believe us."

Joel planned to do that.

"Listen, Gillian. I'm investigating three homicides. Three. All the victims were about your age, and all of them were murdered in the week since your group held a protest here. Okay? Now we're exploring every lead we can think of, and that includes tourists visiting the island."

She didn't respond.

"Look, if no one in your group is involved, there's nothing to worry about. We'll cross them off the list and move on."

"I'm telling you, our group isn't violent."

"Your group, maybe not. But how well do you know every single person?"

She sighed and looked away.

Joel pulled a business card from his wallet and handed it to her. "I need your help, Gillian. If you really have a social conscience, then do the right thing."

CHAPTER

TWENTY-FOUR

"GILLIAN COPELAND, TWENTY-THREE." Nicole taped the mug shot to the whiteboard. "Unlawful possession of a controlled substance. Possession with intent to distribute. She copped a plea in exchange for testimony against someone higher up the chain."

"If she's still in business, might explain how they're financing their road trip," Emmet said from his seat at the conference table.

"It might." Nicole took the empty chair beside him and set down her file. She'd been up late pulling together everything she could about Trevor Keen, his girlfriend, and the organization that they were maybe, maybe-not leading.

"Where'd she meet Keen?" Chief Brady looked at Nicole over his reading glasses. He had a legal pad in front of him and was jotting down updates from the team—which now included a pair of sheriff's deputies.

"I'm not sure," Nicole said. And she hadn't thought to

ask. "This drug bust was in Provo, Utah, but her driver's license shows a Denver address, so maybe they met there, at some point."

The conference room door opened, and Joel walked in with a file under his arm and a can of Dr Pepper in his hand. When Nicole had arrived at work this morning, he'd been on the phone in an interview room, furiously taking notes.

Brady leaned back in his chair. "What's the word?"

"Just got off the phone with Brian Romero." Joel took a seat beside his brother.

"Who's that?" Owen asked.

"An FBI agent in Houston. Counterterrorism team." Joel popped open his drink and took a swill. "He works on domestic terror organizations."

"This group's a terror organization?" Emmet asked.

"Not officially, but the feds have had their eye on it ever since the pipe-bomb incident a while back." Joel flipped his file open. "And listen to this."

"Wait. Pipe-bomb incident? You're talking about the logging company?" Emmet asked.

"Yeah. They're based in Beaumont. Anyway, get this. About six months after the bomb thing, their CEO was murdered."

"Holy shit." Owen leaned forward. "Let me guess. A .38 pistol?"

"Nope. *Conium maculatum.*"

Brady frowned. "Say again?"

"Poison hemlock."

"He was *poisoned*?" Nicole asked.

"That's right. Case is still open. The feds took a look, given the previous incident targeting the company. They did some poking around with Alpha Omega Now but didn't turn up anything. The local police ended up zeroing in on the guy's wife. Evidently, they were having marital problems and she inherited about a million in life insurance."

"So, they think his *wife* poisoned him?" Nicole asked.

"That's one theory. Someone put something in his coffee, and he died at his desk at work."

Nicole shook her head. Another bizarre twist to this thing.

"Do the feds think it might be connected to the murders here?" Brady asked.

"They're now looking into it. This agent, Romero, told me he never liked the wife for it. He always thought it had something to do with the protest organization, but he could never prove it. He's reinterviewed several Alpha Omega members a few times, trying to shake something new loose, but they've stuck to their stories. No one was in Beaumont at the time of the murder, at least no one they turned up."

"So, now we've got a sixth murder, possibly connected, possibly not," Owen said.

Brady took off his reading glasses and tossed them atop his legal pad. "Let's get back to what we know."

The chief sounded frustrated, and Nicole didn't blame him. He'd been burning the candle at both ends for a week—as all of them had—plus fielding relentless questions from the media. He was also under pressure from local business owners to make an arrest soon because summer season was about to start, and everyone was freaking out over all the negative publicity.

"Okay, let me run through it," Joel said. "We've got five people, all killed with the same pistol. That's now confirmed. We don't know if it's the same shooter—"

"Let's assume." Brady crossed his arms.

"All right, assume it is. In four of those five cases a feather was recovered on or near the victim." Joel glanced at the two new guys from the sheriff's office. "We know at least two of the feathers are from endangered South American birds, so we're working the theory that the feathers may be some sort of message from the killer. Also, in the case of the three homicides here on the island, all of them happened within a few days of a protest at a new hotel here. The protest was staged by Alpha Omega Now, and our first two victims were members of the group."

"What about Alexander Kendrick?" The chief looked at Emmet. "Was he a member?"

"According to his girlfriend, no. She'd never even heard of them before."

"How is that possible?" Brady asked. "A big mob of them was just here protesting."

"She doesn't pay attention to the news."

"Okay, what else?" The chief looked at Joel.

"I checked out the story that Trevor Keen and his girlfriend gave us in separate interviews. Sounds like they *did* leave Lost Beach on Sunday and drove down to Padre Island, like they claimed. The motel where they stayed has a record of them, and they were there all week."

"They spent the night there, maybe. It's only an hour away, so they could have driven back," Owen pointed out.

"True," Joel said. "It's not airtight, but it's something. Other thing is, I didn't get the sense that they were lying."

"You thought they were straight with you?" Brady said.

Joel tipped his head to the side. "I wouldn't go that far. They might be hiding something. Maybe drug possession or something like that."

"I agree," Nicole said. "I interviewed Gillian. She wasn't too happy about talking to cops, but she didn't seem nearly nervous enough to be hiding three murders."

"Maybe she doesn't know," Emmet suggested. "Maybe this is the boyfriend's deal, and he left her out of the loop."

"Let's go back to logistics," Brady said. "How'd someone get to and from the first Lost Beach crime scene? I thought we were looking for a boat."

"We are," Joel said.

"Tell us about the boat," one of the sheriff's deputies said, chiming in for the first time. His name was Garza, and he looked to Nicole to be the younger of the two.

"The real estate developer was shot while fishing off his boat dock," Joel said. "I've checked out the property, and the easiest way to approach him there would have been from the water."

"So, someone shot him and took off?" Garza asked.

"It's possible. Same for the two victims in the canoe. They were in the marshes, about a hundred yards from the marina. We think they were approached by someone in a boat."

"Don't forget our witness," Nicole said. "We have a woman who was fishing off her boat dock around the estimated time of the murders, and she saw someone race past in a skiff. Said it was too dark to get much of a description, but someone definitely went by in a hurry, no running lights."

"The boat could have come from the island or the mainland. We don't know," Joel said. "Maybe someone owns it, or it could have been rented, stolen, or borrowed. There's no shortage of boats around here."

"Why don't we take the boat lead," Garza said, looking at the other deputy. "We've got contacts on both sides of the bay. Maybe someone saw a suspicious person coming or going on Monday morning. A lot of the marinas have security cams facing their docks, so we might be able to turn something up."

"Sounds good," Brady said. He looked at Nicole. "Keep checking out Trevor Keen and his girlfriend and vetting their story. You and Owen see what else you can find on that." He turned to Emmet. "How's it coming with Alexander's friends?"

"Still interviewing people, trying to pin down who he saw and what he did in the days before his murder."

The chief looked at Joel. "And where are we on the suspect list?"

"It's coming together," Joel said. "I'm working on cross-referencing persons of interest from all five of these open investigations. I'm hoping to find some overlap."

"Six open investigations, if you include the poisoned logging-company executive," Nicole said.

"Let's put that aside for now," Brady said. "We've got enough on our hands with the other cases, and we know the same weapon was used."

Joel nodded.

"Okay, as of today," the chief said, "the state crime lab is fast-tracking all forensic evidence related to our three cases. That's fingerprints, shoe prints, shell casings, whatever. Anything we recover goes straight to them. Drive it up there if you have to, but make sure they get their hands on it, ASAP."

"What about the stuff we already submitted?" Nicole asked.

"We recovered prints from the victims' trailer," Joel said. "Looked like someone had been snooping around the place, peeking in the windows. Miranda lifted a bunch of stuff and sent it in on Wednesday, but still no word."

"We also sent the backpack from the canoe," Nicole said. "Someone stole cell phones and IDs, so we're hoping to get a print off the zipper."

"The state has everything," Brady said. "And they've promised us a quick turnaround."

Emmet scoffed. "I'll believe it when I see it."

Nicole agreed. Even with a task force in place, she doubted they were going to leapfrog priority cases coming from Houston and Dallas. But at least Brady was trying.

"Okay, I want everyone back here at"—the chief checked his watch—"four o'clock. I want progress and updates. Time's ticking, people."

T HE COFFEE SHOP was busy for a Sunday afternoon. Miranda had intended to get in and out quickly, but given the cluster of people waiting at the pickup bar, this was going to take longer than she'd thought. Peeling off her sunglasses, she scanned the shop and was surprised to see Joel at a table by the window, deep in conversation with a beautiful woman.

The pang of jealousy was sharp and quick. Miranda turned to face the menu board, not really reading it as she tried to process what she'd seen. Was she his ex, maybe? No. His ex was probably on her honeymoon right now. Anyway, it didn't matter who she was. Miranda and Joel weren't a couple, and he could have coffee with whomever he wanted.

The line moved, and the barista smiled up at her.

"What can I get you today?" she asked.

Miranda had been craving a frothy blender drink, but now she just wanted something fast.

"Um . . . a large house blend. To go, please."

Dread filled her stomach as she paid for her coffee and waited. She wanted to slip out before Joel spotted her. But why should she avoid him? Maybe she should make eye contact and wave, as though seeing him with someone was no big deal. Which it wasn't. Acid filled her stomach as she debated what to do.

The barista handed over her drink, and Miranda turned around, darting a look at the window.

Joel was staring right at her.

Crap.

Miranda forced a smile and made her way over. "Hi," she said brightly, trying not to stare at the woman beside him as he stood up.

"Hey." He touched Miranda's waist, and her heart skittered. "I want you to meet my sister, Leyla."

Relief flooded her. And then she felt ridiculous for getting all worked up.

"This is Miranda Rhoads, our new CSI," Joel said.

Joel's sister shot him a look and then smiled at Miranda. "Nice to meet you. I've heard a lot about you."

She had?

"Nice to meet you, too."

Leyla had vivid blue eyes, like her brother's, and her thick dark hair was pulled back in a ponytail. She wore a black apron with the Island Beanery logo.

"Well, break's over." She sent Joel another look as she scooted her chair back. "You can have my spot, Miranda."

"Oh, don't get up."

"No, sit, please."

"I don't mean to run you off."

"You're not at all." Leyla stood and smiled. "Enjoy your coffee." She nodded at the table. "And make him share those croissants with you. They're our last ones."

She walked off, leaving Miranda alone with Joel. He was watching her with amusement, as though maybe he knew she'd jumped to the wrong conclusion.

"Have a seat," he said. "We've got the best table here."

Miranda set her tote bag on the floor and lowered herself into the chair as she glanced out the window. He was right.

The bay-window table had a clear view over the dunes to the beach.

She looked at Joel and picked up her coffee.

"So. That's Leyla."

"Yep."

"The one who took the balloon photo."

"Balloon photo?"

"The hot-air balloons on your refrigerator."

"Oh. Right."

"I didn't know she worked here. I've been in here a million times."

"She's the manager. And the chef."

Miranda watched as Leyla walked behind the counter and into the kitchen. "Wow, that's amazing. They do a ton of business. I've never seen them not busy."

"Yeah."

She turned to Joel, and he was watching her with a look she couldn't read.

"So. What's up with you?" she asked.

"I was giving Leyla an update. She's been worried a lot."

"About safety?"

"About everything." His expression clouded. "We're not used to this kind of thing around here. She's freaked-out."

"Yeah, I understand."

Joel watched her for a long moment, and she felt a flutter of warmth in her stomach.

"How are *you* doing?" he asked.

"Okay."

"Really?"

Miranda sighed. She glanced at the folder sticking out of her tote bag.

"Actually, I was on my way to the police station. I just stopped in for a caffeine fix. Maybe I'm stalling. I've been dreading talking to you."

Joel's brow furrowed. "Why?"

She pulled out her file and set it on the table. "I've been going over the photos from the other night." She opened the file and pulled out a picture. "In particular, I've been looking at the photographs of the shoe print from the flower bed."

Joel slid the picture over and studied it. Based on the shoe print and the shell casing recovered nearby, it looked as though the perpetrator had been standing in the flower bed when he shot Alexander Kendrick through the wire mesh of the storage locker as he was putting away his bike.

"You know, we got the results back on the ballistics," Joel said.

"Any fingerprints?"

"No. But we learned that the rifling marks match the other slugs."

"So, the same weapon as all the others," she said.

"Yep. And since none of the neighbors reported hearing a gunshot, the shooter likely used a suppressor."

"Also like the others."

"Yep."

"I sent this picture to a friend of mine in the crime lab where I used to work," Miranda said.

Joel frowned. "Why? We've got the state helping us now."

"This guy specializes in footwear identification. He's kind of a geek about it, really." Miranda smiled. But then her stomach started churning, as it had been since her phone call with him.

"He tells me this is a Nike running shoe, size eleven, one of their most common styles. So, it doesn't do much to narrow our suspect pool. *However*, there are some distinguishing characteristics about this particular print. So we're lucky." Miranda forced a smile. "This shoe shows a distinctive wear pattern. See the nicks on the side of the tread here? That gives us more to go on in terms of matching it to a specific shoe, if and when you zero in on a suspect."

"Okay."

She took a deep breath.

"Miranda, what is it?" Joel leaned forward, clearly picking up on her stress.

She took another photograph from the file and slid it in front of Joel.

"This photo shows a muddy shoe print that looks remarkably similar. In fact, it's so remarkably similar, my friend believes it was made by the same shoe."

Joel pulled the picture closer and frowned down at it. "Where'd you get this?"

"My deck."

JOEL GLANCED UP, sure he must have heard her wrong. "Your *deck*?"

"The other night—"

"Wait. *When?*"

She took a deep breath. "Wednesday night. After I saw you at the marina."

He leaned closer. "He was at your house?"

"I think so. At least, that's what it looks like. I came home and took Benji out, and I noticed some muddy footprints on my stairs. Looked like someone had walked up to the door and looked inside."

"Miranda, why didn't you tell me?"

"Because I thought it was nothing."

"You thought it was nothing, but you took a photograph?"

"Force of habit." She shrugged. "I wanted to document it. But then I checked with my landlord to see if maybe he'd stopped by the place. He said he hadn't, but he'd sent his handyman by to fix the floodlight on the deck. It's been out for a few weeks. So I figured that was who it was, no big deal."

Joel stared at her, unable to believe what she was telling him. But the photos didn't lie.

"So . . . basically, I'm wondering if this person is maybe aware of me," she said. "And if he has some sort of, I don't know, interest in me because I'm involved in the case."

Joel squeezed his eyes shut. She'd just spelled out the very thing that had been grinding away at him for days.

"Miranda . . ." He leaned forward and took her hand. "I don't want you staying there alone anymore."

"Staying . . . in my house?"

"Not alone."

She watched him.

"Not at all, really. You should come to my place."

He held her hand, hoping she'd listen. She looked wary.

"But . . . what about Benji?"

"Bring him with you."

She continued to watch him, and he could see the debate going on in her head. She was overanalyzing again, making this complicated. But the answer was obvious—he just had to convince her.

"Think about what we know," he said. "The shoe print. The fire. You can't stay at that house by yourself."

"I know. You're right. I'm just—I feel weird about asking you this right now when you're completely slammed with everything else."

"You're not asking. I offered. And anyway, what does it matter?"

"But you're working all the time."

"My place is better than your place. The back of your house is all glass. Mine's got much better security, especially when I'm there."

She stared at him. Then she stared down at the photos.

The undercurrent of anxiety that had been with him all week had become a full-blown fear. Whoever was doing this, whoever was killing these people, had Miranda on his radar. He didn't know why, but they could no longer pretend otherwise.

Joel squeezed her hand. "Miranda, how many crime scene photos have you taken over the years?"

She looked startled by the question.

"How many?" he repeated.

"I don't know. Thousands. Tens of thousands."

"Right. You know what these pictures mean. And you wouldn't be showing them to me if you weren't worried."

She looked down at the photographs side by side on the table.

He was right, and they both knew it.

CHAPTER

TWENTY-FIVE

B ENJI TROTTED ALONG behind her as Miranda mounted the steps. Country music drifted from next door, where a man stood on his boat dock, cleaning a fish at a wooden sink. On a deck across the canal, a couple in lounge chairs watched the sunset. Miranda wondered what they thought of her as she pulled Joel's key from her purse and unlocked his door. Benji waited beside her, wagging his tail as she let herself in.

The house was dim and silent. Benji darted straight inside and started sniffing around the furniture as Miranda secured the lock.

Joel's home smelled like him. She couldn't pinpoint the scent, except that it was good, and it filled her with reassurance as she looked around. The place was just as she remembered it, minus the tuxedo draped over the sofa. He must have returned it. Some file folders were spread across the coffee table, and it looked like he'd been up late—or possibly early—working on the case.

Benji rounded the sofa and then did a lap around the breakfast table, wagging his tail as he checked out the new surroundings.

Joel's words came back to her as she slipped the key into her pocket. *I'll take off as soon as I can. Make yourself at home.*

She dropped her duffel bag onto the sofa and went into the kitchen to unload her grocery bag.

"Over here, Ben," she said, filling one of his bowls with water. She put it on the floor by the sink, and he lapped it up as she filled his second bowl with food. He gave her a curious look and then dug right in. With Benji more or less settled, she stashed his food in the pantry and returned to the living room.

Butterflies filled her stomach as she glanced around. It felt strange to be in Joel's house without him, but he'd insisted. Miranda had pushed back, but not really. She didn't want to tell him, but she was just as worried as he was—probably more. From the moment she'd compared those shoe prints and understood what they meant, the mere thought of being in her secluded cottage by herself unnerved her. She had planned to ask him to stay at her place for a few days. But his place was a better option. It had a solid front door, sturdier locks, and plenty of neighbors just a stone's throw away.

Miranda pulled out her phone and tapped a text. We r here. All good. No need to rush home. Hitting SEND on the message, she felt less like an intruder.

She wandered to the window by the breakfast table and peered outside. Most of the homes on Joel's side of the canal appeared to be occupied by year-round residents. Were his neighbors nosey? Would they take note of her Jeep in the driveway and wonder what she was doing here when Joel wasn't around? Not that she cared, really, but after months of living in her solitary house, it felt weird to be surrounded by people on all sides.

Her phone buzzed as a text landed.

Lock up. Help yourself to anything.

Benji trotted over and circled the sofa again. He sniffed at Joel's running shoes and then went over to check out the back of the house. Miranda followed him. The house's layout was remarkably similar to hers, with two small bedrooms and a shared bathroom off the hallway. Simple but functional.

Miranda leaned her head into the bathroom. It was impressively clean, with a gleaming white tub and a row of shaving products lined up beside the sink.

She checked her watch. He'd said nine o'clock, which gave her half an hour to herself. She turned on the shower and was thrilled to see the powerful water pressure. She retrieved her overnight bag from the living room and shut herself in the bathroom to undress as the air filled with steam. Benji whined and pawed at the door.

She let him in. "No scratching, Ben. This isn't our house."

Benji made a few circles and settled on the bath mat.

Miranda stepped into the tub. Tipping her head back, she stood under the spray and let the blissfully hot water sluice over her. Ten long weeks. That was how long it had been since she'd had a piping-hot shower with actual water pressure. The water pummeled her neck, pounding out the tension as she stood there and tried to decompress. She tried to clear her mind, tried not to think about work or violence or the reason she was here. Instead, she focused on the water streaming over her, relaxing her muscles and washing her worries down the drain.

Benji barked and ran from the room, and Miranda's heart lurched. She peeked around the shower curtain.

"Miranda?"

"In here. I'm almost finished."

Joel stepped into the doorway. He wore his work clothes, minus the gun, and his hair was windblown.

"Hi," she said. "I had to clean up."

His gaze heated as he looked her over.

"Want to join me?"

He stepped into the room and stripped off his shirt.

"Is that a yes?"

"Yes."

She ducked back under the water, heart thrumming as she heard his boots thud to the floor. Then he stepped into the tub behind her, and she glanced over her shoulder.

She smiled. "Hi."

He kissed her. Sliding his arms around her, he turned her to face him and pulled her against him.

"You taste good." He trailed kisses over her neck as she tipped her head back. And then his hands were everywhere, gliding over her wet skin.

"I missed you," she said.

"Me, too."

He turned them both as he stepped under the spray, and she combed her fingers into his hair and brought his head down for a kiss. She'd missed the way he kissed her and touched her, as though he could never get enough. His mouth locked on her nipple, and she felt a jolt of need.

Hot water sluiced between them as he hitched her thigh up to his hip. He looked up from her breast, his gaze intense as he watched her through the steam. He took her hand and wrapped it around his neck.

"Hold on."

She gripped his shoulders as he lifted her up. She

wrapped her legs around him as he eased her back against the cool tile. Then he took her mouth again. The kiss was hard and needy, and her whole body responded. She wanted him inside her.

"Joel. Condom."

"It's on. Hold on to me."

He shifted her weight and carefully eased her onto him.

"Oh my God."

"Don't let go," he said.

She squeezed her legs tighter as he started pumping into her.

"Oh, that's good," she gasped.

"Yeah?"

"Don't stop."

She tipped her head back, clinging to his shoulders as he moved against her, pinning her against the tile.

She wrapped her arms around his neck, clenching him as tightly as she could as he pounded into her, harder and harder.

"Babe." His voice was tight. "Tell me when."

"Yes. *Yes.*"

His skin was slick and warm, and she dug her nails into his shoulders.

"Now. *Please.*"

Another hard thrust, and she came in a blinding flash.

She dropped her head onto his shoulder. The world was spinning. Water streamed down her side, reminding her where they were as her mind reeled.

She blinked up at him, and his head rested against the tile.

He opened his eyes. "You okay?"

She nodded.

"Careful," he said, easing back and setting her on her feet. He held her arm as she got her balance.

He stepped out of the tub, leaving her alone in the cloud of steam.

She rinsed her hair one last time and turned the water off. Joel handed her a folded blue towel. She wrapped it around herself and tucked the corner as she watched him dry off.

He slung the towel around his narrow hips, then leaned over and kissed her. "Hi."

"Hi."

She stepped out of the tub and gazed up at him. His dark hair was slicked back, and his eyes looked even bluer than usual.

"You said make yourself at home, so—"

He cut her off with a kiss. "I meant it." He took her hand and led her from the room, grabbing her overnight bag off the counter. She followed him into his bedroom, where a king-size bed took up most of the space. He dropped her bag beside the bed and slid his arms around her.

He lifted an eyebrow. "You hungry for dinner?"

"A little. You?"

He tugged her towel loose, and it dropped to the floor. "Not yet."

MIRANDA AWOKE TO a clatter of pans. She blinked into the darkness, then sat up and looked around. Beside her the bed was empty. She glanced at the red digits of the alarm clock: 11:45.

Swinging her legs out of bed, she glanced around. She grabbed a T-shirt off the chair in the corner and pulled it over her shoulders. It was roomy and soft and smelled like Joel.

She stopped by the bathroom to wash her face and then followed the sound of Joel's voice into the kitchen, where he stood at the stove talking to Benji. He wore khaki cargo shorts, no shirt, and he had a spatula in his hand.

Benji stood at attention. Joel tossed him a chip.

"I saw that."

Joel turned around. "Uh-oh. Busted."

Benji didn't even look at her. One hundred percent of his attention was focused on his new friend.

"Watch this." Joel grabbed another tortilla chip from the bag on the counter and held it up. He tossed it, and Benji chomped it out of the air.

"Gee, that's impressive." Miranda walked into the kitchen and scratched Benji's head. Then she looked up at Joel. His stubbled jaw and bare chest looked ridiculously sexy. She couldn't believe she was actually here, shacked up at his house.

"Why didn't you wake me?" she asked.

"I tried."

"You did?"

"You were out cold." He slid his arm around her waist. "Hope you're hungry. I'm making *migas*."

"I'm starving."

"Here." He handed her a bottle of water.

"How can I help?"

"You can't. Just relax."

Miranda took a swill of water, and it felt wonderfully cool on her parched throat. She'd worked up a thirst. And an appetite. Just the scent of whatever he was cooking was making her stomach growl.

She hitched herself onto the counter and watched him.

"You crashed." He glanced up from the pan where he was sautéing onions and peppers.

"Yeah, what was that? Two hours?"

"Two and a half. You okay?"

She caught the worry in his tone.

"I haven't been sleeping well," she said. "Guess I needed to catch up."

He took an egg from the carton beside the stove and cracked it one-handed into a cereal bowl. He set the shell on a napkin and cracked two more.

He reached for the drawer beside her, and she scooted over as he opened the drawer and took out a fork.

"Stress?" He glanced up at her as he whisked the eggs.

Miranda studied his face. His tone was casual, but his expression was serious.

Nerves flitted in her stomach. They'd reached a turning point. She sensed it. She could either let him in or keep him at arm's length. The safe bet would be to gloss over his question and keep the conversation light. But after everything he'd done for her over the past three days, that seemed wrong.

She cleared her throat. "I've had insomnia on and off for the last few months."

He didn't look up. "Since you left your job?"

"Since before that."

Using the spatula, he moved the vegetables to one side of the pan and then poured in the eggs.

He looked up. "Bad case?"

"Yeah."

He tipped the pan.

"It was a murder case," she said. "A child murder. It went to trial last fall."

He didn't look up. "The Lindsey Bonner case."

Her stomach clenched. "You heard about it?"

"Yeah."

He stirred the eggs, still not looking up. Miranda watched his expression. His eyes looked somber as he tilted the pan again.

After years of being a cop, Joel would understand. He'd seen violence and cruelty and soul-crushing loss. But still she felt reluctant to talk about this. She didn't want him to think less of her. Just the idea of it put a knot in her stomach.

He switched off the burner. Then he picked up a towel and wiped his hands.

"What happened?"

She took a deep breath. "We got the call one night last August. Me and my team. I was the lead CSI. It was an outdoor crime scene."

"Bexar County?"

"Yeah. This was a rural area at the edge of some woods. Some teenagers were out there shooting beer cans and they found her. He'd left her in a shallow grave, but some animals scattered the remains."

Joel just watched her. He probably knew this already if he'd read about the case. But now that she'd started, she wanted to finish.

"We set up a perimeter around the grave, almost a full acre. Spent about twelve hours combing every inch, photographing everything." Her stomach roiled. "Almost everything. Some of the key evidence was recovered in the first few hours."

"The cigarette butt."

Miranda nodded. He'd read the details.

"The DNA matched a convicted sex offender," she said. "They tracked him down, arrested him. It went to trial. It should have been an open-and-shut case, but my team screwed up. The cigarette butt got tossed, and everything unraveled."

Joel set the towel on the counter. "It wasn't your fault."

She scoffed.

"It wasn't."

"It was."

"I talked to your supervisor, Miranda."

"You . . . what?"

"You listed him as a reference. I talked to him. He told me all about what happened."

A chill came over her.

"What did he say?"

Joel stepped closer. "That you're the best CSI he's ever worked with. That he was sorry you left. That you could have your job back at any time, if you decide you want it."

Tears stung Miranda's eyes. She looked away. She started to slide off the counter, but Joel put his hand on her leg.

"Hey. Talk to me."

"No."

"Why can't we discuss this?"

Benji walked over and licked her ankle. "I don't want to talk about it."

"Why not?"

Emotions flooded her. Anger. Guilt. Confusion. How could he have known this all along and *not* understood what had been eating away at her?

How could he have known this all along and *hired* her?

"It's not your fault, Miranda. You didn't mess up. Someone else did."

"My team, my fault. I was the lead. *Me*. It was my job to make sure every shred of evidence got documented before it was collected. I failed to do that. Hence, the key piece of evidence was inadmissible, and a killer walked." Tears overflowed, and she swiped at her cheeks. "He's out on the street right now because I failed to do my job."

"Someone on your team failed to do their job."

She shook her head. "That's not how it is."

Joel reached up and touched her cheek. The tenderness of the gesture put a hot lump in her throat.

"Look at me."

"No."

"Please?"

She looked up and wiped her cheeks again. "I fucked up. And I can't undo it. It's irreversible. It's done."

"You're right, it is. So you need to stop torturing yourself over it."

"I can't." She looked down at Benji. "I can't stop thinking about it. That's why I came down here. I had to get away from all of it. And then I found that canoe, and I knew it was futile. I can't get away from anything. And now I'm doing the job again, and every time I go to a crime scene, I get this ball of dread in the pit of my stomach."

"It's okay. You have to work through it."

"I hate it."

"I know."

"All I do is doubt myself."

He picked up her hand and kissed her knuckles, and her heart skittered as he looked at her with those intense blue eyes.

"It's not your fault, Miranda. You didn't even have a camera in your hand that night. Did you?"

She took a deep breath. "No."

"And the person who should have taken that photograph isn't working there anymore."

"He was suspended. Then he quit."

Miranda's boss had suspended him after the prosecution's case fell apart at trial because of a technicality. The cigarette butt wasn't in the crime scene photos, so it wasn't at the crime scene, according to the defense. They claimed it could have been planted by detectives desperate to prop up a weak case.

"*I* was in charge of the team that night," Miranda said. "Me. No one else. I should have paid closer attention to every single thing they did and didn't do."

Joel gazed at her, and the sympathy in his eyes made her chest tighten. Where was this coming from?

He slid his arms around her and pulled her against him.

Miranda closed her eyes, inhaling the familiar scent of him. He smelled wonderful. She rested her head on his muscular shoulder.

"Thank you," he said.

"For what?"

"Telling me about it."

She sighed. She hated talking about this. But there was something cathartic about telling someone. The only other person she'd ever really talked to about this was Bailey, and it had been months since their last conversation about it. She hadn't talked about it with anyone since moving to Lost Beach.

Joel pulled back. He brushed a lock of hair from her face and tucked it behind her ear.

"Sorry." She pulled up the T-shirt collar and dabbed her cheeks. "I don't know what the hell's wrong with me. I keep crying on you."

He smiled. "I don't mind."

She sighed and slid off the counter, putting her at eye level with his neck.

"Are you ready for *migas*?" he asked.

"Yes."

He stepped to the stove and took a handful of chips from the bag. He crunched them in his hand and sprinkled them over the eggs.

"You want to heat the tortillas?" He nodded at the package on the counter. "They need about thirty seconds."

Miranda put the tortillas on a plate and slid them into the microwave. When they were done, Joel loaded the plates.

She grabbed a water for herself from the fridge and followed Joel into the living room, where he cleared the coffee table and stacked the files on the armchair.

They sat on the floor beside the table. Miranda watched him chomp into his taco. He took a chip off his plate and tossed it to Benji.

She sighed. "You're spoiling him."

"He's hungry."

She shook her head and picked up her taco. It was hot and spicy, and she polished off half of it in three bites.

They ate in silence, and she watched him across the coffee table. Part of her felt relieved that she'd finally told him, but another part of her felt self-conscious about having another meltdown.

He put his taco down. "You're doing it again."

"What?"

"Stop worrying so much." He swigged his water.

"I don't know what's wrong with me. I've never been a crier."

"Maybe you should stop keeping everything to yourself."

"What, and dump everything on you?"

"Yeah." He picked up her hand and squeezed it. "I can take it."

CHAPTER

TWENTY-SIX

THE BED CREAKED as Joel slid into it. Miranda rolled toward him, not opening her eyes. She felt his hand on her hip, gliding over her skin, gradually waking her up with slow, lazy strokes. He nudged her onto her back and leaned over her.

Sighing contentedly, she opened her eyes.

The room was gray and quiet. Joel's face was shadowed, and he smelled faintly of shaving cream. He'd been in the shower, and she'd totally slept through it. She ran her fingers into his damp hair as he kissed his way down her body.

"Hmm." She wrapped her leg around him.

He slid up and kissed her neck, just below her ear.

"Morning," he murmured.

She glanced at the clock, then at him.

"Are you going in?" she asked.

"Yeah." He propped his weight on his elbow and gazed down at her. "I wish I could stay."

"It's okay."

"What are you doing today?"

Her thoughts jumbled together. She couldn't even think what day it was.

"It's Monday," he said, reading her mind.

"Papers to grade. Calls to make." Her to-do list snapped into focus. "I have an online study session with my students at two."

He kissed her forehead.

"You want to come to our task force meeting?" he asked.

She blinked up at him. "I don't know. Should I?"

"If you want. You're part of the team."

She sighed. She wasn't accustomed to the workings of a small department. Where she'd worked before, CSIs didn't sit in on task force meetings. But Joel's department was a tight-knit group.

"Won't it be awkward if I'm there?" she asked.

"Why?"

"I don't know." She played with his hair. "Don't you think people will pick up on the fact that we're involved?"

"Maybe."

"We're talking about a group of detectives. They're not stupid."

"So what if they know?"

She looked up at him. "Don't you think that could get uncomfortable?"

"Why?"

"Because. You're having a fling with the CSI."

"A fling?" He lifted his eyebrows.

"Okay, sex. Whatever you want to call it."

He smiled down at her.

"What?"

He sat up taller on his elbow. "Can I ask you something?"

She felt her guard going up.

"Have you ever thought of staying?"

"Staying in Lost Beach?" she asked.

"Yeah."

"You mean past the summer?"

He just looked at her. Butterflies filled her stomach as she gazed up at those intense blue eyes. Suddenly, she felt wide awake.

Staying *here*. As in making this move permanent. As in giving up her life in San Antonio, the life she'd always planned to go back to once she sorted through her personal problems.

Joel brushed a lock of hair from her face. He looked down at her and lifted an eyebrow. "Well?"

She swallowed the lump in her throat and decided to be honest. "I've thought about it. A lot, actually."

"Good."

He kissed her. It was soft and tender, and her heart squeezed. Emotions swirled inside her, so many she couldn't put a label on them all. When he eased back, his gaze was intense.

"Joel," she whispered. "What are we doing, exactly?"

"How about seeing where this goes?"

"Where do you want it to go?"

He kissed her again, and her heart started thrumming, distracting her from the conversation. When he kissed her, she couldn't focus on anything—all she could do was melt into the moment with him.

This time when he pulled away, his eyes simmered.

"I like you a lot, Miranda. This doesn't feel like a fling to me." His thigh eased between hers. "What about you?"

Her throat went dry and she could only shake her head.

He smiled. "Damn. You've got that look again."

"What look?"

"Wary."

His leg against hers created a warm friction that made it difficult to think clearly.

"It just feels . . . fast," she said. "And I'm worried you might be reacting to other things."

"Like what?" His hand slid down her body.

"I don't know. Your breakup. The wedding."

He grinned. "Are you saying I'm on the rebound?"

"Maybe."

"Try again." He leaned down and nuzzled her neck.

"How can you be sure?"

"Because I can." He looked at her, still smiling. "I was with Elaina three years, and I never felt this way." His look turned serious as he gazed down at her. "Not even close."

Warmth flooded her, making her feel slightly buzzed. "Really?"

"Really." He kissed her. "Does that freak you out?"

She shook her head.

"No?"

She shrugged. "Maybe a little. I tend to be kind of a worrier. When it comes to relationships."

"No way." He smiled.

"I'm serious."

"So, you're saying you're worried about this?"

"Just that it's all been so intense. Everything's happening so fast."

"True." He moved his thigh, setting off sparks throughout her body. "But that's not necessarily bad, is it?"

She bit her lip.

"How about this?" he said.

Suddenly, she was back at her house their first night together, when he proposed that they just have fun for the night and worry about the rest in the morning.

"How about we take it one day at a time, and see where this goes?"

And once again, she couldn't say no. She didn't want to.

"You're a master at this, aren't you?"

"At what?"

She sighed. "Slow persuasion."

"I'll take that as a compliment."

She pulled his head down to kiss him, but he pulled back.

"Does that mean yes?" he asked.

"Yes."

TWENTY-SEVEN

Nicole watched the sun-kissed coastline as Owen made a wide arc and pulled up to the police station boathouse. A brown pelican on a post flapped away as they motored toward shore. Owen expertly lined up the boat with the empty slip and killed the speed so that they glided straight in.

Joel walked onto the dock, casting a long shadow on the weathered boards. His expression looked grim, and Nicole could tell he'd had a long day.

Joel caught the bow of the boat with his boot. "How'd it go?"

She grabbed a coil of rope and tossed it to him. "Okay."

Joel tied the line to a cleat as Nicole stepped onto the dock. She turned to Owen.

"Hand me that cooler," she said.

"I got it."

He hefted it in his arms, and she turned to Joel.

"We were out for four hours," she said. "Talked to people at every marina on this side of the bay. Flashed the pictures around. No one recognized Trevor Keen or his girlfriend or said they noticed anyone suspicious on Monday morning."

Joel didn't look surprised.

"The sheriff's guys are working the other side," Owen said, stepping from the boat. He set the cooler on the dock and unfastened the plug to drain it. "They said they'd call in when they wrapped up. If they'd gotten anything, I think we would have heard from them already."

"How'd it go here today?" Nicole asked.

Joel raked his hand through his hair. "I spent all afternoon on the phone, tracking down detectives in different jurisdictions."

"Any luck with the suspect list?" she asked, even though she could guess the answer from his body language.

"None of the persons of interest overlap."

"None?" Owen asked.

"Not a one."

"Shit."

"Maybe we should add the sixth case," Nicole said. "The poisoning. It couldn't hurt."

"I'm working on it."

Owen collected the empty water bottles from the cooler. "I'm going to answer some emails and grab dinner. You guys want anything?"

"It's not even five thirty," Nicole said.

"I skipped lunch."

"I'm good," Joel said.

Owen pitched the bottles in the recycle bin and headed inside.

She turned to look at his brother. "Any word from Miranda?"

"No. Why?"

"Just wondering how she's doing." Nicole had been concerned about her ever since this morning's team meeting, when Joel shared the news about the shoe print at Miranda's house that matched the one at the crime scene.

"I think she's fine," Joel said. "She's been at the library with her laptop all afternoon. Said she wanted to work somewhere public today instead of staying home alone."

"I don't blame her," she said. "You headed back inside?"

"Yeah."

"I'll come with you. I've got a theory I want to run by you. Owen's skeptical, but I want to hear what you think."

He lifted an eyebrow at that as they headed toward the back door of the police station. "What's the theory?"

"Well, I keep going through the social media posts of our first two victims, Liz and Will."

"Yeah?"

"On the surface, they're these tree-hugger activists. But maybe it's not as simple as it seems."

"How do you mean?"

The back door opened, and a couple of uniformed officers walked out. They nodded at Nicole and Joel and headed for the parking lot.

"Sit down and explain," Joel said, nodding at an empty picnic table.

Nicole sank onto the bench and pulled off her sweaty baseball cap. It was hot as hell today. Her skin had been spared, though, because she'd spent half the afternoon slathering on sunblock.

"Okay, so the two of them had been road-tripping for months, right? Posting all these pictures of themselves at tourist attractions and national parks and scenic overlooks," she said. "And when they weren't busy taking selfies in front of the Grand Canyon or whatever, they were busy protesting all the evil corporations ravaging the planet, right?"

"Okay."

"But what if they're just as bad as the corporations? Maybe worse?"

Joel frowned. "How?"

"Well, I've been reading the comments on their posts. And not everybody agrees they're exactly saving the world with what they're doing. A lot of the places they've visited— most of them, in fact—are suffering from overtourism."

"Overtourism." Joel sounded just as skeptical as his brother.

"Yeah. It's a problem, and some people are quick to point it out. People like Liz and Will go zipping around in their trendy camper, taking pictures in front of iconic views—like the Half Dome in Yosemite, or the Rainbow Bridge in Utah, or White Dunes Park here on the island, or wherever. And droves of people see their posts and follow in their footsteps, overwhelming all these places that aren't used to such an onslaught of traffic. And a lot of the people who come don't really care about these places at all; they just want to snap a selfie they can post online. Which leads to more traffic and makes the problem worse."

Joel just looked at her.

"It's a serious issue. Look it up if you don't believe me. There are places—in Thailand and the Philippines, for example—where they've had to shut down entire islands because people's social media posts have prompted hordes of people to descend on these little communities and they've been completely overwhelmed with cruise ships and foot traffic and pollution."

Joel folded his arms over his chest. "So, you're saying they're hurting the cause, not helping it."

"Exactly. And they've gotten some blowback about it on some of their social media posts. So, I started thinking, what if *that's* why they were targeted? We have a killer who seems to be motivated by ideology. Defending the environment, preventing the destruction of the planet, however you want to think about it—"

"We don't know that for a fact," he said.

"Okay, but it's our working theory. The best one we have so far that ties all these cases together. Anyway, we've been stuck on the motive for these two young victims—how can they be targeted by someone like that if they're members of this activist group—but maybe not all Alpha Omega Now members are created equal. Maybe some extremist within the group didn't like what these two were doing and thought they were hypocrites."

Joel gazed down at her but didn't respond. She couldn't tell whether he didn't buy her theory or was giving it serious consideration.

"By that logic—twisted though it is—people like Liz and Will are just as bad as a real estate developer or an oil executive or someone who owns a logging company," she said. "They're degrading the environment for personal profit. And maybe the two of them are worse, because their social media posts encourage people to follow in their footsteps, so their negative impact is amplified."

She took a deep breath, watching Joel's reaction. She couldn't read him.

"Owen thinks I'm in the weeds," she admitted. "What do *you* think?"

"It's an interesting take."

"'Interesting' as in you think it has merit? Or you think it's totally out-there?"

"It has merit. We should discuss it at the next task force meeting. Tee it up."

Nicole felt a swell of pride. He thought her theory had merit *and* he wanted her to take credit for it. His support meant a lot.

Nicole's phone vibrated in her pocket and she pulled it out to read a text. She recognized the Houston area code.

"You say Miranda's at the library?" She looked at Joel.

"Yeah. Why?"

"I have a text from my detective contact in Houston. He sent over that photograph she wanted."

Joel frowned. "What photograph?"

"The feather recovered with the Houston murder victim. The oil-and-gas executive. Miranda wanted a close-up of it."

"Why?"

"I don't know. I figure she's investigating it."

JOEL DUCKED INTO the empty conference room and called Miranda. He'd been thinking about her all day but had been determined to give her some space. As much as he could, anyway, given all the shit that had been happening. He deeply regretted getting her involved in his case.

"Hey," she said. "How's it going?"

Just the sound of her voice loosened the knot in his chest.

"Okay," he said. "How are you?"

"Just okay?"

He sat on the table, staring at the crime scene photographs that had been haunting him for days. "Yeah, the suspect list isn't coming together. So far, no overlap."

"Damn."

"What about you? Are you still at the library grading papers?" he asked.

"Actually, I've been doing some research."

"The feather."

Silence on the other end.

"How'd you know?" she asked.

"Nicole mentioned it. You dig up anything interesting?"

"Maybe," she said. "I've been going through books here. They've actually got a nice collection of ornithology references. You must have a lot of birders on the island."

"We do."

"Well, I've narrowed it down, I think. It's definitely a South American parrot, possibly a scarlet macaw. Those aren't endangered, like the indigo macaw and the yellow-browed toucanet. But their habitat is certainly endangered. So, it reinforces our theory about the killer being ideologically motivated."

Joel stepped closer to the board and studied the photograph that had been stuck in his mind for days—the two young victims intertwined in the canoe. From day one, Joel had thought they looked posed. And he wondered now if that might be part of the killer's message.

Their social media posts encourage people to follow in their footsteps, so their negative impact is amplified.

Nicole might be onto something with her theory. He liked that she was thinking creatively.

"Joel?"

"Yeah?"

"So, what are you going to do about your suspect list?"

"Keep working on it. I may have to add the sixth case."

"What sixth case?"

He sighed. "I guess I didn't tell you about the poisoning."

"Someone was *poisoned*?"

"This was that logging company that Alpha Omega Now protested a couple years ago. Turns out their CEO died from hemlock poisoning."

"Hemlock? How awful. That stuff causes paralysis and respiratory failure."

"The police looked at a bunch of people and homed in on his wife," he said. "I need to call them up and find out who else they talked to. It's still an open case."

"Sounds like a bit of a stretch, though," she said.

"Why?"

"Well, typically poison is more of a woman's MO. We're looking for a man with a size eleven shoe, and he uses a gun."

"I know, but I'm running out of leads here."

He turned away from the murder board and stepped to the window. Parting the blinds, he looked out over the parking lot. The big push he'd hoped to make today hadn't materialized, and he was still hours away from being able to wrap up. Which meant Miranda would be going home to an empty house.

"Sounds like you're going to be there late," she said.

"I am. What about you? You're still working?"

"Yeah, but they're about to close here. Maybe I could finish up at the station while you get the rest of your work done."

Joel liked the sound of that. He'd been on edge all day, and having her close by would be a relief.

"Then we could pick up dinner," she suggested. "Or do you plan to be there really late?"

"People can reach me at home if they need to," he said. "Picking up dinner sounds good."

"Okay, I'll be there in an hour or so."

"You have your pepper spray?"

"Yeah."

"Be careful. And pay attention to your surroundings."

"Joel, seriously."

"*Seriously*, Miranda. You need to pay attention."

"I do pay attention. See you soon."

He ended the call, feeling like a nag. But it didn't matter. She needed to be vigilant, and he didn't care if he sounded overprotective. The thought of something happening to her put a ball of dread in his gut. He hated that this case was dragging on, and he wouldn't relax until they had someone in custody.

Joel took out his phone and scrolled through it for the number of his FBI contact. Just as he located the contact, a call came in.

He didn't recognize the number.

"Breda."

No response.

"Hello?"

"Is this . . . Joel Breda with the Lost Beach Police?" It was a woman's voice, and she sounded nervous.

"That's right."

"It's Gillian Copeland."

Joel's pulse gave a kick. And he knew his shit day was about to change.

"Hi, Gillian. What can I do for you?"

"I wanted to see if you could meet me."

"What's going on?"

"There's something I want to show you."

M IRANDA PULLED INTO the parking lot and gazed out over the marsh. The place had cleared out for the day, and she parked in a front-row space close to the entrance. For a minute, she sat behind the wheel and absorbed the quiet. The marsh was lavender in the dusky light of evening, and the breeze off the bay sent ripples through the salt grass. The tall wooden observation tower was empty except for a lone bird-watcher with binoculars.

Miranda gathered her thick accordion file and got out. The air smelled of fresh-cut grass, and a green riding mower sat beside the path. Tucking her file under her arm, she walked up the sidewalk and went around to the back door near the boardwalk. She tried the door and found it unlocked, as promised.

Stepping into the dim lobby of the nature center, she looked at the reception desk and felt a pang of sadness as she pictured Xander Kendrick with his blond ponytail and his laid-back smile. It was hard to believe someone so young and vibrant could suddenly be gone.

Behind the empty reception desk, the science laboratory glowed. Miranda walked across the lobby and spotted a man in a white lab coat standing at a microscope.

"You're early."

She turned around to see Daisy Miller crossing the lobby. She wore her big straw hat and had a silver bucket in her hand.

"Hi," Miranda said.

She smiled. "I was just feeding the turtles."

"Need a hand?"

"Oh, I'm fine. They're done for today." Daisy gestured toward the laboratory. "Come on back."

Miranda followed her to the laboratory. Just inside the door was a tall stainless-steel shelf. Daisy set down her bucket of turtle food and peeled off her hat.

"Thanks for meeting me," Miranda said. "Hope I'm not keeping you here too late."

"Not at all. It takes hours to close this place. All our creatures need to be fed and settled for the night." She smiled. "You need any water or anything?"

"I'm good, thanks."

The guy with the lab coat had disappeared, and Miranda followed Daisy past the empty counter to her computer. Miranda glanced around the lab, taking note of all the microscopes and sinks and cabinets filled with glass beakers.

They must do a lot of research here, and she wished she knew more about it.

"So." Daisy tossed her hat on the desk and ran her hand through her wild gray curls. "You have another feather for me."

"That's right."

Daisy pulled out her swivel chair. "Sit down." She nodded toward the chair at the computer station beside hers. "You can use Jason's chair. He just left."

Miranda sat down and opened the accordion file.

"Once again, I only have a photograph." She pulled out the picture Nicole had sent her. The long red feather with a bluish tip was on a steel table with a ruler positioned beside it.

Daisy fished a pair of reading glasses from a drawer and perched them on the end of her nose. "And where did *this* one come from? Don't tell me there was another murder."

"There was, unfortunately. This one's from Houston." She handed over the picture. "It happened a while ago, actually."

Daisy frowned at the picture. "A scarlet macaw. I can tell just by looking at it."

"You don't need to enter it in your database?"

"Nope." She handed back the photo. "That's a central tail feather, forty-six centimeters, or almost half the bird's length. They're long birds. They're poached for their feathers as well as for food."

"They're not endangered, though, right?"

"No, but their habitat certainly is. Why do you ask?"

"Just a theory we're working on."

"We?"

"Investigators looking at the case."

Daisy looked at her for a long moment. Then she gazed down at the photograph.

"So, I was wondering," Miranda said. "Last time I was here, you said your database—what is it called?"

"The Global Feather Index?"

"Yes, that. You said it's used by law enforcement. People who deal with animal trafficking?"

"That's right."

"Well, I got to wondering. Who keeps the specimens? Is it the law enforcement agencies?"

Daisy tipped her head to the side. "How do you mean?"

"I mean, who has the actual feathers? The ones used as reference samples."

"You mean, who maintains the collection?"

"That's right. Sorry, let me back up," Miranda said. "One of the detectives I work with made a point the other day, that these feathers of endangered birds aren't just floating around, right? And yet someone is planting them at crime scenes. So, I'm wondering who has access to feathers of species that are protected, like the indigo macaw."

Daisy looked down at the photograph on the desk. "Hmm."

"I mean, it's not like you can get these at a pet store. Some feathers, like the scarlet macaw, you can get through online vendors. But the endangered species are another story. Very few of these animals are even in zoos. So that's why I'm wondering."

Daisy pursed her lips as she looked at the photograph. She swayed slightly.

Miranda leaned forward. "Are you all right?"

She glanced up. "Yes. I just remembered something. Would you wait here a minute?"

"Sure."

She got up and looked around. "One minute."

She crossed the lab and walked out, and Miranda stared after her.

Her phone vibrated in her purse, and Miranda pulled it out. Nicole.

"Hey," Miranda said.

"Joel had to run out, but he said he'd be back soon. Are you coming by the station?"

"In a bit. I stopped by the nature center to ask a question about the feather."

"Is it a scarlet macaw, like you thought?" Nicole asked.

"According to their ornithologist, yes. Those aren't endangered, by the way."

"I know. A friend of mine has one as a pet."

Miranda stood up, stretching her legs. She'd been sitting all day.

"When you get here, come find me," Nicole said. "I've made some progress on the social media front, and I want to show you what I found. I'll be in the conference room."

"I'll find you."

Miranda ended the call and looked around. The lab was quiet and still. Where had Daisy gone?

She wandered to a second glass door, which stood ajar. Miranda leaned her head into the next room, which was the Discovery Center. She stepped into the cavernous space and looked up. Mobiles of aquatic animals hung from the ceiling. Miranda stepped over to a tank and examined the array of starfish and sea anemones.

A clatter on the other side of the room caught her attention. She walked over to another glass door, this one leading to a long corridor lined with metal tables on both sides. The space was being used as a greenhouse.

A blur of pink caught her eye.

"Daisy?" Miranda peered down the corridor. She tried the door and found it unlocked.

The greenhouse was dim and silent as she stepped inside. The warm air smelled like compost, and in the corner was a big plastic bag of organic fertilizer. The long steel tables were filled with dozens and dozens of potted plants. Beneath the tables were buckets containing different types of dirt and potting soil.

Miranda approached the nearest table, where clay pots brimmed with leafy green plants. She identified many of them by sight, but little metal placards provided scientific names: *LAVANDULA OFFICINALIS, THYMUS VULGARIS, OCIMUM BASILICUM.* Her gaze fell on a pot of lacy white flowers in the back row. *CONIUM MACULATUM.*

The hair on the back of her neck stood up. She took a step backward. And another.

Thud.

Miranda whirled around.

J OEL PULLED INTO the parking lot and scanned the area. The convenience store was busy, but he saw no sign of Gillian Copeland or the black Honda. Joel pulled into a space on the edge of the lot.

The store's door opened, and Gillian stepped out, looking directly at him.

He slid from his truck and crossed the lot toward her. She wore an actual shirt this time with her cutoff shorts. She also wore a baseball cap, and her long blond ponytail trailed down her back.

She cast a worried look over Joel's shoulder and then motioned for him to follow her around the side of the building. In her hand was a plastic bag filled with Pringles and soft drinks.

"I can't stay long," she said.

"Where's Trevor?"

"Back in the room. I walked." She cast another look over his shoulder. "Are you alone?"

"Yeah."

Joel gazed down at her. Her eyes were bloodshot, and he couldn't tell whether she was high or she'd been crying.

She looked up at him and bit her lip, and Joel tried to tamp down his impatience.

"I've been thinking about what you said. And I want you to know you're wrong about us," she said.

"Wrong about what?"

"Trevor. And me. We'd never hurt anyone. And Trevor— you don't know him, but he's a good person. I mean, he's made some mistakes, but never anything serious, not like what that guy Romero was saying."

"How do you know?"

"Because I know him, all right?"

"All right. So, what did you want to show me?"

No response. She bit her lip again, and Joel felt a swell of frustration.

"I got the names for you."

"Names?"

"Alpha Omega Now. Well, not names, really, but the email list." She tugged a folded paper from her back pocket. "There's five hundred, give or take. You'll have to figure out the names yourself. I just have the emails."

She handed it over, and he saw that it was several papers stapled together.

He looked at her. "Anyone you want to flag?"

"No. I told you. We're not violent." She looked defiant. "I still think you're wrong about this, but you're right that I don't know everyone personally, so . . . whatever. Knock yourself out. Hopefully, you'll find what you're looking for and leave me and Trevor alone."

Joel folded the paper and tucked it away. "Thank you. You're doing the right thing here."

She sniffed and rolled her eyes.

"Stay out of trouble, all right?"

Another eye roll.

Joel walked back to his truck and slid behind the wheel. In his rearview mirror, he watched Gillian walk down the sidewalk toward the inn where Trevor was waiting for his snacks.

Joel unfolded the papers in his lap. It was getting dark, and he flipped on the overhead light to read.

It was a long list of email addresses, no names. Joel gritted his teeth as he scanned the pages. This would take hours to go through. Most of the dot-coms were Internet providers, not private businesses. He noticed a few dot-orgs and dot-edus mixed in.

A name snagged his attention, and Joel's heart skipped a beat. He blinked down at the paper.

"No fucking way."

NICOLE'S PHONE VIBRATED on the table. Joel.

"Hey," she said.

"Where are you?" he demanded.

"At the station. Why?"

"I just got the email list of Alpha Omega Now members."

Nicole sat up straighter. "Where'd you get that?"

"Gillian. Listen, there are *three* names on here from Lost Beach BCNC dot-org."

"BCNC?"

"Birding Center and Nature Conservatory," he said.

"Who are they?"

"Jason Freeman, Daisy Miller, and Tom Miller. All three of them are members."

"Jason is one of their bird experts," she said. "So is Daisy. Who's Tom?"

"The groundskeeper," Joel said. "He's Daisy's husband.

And, listen, Tom's also the person I called to find out who worked at the nature center front desk. Remember when Miranda recognized the guy on the bike, and so we found out who he was and went and interviewed him?"

A chill slithered down Nicole's spine. "And then he ended up dead."

"Yeah."

"Damn, Joel."

"I know. Who all's there? We need to pick up these three suspects and—"

"Joel, oh my God. *Miranda*."

"What about her?"

"She's at the nature center right now."

"What? Why?"

"She wanted to talk to Daisy about a feather."

Silence.

"Joel? Hello?"

He'd hung up.

M IRANDA WALKED BACK to the science laboratory. It was empty. But she couldn't shake the feeling that someone was lurking around.

Her phone chimed. She pulled it from her pocket and wandered back over to the starfish tank.

"Hi," she said to Joel.

"Where are you?"

His sharp tone put her on edge.

"At the nature center. Listen, I just found something *very* strange here. I was about to—"

"Get out of there."

"What?"

"You need to get out of there right now. Three people who work there just jumped to the top of our suspect list."

She went still.

"Miranda?"

"I hear you. Hold on." She muffled her phone against her chest and crept toward the science lab. Keeping out of sight, she peeked inside.

A shadow moved near the window. Someone was in the lab. Miranda spied her purse on the desk beside Daisy's computer. Her car keys were inside it. So was her pepper spray.

The shadow moved and Miranda ducked back into the Discovery Center. She disconnected the call with Joel. With trembling fingers, she sent him a quick text.

Leaving. Do not call.

He responded instantly: On my way.

Ducking low, Miranda hurried to the other end of the greenhouse. The door there was unlocked. Slowly, she pulled it open. She found herself in a soaring atrium surrounded by lush tropical plants. Water gurgled from somewhere nearby. A monarch butterfly fluttered past her face and alighted on a shiny green leaf.

With a glance behind her, Miranda scurried over a wooden footbridge and reached another door. She opened it, hoping for a way outside. But instead she found herself in another science lab, this one dark. A big black table stood in the center and file drawers lined the wall. A red exit sign glowed on the far side of the room. Miranda hurried toward it. Passing the file drawers, she noticed the labels.

Birds.

Miranda stopped. She cast a furtive glance over her shoulder, then tugged open a drawer. The shallow tray held a pair of long blue feathers.

They had a reference collection. Right here *on-site*. She took out her phone and snapped a photo.

Footsteps.

Miranda dashed toward the door. She tried it, but it was locked.

The footsteps drew closer, and she ducked down and crawled under the big black table. Holding her breath, she listened as someone stepped into the room.

"I don't know. She was just here."

It was Daisy. She was on the phone with someone.

"How should I know?" Daisy's voice was closer now.

Miranda stayed stock-still, holding her breath as her heart hammered against her ribs.

"Fine."

A door clicked shut, and the footsteps faded away.

Miranda let out a breath. She scrambled out from under the table and looked around.

She had to get back to her purse. She tiptoed down the corridor, straining for any hint of sound. Through the greenhouse window, she caught a blur of pink as Daisy strode across the Discovery Center and went back into the main lobby.

Miranda jogged back to the science lab. She peeked her head around the corner. The lab was empty. She darted to the desk and grabbed her purse and immediately fished the tube of pepper spray from the bottom as she hurried back to the glass door.

The lobby looked empty. Miranda's heart raced as she paused beside the door, searching for any shadow or movement or even a hint that someone was there.

Miranda set her sights on the back exit. She made a run for it.

The door was still unlocked, thank God. She stepped into the muggy night air and glanced around.

The wooden boardwalk stretched out across the dark marshland. Every fifty feet or so, a small light illuminated the path. The trails looked deserted.

Miranda hurried around the side of the building and spotted her Jeep in the front row. She glanced at the lobby. The science lab still glowed, but everything else was dark. The only other vehicle nearby was a lone white pickup truck on the far edge of the parking lot.

Gripping her pepper spray, Miranda dashed to her Jeep. She hadn't locked it, and she jerked open the door. Her gaze landed on the front tire.

Flat.

Panic zinged through her. The back tire was flat, too. Someone had slashed her tires!

She shot a desperate glance at the highway. Where was Joel?

Pop!

Miranda dove to the ground.

CHAPTER

TWENTY-EIGHT

*G*UNSHOT.

Miranda's heart jackhammered as she crouched by the bumper. She peered around the side of the Jeep as a shadow moved behind the riding mower.

Her pulse skittered, and she scrambled to the other side of the Jeep. She looked at the highway. No police cars, no sirens, no Joel.

The shadowy figure darted from the mower to the building. Was he running away?

She felt like a sitting duck in the vast lot with her disabled car. Gripping her pepper spray, she looked around and tried to think of a plan.

Joel was on his way.

She needed to hide. And warn him.

Not far away was a clump of palmetto trees at the entrance to one of the trails. She eased forward on the balls of her feet, heart racing as she looked around.

She took a deep breath and sprinted for the trees. Her

T-shirt snagged as she darted behind them. She jerked the fabric free and ducked low, looking through the palm fronds.

Had anyone seen her?

She looked at the highway and pulled her phone from her pocket. With trembling fingers she texted a message.

Call backup they r shooting.

J OEL'S HEART JUMPED into his throat as he read the text. He stomped on the gas as he tapped a response.

Almost there. Take cover.

Joel's truck skidded as he whipped into the parking lot. He spied Miranda's Jeep parked near the entrance. The driver's-side door stood open, but she was nowhere in sight. He raced across the lot and screeched to a halt, and his stomach clenched as he noticed the Jeep's tires.

M IRANDA DUCKED LOW as she peered around the clump of trees. Cool water seeped between her toes and she wished she had on sneakers instead of flip-flops. She crept around a shrub, eyeing the wooden boardwalk nearby. The long walkway spanned the marsh and linked up with a gravel trail that led straight into the nearby neighborhood. If she could make it to the trail, she'd be able to duck behind the foliage as she ran for help.

Mud sucked at her flip-flop as she tried to move.

Thwack.

She crouched down, hoping no one had heard the sound. She stepped out of the shoes, and mud oozed between her toes. She surveyed the boardwalk, looking for any sign of movement.

Her gaze landed on a sign. **BEWARE OF ALLIGATORS.**

Miranda stepped onto the boardwalk and made a sprint for the trees. She ran as fast as she could, clutching her pepper spray.

Pop!

She jumped off the path into a clump of cattails. Panicked, she looked around.

Where had that shot come from?

She ducked low, wading through the knee-deep water. She found a dense clump of cattails and squatted down, getting her shorts wet.

Peering through the reeds, she tried to spot the shooter.

She scanned the path but didn't see anyone. Her gaze landed on the turtle tanks. They weren't far away, maybe thirty yards, much closer than the nearest neighborhood. She could hide behind them until the police came.

Ducking behind the reeds, she slowly waded out until the water reached her thighs. What about her phone? She put it in her mouth, clamping it between her teeth as she lowered herself into the cool black water. Heart pounding, she swam toward the dock.

JOEL PRESSED HIS back against the brick and gripped his Glock as he looked around. Where was she? He scanned the dark marshes, looking for any sign of movement. Where the hell was his backup?

A flash of movement at the top of the observation tower caught his eye.

Someone was up there. A lone dark figure, watching over everything with a pair of binoculars.

Was it Jason Freeman? Tom Miller?

Was it Daisy, spotting for her husband?

Dread filled his stomach as he watched the figure move to the edge of the platform. Following the line of sight, Joel zeroed in on the long boardwalk leading to the turtle tanks.

Something moved in the water.

Miranda.

S HE STRAINED TO keep her head above water, along with her phone, as she did a frog-like breaststroke toward the tanks. She was almost there. Almost. She scanned the dock for a ladder but didn't see one. She was going to have to heave herself out of the water. She only hoped she could do it silently.

Miranda's shoulders ached. Her thighs burned. She inched closer and closer to the covered dock with the big blue tanks.

Something cold brushed her leg, and she gasped, dropping her phone.

Tears burned her eyes. She dunked her head under and felt around, but it was no use. She couldn't even touch the bottom here. She glanced back at the nature center, a hulking black shadow that seemed miles away. The only light came from a pair of floodlights aimed at the parking lot.

Salt water stung her eyes as she set her sights on the tanks. She was almost there, and she spied a ladder. She swam toward it, unencumbered now except for the pepper spray still gripped in her hand.

Almost there. Almost there. Almost there.

She took a last hard stroke and glided into the ladder. She tucked the tube of pepper spray into her bra and gripped the ladder's sides. Her foot slipped on the slimy bottom rung, but she hung on and pulled herself up.

She spotted a small skiff tied to the end of the dock. Adrenaline shot through her. Could she use it to get away? But it probably needed a key. And it might have one of those noisy pull-starts. She'd never get it going without drawing attention to herself.

Crouching low, she looked at the nature center. She didn't see a person or even a shadow. Help was *coming*, and she just needed to hide and wait. She scurried behind the big blue tank and sank to her knees.

Please be careful, Joel. Please please please. She hoped he'd called backup, and she hoped to hell they didn't get into a firefight.

Miranda's gaze landed on the skiff. A life jacket was stowed near the motor, along with something else.

A flare gun.

Not the best weapon, but probably better than the pepper spray in her bra. She crawled across the dock and reached into the boat for the gun.

"Well, well."

A tall shadow stepped out from behind a post.

TWENTY-NINE

T HE MAN WALKED out from beneath the overhang, and Miranda's stomach clenched as she got a look at his face. Tom, the groundskeeper. Daisy's husband.

He pointed a pistol at her face.

"Get in the boat."

She stared at him.

"Now." He stepped closer, aiming the gun with a steady hand. "You and me are going for a ride."

Miranda's heart clenched, and she thought of her pepper spray. If she turned away from him, maybe she could reach for it.

"Now."

Miranda scooted over to the boat but didn't get in.

Tom stepped closer, towering over her now. Something moved behind him, about fifty feet away.

Joel.

Miranda tried not to look at him, tried to focus on Tom

and the gun pointed at her as she grabbed the side of the boat and stepped into it.

"Police! Drop it!"

She dove into the water, swimming down down down and holding her breath until her lungs wanted to burst. Still she kept swimming and swimming until she couldn't stand it anymore. Finally, she surfaced and turned around.

A pile of bodies at the end of the dock made her heart lurch.

Joel. And Owen and Emmet.

Tom was pinned beneath them as they handcuffed him.

"Miranda!"

Joel did a racing dive off the dock and swam toward her.

She blinked the salt water from her eyes and paddled toward him, spitting and shaking.

"You okay? You hurt?" His arm wrapped around her, pulling her close. He lifted her with his hip so she could get her face above water.

"Miranda, talk to me. Are you hurt?"

"I'm okay." She gripped his arm. "I'm good."

L IT BY A thousand klieg lights, the nature center looked like a high school football stadium on a Friday night. Nicole traipsed across the parking lot to the mobile command center the sheriff had set up. As opposed to last time, it had taken him less than an hour to descend on the crime scene with a cadre of crime scene techs and eager-beaver deputies. Evidently, the sheriff didn't want to be left out of the news coverage now that they'd made an arrest.

Nicole skirted around the yellow crime scene tape and approached the huddle of cops near Miranda's Jeep. A CSI crouched there now, photographing the slashed tires.

Joel looked up at Nicole.

"It's a match," she told him.

His expression hardened. "Him or her?"

"Her."

"I knew it."

Tom and Daisy Miller had been arrested and printed. Daisy's palm print matched the karate-chop print found on the windows of the Airstream camper. Apparently, Daisy—and possibly her husband—had spied on the victims before killing them.

"Who ran the prints?" Joel asked.

"Miranda did."

She was working at the police station after refusing to go to the clinic and get checked out.

Nicole looked at the nature center entrance, where CSIs were shuttling back and forth with evidence bags and cardboard boxes.

"How's it going here?" Nicole asked.

"So far, we found several pots of hemlock and an interesting collection of feathers," Joel said.

"What about phones and wallets?"

He shook his head. "But our search warrant is on the way. Maybe we'll turn up something at their house."

"If the pistol checks out, we might not need the phones and wallets."

"We need everything we can get."

His tone was sharp, and Nicole studied his face.

Joel's jaw was tense. His clothes were still damp from fishing Miranda out of the bay. He turned and looked toward it now. Several portable klieg lights shone down on the boat dock where Tom Miller had been wrestled to the ground. The motorized skiff there—which was used by the nature center for turtle rescues—was presumed to be the boat that had been used to approach Liz and Will's canoe. It all made sense now. If Alexander Kendrick had passed the nature center on his bike and recognized a car or a person in the parking lot around the time of the murders, he could have figured out that Daisy and Tom Miller were involved. Whether he had realized it or not, he was a possible eyewitness, and someone had wanted him eliminated.

The shoe print in the flower bed suggested that someone was Tom Miller.

But who had pulled the trigger on the others? Was it Daisy? Her husband? Were they working together? The two were being questioned separately right now by FBI agents trained in interrogation, and Nicole knew Joel was pissed. He'd wanted to do it himself, but Brady had made him sit this one out. The chief wasn't clueless. And he evidently thought that Joel's personal connection to one of the victims—namely, Miranda—might be a conflict of interest.

Nicole thought he was right. A case this high-profile was sure to come under intense scrutiny, and the chief couldn't afford any mistakes.

Nicole suspected Joel knew that. But still he looked tense and tired and more than a little frustrated.

"It's a .38, you know."

Joel looked at her. "What's that?"

"The gun Tom had on him. It's already been sent to the lab to see if the slugs match."

He nodded.

"We got him, Joel. No matter what crazy story they come up with. The physical evidence is overwhelming already, even if we never find the cell phones or the wallets or size eleven sneakers. We've got enough to nail them."

Joel raked a hand through his hair. He turned and looked at Miranda's Jeep, which was still swarming with CSIs. One was crouched beside the back bumper measuring the bullet hole near her tire.

Nicole suspected that bullet hole was the real thing driving Joel crazy right now.

She stepped closer. "Hey, we've got things covered here, if you want to head to the station."

Joel wanted to be with Miranda—it was written all over his face.

"Go," she said. "Emmet's here. I'm here. Owen's here. We got this."

Joel looked at his brother, who wasn't known for being the most buttoned-up guy on the planet. But even Owen was rising to the occasion tonight.

"Go, Joel. We've got this covered."

"You sure?"

"Yeah."

He took his keys from his pocket.

"Hey, tell her thanks," Nicole said.

"Who?"

"Miranda. Who do you think? We never could have done this without her."

CHAPTER

THIRTY

SEAGULLS SCREECHED OUTSIDE the window as Miranda dragged herself out of bed. She didn't need to look at the clock to know it was past eight. Benji's bed was empty. Miranda dressed and went into the kitchen.

The light on the coffeepot was on, and she felt a rush of joy. A yellow sticky note sat beside her favorite Snoopy mug.

WENT FOR A RUN.

Miranda poured herself some coffee and took it out onto the deck. A thin fog hung over the beach, and she couldn't see very far up the coast. Grabbing the yellow beach towel off the chair, she went downstairs and crossed the bridge spanning the dunes. Insects trilled all around her, and the vines carpeting the hills were thick with dewy morning glories.

Miranda stepped onto the beach and tipped her head back to look at the sky. She took a deep gulp of fresh air.

She'd slept hard again. Slowly but surely, the anxiety that had had her in its grip for months was loosening its hold.

She spread her towel on the sand and sat down to watch the sandpipers as sunlight glimmered off the water. Her coffee tasted rich and strong. The air around her smelled of fog. Everything was sharp and vibrant, and she couldn't remember the last time she'd felt so alive.

A runner and a dog caught her eye, and Miranda felt a jolt of yearning. Every time she saw them together, her heart swelled. She knew the instant Benji spotted her because he broke into a sprint.

She braced herself as he charged up to her and raced around the towel, kicking up sand. She tried to pet him, but he darted for the waves.

Joel halted beside her, resting his hand on his hips. Sweat streamed down his temples, and his damp T-shirt clung to his body.

"You're up."

"Of course."

He sank to the sand beside her and leaned back on his elbows. "Of course?" he turned and smiled at her, and she saw her disheveled reflection in his shades.

"I just got up," she said.

"No kidding." He turned and kissed her neck, brushing his wet hair against her chin.

"You're slimy!"

He dragged her down and pinned her wrists. "Kiss me."

"Eww."

But she leaned up and kissed him anyway, and he tasted salty and musky and amazing, like he always did, and every cell in her body responded. She slid her hand over his lean waist and dipped her fingers into the back of his shorts.

He smiled down at her. "You save me some coffee?"

"Yep."

They sat up and turned to watch Benji frolicking in the waves. He raced down the shore, scaring up a trio of seagulls.

Joel pulled his shades off and wiped his brow with the back of his arm. "The chief called."

"Oh yeah?" She could tell by his tone that something had happened.

"We got a confession," he said.

"You're kidding."

"Nope."

"From?"

"Him."

The news left her slightly dazed. For three weeks, both Tom and Daisy Miller had refused to talk, leaving investigators to piece together what had happened. As near as they could tell, Daisy was the mastermind behind the killings—a conclusion supported by the extreme reading material they found on her computer, including the Unabomber manifesto, which railed against development and modern technology. Somewhere along the way, her passion had turned into an obsession, and she'd become fixated on local companies that personified what she viewed as evil. So, she developed a hit list.

Who actually carried out the murders was another question.

"What did he confess to?" Miranda asked.

"He shot Alexander."

A bitter lump lodged in her throat. She turned away.

"Why? After three weeks of stonewalling, why talk now?"

"Part of it was the shoe-print evidence," Joel said. "Once they found those Nikes at his house and got a match, there was no way he could wiggle out of it. Plus, he hired his own lawyer a couple days ago, so I guess he got advice that he had to come clean or risk taking the fall for everything. He claims Daisy was responsible for the other murders, and that he didn't even know about them—only suspected—until Liz and Will."

"Why would he kill Alexander?"

"He said Daisy pressured him to. Alexander was a witness who could identify Tom's truck in the parking lot of the nature center at the time of the murders, so she insisted they needed to eliminate him." Joel paused. "It's the same reason, according to Tom, that she set fire to the lighthouse while you were there. Tom said his wife was obsessed with you. She'd been stalking you, just like Liz and Will. She wanted to eliminate anyone who was too close to the truth."

Miranda shivered. Deep down, she'd known someone wanted her to die in that fire, but it felt strange to hear it confirmed.

"But I wasn't even an eyewitness to anything," she said.

"You came up with the lead about the feathers," Joel said. "Maybe she was worried you knew too much."

Miranda looked out at the waves, trying to digest everything. "Why would Tom even admit all this?"

"Who knows? But if he testifies against his wife, he can probably cut a deal and avoid the death penalty."

Tears stung Miranda's eyes, and she shook her head. "So pointless. Such a waste."

"I know."

Benji raced over and shook water all over them. Miranda stroked his fur. It was gritty with sand, but she hugged him anyway, taking comfort in how oblivious he was to all the bad that had happened. She kissed his head, and he zipped off again.

Joel picked up her hand and squeezed it. "You okay?"

"Yeah." She heaved a sigh. "I'm glad it's over."

"Me, too."

She turned to look at him, and his blue eyes were intent on her. His concern for her was palpable, always. She hadn't gotten used to someone caring so much about her feelings and how things affected her. It was a level of intimacy she'd never experienced before.

She looked out at the surf. "So . . . I heard from Bailey yesterday."

"Oh yeah?"

"She and her fiancé want to drive down this weekend."

"Great."

"And since they're coming, my parents will probably drive up from Padre and spend the day."

"Sounds fun."

"Everyone wants to meet you."

"Good. I want to meet them."

She searched his eyes. "Really?"

He smiled. "Yeah, really. Why wouldn't I?"

"I don't know. Everyone all at once might be a little much."

"I think I can handle it." He bumped his shoulder against hers. "Can *you*?"

"Yes. But I don't want to put pressure on you."

"Miranda?"

"What?"

"I love you."

She stared at him, and his smile turned into a grin.

Emotions flooded her. Happiness and nervousness and disbelief.

"You love me," she repeated.

"Yes. I want to meet your family. I want to meet everyone who's important to you." He squeezed her hand. "Why do you look so shocked?"

"I love you, too."

Just saying the words made her heart flutter, especially when he leaned close and kissed her.

"I know," he said.

"You do?"

"Yes."

"How?"

"I've been paying attention." He eased her back against the sand, and his smile turned serious as he hovered over her.

She pulled his head down and kissed him. And like always, it went from sweet to desperate in only a few heartbeats. His hand slid under her shirt, and the burning-hot need took over. She couldn't stop touching him, grasping him, pulling him closer to prove that this was real.

He eased back, and his eyes glinted down at her. "We can't do this here."

"Why not?" She kissed him again, sliding her leg between his.

"Seriously." He pulled back. "Let's go home."

He got up and tugged her to her feet, and she grabbed the towel. She shook the sand from it and looked for Benji, but he was all the way down the beach chasing birds.

Joel gave a sharp whistle. Benji turned and sprinted right up to him.

"How do you get him to do that for you?"

"He knows when I mean business." Joel snagged her empty coffee mug and grabbed her hand. "Come on."

"Wait."

She pulled him close and gazed up at the man who'd turned her life upside down since the moment she'd met him. He was hard and stubborn and brave and tender, and she couldn't believe how fast her life had changed since the day they'd met.

"I love you, Joel Breda." She smiled. "Just had to tell you that again."

He kissed her softly. And then he pulled her down the beach.

"Tell me again at home."

*Read on for Laura Griffin's next
spine-tingling suspense novel,*

LAST SEEN ALONE

Available in fall 2021 from Berkley

H E WAS LATE, and she shouldn't have been surprised.

Vanessa buzzed down the window a few inches and cut the engine. Crisp, piney air seeped into the car, along with the faint scent of someone's campfire. She checked her phone. Nothing. She settled back in her seat to wait.

Her headlights illuminated a clump of trees—spindly fresh ones, along with the pointed gray spires that had burned years ago. She looked at the stars beyond the treetops. Once upon a time, she'd stretched out on a patch of grass not far from here with Cooper, gazing up at the sky and trying to pick out constellations. Orion. Leo. The Big Dipper. The memory seemed strange. Fanciful. Everything like that was gone now, replaced by a dull ache that never went away. Her emotions felt like tar, thick and heavy in her veins, and even swinging her legs out of bed required effort.

Yet here she was.

She was sick of the dread in her stomach. She was sick of being a silent bystander to her own life.

Vanessa eyed the bottle of Jim Beam peeking out from beneath the passenger seat. She reached for it and checked her phone again before twisting off the cap.

Late, late, late.

She took a swig. The bourbon burned the back of her throat, but then she felt a warm rush of courage. She could do this.

Headlights, high and bright, flashed into her rearview mirror. Her shoulders tensed as she listened to the throaty sound of the approaching truck. It pulled up behind her and the lights went dark.

Vanessa stashed the bottle on the floor and wiped her damp palms on her jeans. Her stomach flip-flopped as he slid from the pickup and walked over. She couldn't believe she was doing this.

He stopped by the car, and she pushed the door open. He watched her from beneath the brim of his ratty baseball cap, and she could smell the smoke on his clothes. Marlboro Reds.

"Long time," he said.

"Do you have it?"

He held up a bag.

It was a lunch sack, like her mom used to pack for her. PBJ and a pudding cup. Vanessa took the bag, and the paper felt soft and greasy. She looked inside.

"That's four hundred."

Her head snapped up. "You said three fifty!"

He pulled the bag away. "I need four."

"I don't have it."

His gaze dropped to her breasts, and she knew that look. Her gut clenched. The thought of sex right now made her want to throw up.

Twisting in her seat, she grabbed her leather tote from

the back. She pulled the stack of bills from her wallet and counted twenty twenties. She turned and held them out.

Tucking the sack under his arm, he took the cash and thumbed through it.

"You look different," he said, and she caught the disapproval.

Vanessa gritted her teeth and waited. His attention fell to the bottle on the floor, and his brow furrowed as he leaned on the door.

"You all right, Van?"

"Yeah."

Something flickered across his face. Pity? Tenderness? She had to be imagining it.

"That's not really for your sister, is it?"

Vanessa didn't respond. It was none of his damn business. He stepped away, and she yanked the door shut.

For a moment he didn't move. But then he turned and walked back to his truck, stuffing her money into his back pocket.

The lights flashed on. Wincing, she watched in her rearview mirror as he backed up and made a three-point turn. When he was gone, she rested her hand on her stomach and let out a breath.

Vanessa started her car. She retraced her route over the pitted road until she reached the two-lane highway. When her tires hit smooth pavement, she pressed the gas and a wave of dizziness washed over her—probably the whiskey. She sighed with relief as the Austin skyline came into view.

Done.

She looked at the houses—some with lights on, some without—scattered on either side of the highway. Through a gap in the pines she caught a glimpse of the lake glimmering under the half moon.

Eying the brown bag beside her, she felt a pang of yearning. She checked the mirror, then pulled onto the shoulder and parked. She grabbed the bag and reached inside.

Seventeen ounces.

It felt heavier than she'd imagined. She held the pistol in her palm and ran her thumb over the textured grip. For the first time in months, the knot of fear in her stomach loosened. She'd never been brave, never in her life. But people could change.

Headlights winked into the mirror, and she glanced up. High and bright again, probably a pickup truck. Squinting, she watched them get closer and closer.

Vanessa's nerves skittered. Was it slowing down?

Had someone followed her here? But she'd been careful. Not just careful—vigilant. She'd taken every precaution.

The truck started to slow, and an icy claw of fear closed around her heart.

Vanessa scooted across the seat and reached for the passenger door, jerking back as her sweater snagged on something. She yanked it free, then grabbed the bag and pushed open the door.

The truck rolled to a halt. Vanessa scrambled from the car, tripping as she glanced back at headlights. Adrenaline shot through her, and she sprinted for the trees. The ground sloped down, and she ran faster, faster, losing control as she hurtled toward the woods.

Her toe caught and she crashed to her knees and elbows but managed to hold on to the bag. She pushed herself up and raced toward the tree line.

Then the headlights switched off, and everything went black. She ran blindly through the knee-high weeds, huffing and gasping and clutching the bag to her chest like a football. A car door slammed, sending a jolt of terror through her. She pictured him running after her, closing the distance, grabbing her by her hair.

Thorns stabbed at her as she reached the thicket. She swiped at the branches, desperate for cover as she imagined him behind her. She couldn't see anything, not even her hand in front of her face as she groped through the razor-sharp bushes.

The thorns disappeared as she stumbled into a clearing. Panting, she stopped and glanced up at the moon. Her heart thundered as she looked around and tried to orient herself. An arc of pines surrounded her. She could hide. Take cover. Defend herself if she had to. With trembling hands, she fumbled inside the bag and pulled out the gun. Dear God, was it loaded? She hadn't thought to ask.

He's coming.

On a burst of panic, she raced for the trees.

B RANDON ALMOST MADE it home.
Almost.

His stomach grumbled, and he eyed the pizza box riding shotgun in his truck. Mushroom and pepperoni, thin crust. It wasn't nearly as good cold, but he wasn't picky.

His cell phone buzzed in the holder, and he tapped it.

"Almost there," he told his partner.

"Where are you exactly?" Antonio asked.

"About two minutes out."

"Okay. Take it easy on the curve. You'll see a black-and-white on the eastbound shoulder near my car. That's the best place to park."

"Got it."

Brandon drove another mile down the highway and slowed. He spotted the whirring yellow lights of a tow truck blocking the eastbound lane as it dragged a pickup from the ditch. Brandon passed them, making note of the disabled vehicle—a black Chevy Silverado.

He tapped the brakes before the curve and saw the reason for Antonio's warning. A silver car occupied the shoulder, just barely off the roadway. Traffic flares flickered on the pavement. Directly across the street, Antonio and a uniform stood talking with a man. Tall, goatee, green camo jacket, and a baseball cap turned backward on his head.

Brandon pulled a U-turn and parked behind Antonio's personal vehicle, a black Mazda. Grabbing his phone, he gave his pizza a last wistful look and slid from the warmth of his truck.

A cool October breeze blew off the lake as Antonio trudged over. He wore dark slacks and a white button-down, same as Brandon, but his sleeves were rolled up. Looked like he hadn't made it home yet, either. Their workday had begun at five thirty a.m. with a gas station holdup on the south side of town, and it was almost eleven.

"How's it look?" Brandon asked.

"Weird."

Antonio stopped in front of him and ran a hand through his black buzz cut. His partner was short but powerfully built, like an MMA fighter.

"When did you get here?"

Antonio sighed. "'Bout ten minutes ago."

Brandon turned to look at the man being interviewed by the patrol officer.

"Guy's name is Tom Murray," Antonio said. "He called it in. Says he was driving westbound when a deer ran in front of him. He slammed on the brakes and swerved. Nearly hit the silver car there, then overcorrected and skidded off the road."

Brandon turned back toward the tow truck. The orange flares illuminated twin skid marks leading to the ditch.

"Tire marks corroborate his story," Antonio said. He'd spent five years on highway patrol, so he should know.

"And the driver of the car?" Brandon asked.

"Nowhere. But all her stuff's in the vehicle. Wallet, keys, phone, everything."

"Her?"

"Yeah, Murray said he walked over to see if anyone was inside and found a purse. Vanessa Adams, twenty-six. He checked the wallet."

Brandon muttered a curse.

"I know, right? Now his prints are everywhere."

Shaking his head, Brandon turned back toward the car. "What do you make of the guy?"

"Seems credible. Passed a Breathalyzer." Antonio shrugged. "We ran the name from the wallet. No wants or warrants. Vehicle's registered to her, too." Antonio looked at him, his brow furrowed. "I gave the car a once-over."

"Did you—"

"Didn't touch anything. There's a smear on the door. Looks to me like blood."

Hence, the reason why he and Antonio had been called out to an otherwise routine abandoned vehicle.

Brandon scanned the area. The highway was lined with trees. North of the road, the forest was thick and healthy. South, not so much. Years ago, the highway had acted as a firebreak, but several hundred acres to the south had burned, and now it was a mix of jagged gray points and fresh saplings. The terrain sloped down to an area dense with scrub trees. Beyond the brush was a man-made lake that had been created in an abandoned quarry. East of the lake was a public park.

Brandon opened his truck and reached into the back. "You have time to look around yet?"

"Not yet." Antonio gave a sheepish smile. "I don't have a flashlight."

Rookie mistake. But Brandon didn't state the obvious, even though he was Antonio's training officer.

Brandon reached into his truck and grabbed his high-powered Maglite, then tucked it into the back of his pants and handed his spare to Antonio. Opening the tackle box that lived in the back of his cab, he dug out two pairs of latex gloves and handed one to his partner.

"You want to talk to the driver?" Antonio asked.

"I'll take a look at the car first." Brandon pulled on the gloves. "Tell him to hang out. Then go get started in the woods."

"Roger that."

Antonio headed off, and Brandon took a last look around before approaching the vehicle.

It was a silver Toyota, ten years old, give or take, with a purple NAMASTE sticker on the back bumper. The tires were bald but not flat. A thin layer of grime covered the paint, except for streaks along the back, where someone had opened and closed the trunk a bunch of times. Brandon switched his beam to high and checked the back seat. Empty. He stepped to the driver's side. The door was closed, but the passenger door was wide open. He didn't like that.

No interior light on, no *ding-ding-ding* warning sound. Brandon circled the vehicle, making note of the license plate and the dented side panel. The damage looked old. Taking care not to mar any footprints in the dirt, he approached the open door and leaned in.

The smell hit him immediately. Pina colada. He swept the flashlight over the seat and spotted the pineapple-shaped air freshener tucked inside the door pocket.

Brandon crouched beside the car. On the floor was a half-empty bottle of bourbon and a big leather bag. It seemed more like a tote bag than a purse. A red leather wallet sat on the passenger seat. He shined the light on the Texas driver's license peeking through the plastic window and studied the smiling picture. Vanessa Adams had long auburn hair. She wore red lipstick, and her eyes were accented with gray eyeshadow. *Smokey eyes.* That was how his ex described it when she did her eyes that way before they went out to clubs. Yet another thing he definitely hadn't missed over the past six months.

Brandon swept the flashlight over the door again and found the smear. It wasn't big—just a swipe near the handle. But it looked to him like blood.

In the cupholder was an old iPhone with a glittery white case that had pink heart on the back. The heart case seemed young for a twenty-six-year-old.

Brandon stood and examined the car's exterior again. No sign that she'd hit an animal or anything else. So, what was the deal here? Was it a simple case of car trouble, and she'd hiked out for help?

Brandon could see her leaving her stuff behind, maybe even the tote bag and wallet if she was inebriated enough not to be thinking clearly. But her phone?

He looked over his shoulder toward the dark woods where a white light bobbed behind the trees. He called Antonio, and the light went still.

"Anyone check nearby gas stations?" Brandon asked. "There's an Exxon half a mile east of here, where Old Quarry Road meets the highway."

"I'll get patrol on it."

"Thanks."

Brandon turned back to look at the car. The iPhone bothered him. Even shitfaced, he couldn't see someone leaving it behind. For most twentysomethings, a phone was like an appendage. Plus, it was late. He couldn't picture a woman leaving here without her phone if she'd gone somewhere by choice.

He swept the light over the dashboard. The ashtray was open slightly and a white business card poked out. Brandon took a pen from his pocket and used the end to slide the tray open enough to read the card.

LEIGH LARSON. ATTORNEY AT LAW.

Beneath the name was a Tenth Street address and an Austin phone number. So, was Leigh a man? A woman? What kind of lawyer? The generic white card didn't offer a clue. Brandon took out his cell and snapped a picture, then slid the ashtray shut.

His phone buzzed as he stood up. "Yeah?"

"Hey, I'm in the woods about fifty yards south of you." Antonio sounded out of breath, and Brandon caught the excitement in his voice. He turned and spotted the distant white glow through the row of trees.

"What is it?" Brandon asked.

"Man, you need to come see this."

Ready to find
your next great read?

Let us help.

Visit prh.com/nextread

Penguin
Random
House